Praise for *New York Times* bestselling author

LINDA LAEL MILLER

"Linda Lael Miller is one of the
hottest romance authors writing today."
—*Romantic Times*

"Ms. Miller's unique way of tempering sensuality
with tenderness in her characters makes them
walk right off the pages and into your heart."
—*Rendezvous*

❦ ❦ ❦

Praise for bestselling author

LAURIE PAIGE

"It is always a joy to savor the consistent excellence
of this outstanding author."
—*Romantic Times*

"A dazzling display of creativity. The variation
on a standard plot is extremely fresh, with superb
characterization to carry it off. Readers will hang
on the edge wondering how the situation can be
resolved, but Ms. Paige comes up trumps with
a thoroughly satisfying resolution."
—*Romantic Times* on *Nothing Lost*

LINDA LAEL MILLER

New York Times bestselling author Linda Lael Miller started writing at age ten and has made a name for herself in both contemporary and historical romance with over fifty published novels to her credit. Her bold and innovative style has made her a favorite among readers. She currently makes her home in Arizona.

LAURIE PAIGE

has won many awards for her romances, but one of the best rewards for writing, she says, comes from her readers. Some write to share their experiences, some to share recipes, some to report they grew up in the story locale. Legends and folklore, as well as off-the-beaten-path places, are also part of the fun...and can liven things up for intrepid heroines and exasperated heroes!

LINDA LAEL MILLER
LAURIE PAIGE

CLAIMING HIS OWN

Silhouette Books

Published by Silhouette Books

America's Publisher of Contemporary Romance

SILHOUETTE BOOKS

CLAIMING HIS OWN

Copyright © 2003 by Harlequin Books S.A.

ISBN 0-373-21837-0

The publisher acknowledges the copyright holders
of the individual works as follows:

RAGGED RAINBOWS
Copyright © 1986 by Linda Lael Miller

SOMETHING TO HIDE
Copyright © 2003 by Olivia M. Hall

This edition published by arrangement with Harlequin Books S.A.

® and TM are trademarks of Harlequin Books S.A., used under
license. Trademarks indicated with ® are registered in the United States
Patent and Trademark Office, the Canadian Trade Marks Office and in
other countries.

Visit Silhouette at www.eHarlequin.com

Printed in U.S.A.

CONTENTS

RAGGED RAINBOWS

Linda Lael Miller

For Mary Ann and Stevie,
my cousins and my first friends.
I love you.

Chapter 1

Marvin's toupé was slightly off-center and he was wearing his standard smile, one that promised low mileage to the public in general and headaches to Shay Kendall in particular. She sat up a little straighter in her chair and looked across the wide polished plains of her employer's desk to the view outside the window behind him. Thousands of red, yellow and blue triangular flags were snapping in the wind, a merry contrast to the cloudy coastal sky.

"I'm an office manager, Marvin," Shay said with a sigh, bringing wide hazel eyes back to his friendly face, "not an actress. While I enjoy helping plan commercials, I don't see myself in front of the camera."

"I've been promising Jeannie this trip to Europe for years," Marvin said pointedly.

Richard Barrett, a representative of an advertising agency in nearby Seattle, was leaning back against a burgeoning bookshelf, his arms folded across his chest. He was tall, with nicely cut brown hair, and would have been handsome if not for the old-fashioned horn-rimmed glasses he wore. "You're Rosamond Dallas's daughter," he put in. "Besides, I know a hundred women who would give anything for a chance like this."

Shay pushed back a lock of long, layer-cut brown hair to rub one temple with her fingers, then lifted her head, giving Mr. Barrett an ironic look. "A chance like what, Richard? You make this sound as though it's a remake of *The Ten Commandments* instead of a thirty second TV spot where I get a dump truck load of sugar poured over me and say, 'We've got a sweet deal for you at Reese Motors in Skyler Beach!' Furthermore, I fail to see what my being Rosamond's daughter has to do with anything."

Marvin was sitting back in his leather chair and smiling, probably at the image of Shay being buried under a half ton of white sugar. "There would be a sizable bonus involved, of course," he reflected aloud.

He hadn't mentioned a bonus on Friday afternoon, when he'd first presented Shay with a storyboard for a commercial starring herself rather than the infamous "Low-Margin Marvin."

Shay sighed, thinking of all the new clothes her

six-year-old son, Hank, would need before school started and of the IRA account she wanted to open but couldn't afford. "How much of a bonus?" she asked, disliking Richard Barrett for the smug look that flickered briefly in his blue eyes.

Marvin named a figure that would cover the IRA payment and any amount of jeans, sneakers, jackets and T-shirts for Hank, with money left over.

"Just for one commercial? That's all I'd have to do?" Shay hated herself for wavering, but she was in no position to turn her back on so much money. While she earned a good salary working as Reese Motors's office manager and general all-around troubleshooter, it took all she could scrape together to support herself and her small son and meet the property taxes on her mother's enormous, empty house. Lord in heaven, she thought, if only someone would come along and buy that house....

Marvin and Richard exchanged indulgent looks. "If you hadn't stomped out of here on Friday," Richard said smoothly, "I would have gone on to explain that we're discussing a series of four spots, thirty seconds each. That's a lot of money for two minutes' work, Shay."

Two minutes' work. Shay was annoyed and insulted. Nobody knew better than she did that a thirty second commercial could take days to perfect; she'd fetched enough antacid tablets for Marvin and made enough conciliatory telephone calls to his wife to know. "I'm an office manager," she repeated, somewhat piteously this time.

"And a damned good one!" Marvin thundered. "I don't know what we'd have done without you all this time!"

Shay looked back over the half dozen years since she'd come to work for Marvin Reese. She had started as a receptionist and the job had been so important to her that she'd made any number of mistakes in her attempts to do it well. Marvin had been kind and his wife, Jeannie, had been a real friend, taking Shay out to lunch on occasion, helping her to find a trustworthy baby-sitter for Hank, reassuring her.

In many ways, Jeannie Reese had been a mother to Shay during those harried, scary days of new independence. Rosamond—nobody had suspected that her sudden tendency toward forgetfulness and fits of temper was the beginning of Alzheimer's disease—had been living on a *rancho* in Mexico then, with her sixth and final husband, blissfully unconcerned with her daughter's problems.

Now, sitting there in Marvin's spacious, well-appointed office, Shay felt a sting at the memory. She had telephoned her mother right after Eliott, then principal of a high school in a small town in Oregon, had absconded with the school's sizable athletic fund and left his young and decidedly pregnant wife to deal with the consequences. Rosamond had said that she'd warned Shay not to marry an older man, hadn't she, and that she would love to send money to help out but that that was impossible, since Eduardo had just bought a thoroughbred racehorse and transporting the beast all the way from Kentucky to the Yucatan peninsula had cost so much.

"Shay?"

Shay wrenched herself back to the present moment and met Marvin's fatherly gaze. She knew then that, even without the bonus check, she would have agreed to be in his commercials. He had believed in her when she had jumbled important files and spilled coffee all over his desk and made all the salesmen on the floor screaming mad by botching up their telephone messages. He had paid for the business courses she'd taken at the junior college and given her regular raises and promotions.

He was her friend.

"It's an offer I can't refuse," she said softly. It was no use asking for approval of the storyboards; Marvin's style, which had made him a virtual legend among car dealers, left no room for temperament. Three years before, at Thanksgiving, he'd dressed up as a turkey and announced to the viewing public that Reese Motors was gobbling up good trade-ins.

Marvin unearthed his telephone from piles of factory invoices and lease agreements and dialed a number. "Jeannie? Shay's going to take over the commercials for me. Dust off your passport, honey—we're going on the trip!"

Shay rose from her chair and left Marvin's office for the sanctity of her own smaller one, only to be followed by a quietly delighted Richard.

"I have three of the four storyboards ready, if you'd like to look them over," he offered.

"Why does Marvin want me to do this?" Shay complained belatedly. "Why not one of the salesmen or some actor? Your agency has access to dozens of people...."

Richard grinned. "You know that Marvin believes in the personal touch, Shay. That's what's made him so successful. You should be proud; he must regard you as practically a member of his family."

There was some truth in Richard's words—Jeannie and Marvin had no children of their own, and they had included her and Hank in many of their holiday celebrations and summer camping trips over the past six years. What would she have done without the Reeses?

She eyed the stacks of paperwork teetering in her in-basket and drew a deep breath. "I have a lot to do, Richard. If you'll excuse me—"

The intercom buzzed and Shay picked up her telephone receiver. "Yes, Ivy? What is it?"

Ivy Prescott's voice came over the line. "Shay, that new salesman Mike hired last Tuesday is...well, he's doing something very weird."

Shay closed her eyes tightly, opened them again. With one hand, she opened the top drawer of her desk and rummaged for a bottle of aspirin, and failed to find it. "What, exactly, is he doing?"

"He's standing in the front seat of that '65 Corvette we got in last month, making a speech."

"Standing—"

"It's a convertible," Ivy broke in helpfully.

Shay made note of the fact that Richard was still loitering inside her office door and her irritation redoubled. "Good Lord. Where is Mike? He's the floor manager and this is his problem!"

"He's out sick today," Ivy answered, and there was a note of panic in her normally bright voice. "Shay, what do I do? I don't think we should bother Mr. Reese with this, his heart, you know. Oh, I wish Todd were here!"

"I'll handle it," Shay said shortly, hanging up the receiver and striding out of the office, with Richard right behind her. As she passed Ivy's desk, she gave the young receptionist a look that, judging by the heightened color in her face, conveyed what Shay thought of the idea of hiding behind Todd Simmons, Ivy's fiancé, just because he was a man.

Shay was wearing jeans and a blue cotton blouse that day, and her sneakers made a squeaky sound on the metal steps leading down into the showrooms. She smiled faintly at the customers browsing among glistening new cars as she crossed the display floor and stepped out onto the lot. Sure enough, there was a crowd gathered around the recently acquired Corvette.

She pushed her way between two of the newer salesmen, drew a deep breath and addressed the wild-eyed young man standing in the driver's seat of the sports car. "Get down from there immediately," she said in a clear voice, having no idea in the world what she would do if he refused.

Remarkably, the orator ceased his discourse and got out of the car to stand facing Shay. He was red with conviction and at least one coffee break cocktail, and there was a blue stain on the pocket of his short-sleeved white shirt where his pen had leaked. "I was only—" he began.

Shay cut him off swiftly. "My office. Now."

The errant salesman followed along behind Shay as she walked back into the building, through the show-room and up the stairs. Once they were inside her office, he became petulant and not a little rebellious. "No woman orders me around," he muttered. Shay sat down in her chair, folded her hands in her lap so that—she glanced subtly at his name tag—Ray Metcalf wouldn't see that they were trembling just a little. "This woman, Mr. Metcalf, is ordering you out, not around. If you have any commissions coming, they will be mailed to you."

"You're firing me?" Metcalf looked stunned. He was young and uncertain of himself and it was obvious, of course, that he had a problem. Did he have a family to support?

"Yes," Shay answered firmly.

"You can't do that!"

"I can and I have. Good day, Mr. Metcalf, and good luck."

Metcalf flushed and, for a moment, the look in his eyes was ominous. Shay was a little scared, but she refused to be intimidated, meeting the man's contemptuous glare with a level gaze of her own. He turned and left the office, slamming the door behind him, and Shay let out a long breath in relief. When Ivy bounced in, moments later, she was going over a printout listing sales figures for the month before.

Despite the difference in their ages—Ivy was only twenty while Shay was nine years older—the two women were good friends. Ivy was going to marry Todd Simmons, an up-and-coming young real-estate broker, at Christmas, and Shay would be her matron of honor.

"Todd's taking me out to lunch," Ivy said, and her chin-length blond hair glistened even in the harsh fluorescent lighting of the office. "You're welcome to come along if you'd like."

"How romantic," Shay replied, with a wry twist of her lips, and went on working. "Just the three of us."

Ivy persisted. "Actually, there wouldn't be three of us. There's someone I want you to meet."

Shay laid down her pen and gave her friend a look. "Are you matchmaking again? Ivy, I've told you time and time again—"

"But this man is different."

Shay pretended to assess Ivy's dress size, which, because she was so tiny, would be petite. "I wonder if Marvin still has that turkey suit at home. With a few alterations, my dear, it might fit you. Why didn't I think of this before?" She paused for effect. "I could pull rank on you. How would you like to appear in four television commercials?"

Ivy rolled her blue-green eyes and backed out of the office, closing the door on a number of very interesting possibilities. Shay smiled to herself and went back to work.

The house was a sprawling Tudor mansion perched on a cliff overlooking the Pacific, and it was too damned big for one single, solitary man.

The dining room was formal, lit by two shimmering crystal chandeliers, and there were French doors opening onto a garden filled with pink, white, scarlet and lavender rhododendrons. The walls of the massive library were lined with handcrafted shelves and the fireplaces on the first floor were all large enough for a man to stand upright inside. The master bedroom boasted a checkerboard of tinted and clear skylights, its own hot tub lined with exquisitely painted tiles, and a broad terrace. Yes, the place was definitely too big and too fancy.

"I'll take it," Mitch Prescott said, leaning against the redwood railing of the upstairs terrace. The salt breeze rippled gently through his dark blond hair and the sound of the incoming tide, far below, was a soothing song.

Todd Simmons, soon to be Mitch's brother-in-law, looked pleased, as well he might, considering the commission his fledgling real-estate firm would collect on the sale. Mitch noticed that Todd's hand trembled a little as he extended it to seal the agreement.

Inwardly, Mitch was wondering what had possessed him to meet the outrageous asking price on this monster of a house within fifteen minutes of walking through the front door. He decided that he'd done it for Ivy, his half-sister. Since she was going to marry Simmons, the sale would benefit her, too.

"When can I move in?" Mitch asked, resting against the railing again and gazing far out to sea. His hotel room was comfortable, but he had spent too much of his life in places like it; he wanted to live in a real house.

"Now, if you'd like," Simmons answered promptly. He seemed to vibrate with suppressed excitement, as though he'd like to jump up in the air and kick his heels together. "In this case, the closing will be little more than a formality. I don't mind tell-

ing you that Rosamond Dallas's daughter is anxious
to unload the place.''

The famous name dropped on Mitch's weary mind
with all the grace of a boxcar tumbling into a ravine.
''I thought Miss Dallas was dead,'' he ventured.

A sad expression moved in Todd's eyes as he
shook his head and drew a package of gum from the
pocket of his blue sports jacket. He was good-looking,
with dark hair and a solid build; he and Ivy would
have beautiful children.

''Rosamond has Alzheimer's disease,'' he said, and
he gave a long sigh before going on. ''It's a shame,
isn't it? She made all those great movies, married all
those men, bought this house and half a dozen others
just as impressive all over the United States, and she
winds up staring at the walls over at Seaview Convalescent, with the whole world thinking she's dead.
The hell of it is, she's only forty-seven.''

''My God,'' Mitch whispered. He was thirty-seven
himself; it was sobering to imagine having just ten
good years left. Rosamond, at his age, had been at
the height of her powers.

Todd ran a hand through his dark hair and worked
up a grin. ''Things change,'' he said philosophically.
''Time moves on. Rosamond doesn't have any use
for a house like this now, and the taxes have been a
nightmare for her daughter.''

Mitch was already thinking like a journalist, even
though he'd sworn that he wouldn't write again for

at least a year. He was in the beginning stages of burnout, he had told his agent just that morning. He'd asked Ivan to get him an extension on his current contract, in fact. Now, six hours later, here he was thinking in terms of outlines and research material. "Rosamond Dallas must have earned millions, Todd. She was a star in every sense of the word. Why would the taxes on this place put a strain on anybody in her family?"

Todd unwrapped the stick of gum, folded it, accordion-fashion, into his mouth and tucked the papers into his pocket. "Rosamond had six husbands," he answered after a moment or two of sad reflection. "Except for Riley Thompson—he's a country and western singer and pays for her care over at Seaview—they were all jerks with a talent for picking the worst investments and the slowest horses."

"But the profit from selling this house—"

"That will go to clear up the last of Rosamond's personal debts. Shay won't see a dime of it."

"Shay. The daughter?"

Todd nodded. "You'll meet her tonight. She's Ivy's best friend, works for Marvin Reese."

Mitch couldn't help smiling at the mention of Reese, even though he was depressed that someone could make a mark on the world the way Rosamond Dallas had and have nothing more to pass on to her daughter than a pile of debts. Ivy had written him often about her employer, who was something of a local celebrity and the owner of one of the largest new-and-used car operations in the state of Washington. Television commercials were Reese's claim to fame; he had a real gift for the ridiculous.

Mitch's smile faded away. "Did Shay grow up in this house, by any chance?" he asked. He couldn't think why the answer should interest him, but it did.

"Like a lot of show people, Rosamond was something of a vagabond. Shay lived here when she was a little girl, on and off. Later, she spent a lot of time in Swiss boarding schools. Went to college for a couple of years, somewhere in Oregon, and that's when she met—" Todd paused and looked sheepish. "Damn, I've said too much and probably bored you to death in the process. I should be talking about the house. I can have the papers ready by tonight, and I'll leave my keys with you."

He removed several labeled keys from a ring choked with similar ones and they clinked as they fell into Mitch's palm. "Ivy mentioned dinner, didn't she? You'll be our guest, of course."

Mitch nodded. Todd thanked him, shook his hand again and left.

When he was alone, Mitch went outside to explore the grounds, wondering at himself. He hadn't intended to settle down. Certainly he hadn't intended to buy a house. He had come to town to see Ivy and meet her future husband, to relax and maybe fish and sail a little, and he'd agreed to look at this house only because he'd been intrigued by his sister's descriptions of it.

Out back he discovered an old-fashioned gazebo, almost hidden in tangles of climbing rosebushes. Pungently fragrant pink and yellow blossoms nodded in the dull, late morning sunshine, serenaded by bees. The realization that he would have to hire a gardener as well as a housekeeper made Mitch shake his head.

He rounded the gazebo and found another surprise, a little girl's playhouse, painted white. The miniature structure was perfectly proportioned, with real cedar shingles on the roof and green shutters at the windows. Mitch Prescott, hunter of Nazi war criminals, infiltrator of half a dozen chapters of the Ku Klux Klan, trusted confidant of Colombian cocaine dealers, was enchanted.

He stepped nearer the playhouse. The paint was peeling and the shingles were loose and there were, he could see through the lilliputian front window, repairs to be made on the inside as well. Still, he smiled to imagine how Kelly, his seven-year-old daughter, would love to play here, in this strangely magical place, spinning the dreams and fantasies that came so easily to children.

Shay stormed out of Marvin's office muttering, barely noticing Ivy, who sat at her computer terminal in the center of the reception room. "Bees…a half-ton of sugar…that could kill me…."

"Todd sold the house!" Ivy blurted as Shay fumbled for the knob on her office door.

She stopped cold, the storyboards for the outrageous commercials under one arm, and stared at Ivy, at once alarmed and hopeful. "Which house?" she asked in a voice just above a whisper.

Ivy's aquamarine eyes were shining and her elegant cheekbones were tinted pink. "Yours—I mean, your mother's. Oh, Shay, isn't it wonderful? You'll be able to clear up all those bills and Todd will make the biggest commission ever!"

Shay forgot her intention to lock herself up in her office and wallow in remorse for the rest of the afternoon. She set the storyboards aside and groped with a tremulous hand for a chair to draw up to Ivy's desk. Of course she had been anxious to see that wonderful, magnificent burden of a house sold, but the reality filled her with a curious sense of sadness and loss. "Who bought it? Who could have come up with that kind of money?" she asked, speaking more to the cosmos than to Ivy.

Her friend sat up very straight in her chair and beamed proudly. "My brother, Mitch."

Shay had a headache. She pulled in a steadying breath and tried to remember all that Ivy had told her, over the years, about her brother. He and Ivy did not share the same mother; in fact, Mitch and his stepmother avoided each other as much as possible. Shay had had the impression that Mitch Prescott was very successful, in some nebulous and unconventional way, and she remembered that he had once been married and had a child, a little girl if she remembered correctly. Probably because of the rift between himself and Ivy's mother, he had rarely been to Skyler Beach.

Ivy looked as though she would burst. "I knew Mitch would want that house, if I could just get him to look at it," she confided happily. But then she peered at Shay, her eyes wide and a bit worried. "Shay, are you all right? You look awful!"

Shay stood up and moved like a sleepwalker toward the privacy of her office.

"Shay?" Ivy called after her. "I thought you'd be pleased. I thought—"

Shay turned in the doorway, the storyboards leaving stains of colored chalk on her jeans and her pale blue blouse. She smiled shakily and ran the fingers of her left hand through her hair, hoping the lie didn't show in her eyes.

"I am happy," she said. And then she went into the office, closed the door and hurled the storyboards across the room.

"Dinner?"

Ivy was clearly going to stand fast. "Don't you dare say no, Shay Kendall. You wanted to be free of that house and Todd sold it for you and the least you can do is let us treat you to dinner to celebrate."

Shay gathered up the last of the invoices she had been checking and put them into the basket on her desk. It had been a difficult day, what with the planning of the commercials and that salesman making his speech on the front lot. Of course, it was a blessing that the house had been sold and she was relieved to be free of the financial burden it had represented, but parting with the place was something of an emotional shock all the same. She would have preferred to spend the evening at home, lounging about with a good book and maybe feeling a little sorry for herself. "Your brother will be there, I suppose."

"Of course," Ivy replied with a shrug. "After all, he's the buyer."

Shay felt a nip of envy. What would it be like to be able to buy a house like that? For a very long time, she had nursed a secret dream of starting her own catering business and being such a smashing success that she could afford to keep the place for herself and Hank. "I have to stop by Seaview to see Rosamond on my way home," she said, hoping to avoid having dinner out. "And then, of course, there's Hank...."

"Shay."

She sighed and pushed back her desk chair to stand up. "All right, all right. I'll spend a few minutes at Seaview and get a sitter for the evening."

Ivy's lovely face was alight again. "Great!" she chimed, turning to leave Shay's office.

"Wait," Shay said firmly, stopping her friend in the doorway.

Ivy looked back over one shoulder, her pretty hair following the turn of her head in a rhythmic flow of fine gold. "What?"

"Don't get any ideas about fixing me up with your brother, Ivy, because I'm not interested. Is that clear?"

Ivy rolled her eyes. "Oh, for pity's sake!" she cried dramatically.

"I mean it, Ivy."

"Meet us at the Wharf at eight," Ivy said, and then she waltzed out, closing Shay's door behind her.

Shay locked her desk, picked up her purse and cast one last disdainful look at the storyboards propped along the back of her bookshelf before leaving. She tried to be happy about the assignment and the money it would bring in, tried to be glad that the elegant house high above the beach was no longer her responsibility, tried to look forward to a marvelous dinner at Skyler Beach's finest restaurant. But, as she drove toward Seaview Convalescent Home, it was all Shay could do to keep from pulling over to the side of road, dropping her forehead to the steering wheel and crying.

Chapter 2

Shay Kendall looked nothing like her illustrious mother, Mitch thought as he watched her enter the restaurant. No, she was far more beautiful: tall with lush brown hair that fell past her shoulders in gentle tumbles of curl, and her eyes were a blend of green and brown, flecked with gold.

She wore a simple white cotton sundress and high-heeled sandals and when Ivy introduced her and she extended her hand to Mitch, something in her touch crackled up his arm and elbowed his heart. It was a sudden, painful jolt, a Sunday punch, and Mitch was off balance. To cover this, he made a subtle production of drawing back her chair and took his time rounding the table to sit down across from her.

Ivy and Todd, having greeted Shay, were now standing in front of the lobster tank, which ran the length of one wall, eagerly choosing their dinner. Their easy laughter drifted over the muted chatter of the other guests to the table beside the window.

Shay was looking out through the glass; beyond it, spatters of fading daylight danced on an ocean tinted with the pinks and golds and deep lavenders of sunset. Her eyes followed the gulls as they swooped and dived over the water, giving their raucous cries, and a slight smile curved her lips. An overwhelming feeling of tenderness filled Mitch as he watched her.

He had to say something, start a conversation. He sliced one irate glance in Ivy's direction, feeling deserted, and then plunged in with, "Ivy tells me that the house I bought belonged to your mother."

The moderation with which Mitch spoke surprised him, considering that he could see the merest hint of rosy nipples through the whispery fabric of Shay's dress. He took a steadying gulp of the white wine Todd had ordered earlier.

The hazel eyes came reluctantly to his, flickered with pain and then inward laughter at some memory. Mitch imagined Shay as a little girl, playing in that miniature house behind the gazebo, and the picture slowed down his respiration rate.

"Yes." Her voice was soft and she tossed a wistful glance toward Ivy and Todd, who were still studying their unsuspecting prey at the lobster tanks. In that instant Shay was a woman again, however vulnerable, and Mitch was rocked by the quicksilver change in her.

He tried to transform her back into the child. "That little house in back, was that yours?"

Shay smiled and nodded. "I used to spend hours there. At the time, it was completely furnished, right down to china dishes—" She fell silent and her beautiful eyes strayed again to the water beyond the window. "I only lived there for a few years," she finished quietly.

Mitch began to wish that he had never seen Rosamond Dallas's house, let alone bought it. He felt as though he had stolen something precious from this woman and he supposed that, in a way, he had. He was relieved when Ivy and Todd came back to the table, laughing between themselves and holding hands.

He was so handsome.

Nothing Ivy had ever said about Mitch Prescott had prepared Shay for the first jarring sight of him. He was a few inches taller than she was, with broad shoulders and hair of a toasted caramel shade, but it was his eyes that unsettled her the most. They were a deep brown, quick and brazen and tender, all at once. His hands looked strong, and they were dusted with butternut-gold hair, as was the generous expanse of chest revealed by his open-throated white shirt. He had just the suggestion of a beard and the effect was one of quiet, inexorable masculinity.

Here was a man, Shay decided uneasily, who had no self-doubts at all. He was probably arrogant.

She sat up a little straighter and tried to ignore him. His vitality stirred her in a most disturbing way. What would it be like to be caressed by those deft, confident hands?

Shay's arm trembled a little as she reached out for her wineglass. Fantasies sprang, scary and delicious, into her mind, and she battled them fiercely. God knew, she reminded herself, Eliott Kendall had taught her all she needed or wanted to know about men.

Ivy was chattering as she sat down, her eyes bright with the love she bore Todd Simmons and the excitement of having her adored brother nearby. "Aren't you going to pick out which lobster you want?" she demanded, looking from Shay to Mitch with good-natured impatience.

"I make it a point," Mitch said flatly, "never to eat anything I've seen groveling on the bottom of a fish tank. I'll have steak."

Ivy's lower lip jutted out prettily and she turned to Shay. "What about you? You're having lobster, aren't you?"

Shay grabbed for her menu and hid behind it. Why hadn't she followed her instincts and stayed home? She should have known she wouldn't be able to handle this evening, not after the day she'd had. Not after losing—*selling* the house.

"Shay?" Ivy prodded.

"I'll have lobster," Shay conceded, mostly because she couldn't make sense of the menu. She felt silly. Good Lord, she was twenty-nine years old, self-supporting, the mother of a six-year-old son, and here she was, cowering behind a hunk of plastic-covered paper.

"Well, go choose one then!"

Shay shook her head. "I'll let the waiter do that," she said lamely. I'm in no mood to sign a death warrant, she thought. Or the papers that will release that very special house to a stranger.

She lowered the menu and her eyes locked with Mitch Prescott's thoughtful gaze. She felt as though he'd bared her breasts or something, even though there was nothing objectionable in his regard. Beneath her dress her nipples tightened in response, and she felt a hot flush pool on her cheekbones.

Mitch smiled then, almost imperceptibly, and his eyes—God, she had to be imagining it, she thought—transmitted a quietly confident acknowledgment, not to mention a promise.

A wave of heat passed over Shay, so dizzying that she had to drop her eyes and grip the arms of her chair for a moment. Stop it, she said to herself. You don't even know this man.

A waiter appeared and, vaguely, Shay heard Todd ordering dinner.

Ivy startled her back to full alertness by announcing, "Shay's going to be a star. I'll bet she'll be so good that Marvin will want her to do all the commercials."

"Ivy!" Shay protested, embarrassed beyond bearing. Out of the corner of one eye she saw Mitch Prescott's mouth twitch slightly.

"What's the big secret?" Ivy complained. "Everybody in western Washington is going to see you anyway. You'll be famous."

"Or infamous," Todd teased, but his eyes were gentle. "How is your mother, Shay?"

Shay didn't like to discuss Rosamond, but the subject was infinitely preferable to having Ivy leap into a full and mortifying description of the commercials Shay would begin filming the following week, after Marvin and Jeannie departed for faraway places. "She's about the same," she said miserably.

The salads arrived and Shay pretended to be ravenous, since no one would expect her to talk with her mouth full of lettuce and house dressing. Mercifully, the conversation shifted to Todd's dream of building a series of condominiums on a stretch of property south of Skyler Beach.

Throughout dinner, Ivy chattered about her Christmas wedding, and when the plates had been removed, Todd brought out the papers that would transfer own-

ership of Rosamond's last grand house to Mitch. Shay
signed them with a burning lump in her throat and,
when Ivy and Todd went off to the lounge to dance,
she moved to make her escape.

"Wait," Mitch said with gruff tenderness, and
though he didn't touch Shay in any physical way, he
restrained her with that one word.

She sank back into her chair, near tears. "I know
I haven't been very good company. I'm sorry...."

His hand came across the table and his fingers were
warm and gentle on Shay's wrist. A tingling tremor
moved through her and she wanted to die because she
knew Mitch had felt it and possibly guessed its meaning. "Let me take you home," he said.

For a moment Shay was tempted to accept, even
though she was terrified at the thought of being alone
with this particular man. "I have my car," she managed to say, and inwardly she despaired because she
knew she must seem colorless and tongue-tied to
Mitch and a part of her wanted very much to impress
him.

He rose and pulled back her chair for her, escorted
her as far as her elderly brown Toyota on the far side
of the parking lot. There were deep grooves in his
cheeks when he smiled at Shay's nervous efforts to
open the car door. When she was finally settled behind the steering wheel, Mitch lingered, bending
slightly to look through the open window, and there
was an expression of bafflement in his eyes. He prob-

ably wondered why there were three arthritic French fries, a fast-food carton and one worn-out sneaker resting on the opposite seat.

"I'm sorry, Shay," he said.

"Sorry?"

"About the house. About the hard time Ivy gave you."

Shay was surprised to find herself smiling. She started the car and shifted into reverse; there was hope, after all, of making a dignified exit. "No problem," she said brightly. "I'm used to Ivy. Enjoy the house."

Mitch nodded and Shay backed up with a flourish, feeling oddly relieved and even a bit dashing. Oh, for an Isadora Duncan-style scarf to flow dramatically behind her as she swept away! She was her mother's daughter after all.

She waved at Mitch Prescott and started into the light evening traffic and the muffler fell off her car, clattering on the asphalt.

Mitch was there instantly, doing his best not to grin. Shay went from wanting to impress him to wanting to slap him across the face. The roar of the engine was deafening; she backed into the parking lot and turned off the ignition.

Without a word, Mitch opened the door and when Shay got out, he took her arm and escorted her toward a shiny foreign status symbol with a sliding sunroof and spoked wheels. The muffler wouldn't dare fall off this car.

"Where do you live?" Mitch asked reasonably.

Shay muttered directions, unable to look at him. Damn. First he'd seen her old car virtually fall apart before his eyes and now he was going to see her rented house with its sagging stoop and peeling paint. The grass out front needed cutting and the mailbox leaned to one side and the picture windows, out of keeping with the pre-World War II design, gave the place a look of wide-eyed surprise.

By the time Mitch's sleek car came to a stop in front of Shay's house, it was dark enough to cover major flaws. The screen door flew open and Hank burst into the glow of the porchlight, his teenage baby-sitter, Sally, behind him.

"Mom!" he whooped, bounding down the front walk on bare feet. "Wow! That's some awesome car!"

Shay was smiling again; her son had a way of putting things into perspective. Sagging stoop be damned. She was rich because she had Hank.

She turned to Mitch, opening her own door as she did so, and put down a foolish urge to invite him inside. "Good night, Mr. Prescott, and thank you."

He inclined his head slightly in answer and Shay felt an incomprehensible yearning to be kissed. She got out of the car and cut Hank off at the gate.

"Who was that?" the little boy wanted to know.

Shay ruffled his red-brown hair with one hand and ushered him back down the walk. "The man who bought Rosamond's house."

"Uncle Garrett called," Hank announced when they were inside.

Shay paid the baby-sitter, kicked off her high-heeled sandals and sank onto her scratchy garage-sale couch. Garrett Thompson had been her stepbrother, during Rosamond's Nashville phase, and though Shay rarely saw him, their relationship was a close one.

Hank was dancing from one foot to the other, obviously ready to burst. "Uncle Garrett called!" he repeated.

"Did he want me to call him back?" Shay asked, resting her feet on the coffee table with a sigh of relief.

Hank shook his head. "He's coming here. He bought a house you can drive and he's going fishing and he wants me to go, too!"

Shay frowned. "A house—oh. You mean a motor home."

"Yeah. Can I go with him, Mom? Please?"

"That depends, tiger. Maggie and the kids will be going, too, I suppose?"

Hank nodded and Shay felt a pang at his eagerness, even though she understood. He was a little boy, after all, and he needed masculine companionship. He adored Garrett and the feeling appeared to be mutual. "We'd be gone a whole month."

Shay closed her eyes. "We'll talk about this tomorrow, Hank," she said. "I've had a long day and I'm too tired to make any decisions."

Anxious to stay in his mother's good graces, Hank got ready for bed without being told. Shay went into his room and gave his freckled forehead a kiss. When he protested, she tickled him into a spate of sleepy giggles.

"I love you," she said moments later, from his doorway.

"Ah, Mom," he complained.

Smiling, Shay closed the door and went into her own room for baby-doll pajamas and a robe. After taking a quick bath and brushing her teeth, she was ready for bed.

She was not, however, ready for the heated fantasies that awaited her there, in that empty expanse of smooth sheets. She fell asleep imagining the weight of Mitch Prescott's body resting upon her own.

The next day was calm compared to the one before it. Shay's car had been brought to Reese Motors and repaired and she left work early in order to spend an hour with her mother before going home.

Rosamond sat near a broad window overlooking much of Skyler Beach, her thin, graceful hands folded in her lap, her long hair a stream of glistening, gray-marbled ebony tumbling down her back. On her lap she held the large rag doll Shay had bought for her six months before, when Rosamond had taken to wandering the halls of the convalescent home, day and night, sobbing that she'd lost her baby—couldn't someone please help her find her baby?

She had seemed content with the doll and even now she would clutch it close if anyone so much as glanced at it with interest, but Rosamond no longer cried or questioned or walked the halls. She was trapped inside herself forever, and there was no knowing whether or not she understood anything that happened around her.

On the off chance that some part of Rosamond was still aware, Shay visited often and talked to her mother as though nothing had changed between them. She told funny stories about Marvin and his crazy commercials and about the salesmen and about Hank.

Today there were no stories Shay wanted to tell, and she couldn't bring herself to mention that the beautiful house beside the sea, with its playhouse and its gazebo and its gardens of pastel rhododendrons, had been sold.

She stepped over the threshold of her mother's pleasant room and let the door whisk shut behind her, blessing Garrett's father, Riley Thompson, for being willing to pay Seaview's hefty rates. It was generous of him, considering that he and Rosamond had been divorced for some fifteen years.

"Hello, Mother," she said quietly.

Rosamond looked up with a familiar expression of

bafflement in her wide eyes and held the doll close. She began to rock in her small cushioned chair.

Shay crossed the room and sank into another chair, facing Rosamond's. There was no resemblance between the two women; Rosamond's hair was raven-black, though streaked with gray now, and her eyes were violet, while Shay's were hazel and her hair was merely brown. As a child Shay had longed to be transformed into a mirror image of her mother.

"Mother?" she prompted, hating the silence.

Rosamond hugged the doll and rocked faster.

Shay worked up a shaky smile and her voice had a falsely bright note when she spoke again. "It's almost dinnertime. Are you getting hungry?"

There was no answer, of course. There never was. Shay talked until she could bear the sound of her own voice no longer and then kissed her mother's papery forehead and left.

The box, sitting in the middle of the sidewalk in front of Shay Kendall's house, was enormous. The name of a local appliance store was imprinted on one side and, as Mitch approached, he saw the crooked coin slot and the intriguing words, Lemmonad, Ten Sens, finger-painted above a square opening. He grinned and produced two nickels from the pocket of his jeans, dropping them through the slot.

They clinked on the sidewalk. The box jiggled a bit, curious sounds came from inside, and then a small freckled hand jutted out through the larger opening, clutching a grubby paper cup filled with lemonade.

Mitch chuckled, crouching as he accepted the cup. "How's business?"

"Vending machines don't talk, mister," replied the box.

Some poor mosquito had met his fate in the lemonade and Mitch tried to be subtle about pouring the stuff into the gutter behind him. "Is your mother home?" he asked.

"No," came the cardboard-muffled answer. "But my baby-sitter is here. She's putting gunk on her toenails."

"I see."

A face appeared where the cup of lemonade had been dispensed. "Are you the guy who brought my mom home last night?"

"Yep." Mitch extended a hand, which was immediately clasped by a smaller, stickier one. "My name is Mitch Prescott. What's yours?"

"Hank Kendall. Really, my name is Henry. Who'd want people callin' 'em Henry?"

"Who indeed?" Mitch countered, biting back another grin. "Think your mom will be home soon?"

The face filling the gap in the cardboard moved in a nod. "She visits Rosamond after work sometimes. Rosamond is weird."

"Oh? How so?"

"You're not a kidnapper or anything, are you?

Mom says I'm not supposed to talk to strangers. Not ever.''

"And she's right. In this case, it's safe, because I'm not a kidnapper, but, as a general rule—''

The box jiggled again and then toppled to one side, revealing a skinny little boy dressed in blue shorts and a He-Man T-shirt, along with a pitcher of lemonade and a stack of paper cups. "Rosamond doesn't talk or anything, and sometimes she sits on my mom's lap, just like I used to do when I was a little kid.''

Mitch was touched. He sighed as he stood upright again. Before he could think of anything to say in reply, the screen door snapped open and the baby-sitter was mincing down the walk, trying not to spoil her mulberry toenails. At almost the same moment, Shay's Toyota wheezed to a stop behind Mitch's car.

He wished he had an excuse for being there. What the hell was he going to say to explain it? That he'd been awake all night and miserable all day because he wanted Shay Kendall in a way he had never before wanted any woman?

Mitch was wearing jeans and a dark blue sports shirt and the sight of him almost made Shay drop the bucket of take-out chicken she carried in the curve of one arm. Go away, go away, she thought. "Would you like to stay to dinner?'' she asked aloud.

He looked inordinately relieved. "Sounds good,'' he said.

Sally wobbled, toes upturned, over to stand beside Shay. "Who's the hunk?" she asked in a stage whisper that sent color pulsing into her employer's face.

Shay stumbled through an introduction and was glad when Sally left for the day. Mitch watched her move down the sidewalk to her own gate with a grin. "I hope her toenails dry before the bones in her feet are permanently affected," he said.

"Dumb girl," Hank added, who secretly adored Sally.

The telephone was ringing as Shay led the way up the walk; Hank surged around her and bounded into the house to grab the receiver and shout, "Hello!"

"Why are you here?" Shay asked softly as Mitch opened the screen door for her.

"I don't know," he answered.

Hank was literally jumping up and down, holding the receiver out to Shay. "It's Uncle Garrett! It's Uncle Garrett!"

Shay smiled at the exuberance in her son's face, though it stung just a little, and handed the bucket of chicken to Mitch so that she could accept the call.

"Hi, Amazon," Garrett greeted her. "What's the latest?"

Shay was reassured by the familiar voice, even if it was coming from hundreds of miles away. The teasing nickname, conferred upon Shay during the adolescent years when she had been taller than Garrett, was welcome, too. "You don't want to know," she answered, thinking of the upcoming commercials and the attraction she felt toward the man standing behind her with a bucket of chicken in his arms.

Garrett laughed. "Yes, I do, but I'll get it out of you later. Right now, I want to find out if Maggie and I can borrow Hank for a month."

Shay swallowed hard. "A month?"

"Come on, mother hen. He needs to spend time with me, and you know it."

"But…a month."

"We've got big stuff planned, Shay. Camping. Fishing." There was a brief pause. "And two weeks at Dad's ranch."

Shay was fond of Riley Thompson; of all her six stepfathers, he had been the only one who hadn't seemed to regard her as an intruder. "How is Riley?"

"Great," Garrett answered. "You've heard his new hit, I assume. He's got a string of concerts booked and there's talk that he'll be nominated for another Grammy this year. You wouldn't mind, would you, Shay, our taking Hank to his place, I mean? Dad wants to get to know him."

"Why?"

"Because he's your kid, Amazon."

Shay felt sad, remembering how empty that big beautiful house overlooking the sea had been after Riley and Garrett had moved out. Everyone knew that the divorce had nearly destroyed Riley; he'd loved Rosamond and chances were that he loved her still.

"I want you to tell him, for me, how much I appreciate all he's done for my mother. God knows what kind of place she'd have to stay in if he weren't paying the bills."

"Shay, if you need money—"

Shay could hear Hank and Mitch in the kitchen. It sounded as though they were setting the table, and Hank was chattering about his beloved Uncle Garrett, who had a house that could be "drived" just like a car.

"I don't need money," she whispered into the phone. "Don't you dare offer!"

Garrett sighed. "All right, all right. Maggie wants to talk to you."

Garrett's wife came on the line then; she was an Australian and Shay loved the sound of her voice. By the time the conversation was over, she had agreed to let Hank spend the next four weeks with the Thompsons and their two children.

She hung up, dashed away tears she could not have explained, and wandered into the kitchen, expecting to find Mitch and Hank waiting for her. The small table was clear.

"Out here, Mom!" Hank called.

Shay followed the voice onto the small patio in back. The chicken and potato salad and coleslaw had been set out on the sturdy little picnic table left behind by the last tenant, along with plates and silverware and glasses of milk.

"Do I get to go?" Hank's voice was small and breathless with hope.

Shay took her seat on the bench beside Mitch, because that was the way the table had been set, and smiled at her son. "Yes, you get to go," she answered, and the words came out hoarsely.

Hank gave a whoop of delight and then was too excited to eat. He begged to be excused so that he could go and tell his best friend, Louie, all about the forthcoming adventure.

The moment he was gone, Shay dissolved in tears. She was amazed at herself—she had not expected to cry—and still more amazed that Mitch Prescott drew her so easily into his arms and held her. There she was, blubbering all over his fancy blue sports shirt like a fool, and all he did was tangle one gentle hand in her hair and rock her back and forth.

It had been a very long time since Shay had had a shoulder to cry on, and humiliating as it was, silly as it was, it was a sweet indulgence.

Chapter 3

Tell me about Shay Kendall," Mitch said evenly, and his hand trembled a little as he poured coffee from the restaurant carafe into Ivy's cup.

Ivy grinned and lifted the steaming brew to her lips. "Are you this subtle with stool pigeons and talkative members of the Klan?"

"Damn it," Mitch retorted with terse impatience, "don't say things like that."

"Sorry," Ivy whispered, her eyes sparkling.

Mitch sat back in the vinyl booth. The small downtown restaurant was full of secretaries and businessmen and housewives with loud little kids demanding ice cream; after a second night in that cavernous house of his, he found the hubbub refreshing. "I asked about Ms. Kendall."

Ivy shrugged. "Very nice person. Terrific mother. Good office manager. Didn't you find out anything last night? You said you had dinner with Shay."

Mitch's jaw tightened, relaxed again. "She was married," he prompted.

Ivy looked very uncomfortable. "That was a long time ago. I've never met the guy."

Mitch sipped his coffee in a leisurely way and took his time before saying, "But you know all about him, don't you? You're Shay's friend."

"Her best friend," Ivy confirmed with an element of pride that said a great deal about Shay all by itself. A second later her blue eyes shifted from Mitch's face to the sidewalk just on the other side of the window and her shoulders slumped a little. "I don't like talking about Shay's private life. It seems…it seems disloyal."

He sighed. "I suppose it is," he agreed.

Ivy's eyes widened as a waitress arrived with club sandwiches, set the plates down and left. "Mitch, you wouldn't—you're not planning to write a book about Rosamond Dallas, are you?"

Mitch recalled his telephone conversation with his agent that morning and sorely regretted mentioning that the house he'd just bought had once belonged to the movie star. Ivan had jumped right on that bit of information, reminding Mitch that he was under contract for one more book and pointing out that a biography of Ms. Dallas, authorized or not, would sell faster than the presses could turn out new copies.

He braced both arms against the edge of the table and leaned toward his sister, glaring. "Why would I, a mild-mannered venture capitalist, want to write a book?"

Ivy was subdued by the reprimand, but her eyes were suspicious. "Okay, okay, I shouldn't have put it quite that way." She lowered her voice to a whisper. "Are you writing about Shay's mother or not?"

Mitch rolled his eyes. "Dammit, I don't know," he lied. The truth was that he had already agreed to do the book. Rosamond Dallas's whereabouts, long a mystery to the world in general, were now known, thanks to the thoughtless remark he'd made to Ivan. Mitch knew without being told that if he didn't undertake the project, his agent would send another writer to do it, and unless he missed his guess, that writer would be Lucetta White, a barracuda in Gucci's.

Lucetta was no lover of truth, and she made it a practice to ruin at least three careers and a marriage every day before breakfast, just to stay in top form. If she got hold of Rosamond's story, the result would be a vicious disaster of a book that would ride the major best-seller lists for months.

"Shay's husband was a coach or a teacher or something," Ivy said, jolting Mitch back to reality. "He was a lot older than she was, too. Anyway, he em-

bezzled a small fortune from a high school in Cedar
Landing, that's a little place just over the state line,
in Oregon.''

"And?"

"And Shay was pregnant at the time. She found
out at her baby shower, if you can believe it. Somebody just walked in and said, 'guess what?'''

"My God."

"There was another woman involved, naturally.''

Mitch was making mental notes; he would wait until later to ask his sister what had prompted her to
divulge all this information. For the moment, he
didn't want to chance breaking the flow. ''Does anybody know where they are, Shay's ex-husband and
this woman, I mean?"

Ivy shrugged. ''Nobody cares except the police.
Shay received divorce papers from somewhere in
Mexico a few weeks after he left, but that was over
six years ago. The creep could be anyplace by now.''

"Who was the other woman?''

"Are you ready for this? It was the local librarian.
Everybody thought she was so prim and proper and
she turned out to be a mud wrestler at heart.''

If it hadn't been for an aching sense of the humil-
iation Shay must have suffered over the incident,
Mitch would have laughed at Ivy's description of the
librarian. ''Appearances are deceiving,'' he said.

"Are they, Mitch?'' Ivy countered immediately. ''I

hope not, because when I look at you, I see a person I can trust.''

"Why did you tell me about Shay's past, Ivy? You were dead set against it a minute ago.''

Ivy lifted her chin and began methodically removing frilled toothpicks from the sections of her sandwich. "I just thought you should know why she's... why she's shy.''

Mitch wondered if "shy" was the proper word to describe Shay Kendall. Even though she'd wept in his arms the night before, on the bench of a rickety backyard picnic table, he sensed that she had a steel core. She was clearly a survivor. Hadn't she picked herself up after what must have been a devastating blow, found herself a good job, supported herself and her son? "Didn't Rosamond do anything to help Shay after Kendall took off with his mud wrestler?''

Ivy stopped chewing and swallowed, her eyes snapping. "She didn't lift a finger. Shay makes excuses for her, but I think the illustrious Ms. Dallas must have been an egotistical, self-centered bitch.''

Mitch considered that a distinct possibility, but he decided to reserve judgment until he had the facts.

After they had eaten their club sandwiches, Mitch drove his sister back to Reese Motors and her job. One hand on the inside handle of the car door, she gazed at her brother with wide, frightened eyes. "All those things in your books, Mitch—did you really know all those terrible people?''

He had hedged enough for one day, he decided. "Yes. And unless you want all those 'terrible people' to find out who and where I am, you'd better learn to be a little more discreet."

Tears sparkled in Ivy's eyes and shimmered on her lower lashes. "If anything happened to you—"

"Nothing is going to happen to me." How many times had he said that to Reba, his ex-wife? In the end, words hadn't been enough; she hadn't been able to live with the fears that haunted her. The divorce had at least been amicable; Reba was married again now, to a chiropractor with a flourishing practice and a suitably predictable life-style. He made a mental note to call and ask her to let Kelly come to visit for a few weeks.

Ivy didn't look reassured, but she did reach over and plant a hasty kiss on Mitch's cheek. A moment later she was scampering toward the entrance to the main showroom.

Mitch went shopping. He bought extra telephones in one store, pencils and spiral notebooks in another, steak and the makings of a salad in still another. He reflected, on his way home, that it might be time to get married again. He didn't mind cooking, but he sure as hell hated eating alone.

Shay carried a bag of groceries and several sacks containing new clothes for Hank's trip with Garrett and Maggie. She resisted an urge to kiss the top of her son's head after setting her purchases down on the kitchen table.

"How was work?" he asked, crawling onto a stool beside the breakfast bar that had, like the picture windows in the living room, been something of an architectural afterthought.

Shay groaned and rolled her eyes. "I spent most of it being fitted for costumes."

Hank was swinging his bare feet back and forth and there was an angry-looking mosquito bite on his right knee. "Costumes? What do you need costumes for? Halloween?"

Shay brought a dozen eggs, a pound of bacon and other miscellaneous items from the grocery bag. "Something similar, I'm afraid," she said ruefully. "I'm going to be doing four commercials."

Hank's feet stopped swinging and his brown eyes grew very wide. "You mean the kind of commercials Mr. Reese does? On TV?"

"Of course, on TV," Shay answered somewhat shortly. "Mr. and Mrs. Reese are going to be away, so I'll have to take Mr. Reese's place."

"Wow," Hank crowed, drawing the word out, his eyes shining with admiration. "Everybody will see you and know you're my mom! I betcha I could get a quarter for your autograph!"

A feeling of sadness washed over Shay; she recalled how people had waited for hours to ask Rosamond for her autograph. She had signed with a loopy flourish, Rosamond had, so friendly, so full of life, so certain of her place in a bright constellation of stars. Did that same vibrant woman exist somewhere inside the Rosamond of today?

"You're thinking about your mom, aren't you?" Hank wanted to know.

"Yes."

"Sally's mother says you should write a book about Rosamond. If you did, we'd be rich."

Shay took a casserole prepared on one of her marathon cooking days from the small chest freezer in one corner of the kitchen and slid it into the oven. She'd been approached with the idea of a book before, and she hated it. Telling Rosamond's most intimate secrets to the world would be a betrayal of sorts, a form of exploitation, and besides, she was no writer. "Scratch that plan, tiger," she said tightly. "There isn't going to be a book and we're not going to be rich."

"Uncle Garrett is rich."

"Uncle Garrett is the son of a world-famous country and western singer and a successful businessman in his own right," Shay pointed out.

"Rosamond was famous. How come you're not rich?"

"Because I'm not. Set the table, please."

"Sally's mother says she had a whole lot of husbands. Which one was your dad, Mom? You never talk about your dad."

Shay made a production of washing her hands at the sink, keeping her back to Hank. How could she explain that her father had never been Rosamond's husband at all, that he'd been the proverbial boy back home, left behind when stardom beckoned? "I didn't know my father," she said over the sound of running water. In point of fact, she didn't even know his name.

Hank was busily setting out plates and silverware and plastic tumblers. "I guess we're alike that way, huh, Mom?"

Shay's eyes burned with sudden tears and she cursed Eliott Kendall for never caring enough to call or write and ask about his own son. "I guess so."

"I like that guy with the blue car."

Mitch. Shay found herself smiling. She sniffled and turned to face Hank. "I like him, too."

"Are you going to go out with him, on dates and stuff?"

"I don't know," Shay said, unsettled again. "Hey, it'll be a while until dinner is ready. How about trying on some of this stuff I bought for your camping trip? Maggie and Garrett will be here Saturday, so if I have to make any exchanges, I'd like to take care of it tonight."

The telephone rang as Shay was slicing cucumbers for a salad, and there was a peculiar jiggling in the pit of her stomach as she reached out one hand for the receiver. She hoped that the caller would be Mitch

Prescott and then, at the nervous catching of her breath in her throat, hoped not.

"Shay?" The feminine voice rang like crystal chimes over the wires. "This is Jeannie Reese."

Mingled relief and disappointment made Shay's knees weak; she reached out with one foot for a stool and drew it near enough to sit upon. With the telephone receiver wedged between her ear and her shoulder, she went on slicing. "All ready for the big trip?" she asked, and her voice was as tremulous as her hands. If she didn't watch it, she'd cut herself.

"Ready as I'll ever be, I guess. We couldn't get away if it weren't for you. Shay, I'm so grateful."

"It was the least I could do," Shay replied, thinking of how frightened and alone she'd been when she had come back to Skyler Beach hoping to take refuge in her childhood home and found herself completely on her own. The Reeses had made all the difference. "What's up?"

"I know it's gauche, but I'm throwing my own going-away party. It'll be at our beach house, this Saturday night. Can I count on you to be there?"

By Saturday night, Hank would be gone. The house would be entirely too quiet and the first television commercial would be looming directly ahead. A distraction, especially one of the Reeses' elegant parties, would be welcome. "Is it formal?"

"Dress to the teeth, my dear."

Shay tossed the last of the cucumber slices into the

salad bowl and started in on the scallions. Her wardrobe consisted mostly of jeans and simple blouses; she was either going to have to buy a new outfit or drag the sewing machine out of the back of her closet and make one. "What time?"

"Eight," Jeannie sang. "Ciao, darling. I've got fifty-six more people to call."

Shay grinned. "Ciao," she said, hanging up.

Almost instantly, the telephone rang again. This time the caller was Ivy. "You've heard about the party, I suppose?"

"Only seconds ago. How did you find out so fast?"

"Mrs. Reese appointed me to make some of the calls. Shay, what are you going to wear?"

"I don't know." The answer was sighed rather than spoken.

"We could hit the mall tomorrow, after work."

"No chance. I've got too much to do. It's tonight or nothing."

Ivy loved to shop and her voice was a disappointed wail. "Oh, damn! I can't turn a wheel tonight! I've got to sit right here in my apartment, calling all the Reeses' friends. Promise me you'll splurge, buy something really spectacular!"

Shay scraped a pile of chopped scallions into one hand with the blade of her knife and frowned suspiciously. "Ivy, what are you up to?"

"Up to?" Ivy echoed, all innocence.

"You know what I mean."

"No, I don't."

"You're awfully concerned, it seems to me, about how I plan to dress for the Reese party."

"I just want you to look good."

"For your brother, perhaps?"

"Shay Kendall!"

"Come on, Ivy. Come clean. He's going to be there, isn't he?"

"Well, I did suggest..."

Shay laughed, even though the pit of her stomach was jumping again and her heart was beating too fast. "That's what I thought. Has it occurred to you, dear, that if Mitch wanted to see me again he would call me himself?"

"He did drop in for chicken last night," Ivy reminded her friend.

Shay blushed to remember the way she had sobbed in Mitch's arms like a shattered child. She'd probably scared him off for good. "That didn't go too well. Don't get your hopes up, Ivy."

"Buy something fabulous," insisted the irrepressible Ivy. And then she rang off.

By the time Hank had paraded through the kitchen in each of his new outfits—by some miracle, only one pair of jeans would have to be returned—the casserole was finished. Mother and son sat down to eat and then, after clearing the table and leaving the dishes to soak, they went off to the mall.

Exchanging the jeans took only minutes, but Shay

spent a full hour in the fabric store, checking out patterns and material. Finally, after much deliberation, she selected floaty black crepe for a pair of dressy, full-legged pants. In a boutique across the way, she bought a daring top of silver, black and pale blue sequins, holding her breath the whole while. The blouse, while gorgeous, was heavy and impractical and far too expensive. Would she even have the nerve to wear it?

Twice, on the way back to her car, Shay stopped in her tracks. What was she doing, spending this kind of money for one party? She had to return the blouse.

It was Hank who stopped her from doing just that. "You'll look real pretty in that shiny shirt, Mom," he said.

Shay drew a deep breath and marched onward to the car. Every woman needed to wear something wickedly glamorous, at least once in her life. Rosamond had owned closetfuls of such things.

The telephone was ringing when Shay entered the house, and Hank leaped for the living room extension. He was a born positive-thinker, expecting every call to bring momentous news.

"Yeah, she's here. Mom!"

Shay dropped her purchases on the couch and crossed the room to take the call. She was completely unprepared for the voice on the other end of the line, much as she'd hoped and dreaded to hear it earlier.

"You've heard about the party, I presume?" Mitch

Prescott asked with that quiet gruffness that put everything feminine within Shay on instant red alert.

"Yes," she managed to answer.

"I don't think I can face it alone. How about lending me moral support?"

Shay couldn't imagine Mitch shrinking from anything, or needing moral support, but she felt a certain terrified gladness at the prospect of being asked to go to the party with him. "Being a sworn humanitarian," she teased, "I couldn't possibly refuse such a request."

His sigh of relief was an exaggerated one. "Thank you."

Shay laughed. "Were you really that afraid of a simple party?"

"No. I was afraid you'd say no. That, of course, would have been devastating to my masculine ego."

"We can't have that," Shay responded airily, glad that he couldn't see her and know that she was blushing like a high-schooler looking forward to her first prom. "The Reeses' beach house is quite a distance from town. We'd better leave at least a half an hour early."

"Seven?"

"Seven," Shay confirmed. The party, something of an obligation before, was suddenly the focal point of her existence; she was dizzy with excitement and a certain amount of chagrin that such an event could be so important to her. Shouldn't she be dreading her son's imminent departure instead of looking past it to a drive along miles and miles of moon-washed shore?

While Hank was taking his bath, under protest, Shay washed the dishes she'd left to soak and then got out her sewing machine. She was up long after midnight, adjusting the pattern and cutting out her silky, skirtlike slacks and basting them together. Finally she stumbled off to bed.

The next day was what Hank would have called "hairy." Three salesmen quit, Ivy went home sick and the people at Seaview called to say that Rosamond seemed to be in some kind of state.

"What kind of 'state'?" a harried Shay barked into the receiver of the telephone in her office.

"She's curled up in her bed," answered the young and obviously inexperienced nurse. "She's crying and calling for the baby."

"Have you called her doctor?"

"He's playing golf today."

"Oh, at his rates, that's just terrific!" Shay snapped. "You get him over there, my dear, if you have to drag him off the course. Does Mother have her doll?"

"What doll?"

"The rag doll. The one she won't be without."

"I didn't see it."

"Find it!"

"I'll call you back in a few minutes, Mrs. Kendall."

"See that you do," Shay replied in clipped tones just as Richard Barrett waltzed, unannounced, into her office.

"Bad day?"

Shay ran one hand through her already tousled hair and sank into the chair behind her desk. "Don't you know how to knock?"

Richard held up both hands in a concessionary gesture. "I'm sorry."

Shay sighed. "No, I'm sorry. I didn't mean to snap at you that way. How can I help you?"

"I just wanted to remind you that we're going to shoot the first commercial Monday morning. You've memorized the script, I assume?"

The script. If Shay hadn't had a pounding headache, she would have laughed. "I say my line and then read off this week's special used-car deals. That isn't too tough, Richard."

"I thought we might have a rehearsal tonight."

Shay shook her head. "No chance. My mother is in bad shape and I have to go straight to the convalescent home as soon as I leave here."

"After that—"

"My son is leaving on a camping trip with his uncle, Richard, and he'll be gone a month. I want to spend the evening with him."

"Shay—"

Now Shay held up her hands. "No more, Richard. You and Marvin insisted that I take this assignment and I agreed. But it will be done on my terms or not at all.''

A look of annoyance flickered behind Richard's glasses. ''Temperament rears its ugly head. I was mistaken about you, Shay. You're more like your mother than I thought.''

The telephone began to jangle, and Ivy wasn't out front to screen the calls. Shay dismissed Richard with a hurried wave of one hand and snapped ''Hello?''

A customer began listing, in irate and very voluble terms, all the things that were wrong with the used car he'd bought the week before. While Shay tried to address the complaint, the other lines on her telephone lit up, all blinking at once.

It was nearly seven o'clock when Shay finally got home, and she had such a headache that she gave Hank an emergency TV dinner for supper, swallowed two aspirin and collapsed into bed.

Bright and early on Saturday morning, Garrett and his family arrived in a motor home more luxuriously appointed than many houses. While Maggie stayed behind with her own children and Hank, Shay and Garrett drove to Seaview to visit Rosamond.

Because the doll had been recovered, Rosamond was no longer curled up in her bed weeping piteously for her ''baby.'' Still, Garrett's shock at seeing a woman he undoubtedly remembered as glamorous and flippant staring vacantly off into space showed in

his darkly handsome face and the widening of his
steel-gray eyes.

"My God," he whispered.

Rosamond lifted her chin—she was sitting, as always, in the chair beside the window, the rag doll in
her lap—at the sound of his voice. Her once-magical
violet eyes widened and she surprised both her visi-
tors by muttering, "Riley?"

Shay sank back against the wall beside the door.
"No, Mother. This is—"

Garrett silenced her with a gesture of one hand,
approached Rosamond and crouched before her chair.
Shay realized then how much he actually resembled
his father, the Riley Thompson Rosamond would remember and recognize. He stretched to kiss a faded
alabaster forehead and smiled. "Hello, Roz," he said.

The bewildered joy in Rosamond's face made Shay
ache inside. "Riley," she said again.

Garrett nodded and caught both his former stepmother's hands in his own strong, sun-browned ones.
"How are you?" he asked softly.

Tears were stinging Shay's eyes, half blinding her.
Through them, she saw Rosamond hold out the doll
for Garrett to see and touch. "Baby," she said
proudly.

As Garrett acknowledged the doll with a nod and
a smile, Shay whirled away, unable to bear the scene
any longer. She fled the room for the small bathroom
adjoining it and stood there, trembling and pale, bat-

tling the false hopes that Rosamond's rare moments of lucidity always stirred in her.

When she was composed enough to come out, Rosamond had retreated back into herself; she was rocking in her chair, her lips curved into a secretive smile, the doll in her arms. Garrett wrapped a supportive arm around Shay's waist and led her out of the room into the hallway, where he gave her a brotherly kiss on the forehead.

"Poor baby," he said, and then he held Shay close and rocked her back and forth in his arms. She didn't notice the man standing at the reception desk, watching with a frown on his face.

Chapter 4

When Hank disappeared into Garrett and Maggie's sleek motor home, a lump the size of a walnut took shape in Shay's throat. He was only six; too young to be away from home for a whole month!

Garrett grinned and kissed Shay's forehead. "Relax," he urged. "Maggie and I will take good care of the boy. I promise."

Shay nodded, determined not to be a clinging, neurotic mother. Six or sixty, she reminded herself, Hank was a person in his own right and he needed experiences like this one to grow.

Briefly, Garrett caressed Shay's cheek. "Go in there and get yourself ready for that party, Amazon," he said. "Paint your toenails and slather your face with gunk. Soak in a bubble bath."

Shay couldn't help grinning. "You're just full of suggestions, aren't you?"

Garrett was serious. "Devote some time to yourself, Shay. Forget about Roz for a while and let Maggie and me worry about Hank."

It was good advice and Shay meant to heed it. After the motor home had pulled away, a happy chorus of farewell echoing behind, she went back into the house, turned on the stereo, pinned up her hair and got out the crepe trousers she'd made for the party. After hemming them, she hurried through the routine housework and then spent the rest of the morning pampering herself.

She showered and shampooed, she pedicured and manicured, she gave herself a facial. After a light luncheon consumed in blissful silence, she crawled into bed and took a long nap.

Upon rising, Shay made a chicken salad sandwich and took her time eating it. Following that, she put on her makeup, her new crepe slacks and the lovely, shimmering sequined top. She brushed her hair and worked it into a loose Gibson-girl style and put on chunky silver earrings. Looking into her bedroom mirror, she was stunned. Was this lush and glittering creature really Shay Kendall, mother of Hank, purveyor of "previously owned" autos, wearer of jeans and clear fingernail polish?

It was. Shay whirled once, delighted. It was!

Promptly at seven, Mitch arrived. He wore a pearl-

gray, three-piece suit, expertly fitted, and the effect
was at once rugged and Madison Avenue elegant. He
was clean shaven and the scent of his cologne was
crisply masculine. His brown eyes warmed as they
swept over Shay, and the familiar grooves dented his
cheeks when he smiled.

"Wow," he said.

Shay was glad that it was time to leave for the
Reeses' beach house; she had rarely dated in the six
years since her divorce and she was out of practice
when it came to amenities like playing soft music and
serving chilled wine and making small talk. "Wow,
yourself," she said, because that was what she would
have said to Hank and it came out automatically. She
could have bitten her tongue.

Mitch laughed and handed her a small florist's box.
There was a pink orchid inside, delicate and fragile
and so exotically beautiful that Shay's eyes widened
at the sight of it. It was attached to a slender band of
silver elastic and she slid it onto her wrist.

"Thank you," she said.

Mitch put a gentlemanly hand to the small of her
back and steered her toward the door. "Thank you,"
he countered huskily, and though Shay wondered
what he was thanking her for, she didn't dare ask.

As his fancy car slipped away from the curb, Mitch
pressed a button to expel the tape that had been blaring a Linda Ronstadt torch song.

The drive south along the coastal highway was a

pleasant one. The sunset played gloriously over the rippling curl of the evening tide and the conversation was comfortable. Mitch talked about his seven-year-old daughter, Kelly, who was into Cabbage Patch Kids and ballet lessons, and Shay talked about Hank.

She wanted to ask about Mitch's ex-wife, but then he might ask about Eliott and she wasn't prepared to discuss that part of her life. It was possible, of course, Shay knew, that Ivy had told him already.

"Have you started furnishing the house yet?" Shay asked when they'd exhausted the subject of children.

Mitch shook his head and the warm humor in his eyes cooled a little, it seemed to Shay, as he glanced at her and then turned his attention back to the highway. "Not yet."

Shay was stung by his sudden reticence, and she was confused, too. "Did I say something wrong?"

"No," came the immediate response, and Mitch flung one sheepish grin in Shay's direction. "I was just having an attack of male ego, I guess."

Intrigued, Shay turned in her seat and asked, "What?"

"It isn't important."

"I think maybe it is," Shay persisted.

"I don't have the right to wonder, let alone ask."

"Ask anyway." Suddenly, Shay was nervous.

"Who is that guy who was holding you in the hall-way at Seaview this morning?" The question was blurted, however reluctantly, and Shay's anxieties fled—except for one.

"That was Garrett Thompson. His father was married to my mother at one time." Shay folded her hands in her lap and drew a deep breath. "What were you doing at Seaview?"

The Reeses' beach house was in sight and Mitch looked longingly toward it, but he pulled off the highway and turned to face Shay directly. "I was asking about your mother," he said.

Shay had been braced for a lie and now, in the face of a blunt truth, she didn't know how to react. "Why?" she asked after several moments of silence.

"I don't think this is a good time to talk, Shay," Mitch replied. "Anyway, it isn't anything you need to worry about."

"But—"

His hand closed, warm and reassuring, over hers. "Trust me, okay? I promise that we'll talk after the party."

Mitch had been forthright; he could have lied about his reason for visiting Seaview, but he hadn't. Shay had no cause to distrust him. And yet the words "trust me" troubled her; it didn't matter that Mitch had spoken them: she heard them in Eliott's voice. "After the party," she said tightly.

Moments later she and Mitch entered the Reeses' spacious two-story beach house. It was a beautiful place with polished oak floors and beamed ceilings and a massive stone fireplace, and it was crowded with people.

Marvin took one look at Shay's sequined blouse and bounded away, only to return moments later wearing a pair of grossly oversized sunglasses that he'd used in a past commercial. Shay laughed and shook her head.

"I hope his tie doesn't squirt grape juice," Mitch commented in a discreet whisper.

Shay watched fondly as Marvin turned away to rejoin the party. "Don't let him fool you," she replied. "He reads Proust and Milton and speaks two languages other than English."

Mitch was still pondering this enlightening information—Marvin's commercials and loud sports jackets were indeed deceptive—when Ivy wended her way through the crowd, looking smart in a jump suit of pale blue silk belted with a slender band of rhinestones. Her aquamarine eyes took in Shay's outfit with approval. "Jeannie sent me to bid you welcome. She's in the kitchen, trying to pry an ice sculpture out of the freezer. Would you believe it's a perfect replica of *Venus de Milo?*"

"Now we know why the poor girl has no arms," Todd quipped, standing just behind Ivy.

Both Ivy and Shay groaned at the joke, and Ivy added a well-aimed elbow that splashed a few drops of champagne out of Todd's glass and onto his impeccable black jacket.

"Six months till the wedding and I'm already henpecked," he complained.

"I've been thinking about those condos," Mitch reflected distractedly. "From an ecological standpoint..."

"Business!" Ivy hissed, dragging Shay away by one arm. They came to a stop in front of a table spread with plates of wilted crab puffs, smoked oysters, crackers and cheeses.

Shay cast one look in Mitch's direction and saw that he was engrossed in his conversation with Todd. It hurt a little that he apparently hadn't even noticed that she was gone. She took a crab puff to console herself.

Ivy frowned pensively at the morsel. "Isn't that pathetic? You'd think a place as big as Skyler Beach would have one decent caterer, wouldn't you? Mrs. Reese had to have everything brought in from Seattle."

The crab puffs definitely showed the rigors of the journey, and it was a miracle that *Venus de Milo* had made it so far without melting into a puddle. Shay's dream of starting her own catering business surfaced and she pushed it resolutely back onto a mental shelf. She had a child to support and there was no way she could afford to take the financial risks such a venture would involve.

"You look fantastic!" Ivy whispered. "Is that blouse heavy?"

"It weighs a ton," Shay confided. Her eyes were following Mitch; she was memorizing every expression that crossed his face.

"Let's separate those two before they start drawing up plans or something," Ivy said lightly.

Shay wondered how long it would be before Todd balked at Ivy's gentle commandeering but made no comment. A buffet supper was served soon afterward, and she and Mitch sat alone in a corner of the beach house's enormous deck, listening to the chatter of the tide as they ate. Stars as bright as the sequins on Shay's blouse were popping out all over a black velvet sky and the summer breeze was warm.

When silences had fallen between herself and Eliott, Shay had always been uncomfortable, needing to riddle the space with words. With Mitch, there were no gaps to fill. It was all right to be quiet, to reflect and to dream.

Presently, a caterer's assistant came and collected their empty plates and glasses, but Mitch and Shay remained in that shadowy corner of the deck. When the Reeses' stereo system began to pipe soft music into the night, they moved together without speaking. They danced, and the proximity of Mitch's blatantly masculine body to Shay's softer one was an exquisite misery.

Shay saw his mouth descending to claim her own and instead of turning to avoid his kiss, she welcomed it. Unconsciously she braced herself for the crushing ardor Eliott had taught her to expect, but Mitch's kiss was gentle, tentative, almost questioning. She felt the tip of his tongue encircle her lips and a delicious tingling sensation spread into every part of her. His nearly inaudible groan rippled over her tongue and tickled the inner walls of her cheeks as she opened her mouth to him.

Gently, ever so gently, he explored her, his body pinning hers to the deck railing in a tender dominance that she welcomed, for rather than demanding submission, the gesture incited a passion so intense that Shay was terrified by it. Had it been feelings like these that had caused Rosamond to flit from one husband to another, dragging one very small and frightened daughter after her?

Shay turned her head, remembering the bewilderment and the despair. No one knew better than she did that the price of a grand passion could be a child's sense of security, and she wasn't going to let that happen to Hank.

"I'd like to go home," she managed to say.

Mitch only nodded, and when Shay dared risk a glance at his profile, turned now toward the dark sea, she saw no anger in the line of his jaw or the muscles in his neck.

They left minutes later, pausing only to make plausible excuses to Marvin and Jeannie Reese, and they had traveled nearly half an hour before Mitch broke the silence with a quiet, "I'm sorry, Shay."

Shay was miserable; she was still pulsing with the raw desire Mitch had aroused in her. Her breasts were weighted, as though bursting with some nectar only he could relieve them of, the nipples pulled into aching little buds, and a heavy throbbing in her abdomen signaled her body's preparation for a gratification that would be denied it. "I just—I guess I'm just not ready." Like hell you're not ready, she taunted herself.

"I wasn't going to make love to you with half of Skyler Beach just a wall away," Mitch pointed out reasonably. "Nor did I intend to fling you down in the sand, though now that I think about it, it doesn't sound like such a bad idea."

Shay had forgotten all about the party while Mitch was kissing her anyway and the reminder of that stung her to fury. "What exactly was your plan?" she snapped.

"I was in no condition to plan anything, lady. We're talking primitive responses here."

Shay lowered her head. She'd been trying to lay all the blame for what had nearly happened on Mitch and that was neither fair nor realistic. The only sensible thing to do now was change the subject. "You said we would talk after the party. About why you were at Seaview this morning."

"And we will. My place or yours?"

Did he think she was insane? Either place would be too private and yet a restaurant might be too public. "Mitch, I want to know why you're interested in my mother's illness, and I want to know right now."

"I never explore potentially emotional subjects in a moving vehicle."

"Then stop this car!"

"Along a moonlit beach? Come on, Shay. Surely you know what's going to happen if I do that."

Shay did know and she still wanted him to stop, which made her so mad that she turned in her seat and ignored him until they reached Skyler Beach. He drove toward her house, chivalrously giving her a choice between asking him in or spending a whole night in an agony of curiosity about his visit to Seaview. There would be agony aplenty without that.

"I'll make some coffee," Shay said stiffly.

He simply inclined his head, that brazen tenderness dancing in his eyes. Moments later he was seated at the table in Shay's small spotless kitchen, his gray jacket draped over the chair back. "What did Ivy tell you about me?"

Shay, filling the coffeepot with cold water, stiffened. "Not much. Come to think of it, I don't even know what you do for a living." It was humiliating, not knowing even that much about a man who had nearly made love to her on a sundeck.

"I'm a journalist."

Shay set the coffeepot aside, water and all, not even bothering to fill the basket with grounds. She fell into a chair of her own. "I don't understand."

"I think you do understand, Shay," he countered gently.

Shay felt tears gather in her eyes, stinging and hot. To hide them, she averted her face. "You plan to write about my mother, I suppose."

"Yes."

Swift, simmering anger made Shay meet his gaze. Damn, but it hurt to know that he hadn't taken her to the party just because he found her attractive and wanted her company! "I think you'd better leave."

Mitch sat easily in his chair, giving no indication whatsoever that he meant to do as Shay had asked. "I could have lied to you, you know. Won your confidence and then presented you with a fait accompli."

"I imagine you're very practiced at that, Mr. Prescott. Winning people's confidence, I mean, and then betraying them." She remembered the coffeepot and went back to measure in the grounds, which sprinkled the counter because she was shaking, put the lid on and plug the thing in. "Surely you don't write for one of those cheap supermarket scandal sheets—that would never pay you enough money to buy a house like yours."

"I write books," he said, unruffled. "Under a pen name."

Shay leaned back against the counter's edge, the coffeepot chortling behind her, and folded her arms across her glitzy chest. "So my mother rates a real book, does she? Well, I'm sorry, Mr. Prescott, but there will be no book!''

"I'm afraid there will."

Shay went back to the table and sat down again. "I won't permit it! I'll sue!"

"You don't have to permit anything—unauthorized biographies are perfectly legal. Moreover, nothing would make my publisher happier than a lawsuit filed by Rosamond Dallas's daughter. The publicity would be well worth any settlement they, or I, might have to pay."

Shay felt the color drain from her face. What Mitch said made a dreadful sort of sense.

"I would have turned the project down cold, Shay," he went on, "except for one thing."

Shay sat up a little straighter. "What 'one thing' was that? Money?"

"I have plenty of money. Have you ever heard of Lucetta White?"

Lucetta White. Shay searched her memory and remembered the woman as the one person Rosamond had truly feared. Ms. White's books could be lethal to a career, every word as sharply honed as a razor's edge. "She ruined half a dozen of my mother's friends."

Mitch nodded. "Lucetta and I have the same agent. If I don't write this book, Shay, she will."

Shay felt sick at the prospect. "What assurance do I have that you'll be any kinder?"

"This. I'd like you to co-author the book. The by-line is yours, if you want it."

Thinking of other books written by the children of movie stars, Shay shook her head. "I couldn't."

"You couldn't help, or you couldn't claim the by-line?"

"I won't exploit my own mother," Shay said firmly. "Besides, I'm no writer."

"I'll handle that part of it. All I want is your input: memories, old scrapbooks, family pictures. In return, I'll pay you half of the advance and half of the roy-alties."

Shay swallowed hard. "You're talking about a con-siderable amount of money."

Again he nodded.

A kaleidoscope of possibilities fanned out and then merged in Shay's mind. She could provide for Hank's education, start her catering business....

"Would I have full control?"

Mitch was turning a teaspoon from end to end on the tabletop. "'Full control' is a very broad term. You can read all the material as we go along. I'll be as kind as I can, but I won't sugarcoat anything, and if I find a skeleton, I'll drag it out of the closet."

Shay's color flared, aching on her cheekbones and flowing in a hot rush down her neck. "That sounds like Lucetta White's method."

"Read a few of her books," Mitch answered

briskly. "Lucetta invents her own skeletons, bone by grizzly bone."

The coffee was done, but Shay couldn't offer any, couldn't move from her chair. She rested her forehead in her palms. "I'll have to think about this."

She heard Mitch's chair scrape the linoleum floor as he stood up to go. "Fair enough. I'll call you in a few days."

Shay did not move until she had heard the front door open and close again. Then she went and locked it and watched through one of the picture windows as Mitch Prescott's Italian car pulled away.

Mitch waited for three days.

During those seventy-two endless hours, he hired a cook and a housekeeper and a gardener. He sent for the contents of his apartment in San Francisco, he sat at the microfilm machine in the public library, reading everything he could find concerning Rosamond Dallas, until the muscles in the small of his back threatened spasmodic rebellion.

On Tuesday morning, he drove to Reese Motors.

"Damn," Shay grumbled as she came out of the plush RV on the back lot.

Ivy tried very hard not to smile as she took in the yellow-and-black striped suit Shay was wearing. "I think you make a terrific bee," she said.

"Flattery," Shay answered bitterly, "will get you nowhere. Don't you dare laugh!"

Ivy put one hand over her mouth and the diamonds in her showy engagement ring sparkled in the sunshine. "Put the hat on. Here, let me help you."

Shay submitted to the hat, which was really more of a hood. It was black, with nodding antennae on top.

Richard Barrett approached with long strides. "The wings!" he thundered. "Where are the wings?"

"He thinks he's Cecil B. DeMille," Ivy whispered.

Shay, standing there in the hot sun, sweltering in her padded velveteen bee suit, wanted to slap him. "Wings?" she hissed.

"Of course," Richard replied with the kind of patience usually reserved for deaf dogs. "Bees do have wings, you know."

The wings were hunted down by Richard's curvaceous young assistant, who was taking this taste of show biz very seriously. She wore her sunglasses on top of her head and constantly consulted her clipboard.

"I don't need this job, you know," Shay muttered to no one in particular as she was shuffled onto an *X* chalked on the asphalt in front of an '82 Chrysler with air-conditioning.

"Do you remember your lines?" Richard's cretin assistant sang, blowing so that her fluffy auburn bangs danced in midair.

"Sure," Shay snapped. "To bee or not to bee, that is the question."

"Sheesh," the assistant marveled, not getting the joke.

"All right, Shay," Richard said, indicating one of two portable video cameras with a nod of his head. "We'll be filming from two angles, but I want you to look into this camera while you're delivering your line."

"Since when is 'bzzzz' a line?"

"Just do as I tell you, Shay." A muscle under Richard's right eye was jumping. Shay had never noticed that he had a twitch before.

"I'm ready," she conceded.

The cameras made an almost imperceptible whirring sound and a clapboard was snapped in her face.

"Take One!" Richard cried importantly.

"Bzzzzzz," said Shay, dancing around the hood of the Chrysler as though to pollinate it. "Come to Reese Motors, in Skyler Beach, 6832 Discount Way! You can't afford to miss a honey of a deal like this!" She moved on to a '78 Pinto. So far, so good. "Take this little model right here, only nineteen-ninety—nineteen-ninety—"

Shay's voice froze in her throat and her concentration fled. Mitch Prescott was standing beside Ivy, looking stunned.

"Cut!" Richard bellowed.

Shay swallowed, felt relieved as she watched Mitch turn and walk resolutely away. Were his shoulders shaking just a little beneath that pristine white shirt of his?

"I'm sorry," she said to Richard, who looked apoplectic. It seemed to Shay that he took commercials a mite too seriously.

"Take Two," Richard groaned. "God, why do I work with amateurs? Somebody tell me why!"

He wouldn't have dared to talk to Marvin that way, Shay thought. And why had she apologized, anyway? Nobody got a commercial right on the first take, did they?

Shay waited for the camera to click into action and then started over, offering the folks in Skyler Beach a bunny of a deal.

"That's Easter!" Richard screamed, frustrated beyond all good sense.

"Don't get your stinger in a wringer!" the bee screamed back and every salesman on the lot roared with laughter.

On the third take the spot was flawless. Shay scowled at Richard and stomped into the RV with Ivy right behind her. The younger woman kept biting back giggles as she helped with the cumbersome costume.

When Shay was back in her white slacks and golden, imitation-silk blouse, her hair brushed and her makeup back to normal, she left the RV with her chin held high. The salesmen formed a double line, a sort of good-natured gauntlet, and applauded and cheered as she passed.

Shay executed a couple of regal bows, but her cheeks were throbbing with embarrassment by the time she closed her office door behind her and sank against it. It was bad enough that half of Washington state would see that stupid commercial. Why had Mitch had to see it, too?

Chapter 5

The very fact of Marvin's absence seemed to generate problems and Shay was grateful for the distraction. Dealing with the complaints and questions of customers kept her from thinking about the three commercials yet to be filmed and the very enticing dangers of working closely with Mitch Prescott.

At five minutes to five, Ivy waltzed into Shay's office with a mischievous light in her eyes and a florist's bouquet in her hands. "For you," she said simply, setting the arrangement of pink daisies interspersed with baby's breath and white carnations square on top of Shay's paperwork.

At the sight and scent of the flowers, Shay felt a peculiar shakiness in the pit of her stomach. Reason said the lovely blossoms had been sent by the sales-men downstairs or perhaps the Reeses. Instinct said something very different.

Her hands trembling just slightly—she couldn't remember the last time anyone had sent her flowers—Shay reached out for the envelope containing the card. Instinct prevailed. "If you're free tonight, let's discuss the book over dinner at my place. Strictly business, I promise. R.S.V.P. Mitch."

Strictly business, he said. Shay remembered Mitch's kiss and the sweet, hard pressure of his body against her own on the Reeses' darkened deck the night of the party and wondered who the hell he thought he was kidding. She felt a certain annoyance, a tender dreading, but mingled with these emotions was a sensation of heady relief. With a sigh, Shay admitted to herself that she would have been very disappointed if the flowers had come from anyone else on the face of the earth.

"Mitch?" Ivy asked, the impish light still dancing in her eyes.

Shay grinned. "How very redundant of you to ask. You knew."

"I did not!" Ivy swore with conviction and just a hint of righteous indignation. "I just guessed, that's all."

Shay's weariness dropped away and she moved the vase of flowers to clear the paperwork from her desk. She sensed all the eager questions Ivy wanted to ask and enjoyed withholding the answers. "Well," she said with an exaggerated sigh, picking up her purse and the flowers and starting toward the door, "I'll see you tomorrow. Have a good evening."

Ivy was right on her heels. "Oh, no you don't, Shay Kendall! Did my brother ask you out or what? Why did he send you flowers? What did the card *say*, exactly?"

Smiling to herself, Shay walked rapidly toward the stairs. To spare her friend a night of agonizing curiosity, she tossed back an off-handed "He wants to start work on the book about Rosamond. Good night, Ivy."

"What book?" Ivy cried desperately, hurrying to keep up with Shay as she went down the stairs and across the polished floor of the main display room. "You don't mean—you're not actually—you said you'd never—"

Fortunately, Todd was waiting for Ivy outside, or she might have followed Shay all the way to her car, battering her with questions and fractured sentences.

Ivy looked so pained as her fiancé ushered her into the passenger seat of his car that Shay called out a merciful, "I promise I'll explain tomorrow," as she got behind the wheel of her own car.

Shay did not drive toward home; Hank wouldn't be there and she needed some time to prepare herself for the strange quiet that would greet her when she unlocked her front door. She decided to pay her mother a visit.

More than once during the short drive to Seaview Convalescent Home, Shay glanced toward the flowers so carefully placed on the passenger seat and wondered if it wouldn't be safer, from an emotional standpoint anyway, to forget Mitch Prescott and this collaboration business altogether and take her chances with Lucetta White. Granted, the woman was a literary viper, but Ms. White couldn't hurt Rosamond, could she? No one could hurt Rosamond.

Shay bit her lower lip as she turned into the spacious asphalt parking lot behind the convalescent home. Rosamond was safe, but what about Hank? What about Riley and Garrett? What about herself?

Stopping the car and turning off the ignition, Shay rested her forehead on the steering wheel and drew a deep breath. Each life, she reflected, feeling bruised and cornered, touches other lives. If Miss White chose to, she could drag up all sorts of hurtful things, such as Eliott's theft all those years before, and his desertion. Shay had long since come to terms with Eliott's actions, but how could Hank, a six-year-old, be expected to understand and cope?

Shay drew another deep breath and sat up very straight. Except for his personal word, she had no assurances that Mitch Prescott would be any fairer or any kinder in his handling of the Rosamond Dallas story, but he did seem the lesser of two evils, even considering the unnerving effect he had on Shay's emotions. The book would be written, one way or the other, and there was no going back.

She got out of the car, crossed the parking lot and entered the convalescent home resolutely. Shay was not looking forward to another one-sided visit with her mother and the guilt inspired by that fact made her spirits sag. What was she supposed to say to the woman? "Hello, Mother, today I dressed up as a bee?" Or maybe she could announce, "Guess what? I've met a man and he wants to tell all your most intimate secrets to the world and I'm going to help him and for all that, Mother, I do believe he could seduce me without half trying!"

As Shay hurried through the rear entrance to the building and down the immaculate hallway toward her mother's room, the inner dialogue gained momentum. *I'm afraid, Mother. I'm afraid. I'm starting to care about Mitch Prescott and that's going to make everything that much more difficult, don't you see? We'll make love and that will change me for always but it will just be another affair to him. I don't think I could bear that, Mother.*

Overcome, Shay stopped and rested one shoulder against the wall beside Rosamond's door, her head lowered. The fantasy was futile: Rosamond couldn't advise her, probably wouldn't bother even if she were well. That was reality.

A cold, quiet anger sustained Shay, made her

square her shoulders and lift her chin. She walked into her mother's room, crossed to her chair, bent to bestow the customary forehead kiss. Then, because her own reality was that she loved her mother, whether that love had ever been returned or not, Shay sat down facing Rosamond and told her about being a bee in a car-lot commercial, about a bouquet of pink daisies, about a man with brash brown eyes and a smile that made grooves in his cheeks.

After half an hour, when Rosamond's dinner was brought in, Shay slipped out. She hesitated only a moment before the pay phone in the hallway, then rummaged through her purse for a quarter. Mitch answered on the second ring.

"Thank you for the flowers," Shay said lamely. She'd planned a crisper approach, but at the sound of his voice, the words had evaporated from her mind in a shimmering fog.

His responding chuckle was a low, tender sound, rich with the innate masculinity he exuded so effortlessly. "You're welcome. Now, what about dinner and the book?"

Shay, whose job and personal responsibilities had always forced her to be strong, suddenly ached with shyness. "Strictly business?" she croaked out.

Mitch's silence was somehow endearing, as though he had reached out to caress her cheek or smooth her hair back from her face, but it was also brief. "Until we both decide otherwise, princess," he said softly.

"You're not walking into any heavy scenes, so relax. You're safe with me."

Tears filled Shay's eyes, coming-home tears, in-out-of-the-rain tears. She would be safe with Mitch, and that was a new experience for Shay, one she had never had with Rosamond or Eliott. "Thanks," she managed to say.

"No problem," came the velvety yet gruff reply. "Remember, though, I'm not promising that I won't tease you about this morning."

Shay found herself laughing, a moist sound making its way through receding tears. "If you think the bee debacle was bad, wait until you hear about my next epic."

"The suspense is killing me," Mitch replied with good-natured briskness, but then his voice was soft again, at once vulnerable and profoundly reassuring. "It looks as though it might rain. Drive carefully, Shay."

"What time do you want me?"

Mitch laughed. "You name a time, baby, and I want you."

"Let me rephrase that," retorted Shay, smiling. "What time is dinner?"

"Now. Whenever." He paused, sighed in exasperation. "Shay, just get over here, before I go crazy."

"Can you stay sane for half an hour? I want to change clothes."

She could almost see his eyebrows arch. "Wear the bee suit," he answered. "It really turns me on."

Shaking her head, Shay said goodbye and hung up. Her step was light as she hurried down into the hallway and outside to her car. The sky had clouded over, just as Mitch had said, and there was a muggy, pre-storm heaviness in the summer air. Shay blamed her sense of sweet foreboding on the weather.

At home, she quickly showered, put on trim gray slacks and a lightweight sweater to match, reapplied her makeup and gave her damp hair a vigorous brushing. It was a glistening mane of softness, tumbling sensuously to her shoulders and she decided that the look was entirely too come-hither. With a few brisk motions, she wound it into a chignon and then stood back from the bathroom mirror a little way to assess herself. Yes, indeed, she looked like the no-nonsense type all right. "Strictly business," she reminded her image aloud, before turning away.

Since his new housekeeper, Mrs. Carraway, had left for the day, Mitch answered the door himself. He knew the visitor would be Shay, and yet he felt surprised at the sight of her, not only surprised, but jarred.

She was wearing gray slacks and a V-necked sweater to match. Her makeup was carefully understated and her hair was done up, instead of falling gracefully around her shoulders as it usually did, and

Mitch suppressed a smile. Obviously she had made every effort to look prim, but the effect was exactly the opposite: she had achieved a sexy vulnerability that made him want her all the more.

For several moments, Mitch just stood there, staring at her like a fool. The cymballike clap of thunder roused him, however, and he remembered his manners and moved back from the doorway. "Come in."

Shay stepped into the house with a timid sort of bravado that touched Mitch deeply. Were her memories of the place sad ones, or were they happy? He wanted to know that and so much more, but getting close to this woman was a process that required a delicate touch; she was like some wild, beautiful, rarely seen creature of the forests, ready to flee at the slightest threat.

"Your things haven't arrived," she said, her eyes sweeping the massive empty foyer swiftly, as though in an effort not to see too much.

Gently, Mitch took her elbow in his hand, still fearing that she would bolt like a unicorn sensing a trap. "Actually," he answered in a tone he hoped sounded casual, "some of them have. All the most impractical things, anyway: pots and pans but no plates, sheets and pillows but no bed..."

He instantly regretted mentioning the bed.

Shay only smiled. She was relaxing, if only slightly.

They ate in the library, picnic-style, before a snapping, summer-storm fire, their paper plates balanced on their laps, their wine contained in supermarket glasses. For all that, there was an ambiance of elegance to the scenario, and Mitch knew that it emanated from the woman who sat facing him. What a mystery she was, what a tangle of vulnerability and strength, softness and fire, humor and tragedy.

Mitch felt his own veneer of sophistication, something he had long considered immutable, dissolving away. His reactions to that were ambivalent, of course; he was a man who controlled situations—at times his life had depended on that control—but now, in the presence of this woman, he was strangely powerless. The surprising thing was that he was comfortable with that.

When the meal was over he disposed of the plates and the plastic wineglasses and returned to the library to find Shay standing in the center of the room, studying every bookcase, every stone in the fireplace.

"Were you happy here?" he asked, without intending to speak at all.

She started and then turned slowly to face him. "Yes," she said.

The ache in Shay's wide hazel eyes came to settle somewhere in the middle of Mitch's chest. "Feel free to explore," he said after a rather long silence.

A quiet joy displaced the pain in Shay's face and Mitch was relieved. "But we were going to work," she offered halfheartedly. "I brought the photo albums you wanted. They're in the car and—"

Mitch spoke with the abruptness typical of nervous people. "I'll get them while you look around. Maybe you can give me a few decorating ideas. Right now, this place has all the cozy warmth of an abandoned coal mine."

She looked grateful and just a little suspicious. "Well…"

Mitch pretended that the matter had been settled and left the house. Her car was parked in the driveway, only a few strides from the front door, and the box containing Rosamond Dallas's memorabilia was sitting in plain sight on the seat. He took his time carrying the stuff inside, setting it on the library floor, sorting through it. Instinctively he knew that Shay needed time to wander from room to room, settling memories.

The room that had been Shay's was empty, of course. The built-in bookshelves were bare and dusty, the French provincial furniture and frilly bedclothes had been removed, along with the host of stuffed animals and the antique carousel horse, a gift from Riley Thompson, that had once stood just to the left of the cushioned windowseat. The nostalgia Shay had braced herself for did not come, however; this had been the room of a child and she felt no desire to go backward in time.

She wandered across the wide hallway and into the suite that had been Rosamond's, in a strange, quiet mood. The terrace doors were open to the rising rain-and-sea misted wind and Shay crossed the barren room to close them. She smiled as she stepped over the tangled sleeping bag that had been spread out on the floor, and a certain scrumptious tension gripped her as she imagined Mitch lying there.

He was downstairs, waiting for her, but Shay could not bring herself to hurry. She reached down and took a pillow from the floor and held it to her face. Its scent was Mitch's scent, a mingling of sun-dried clothing and something else that was indefinably his own.

Shay knelt on the sleeping bag, still holding the pillow close and, unreasonably, inexplicably, tears filled her eyes. She couldn't think why, because she didn't feel sad and she didn't feel happy, either. She felt only a need to be held.

It was as though she had called out—in the future Shay would wonder many times whether or not she had—because Mitch suddenly appeared in the double doorway of the suite. "Are you all right?" he asked, and Shay knew that he was keeping his distance, honoring his promise that she would be safe with him.

And she didn't want to be safe. "No," she answered. "Actually, no."

Mitch crossed the room then, knelt before her, removed the pillow from her grip and cupped her face in his strong hands, his thumbs moving to dry away her tears.

Shay was reminded of that other time when he'd held her, before the party, when she had dissolved over a bucket of take-out chicken at the backyard picnic table. "I'm not usually such a c-crybaby," she stammered out. "You must think—"

"I think you're beautiful," he said. It was what any healthy man on the verge of a seduction would say, Shay supposed, but coming from Mitch Prescott it sounded sincere. A tremulous, electric need was surging through her, starting where his hands touched her face so gently, settling into sweet chaos in her breasts and deep within her middle. She couldn't think.

"Hold me," she said.

Mitch held her and she knew that the line had been irrevocably crossed. He kissed her, just a tentative, nibbling kiss, and the turmoil within her grew fierce. This facet of Shay's womanhood, denied for six years and largely unfulfilled before that, was now beyond the realm of good judgment: it was a thing of instinct.

But Mitch drew back, his hands on Shay's shoulders now, his expression somber in the shadowy half light of that enormous, empty room. "Remember what I said earlier, Shay? About both of us being ready?"

Shay couldn't speak; her throat was twisted into a raw knot. She managed to nod.

The low timbre of Mitch's voice resounded with misgivings. "I don't want this to be something you regret later, Shay, something that drives a wedge between us. Being close to you is too important to me."

Shay swallowed hard and was able to get out a soft, broken "I need you."

"I know," came the unhurried answer, "and I feel the same way. But for you this house is full of ghosts, Shay. What you need from me may be something entirely different than what I need from you." As if to test his theory, he held her, his hands strong on her back, comforting her but making no demands.

She rested her forehead against his shoulder, breathing deeply, trying to get control of herself. "You're wrong," she said after a long, careful silence. "I'm not Rosamond Dallas's little girl, haunting this house. I'm—I'm a woman, Mitch."

He chuckled, his breath moving warm in her hair, his hands still kneading the tautness of her back. "You are definitely a woman," he agreed. "No problems there."

Shay moved her hands, sliding them boldly beneath his sweater so that she could caress his chest, and her touch brought an involuntary groan from him, along with a muttered swearword.

Shay laughed and fell to the down-filled softness of the sleeping bag, and Mitch descended with her, one of his hands coming to rest on her thigh with a reluctant buoyancy that made it bounce away and then return again, albeit unwillingly.

"We're both going to regret this," he grumbled, but his hand was beneath her sweater now, caressing the inward curve of her waist.

That remark made sense to Shay, but she was beyond caring. There was only the needing now. "It was inevitable...."

Mitch was kissing the pulsing length of her neck, the outline of her jaw. "That it was," he agreed, and then his mouth reached hers, claiming it gently.

Shay shuddered with delicious sensations as his hand roamed up her rib cage to claim one lace-covered breast. With a practiced motion that would have been disturbing if it hadn't felt so wonderful; he displaced her bra and took her full into his hand, stroking the nipple with the side of his thumb.

She felt a shudder to answer her own move through his body as he stretched out beside her, the kiss unbroken. A primitive, silent whimpering pounded through Shay and she was glad that Mitch couldn't hear it. She wriggled to lie beneath him, needing the weight and pressure of him as much as she needed the ultimate possession they were moving toward.

He groaned at this and ended the kiss, but only to slide Shay's sweater upward, baring her inch by inch. She felt the garment pass away, soon followed by the skimpy bra beneath. She wondered why she'd worn that bra, when she'd dressed to fend off just what was happening now. Or had she dressed to invite it?

"Oh," she said, gasping the word, as Mitch's mouth closed boldly around her nipple and drove all coherent thought from her mind. His hand found the junction of her thighs, still covered by her slacks and panties, and the skilled motions of his fingers caused her hips to leap in frenzied greeting. Just when she would have begged for closer contact, he gave it, deftly undoing the button and zipper of her slacks, sliding them away into the nothingness that had taken her sweater and all her inhibitions. Her panties and sandals were soon gone, too.

"God in heaven," Mitch muttered as he drew back to look at her. He stripped off his own clothes and returned to her unwillingly, as though flung to her by forces he could not resist.

Mitch's hands caressed and stroked every part of her, until she was writhing in a tender delirium, searching him out with her fingers and her mouth, with every part of her. Finally he sat back on his muscled haunches and lifted Shay to sit astraddle of him, and she cried out as they became one in a single, leisurely stroke.

Even at the beginning, the pleasure was so great as to be nearly unbearable to Shay; she flung her head back and forth in response to the glorious ache that became greater with every motion of their joined bodies, and her hair fell from its pins and flew about her face and shoulders in a wild flurry of femininity.

All that was womanly in Shay called out to all that was masculine in Mitch and they moved as one to lie prone on the tangled sleeping bag, their bodies quickening in the most primal, most instinctive of quests. And then there was no man and there was no woman, for in the blinding explosion of satisfaction that gripped them and wrung a single shout of triumph from them both, they were one entity.

Afterward, as Shay lay trembling and dazed upon that sleeping bag, she tried to brace herself for the inevitable remorse. Incredibly she felt only brazen contentment. It was fortunate, in her view, that she didn't have the strength to talk.

Apparently, Mitch didn't either. He was lying with one leg thrust across hers, his chest moving in breaths so deep that they must have been carrying air all the way to his toes, his face buried in the warm curve where Shay's neck met her shoulder.

Long minutes had passed before he withdrew from her and crossed the room to take a robe from the closet and pull it on. The wrenching motions of his arms were angry, and the glorious inertia that had possessed Shay until that moment fled instantly.

Mitch left the room without speaking and Shay was too proud to call him back. She sat upright on the sleeping bag and covered herself with his shirt, chilled now that the contact had been broken not only physically, but emotionally. She waited in a small hell of confusion and shame, willing herself to put on her clothes and leave but unable to do so.

Finally, Mitch returned. He flipped on the lights, revealing the starkness of the room, the scattering of Shay's clothes and his own, the reality of the situation. Shay closed her eyes and let her forehead fall to her upraised knees.

He nudged her shoulder with something cold and she looked up to see that he was offering a glass of chilled wine. Blushing, Shay took it in both hands, but she could not meet his eyes.

"You're angry," she said miserably.

"Shocked would be a more appropriate word," he answered, sitting down nearby and clinking his own glass against hers.

Now, Shay's eyes darted to his face. She was stung to an anger that made her forget the one she had sensed in Mitch. "Shocked? You? The adventurer, the sophisticate?"

His expression had softened; in his eyes Shay saw some lingering annoyance, but this was overshadowed by a certain perplexity. "I wasn't casting aspersions on your moral character, Shay, so settle down."

"Then what were you doing?"

He only smiled at the snap in her voice, setting his wineglass aside with a slow, lazy motion of one hand. "From the moment I met you, you've been trying to keep me at a distance. You might as well have worn a sign saying Look, but Don't Touch. Yet tonight, you—''

She couldn't bear for him to say that she'd seduced him, though it was true, in a manner of speaking. ''I'm a woman of the eighties!'' she broke in, shrugging nonchalantly and lifting her wineglass in an insolent salute, though in truth she felt like sliding down inside the sleeping bag and hiding there.

''Yes,'' Mitch replied wryly. ''The eighteen-eighties.''

''I resent that!''

He took her wineglass and set it aside. ''Strange. That's one of the most interesting things about you, you know. Despite what we just did, you're an innocent.''

''Is that bad or good?''

He took the shirt she'd been clutching and flung it away, giving her bare breasts a wicked assessment with those quick, bold eyes of his. ''I haven't decided yet,'' he said, and then they made love again, this time in the light.

Chapter 6

The box containing what remained of the Rosamond Dallas legend was a silent reprimand to Mitch. He rolled his head and worked the taut muscles in his neck with one hand. *You'll be safe with me,* he'd told Shay. No heavy scenes, he'd said.

He heard that ridiculous old car of hers grind to a start in the driveway and swore. She'd come there to have dinner and to work and instead she was making a getaway in the gray light of a drizzling dawn, afraid of encountering his housekeeper.

Mitch shook his aching head and swore again, but then a slow, weary smile broke over his face. He regretted buying the house and he regretted ever mentioning Rosamond Dallas to his agent, but he couldn't regret Shay. For better or for worse, she was the answer to all his questions.

He walked to the middle of the library floor, knelt on the carpet and began going through the photographs, diaries and clippings that made up Rosamond Dallas's life.

At home Shay took a hot, hasty shower and dressed for work. She kept waiting for the guilt, the remorse, the regret, but there were no signs of any such emotion. Her body still vibrated, like a fine instrument expertly played, and her mind, for the first time in years, was quiet.

While she brushed her hair and applied her makeup with more care than usual, Shay remembered the nights with Eliott and wondered what she'd seen in him.

She paused, lip pencil in midair, and gazed directly into the mirror. "Hold it, lady," she warned her reflection out loud. "One night on a man's sleeping bag does not constitute a pledge of eternal devotion, you know. Don't forget that you threw yourself at him like a—like a brazen hussy!" Shay frowned hard, for emphasis, but even those sage words, borrowed in part from one of her mother's early movies, could not dampen her soaring spirits. She was in love with Mitch Prescott, really in love, for the first time in her life, and for the moment, that was enough.

Of course, it made no sense to be so happy—there

was every chance that she'd just made a mistake of epic proportions—but Shay didn't let that bother her either. Mitch's feelings, whatever they might be, were his own problem.

She drove to Reese Motors and soared into her office, only to find Ivy waiting in ambush. Even though the phones were ringing and Richard's camera crew was crowded into the reception room, Ms. Prescott sat quietly on Shay's couch, her legs crossed, her hands folded in her lap.

Shay smiled and shook her head. Love was marvelous. Richard's crew was proof positive that she was going to have to film another commercial that very day and here was Ivy, waiting to grill her about the evening with Mitch, and she still felt wonderful. "I hate to pull rank, Ivy," she said brightly, "but get out there and take care of business. Now."

Ivy looked hurt but nonetheless determined as she stood up and smoothed the skirt of her blue cotton dress. "At least promise to have lunch with me," she said with dignity. "You did say that you'd tell me all about everything, you know."

Shay thought about "everything" and blushed. There was no way she was going to tell everything. "We may not have time for lunch today, Ivy. There's another commercial scheduled, isn't there? And by the way that phone is jumping around on the desk, I'd say it's going to be a crazy day."

Ivy was sulking and just reaching for the doorknob

when the door itself suddenly sprang open, the chasm filled by an earnest and somewhat testy Richard. "I know we planned to wait a week before we filmed the second spot, but something has come up and—"

Shay smiled placidly, knowing that the advertising executive had been prepared for a battle. "Come in, Richard," she said in a sweet voice. "Don't bother to knock."

Richard looked sheepish and somewhat baffled. He ran one hand through his already mussed hair and stared at Shay in speechless bewilderment.

She laughed. "Which one are we doing today?" she prompted lightly as Ivy dashed out and began answering the calls that were lighting up all the buttons on the telephone.

"The one you hated."

Shay was still unruffled. "That figures. When are they airing yesterday's artistic triumph?"

"Next week," Richard answered distractedly, glancing at his watch and frowning as though it had somehow displeased him. "Do you want the makeup done here, or down on the lot, in the RV?"

"I don't want it done at all, but I know wishful thinking when I see it. I'll be on down there in five or ten minutes."

Shay's intercom buzzed and she picked up the telephone receiver. "Yes, Ivy?"

"Hank's on line two," the secretary said pleasantly, her ire at being put off having faded away.

Delighted, Shay punched the second button on her telephone. "Hi, tiger!" she cried. "How are you?"

The sound of Hank's voice was the reward, Shay supposed, for some long-forgotten good deed. "I'm great, Mom! We're at this lake in Oregon and we caught two fish already!"

"That's fantastic!" Shay ignored Richard Barrett's alternating glares of impatience and consultations with his watch and turned to the windows. The sky was gray and drops of rain were bouncing off the cars in the rear lot. It was strange, she reflected fancifully, that she hadn't noticed the weather on her way to work. "Is it raining there?"

The conversation with her son was sweetly mundane and when it ended, five minutes later, Shay stoically followed Richard through the outer office and down the stairs. Due to the rain, the RV had been parked close to one of the rear entrances and the showroom itself would be the set.

Inside the roomy motor home, Shay was helped into a neck-to-toe bodysuit with metallic bolts of thunder stitched to it, and glittery cartoon superheroine makeup was applied to her face. As gooey styling mousse was poured into her hair, she tried to be philosophical. This was the silliest commercial of the lot, but it was also the easiest. She had only to say one line, and the remainder of the spot would show used cars with prices painted on their windshields.

"I bet you hate having your friends see you like

this," commiserated Richard's assistant, she of the fluffy bangs and ever-present clipboard, as she pulled Shay's mousse-saturated tresses into points that stuck straight out, all over her head.

Shay only rolled her eyes, telling herself that the girl was young.

"I'd die," insisted the little helper.

"If you keep working for Richard," Shay replied, "your life will probably be short."

"Huh?"

"Here but for the grace of God go you, my dear."

"I still don't get it."

"Never mind," Shay said with a sigh. The mousse was drying and her scalp itched. The bodysuit was riding up in all the wrong places. She told herself that that was why she suddenly felt so uncharitable.

The door of the RV squeaked open and made the hollow sound typical of all motor homes when it closed behind Richard. He looked at Shay as though he'd just beaten her at some game and his mouth twitched. "I," he said with quiet pomposity, "am a genius."

"Don't press your luck, Richard," Shay snarled. Her body was no longer vibrating, and there was a headache unfolding behind her right temple.

"I said I'd die if I had to dress like that and she said my life might be short if I went on working for you," broke in the assistant in a breathless babble.

"What'd she mean by that, Richard? She won't tell me what she meant!"

"Wait outside, Chrissie," Richard said, all but patting the girl on the head.

Reluctantly, Chrissie obeyed.

"Does your wife know about her?" Shay asked, just to be mean.

Richard cleared his throat and pressed at his hopelessly old-fashioned glasses with one index finger. Despite this display of nervousness, he was not an easy opponent. "You have an audience outside," he said. "Why, darlin', your fame is spreadin' like wildfire!"

Shay stood up with a sigh. "That was the worst imitation of J.R. Ewing I've ever heard," she snapped.

Richard only shrugged, and when they entered the showroom moments later, Shay was even more annoyed to find that she did indeed have an audience. All of the salesmen were there, along with their wives and even a few children. It was the presence of the children that kept Shay from showing them that she was Rosamond Dallas's daughter by making a scene.

"Stand right there on your *X*, darlin'," Richard drawled in the same bad Texas accent. "This'll be over before you can say—"

"Oh, shut up!" Shay grumbled, taking her mark.

The lights were blaring in her face. She drew a deep breath and tried to be professional, which wasn't easy in a thunderbolt bodysuit and outrageous makeup. Mentally she went over her line. Oh, to do this in one take and have it behind her!

The clapboard snapped in her face and Shay smiled broadly, trying not to think of how her hair was standing out from her head in mousse-crusted points. She knew she looked as though she had just stuck her finger into a light socket, and that, of course, was the whole idea. "Come out and see for yourselves, folks," she crowed winningly. "Our prices here at Reese Motors, 6832 Discount Way, are so low that they'll shock you!"

It was a wrap! Shay wanted to jump up into the air, Mickey Rooney-style, and click her heels together.

"Do it again," Richard said with exaggerated patience.

Shay couldn't have been more surprised if he'd doused her in cold water. "What?" she demanded. "Richard, that take was perfect!"

"It wasn't anything of the sort. I want more emphasis on the word 'shock.'"

He was repaying her for the barbs they'd exchanged inside the RV and that knowledge infuriated Shay. "I think this gunk in my hair makes that point on its own, don't you?"

"No," Richard responded flatly.

He made her go through the scene half a dozen

times before he would admit to any sort of satisfaction
with it, and that, when he gave it, was grudging.

Shay muttered as she stomped back into the RV
and slammed the door behind her. Refusing help from
the vacuous Chrissie, she slathered cleansing cream
onto her face and carefully wiped away the glittery
makeup. After that, she squeezed into the vehicle's
miniature bathroom and took a tepid shower, muttering through shampoo after shampoo. A bathrobe that
probably belonged to Marvin was hanging on the
hook inside the door, and Shay helped herself to it.

When she left the bathroom she was startled to find
Mitch Prescott sitting at the RV's tiny table, his hair
moussed into an elongated crew cut rising a good four
inches above his head. "May I say," he told her blandly,
"that I was shocked by your behavior this morning?"

The utter ridiculousness of the moment dissolved
Shay's foul mood, and she began to laugh. "You're
crazy!"

Mitch caught her hand and pulled her onto his lap.
"About you," he said, on cue.

Shay knew that she shouldn't be sitting on this
man's lap in an oversized bathrobe with all of Reese
Motors's employees gathered outside, but she was
powerless to move away. She looked at Mitch's hair
and into his laughing brown eyes and she thought, *I
love you. God help me, I love you.*

Mischievously he opened the front of her robe, revealing her breasts, and she could not lift a hand to

stop him. ''It's a good thing you washed that stuff out of your hair,'' he mumbled distractedly, and she could feel his breath on her right breast, feel the nipple tensing for the touch of his tongue. It came soon enough, and Shay gasped, the sensation was so wickedly delicious.

''Why?'' she groaned.

''Because we might have mated and produced a punk rocker,'' he answered sleepily, still busy with her breast.

Using laughter and the last bit of her willpower, Shay thrust herself off Mitch's lap and out of his reach. Watching her, he helped himself to a hairbrush left behind by Chrissie and returned his hair to some semblance of normalcy. Shay wanted to use that time to dress and escape, but she couldn't seem to work up the momentum.

When the maestro held out his hands, she moved into them, moaning softly as she stood before Mitch, shivering as she felt the robe open. The intermezzo was a sweet one, brief and soaring, underscored by Shay's own soft cries of pleasure as she was taught a new tune, note by glorious note.

Minutes later, fully dressed, she left the RV with her head held high and her body humming. The vibrations carried her through the rest of the day.

If the night before had been given over to dalliance, that one was all business. The rest of Mitch's furniture had arrived and he and Shay sat on a sinfully soft burgundy sofa in his library, facing each other instead of the crackling fire, half-buried in scrapbooks and old photographs.

As she explained what she knew of her mother's life, Shay found herself thrust from one emotional extreme to another, from laughter to tears, from love to anger. Mitch only listened, making no move to touch her.

"Sometimes," Shay confided pensively as the long evening drew toward a close, "I think she was the most selfish person on earth. Riley loved her so much, and yet..."

The small cassette recorder between them hummed and whirred. "Yes?" prompted Mitch.

"I think that was the very reason that Rosamond began to lose interest in him. Finally she seemed to feel nothing but contempt. But Riley was such a good man, so decent and solid—it just doesn't make sense!"

"Since when are legendary movie stars expected to make sense?"

Shay shrugged and then yawned. "Rosamond certainly didn't."

"She must have made you angry," Mitch remarked, snapping off the recorder with a motion of his hand.

The words jarred Shay out of her sleepy stupor.

Suddenly she didn't want to talk about Rosamond anymore, and she didn't want to talk about herself. "I'd better be going," she said, moving to rise off the sofa.

Mitch stopped her by taking her arm in a gentle grasp. "She did make you angry, didn't she?" he persisted quietly.

"No."

"You're lying."

Shay bounded off the couch and this time there was no stopping her. "Who do you think you are?" she snapped. "Sigmund Freud?"

Mitch sat back in that cushy sofa, damn him, and cupped his hands behind his head, not saying so much as a word. Shay was reminded of the scandalous way he'd loved her in the RV earlier and she sat down in a nearby chair, her knees weak.

"Everybody has hang-ups about their mother," she sputtered when the silence grew too long and too damning. She glared at Mitch, remembering all that Ivy had told her over the past few years. "Or their stepmother."

Mitch sighed and stared up at the ceiling, still maintaining his attitude of relaxed certainty. "The difference is, my dear, that I can talk about my stepmother. She and I don't get along because she was my father's mistress before he and my mother were divorced. In effect, you could say that she took him away from us."

"My God," Shay whispered, feeling sympathy even though there was nothing in Mitch's voice or manner that asked for it.

"It was traumatic at the time," Mitch said evenly. "But Dad was a good father to me and, eventually, my mother remarried. She's disgustingly happy."

"But Ivy's mother—"

"Elizabeth does the best she can. She loved my father."

Shay was silent.

"Your turn," Mitch prompted.

She stared into the snapping fire for a while, drifting back to another night. "Rosamond was her own greatest fan," she said. "And yet she could humiliate herself so easily. I remember one of her lovers—a tennis bum—he was good-looking but if you tapped on his forehead, nobody would answer the door."

Mitch chuckled. "Go on."

"He was part of the reason that Mother got bored with Riley, I guess. After Riley and Garrett were gone, he decided that it was time to get back on the old circuit. He was going to walk out and I'll never forget—I'll never forget the way Mother acted. He was trying to get into his car and she was on her knees in the driveway, with her arms wrapped around his legs, begging him to stay." Shay turned shadowed, hurting eyes to Mitch's face. "It was awful."

"You saw that?" Mitch must have tried, but he failed to keep the annoyance out of his voice.

"I've seen a lot worse," she answered.

"Stay with me," he said, clearing away aging memorabilia to make a space beside him on the sofa.

Shay couldn't leave, but she suddenly felt too broken and vulnerable to stay. "I don't want—"

"I know," he said, standing up and extending one hand to her. After a moment or so, she rose and took the offered hand and Mitch led her gently up the stairs and into his bedroom.

Furnished now with a massive waterbed, chairs and bureaus and a freestanding chess table set up for play, the room didn't seem so vast.

Deftly, as though he did such things as a part of his daily routine, Mitch undressed Shay and then buttoned her into one of his pajama tops, a royal blue silk affair with piping and a monogram on the pocket.

"You do not strike me as a man who wears pajamas," she said, aware of the inanity of her remark but too shaky to say anything heavier.

"A Christmas present from Ivy," he explained, disappearing into the adjoining bathroom. A moment later Shay heard the shower running.

"Why am I staying here?" she asked the cosmos, holding her arms out from her sides.

When the cosmos didn't answer, she followed Mitch into the steamy chamber and helped herself to one of the new toothbrushes she found in the cabinet drawer. As she brushed, she fumed. Six toothbrushes, still in their boxes. The man expected to entertain a harem!

Behind the beautifully etched door of the double shower, Mitch sang at the top of his lungs. Shay glared at her reflection in the steamy mirror. "If you had any sense at all," she muttered, "you'd go home! This is a man who keeps extra toothbrushes, for God's sake!"

Having said all this, Shay went back to the bedroom and crawled into bed. The sheets were as smooth as satin and the lulling motion of the water-filled mattress, coupled with the song of the tide coming in through the terrace doors, reduced her to a sleepy, languid state.

She felt the bed sway as Mitch got into it, heard the click of the lamp switch, stirred under the sweet weight of the darkness. "Are you going to make love to me?" she asked.

He chuckled and drew her close, holding her. "No," he said.

Shay yawned. "Don't let go, okay?"

"Okay," came the hoarse reply.

They both slept soundly, huddled close in that gigantic bed, neither asking anything of the other except their nearness.

Mitch awakened to an exquisite caress and opened his eyes to see a tumble-haired vamp kneeling on the bed beside him, her whole face lit by a wicked grin.

"Ummm," he said, stretching, luxuriating in the pleasure she was creating. "The truce is over, I take it?"

"Every man for himself," she agreed.

"In that case..." He stretched again, with deceptive leisure, and then flipped over suddenly, carrying Shay with him, imprisoning her soft body beneath his own.

Her eyes widened in mock surprise and he laughed, using his nose to spar with hers.

She caught her hands together at the back of his neck and drew him into her kiss; it was a soft, nurturing thing, and yet it sent aching waves of desperate need crashing through him. He sensed that she was exerting some tender vengeance for the way he'd pleasured her in the RV the day before and he was all for it.

When the opportunity afforded itself some moments later, Mitch pulled back far enough to rid Shay of the pajama top and then fell to her again, settling against her but reluctant to take her.

Suddenly she parted her legs and the warmth of her was too compelling to be resisted. He entered her almost involuntarily, thrust into the agonizing comfort she offered by the strength of her hands and the upward thrust of her hips.

She guided him, she taunted him, she rendered him mindless with need. For all Shay's beautiful treachery, however, her moment came first and Mitch marveled at the splendor in her face as she cried out, tossing her head back and forth on the pillow and grasping at his shoulders with her hands.

"I love you," he said.

It was clear enough that Ivy's feelings were hurt. Entering the office, after a hasty shower and change of clothes at home, Shay remembered her promise to have lunch with her friend the day before and was chagrined, even though there had been no time to go out to eat.

"Hi," she said, standing before Ivy's desk.

Ivy kept her eyes on her computer screen. "Hi," she said remotely.

"Free for lunch?"

Ivy looked up quickly, and the clouds separated, revealing the sunlight that was integral to her nature. "We might have to stay in. I got kind of behind yesterday."

Shay was relieved that no permanent damage had been done to this most cherished friendship. Ivy might be nosy, but it was only because she cared so much. "We could always call Screaming Hernando's and have them send over a guacamole pizza."

Ivy made a face and then giggled.

The morning went smoothly, and when noon came, Ivy and Shay were able to slip away, Ivy having set the office answering machine to pick up any incoming calls. They had chicken sandwiches at the coffee shop across the street.

"I thought you were mad at me," Ivy confided between delicate bites from her sandwich. "I guess I shouldn't have called Mitch and told him you were filming another commercial."

Shay leaned forward, forgetting her sandwich. "So that was how he knew. I should have guessed. Ivy Prescott, what possessed you?"

"Actually," Ivy replied, "it wasn't anything quite as dramatic as possession. It was plain old bribery. Mitch promised to try to get along with my mother if I would call him whenever you were doing a spot."

"Traitor!"

"What can I tell you? I love my mother and I love Mitch and I want to see them bury the hatchet, especially with the wedding coming up."

Shay remembered what Mitch had told her the night before, when they were talking about hang-ups. "Is it working?"

"They've been civil to each other," Ivy said, shrugging. "I guess that's a start. So, are you and Mitch an item, or what?"

"An 'item'? Have you been reading old movie magazines or something?"

Ivy executed a mock glare. "Stop hedging, Shay. You don't need to tell me, you know. You can just sit by and see me consumed by my own curiosity."

Shay sighed. "If you're talking about the love-and-marriage kind of item, we're not."

Ivy's eyes were wide with delight. "That's what

they all say," she replied. "So the gossip is true! You and Mitch are doing more than working together!"

"Now that is definitely none of your business, Ivy Prescott," Shay said firmly. "And exactly what gossip is this?"

"Well, you two were inside the RV together for quite a while yesterday...."

Shay willed herself not to blush at the memory and failed. She hoped Ivy would ascribe the high color in her face to righteous indignation. "What were you doing, standing out there with a stopwatch?"

"Of course not!" Ivy's feathers were ruffled. She squirmed in her chair and looked incensed and then said defensively, "I don't even own a stopwatch!"

Chapter 7

"This is some pile of bricks," Ivan announced, gazing appreciatively up at the walls of the house while Mitch was still recovering from the surprise of finding his agent standing on his doorstep. "Pretty big for one person, isn't it?"

Mitch stepped back to admit the small, well-dressed man with the balding pate. Ignoring Ivan's question, he offered one of his own. "What's so important that it couldn't have been handled by telephone, Ivan?"

Ivan patted his breast pocket and grinned. "An advance check of this size warrants personal delivery," he answered.

Mitch turned and walked back toward the library

where he'd been working over his notes for the Rosamond Dallas book, leaving Ivan to follow. Mrs. Carraway, who had been upstairs cleaning most of the morning, magically appeared with coffee and warm croissants.

Once the pleasant-faced woman had gone, Ivan helped himself to a cup of coffee and a croissant. "Nice to see you living the good life at last, Prescott. I was beginning to think you were going to spend the rest of your days crawling through jungles on your belly and hobnobbing with the Klan."

Despite his sometimes abrasive manner, Mitch liked and respected Ivan Wright. The man was always direct, and he played hardball in all his dealings. "I guess I'm ready to settle down," he said, and his mind immediately touched on Shay.

"That could be good, and it could be bad," Ivan replied. "What are your plans for after?"

"After what?"

"After you finish the Rosamond Dallas book." Ivan added jam and cream to his croissant.

"I haven't made any plans for another project, if that's what you're getting at. I may retire. After all, I'm a rich man."

"You're also a young man," Ivan pointed out. "What are you, thirty-seven, thirty-eight?" Without waiting for an answer, the agent went on. "Your publishers want another book, Mitch, and they're willing to pay top dollar to get your name on the dotted line."

The thought made Mitch feel weary. He was having a hard enough time working up enough enthusiasm to write about Rosamond, but he supposed that was because of Shay. No matter how delicately the project was handled, she would, to some degree, be hurt by it. "We're talking about a specific subject here, I assume."

Ivan nodded, licking a dab of cream from one pudgy finger. "You've heard of Alan Roget, haven't you? That serial murderer the FBI picked up in Oklahoma a few months back?"

Mitch remembered. The man had been arraigned on some thirty-two counts of homicide. "Sweet guy," he reflected.

"Roget may be a pyscho, but he's a fan of yours. If anybody writes his story, he wants it to be you."

"They don't need his permission to do a book," Mitch pointed out, and he remembered saying a similar thing to Shay.

"No," Ivan agreed readily, calmly. "The difference is that he's willing to talk to you, tell you the whole disgusting saga from his point of view. Another writer could do the job, of course, but they'd be operating on guesswork."

"What about my anonymity? How could we trust this maniac to respect that?"

"He wouldn't have to know your real name. That can be handled, Mitch, in the same way we've handled it in the past. What do you say?" A master of timing, Ivan waited a moment and then laid the sizable check Mitch and Shay would share on the coffee table between them.

"I need time to think, Ivan. For one thing, I'm not sure I even want to hear all the rot this space-case probably plans to spill."

"Going soft, Prescott?"

"Maybe."

Ivan gave a delicate sigh and stood up. "Well, I've got a cab waiting. Got to get back to the airport, you know."

Mitch only shook his head. He was half Ivan's age, but even in his jungle-crawling, Klan-breaking days, he hadn't lived at the pace that Ivan did.

"You'll call?" Ivan asked, tugging at the jacket of his Brooks Brothers' suit to straighten it.

"I'll call." Mitch sighed the words.

Shay raised one eyebrow when Ivy informed her that the bank was calling. She couldn't be overdrawn, could she? She'd just deposited the bonus check Marvin had signed before he left, making payment for the four commercials.

"Ms. Kendall?"

Shay drew a deep breath and set aside the stack of paperwork, also left behind by Marvin, that she'd been wading through. "Yes?"

"My name is Robert Parker and I'm calling in reference to your account."

Shay tensed and then willed herself to relax. She had balanced her checkbook only a few days before, and her figures had tallied with the bank's. "Yes?"

"It seems that a sizable amount of money has been deposited and, well, we were just wondering if a mistake had been made. This sum is well beyond what the Federal Reserve will insure in any single account, you know."

"I don't understand," Shay said, resting her forehead in the palm of one hand. "Surely a four thousand dollar bonus check—"

"Four thousand dollars?" The bank officer laughed nervously. "My, my, this deposit is many times that amount. I was certain that there had to be some error."

Shay was a little stung that the banker could be so incredulous, even though she was incredulous herself. Maybe she'd never had more than eight hundred dollars in her account at any one time, but she wasn't a deadbeat and if she'd been overdrawn a time or two, why, that had been accidental. "Wait just a moment, Mr. Parker, wasn't it? Where did this deposit come from?"

"The check itself was drawn on the account of a Mr. Mitch Prescott."

It was a moment before Shay remembered the book she and Mitch were supposed to be writing together; her mind hadn't exactly been on the professional aspects of their relationship. "Then the money is

mine,'' she said, as much to herself as to Mr. Parker.
''Would you mind telling me the exact amount?''

The sum Mr. Parker replied with made the pit of
Shay's stomach leap and sent her head into a dizzying
spin. Mitch had told her that her share would be a
''lot'' of money, but never in Shay's wildest dreams
had she expected so much.

''We'll have to verify this, of course,'' Parker said
stiffly, seeming to find Shay's good fortune suspect
in some way.

''Of course,'' Shay answered. And then she hung
up the receiver, folded her arms on the desktop and
lowered her head to them.

She was rich.

The more Mitch thought about the Alan Roget project, the more it appealed to him. It would be a study in
human ugliness, that book, but for once in his life he
had something to counterbalance that. He had Shay.

Eager now to get the Rosamond Dallas book behind him, he unpacked his computer equipment and
the attending paraphernalia and brought the machine
on-line. Working from his notes and the tapes containing Shay's observations about her mother, he began composing a comprehensive outline of the material he had on hand.

He was interrupted, at intervals, by the telephone.
Mrs. Carraway tried to field his calls, but there were
several that could not be avoided, one from a pedantic

bank clerk questioning the deposit he'd made to Shay's account after Ivan had left, one from his daughter, Kelly, who wanted to tell him that she could visit over Christmas vacation, and one from Lucetta White. Lucetta had heard, through the grapevine, that he'd landed a "plum" of an assignment and asked for details. Mitch had talked for fifteen minutes and told Ms. White exactly nothing.

He was sitting back in his desk chair, his hands cupped behind his head, when the telephone rang again. To spare Mrs. Carraway the problem, he answered it himself with a crisp "Hello?"

"Hello," Shay replied, and the single word resounded with bewilderment. "About that money..."

Mitch waited for her to go on, but she didn't, so he replied, "Your share, as agreed. Is anything wrong?"

"Wrong? Well, no, of course not. A-are we working tonight?"

"I'm working. From now on, your part will be an occasional consultation. Of course, I'll need you to read over the material, too, as I write it."

"Oh," she said, and she sounded disappointed. Perhaps even a little hurt.

"Shay, what's the matter?"

She sighed. "I feel a little—a little superfluous, I guess. And overpaid for it in the bargain."

Mitch laughed. "You could never be superfluous, my love. Listen, if you want a more active part in writing the book, you can have it."

He could almost see her shaking her beautiful, leonine head. "No, no. I have things of my own to do, now that I'm a woman of means."

Mitch arched an eyebrow, not sure he liked the sound of that. "Like what?"

"Oh, getting solid financial advice, talking to the tax people, starting my catering service. Things of that nature."

Mitch hadn't known that Shay had aspirations to go into business for herself and he was a little peeved that she'd failed to confide something so important. He scowled down at his watch and saw that it was nearly five o'clock. "I won't keep you, then," he said stiffly, and even as he spoke the words he wondered what it was that made him want to put space between himself and this woman when he needed her so much.

There was a brief silence, and then Shay answered, "No. Well, thank you." She hung up and Mitch sat glaring at the receiver in his hand.

No. Well, thank you, he mimicked in his mind. She had what she wanted now, the money; apparently their lovemaking and the special rapport they'd formed weren't important anymore. Mitch hung up with a bang that was no less satisfying for Shay's not hearing it.

As Shay wandered up and down the aisles of the public library that evening, choosing books on the operation of small businesses, she was awash in a numbing sort of despair. All of her dreams were suddenly coming true, or, at least, most of them, and she should have been happy. She hugged the stack of self-help books close to her chest. Why wasn't she happy?

She knew the answer, of course and was only torturing herself with the question. She had thought she meant something to Mitch Prescott and found out differently. She had provided the research material he needed for his book and he'd paid her and, as far as he was concerned, the transaction was complete. There would be a few "consultations," and he wanted her input as the book progressed, but he'd made it clear enough that she wasn't to expect anything more.

Shay drove home slowly, heated a can of soup for her supper and immersed herself in the books she had checked out at the library, making notes in a spiral notebook as she read. It wasn't as though she needed Mitch Prescott to be happy, she told herself during frequent breaks in her concentration. She had Hank, she had her job, and she had the money and the determination to make her life what she'd always dreamed it could be.

Well, almost what she'd dreamed it could be.

For the rest of that week, Shay concentrated on her job at Reese Motors, grateful that she would have a little time before she had to do another commercial.

She talked to Hank frequently by telephone and visited Rosamond every afternoon. From the convalescent home she invariably went to the public library, exchanging the books she'd scanned the night before for new ones. She told herself that she was preparing for her own entry into the world of private enterprise and she was learning a great deal, but the main reason for her marathon study fests was Mitch Prescott. Being absorbed in business theories kept her from thinking about him.

By Saturday morning, she was haggard. Ivy, showing up on her doorstep bright and early, was quick to point that out.

Shay yawned, feeling rumpled and dissolute in her old chenille bathrobe. "How do you expect me to look at nine o'clock on a Saturday morning? Don't you ever sleep in?"

The weather was nice and Ivy looked disgustingly vibrant in her old blue jeans and summery cotton blouse. "Sleep in?" she chimed. "And let the world pass me by?"

"The world wouldn't dare pass you by," Shay responded dryly, staggering toward the kitchen, homing in on the coffeepot which, blessedly, operated on a small timer set the night before. "Where's Todd?"

Ivy settled herself in a chair at Shay's table, shoving aside the current stack of business books with a slight frown. "He's working. Ambition is his curse, you know." She stopped for a breath. "I'm going to this great auction today. Want to come along?"

Shay poured coffee for herself and Ivy and stumbled over to the table to collapse into a chair. "Why would I want to go to an auction?"

"To buy something, silly. This is an estate sale, and they're holding it in a barn."

"I'm not in the market for harnesses and milk stools," Shay muttered, beginning to come alive as caffeine surged through her veins.

"The newspaper ad says they have a lot of great stuff, Shay. Antiques."

"Milk stools."

"You're impossible. I bought my brass bed at a sale like this, and for a song, too."

"They probably just wanted you to stop singing."

"Very funny. Come on, Shay, come with me. For the drive. For the fresh air. Good Lord, you look terrible."

Shay knew she couldn't face another day of studying. Maybe it would be fun to poke through a lot of junk in some old barn and then treat Ivy to lunch. "You haven't asked me why I look terrible, Ivy. For you, that's a drastic oversight."

Ivy sat up very straight and smiled. "I haven't asked because I already know. You and Mitch are on the outs."

"You're pleased about that?"

"I know it's temporary. Now, are you going to the sale with me or not?"

"I'm going. Just let me finish my coffee."

"No." Ivy shook her head. "They sell coffee at the sale. They sell it in little stands along the road. They sell it everywhere. Take your shower and let's go!"

Muttering, Shay abandoned her coffee and made her way to the bathroom.

The carousel horse stood, its once-bright paint chipped and faded, in the middle of the barn where the auction would be held, as though waiting for Shay.

She drew in her breath and moved toward it, her eyes wide. It couldn't be Clydesdale!

Shay crouched to look at the horse's right rear hoof. Sure enough, splotches of Rosamond's favorite fire-engine red fingernail polish still clung to the wood. The marks had been made one glum and rainy afternoon in the long-ago, by Shay herself.

Another woman came to look at the horse. "Wouldn't that make a marvelous planter, Harold?" she was saying. "We could strip off the paint and then varnish it...."

Shay put down an urge to slap the woman away and glanced back over one shoulder at Ivy, who was inspecting a sterling-silver butter dish, one of hundreds of items set out on portable display tables.

The carousel horse, like the playhouse, had been a gift from Riley, before his divorce from Rosamond, and Shay had cherished it. The piece was valuable, and, after shipping Shay off to a summer camp, Rosamond had sold it on a whim.

The anger came back to Shay—or maybe it had never left. In any case, it was all she could do not to fling one arm over the neck of that battered, beloved old horse and cling to it, fending off all prospective buyers with her purse.

"That's nice," Ivy said suddenly from beside Shay, her eyes moving over the hand-carved and painted relic. "Are you going to bid on it?"

The woman and Harold were still standing nearby, pondering their plans to make a planter of Shay's horse. "I might," she said through tight lips, shrugging to give her words an air of indifference and nonchalance.

By the time the bidding finally began, Shay was in a state of anxiety, though she managed to appear calm. When Clydesdale—Garrett and Shay had considered a multitude of names for the horse before coming up with that one—came on the docket, she waited until the auctioneer had gotten a number of bids before entering one of her own.

Harold and the missus drove the price well beyond what Riley had paid for the piece originally, and it had been expensive then, but Shay didn't care. When the competition fell away and hers was the highest bid, she had to choke back a shout of triumph.

"What are you going to do with that, Shay?" Ivy whispered, sounding honestly puzzled.

It was a reasonable question. While Hank would consider the horse an interesting addition to their hodge-podge decorating scheme, he would not see it as a spinner of magic. "I'll explain later," Shay whispered back.

Ivy shrugged and jumped into the bidding for the silver butter dish. Later, after Shay had written a check and arranged for the horse to be delivered, she posed her original question.

Settled into the passenger seat of Ivy's car, Shay shrugged self-consciously. "He was mine, once. One of my mother's husbands gave him to me when I was a little girl. I'd just had my tonsils out, and Riley wanted to spoil me."

"Oh," said Ivy, in a fondly sentimental tone. "That's sweet."

They stopped for a late lunch and Shay was ravenous, but she was also anxious to get home. The horse would be delivered around six o'clock that evening, and she wanted to have sandpaper and fresh paints ready.

In fact, she did. She had newspapers spread out on her living room floor, too, and the deliverymen made jokes about that as they set the beloved old toy on the paper and unwrapped the blankets that had protected it.

Shay smiled wanly at their attempt at humor and had to restrain herself from shooing them out so that she could begin the restoration project. Once they'd been given their tip, they left.

Gently, Shay applied a special paint-stripping compound to the horse, removing as much of the scratched and faded finish as she could. Then she sanded. And sanded. And sanded.

It was therapy, she said to herself. She would restore Clydesdale to his former glory and when she opened her catering service, he would stand in the office, where customers could admire him. Maybe he would even become her personal insignia, his image emblazoned on her letterhead....

Letterhead. Shay smiled and shook her head. Before there could be letterhead, there had to be a business, didn't there?

As she knelt beside the carousel horse, sanding away what remained of the silver paint on one hoof, Shay felt real trepidation. It wouldn't be easy to hand in her resignation; while she could go no further in her job at Reese Motors, it was a secure position and it paid decently. The work might be trying sometimes, but it was never dull, and Marvin and Jeannie had been so kind to her.

On the other hand, Shay had money now, and a

chance to follow her dreams. How many people got an opportunity like this? she asked herself. How many?

Shay sanded more vigorously, so intent on her task and her quandary that, when the doorbell rang, she was startled. Rubbing her hands down the front of an old cotton work shirt that Eliott had left behind, she got to her feet and hurried to answer the persistent ringing.

Mitch Prescott was standing on the worn doormat, looking both exasperated and contrite. He was wearing a white T-shirt and jeans, his hands wedged into his hip pockets.

Shay's heart slid over one beat and then steadied. She was painfully conscious of her rumpled hair and solvent-scented clothes. "Yes?" she said with remarkable calm.

"Dammit, Shay," he grumbled. "Let me in."

Shay stepped back and Mitch opened the screen door and came inside the now-cluttered living room. His dark eyes touched on the carousel horse, now stripped nearly to bare wood, but he made no comment.

Remembering his coolness on the telephone, Shay was determined to keep a hold on her composure, such as it was. She wasn't about to let Mitch know how his disinterest had hurt her. "May I help you?" she asked stiffly.

He looked patently annoyed. "I came here to apologize," he snapped. "Though I'm not exactly sure what it was that I did wrong."

Coolness be damned. Shay simmered, and her voice came out in a furious hiss. "You made love to me, Mitch Prescott. You laughed with me and you held me and you listened to my deepest secrets! Then, when you'd found out all you wanted to know about my mother, when you'd paid me for my trouble—"

Mitch's strong, beard-stubbled jawline tensed, and his coffee-colored eyes snapped. "That's not fair, Shay," he broke in. "The deal we made has nothing to do with what's going on between us."

"Doesn't it? Strange, but I noticed a definite decrease in your interest level once I'd told you about my mother and shared your bed a couple of times!"

"You think that's why I slept with you? To get the inside skinny on your mother?" He paused, made an angry sound low in his throat, and then ran one hand through his hair in frustration. "Good God, Shay, don't you see how neurotic that is?"

"Neurotic? You're calling me *neurotic?*"

His expression, in fact his whole demeanor, softened. "No. No, sweetheart. I'm not. You're probably the sanest person I know. But when it comes to intimate relationships, you've got some problems." Mitch sighed and spread his hands. "Little wonder, considering your mother's exploits and that bastard you married."

Shay wavered, not sure whether to be angry or

comforted. There was something inside her that needed to believe Mitch, no matter what he said, and down that path lay risks that she couldn't take. She'd believed Eliott, after all, and she'd believed Rosamond's promises that each marriage would be the one that would last. "Don't you dare slander my mother," she whispered.

"Rosamond hurt you, Shay. You're angry. Why can't you admit that?"

"She's a poor, sick woman!" Shay cried. "How could I be angry at her? How?"

"You couldn't—not at the Rosamond of today, anyway. But that other Rosamond, the young, vital one who didn't have time for her own daughter—"

Shay whirled away, furious and afraid. "Why are you doing this to me? Why are you pushing me, pestering me? Why?"

He caught her upper arms in his hands and gently turned her to face him. "Shay, get mad. Admit that the woman hurt you, disappointed you. You're not going to be able to let go of that part of your life unless you face what you really feel."

Shay's chin quivered, but her eyes flashed as she looked up into Mitch's face. "How do you know what I feel?" she choked out. "How could anybody know what it's like to mean less than the latest tennis pro in your mother's life? Less than a racehorse, for God's sake?"

"Tell me what it's like, Shay. I'll listen."

Shay trembled. "Making mental notes for your book all the while, I'm sure! Get out of here, Mitch, leave me alone. I've told you all I can."

He gave her a slight shake. "Will you forget that damned book? I'm not talking about Rosamond, I'm talking about you, about us!"

"What about us, Mitch?" The question was a challenge, a mockery, an attempt to drive this man away before he could become important enough to Shay to hurt her. He already had become just that, of course, but there was such a thing as cutting one's losses and making a run for it. God knew, she thought frantically, Rosamond had taught her that if nothing else.

Mitch's hands fell slowly from Shay's shoulders and, once again, he looked toward the carousel horse. She sensed that he knew all about Clydesdale.

After a long time, Mitch sighed and started toward the door. In the opening, he paused, his eyes searching Shay's face for a moment and then shifting away. "You know, I really thought we'd be able to communicate, you and I. I really thought we had a chance."

Shay's throat tightened and tears burned in her eyes. She turned away from Mitch and took up her sandpaper.

"You can't bring back your childhood, Shay," he said, and then the door closed quietly behind him.

Shay wiped her eyes on the sleeve of her work shirt and sanded harder.

Chapter 8

Shay stood back from the carousel horse, her hands on her hips, her head tilted to one side. She had been working on the project every night for a week and now it was done: Clydesdale was restored to his former pink, silver and pale blue glory. He looked fabulous.

She sighed, wiping her hands on her shirt. Now what was she going to do to keep herself from going mad? Hank wouldn't be home for another ten days and Shay couldn't stand the thought of reading another book on the management of a small business. She'd reached her saturation point when it came to studying. Besides, she had learned the rudiments of free enterprise by working for Marvin Reese; it was time to take real action.

Shay glanced at the clock on the wall above the TV and grimaced. It was nearly two in the morning, and the third commercial was scheduled for nine-fifteen. If she didn't get some sleep, she would never get through it.

Though Shay kept herself as busy as she possibly could, teetering always on the brink of utter exhaustion, she dreaded lying down in bed and closing her eyes. When she did, she always saw Mitch on the inner screen of her mind, heard him saying that she couldn't bring back her childhood.

She turned her gaze to the beautiful wooden horse and wondered why anyone would want to bring back a childhood like hers. There had been so many disappointments, so many tears; she'd lived in luxurious neglect, having about as much access to Rosamond as any other adoring fan.

Shay bit her lower lip and shook her head in an effort to curtail that train of thought. No, Mitch Prescott had been wrong: she had no desire to relive those little-girl days. Clydesdale was merely a pleasant reminder that there had been happy, whimsical times, as well as painful ones.

With one hand, Shay tried to rub away the crick in her neck and started off toward the bathroom, looking forward to a hot, soothing shower. But she paused and looked back and it occurred to her that Clydesdale might not be just a memento—he might be a sort of emotional Trojan horse.

* * *

"May I say that you look absolutely dreadful?"
Richard Barrett asked as Shay riffled through the mail
on her office desk and picked out a postcard from
Jeannie and Marvin. There was a picture of the Eiffel
Tower on the front of the card, and Shay felt a pang
at the thought of telling the Reeses about her decision
to resign and start her own business.

"You have bags under your eyes, for God's sake!"
Richard persisted.

Shay smiled ruefully and reread the almost illegible
script on the back of the postcard. The Reeses would
be home in another week and a half; she would break
the news to them once they'd had time to get over
their jet lag and settle in. "That gives me an idea,"
she teased, enjoying Richard's annoyance over the
smudges that betrayed her lack of sleep. "For a commercial, I mean. You could show me, close up, and
I could say, 'Come down to Reese Motors and bag
yourself a good deal!' Get it, Richard? *Bag* yourself
a good deal?"

"You're not only exhausted, you're insane. Shay,
what's the matter with you?"

"Nothing a half ton of sugar wouldn't cure. This
is Sugar Day, isn't it, Richard?"

Richard had the good grace to look just a little
shamefaced. "Yes. Shay, it's safe, really. I wouldn't
ask you to do anything dangerous."

"By all means, let's confine ourselves to the merely ridiculous."

Mr. Barrett sighed dramatically and flung up his hands. "You knew what doing these commercials entailed, Shay, and you agreed to it all!"

"At the time, I needed the money."

"Are you trying to back out of the deal?" Richard's voice was a growl.

Shay shook her head. "No. When I make a promise, I keep it. Even when it means making a fool of myself." Her association with Mitch Prescott and his stupid book, she added, to herself, was a case in point.

"Well, let's get this over with before it rains or something. I've got a dump-truck load of sugar down there waiting." Richard looked truly beleaguered. "I'll be just as glad when that last commercial is in the can as you will, you know!" he barked.

"Nobody could possibly be that glad, Richard," Shay replied tartly. "Now get out of my office, will you please? I need some time to prepare for my big scene."

Richard muttered a single word as he left. It might have been "witch," but Shay wasn't betting on it.

The moment she was alone, she punched the button on her intercom. "Ivy? Would you get Todd on the phone, please?"

Instead of giving her answer over the wire, Ivy dashed into the office to demand in person, "Why? Shay, what are you planning to do?"

Shay sank into her desk chair with a sigh. Because she didn't have the strength to spar with Ivy, she answered readily. "I've decided that it's time to step out on my own, Ivy. I'm going to open my catering business and I'll need a place to work from."

Ivy's expression revealed two distinct and very different emotions: admiration and disappointment. "Wow," she said.

"Make the call, Ivy," Shay replied briskly, shuffling papers around on her desk in a pretense of being too busy to talk.

Five minutes later Todd was on the line. He listened to Shay's comments on the sort of building she needed and, bless him, asked no personal questions whatsoever. He had two good prospects, in fact: a Victorian house on Hill Street and a small restaurant overlooking the ocean. Both were available for lease with options to buy, and both had been abandoned for a considerable length of time.

Shay smiled into the telephone receiver. "You're telling me that they're fixer-uppers, aren't you, Todd?"

Todd laughed. "Yes, but the prices are right. Do you want to look at them?"

"Oh, yes, and as soon as possible."

"How about tonight, after you get off work?"

Despite her weariness, Shay felt a thrill of excitement. After all, she was doing something she had only dreamed about before: she was starting her own business. "That will be great. Why don't we make an evening of it? I'll order a pizza and throw together a salad and you and Ivy can have dinner with me."

"Sounds terrific," Todd agreed warmly. "See you at five."

"Five-thirty would be better. I've got a commercial to do this morning, and that always makes me fall behind on everything else."

"Five-thirty, then," Todd confirmed.

To save Ivy the trouble of an inquisition, Shay went out to her desk and relayed the plan. Ivy, who loved any sort of get-together no matter how casual or how highbrow, was delighted.

Chuckling, Shay started toward the stairs, ready for the third commercial. On the top step, she paused and turned to look back at her friend. "Don't you dare call your brother, either!"

Ivy beamed, sitting up very straight behind her computer terminal. "Too late!" she sang back.

Shay's hopeful mood faded instantly. She glared at her friend and stomped down the metal stairs to meet her singular and ignoble fate.

The dump truck was parked in the rear lot, as Richard had said, and the camera people were checking angles. Surreptitiously, Shay looked around as she walked toward the RV allotted for her use. If Mitch was there, she didn't see him.

This time her makeup was simple; merely a heavier version of what she normally wore. She shooed Richard's chattering assistant out of the RV and got ready, leaving the coveralls she would wear for last.

Outside—thank heaven, there was still no sign of Mitch—she read off the list of special car deals Marvin had authorized before his departure for Europe and then braced herself as the clapboard snapped and the cameras focused on her and on the dump truck parked nearby.

Smiling brightly, she announced, "Come on down to Reese Motors, folks! We guarantee you a sweet deal!"

On cue, the back of the dump truck ground upward and an avalanche of white sugar cascaded down onto Shay, burying her completely. She fought her way to the surface, sputtering and coughing, silently vowing that she would kill Richard Barrett if he wasn't satisfied with the first take.

"It's a wrap!" Richard shouted joyously and a laughing cheer went up from the salesmen, who had, as usual, gathered to watch.

Shay's hair and eyelashes were full of sugar. It filled her shoes, like sand, and even made its way under her clothes to chafe against her skin. She vowed she'd never put the stuff in her coffee again as she hurried back toward the RV, desperate to shower and change her clothes.

She began ripping them off the moment she'd closed the door behind her, flinging them in every direction. When the RV's engine suddenly whirred to

life and the vehicle lurched into motion, she was stark
naked.

Her first thought was that the salesmen were playing some kind of prank. Half amused and half furious,
she wrenched a blanket from the bed above the RV's
cab and wrapped it around herself.

"Stop!" she yelled.

The RV stopped, but only for a second. It was soon
swinging into mid-morning traffic. Just when Shay
would have screamed, a familiar masculine voice
called from the front, "Don't worry, it's all arranged!
You have the day off!"

Too furious to think about the fact that she was
crusted with white sugar and wrapped in a blanket,
Shay flung aside the little curtain that separated the
cab of the RV from the living quarters and raged,
"Mitch Prescott, you stop this thing right now! I'm
getting out!"

He looked back at her, his mouth serious, his eyes
laughing. "In this traffic? Woman, are you mad?
You'd make the six o'clock news, and if you think
the commercials were embarrassing..."

"You'll be the one who makes the news, bucko!"
Shay screamed, outraged. "This is not only kidnapping, it's grand theft auto!"

"I'll have you know that I rented this rig," he answered calmly.

"Well, you didn't rent me! Turn this thing around,
now!"

"I'd need a football field to do that, sweets," came the happily resigned reply. "We're in this for twenty-four hours, plus mileage, I'm afraid."

"You idiot! You—you *caveman*—" Shay paused, breathless, and looked around for something to throw.

"I like the idea of dragging you off to a cave, I must admit," Mitch reflected good-naturedly. "It's the whacking you over the head with a club and hauling you off by the hair that I can't quite deal with."

"You'd never prove that by me!"

Mitch laughed and someone honked as he switched lanes to fly up a freeway ramp. Shay gave a choked little cry and slumped down on the floor in a bundle of sugared synthetic wool. There, she considered her options.

Jumping out of a vehicle traveling at fifty-five miles per hour was definitely out. So was putting her clothes back on without showering first, and she couldn't face the thought of taking a shower with this maniac at the wheel.

A sweet, throbbing warmth moved beneath Shay's skin as she reviewed her situation. There were worse things than being alone with Mitch Prescott, whatever their differences. "Was Ivy in on this?"

"I'm pleading the fifth on that one, sugar plum."

Just the mention of sugar made Shay itch all over. She squirmed in her blanket and wailed, "When I get my hands on her—"

There was, for the first time since that crazy ride

had begun, a serious note in Mitch's voice. "We have to talk, Shay."

"You didn't have to kidnap me for that!"

"Didn't I? The last time I tried, you were something less than receptive."

Shay yawned. It was crazy, but all her sleepless nights seemed to be catching up to her, demanding their due. Now, of all times! She curled up in her blanket and closed her eyes. The swaying, jostling motion of the RV lulled her into a languorous state of half slumber. "Why…are you…doing this?" she asked again.

She could have sworn he said it was because he loved her….

Nah. She'd only dreamed that.

Mitch paced the length of the secluded beach, his hands pushed into the hip pockets of his jeans. What had he done? Was he losing his reason? For all his exploits, he'd never stooped to anything like this. Never.

He looked back at the RV he'd taken such pains to rent and sighed a raspy sigh that grated in his throat. Shay was still asleep, he supposed. When she woke up, she was going to fly into his face like a mother eagle defending her nest. He bent and grasped a piece of driftwood in one hand, and flung it into the surf.

Maybe it was that week of twenty-hour workdays. Maybe that had shorted out his brain or something.

The door of the RV creaked open and Mitch braced himself. Shay was going to give him hell, and the knowledge that he deserved whatever she might say didn't make the scenario any easier to prepare for.

She was still wearing the blanket, and little grains of sugar glimmered like bits of crystal in her hair, in her eyebrows, on her skin. Barefoot, she made her way toward him through the clean brown sand.

"I'm sorry, Shay," he said gruffly when she finally stood facing him, her wide hazel eyes unreadable. "I don't believe I did this—"

She raised the fingers of one hand to his lips, silencing him. Hidden birds chirped in the towering pine trees that edged the beach; gulls squawked in the distance; the tide made whispery music against the shore. It was a poetic interlude where only the earth and the waters spoke.

A primitive, grinding need possessed Mitch; he wanted Shay, craved her. But he didn't dare touch her, or even speak. How was he going to explain this?

Her fingers moved from his lips to caress his jawline and then trace the length of his neck. He shuddered with the aching need of her.

"They forgot to fill the water tank," she announced.

Mitch had been expecting a glorious, violent rage, expecting anything but this inane remark. He gaped at her, and his breath sawed at his lungs as it moved in and out. "What?"

"There isn't any water for the shower," Shay answered, holding the blanket in place with one hand and stroking Mitch's neck with the other. "In the RV, I mean."

She was a constant surprise to Mitch; just when he expected her to be furious, she was quiet. Or was this just the calm before the storm? "A shower?" he echoed stupidly.

Shay's lush lips curved into a smile. "If you'd just had a half ton of sugar dumped on you, you'd want a shower, too."

His frustration doubled and redoubled. Was she tormenting him deliberately? Was she making him want her, just so she could exact revenge by denying him when his need was greatest? "Dammit, Shay, I just shanghaied you and you're standing there talking about showers! Get back in the RV and I'll take you home."

The sweet lips made a pout. "I told you," she said. "I'm covered with sugar. I can't go home like this."

It was revenge; Mitch was sure of it. He made a growling sound in his bafflement and started to turn away. She caught his arm in her small, strong hand and urged him back around to face her.

The blanket seemed to waft to the sand in slow motion and Mitch couldn't breathe, couldn't move, couldn't think.

Shay stood on tiptoe, and when her lips touched Mitch's, he was lost. He groaned and gathered her to him with both hands, her soft flesh warm and gritty beneath his palms. He lowered her to the blanket, taking no time to smooth it, his mouth desperate for hers, his hands stroking her, shaping her for the taking. But he denied himself that possession, denied her, choosing instead to break the kiss and taste Shay's sugared breasts, her stomach, her thighs.

She writhed in pleasure, tossing her head back and forth, her fingers fierce in his hair. If she was setting him up for a last-second denial, she was doing a damned good job of it; Mitch wasn't sure he'd be able to stop if she asked that of him. He felt as though he'd stumbled into some jungle river, as though he were being flung along by currents too strong to swim against.

He didn't remember taking off his clothes, but suddenly he was naked, his flesh pressed against the strange roughness of hers. In silence she commanded his entry, in obedience and passion he complied.

They moved together in a ferocious rhythm, every straining thrust of their bodies increasing the pace until they both cried out, each consumed by the other, their flesh meeting in a final quivering arch. They fell slowly from the heights, gasping, sinking deep into the warm sand.

It took some time for Shay to coerce her lax, passion-sated muscles to lift her from that tangled blanket on the sand. When she managed to stand up, she stumbled toward the surf, into it.

The water was cold, even though it was August, and the chill of it nipped at Shay's knees and thighs and hips as she waded farther out. Mitch was beside her in a moment and she smiled to think that he might be afraid for her.

Shivering, his lips blue with cold, he caught her upper arms in his hands. "Shay."

She didn't want to hear an apology. Nothing could be allowed to spoil the sweet ferocity of the minutes just past. She cupped both hands in the sea and flung salty water into Mitch's face, laughing as he cursed, lost his balance and came up sputtering with cold and fury.

Shay held her breath and submerged herself, letting the ocean wash away the last of the sugar from her body and came up to be pulled immediately into a breathless kiss.

When that ended, Mitch lifted her into his arms, carried her back onto the shore. He lowered her to the sand, the blanket forgotten, and made slow, sweet love to her. Her cries of pleasure carried high into the blue summer sky, tangling with the coarse calls of the seabirds.

"I really have to go back," Shay said quietly. She was dressed again, the dream was over. "Todd has a couple of buildings to show me."

"Buildings?" Mitch, too, was fully dressed, and he sat across the RV's tiny table from Shay, looking strangely defeated.

"I've decided to take the plunge and start my catering business."

Mitch's jaw tightened. "Oh."

"Why does that bother you so much?" Shay asked. "Despite your caveman tactics this afternoon, you don't give the impression of being a chauvinist."

"I'm not a chauvinist, dammit!" Mitch snapped, looking for all the world like a wounded and outraged little boy. "We made love, Shay. We worked together. Maybe we haven't known each other very long, but we've shared a lot. It hurt that you didn't mention something that important."

Shay shrugged, confused. "Until you gave me that money for helping with the book, it was just a dream, Mitch. I have a child to support and I couldn't have taken the risks. What would be the point in talking about something I didn't expect to be able to do?"

There was a short silence while Mitch absorbed the things Shay had said. "I guess I did overreact a little," he finally admitted. His eyes met hers. "I'm sorry about this morning, too. I had no right to do that."

"It was pretty crazy," Shay agreed, but she couldn't bring herself to be angry. Instead her whole being seemed to resonate with a feeling of contentment. "What made you do it?"

Mitch's broad shoulders moved in a shrug and he rubbed his beard-stubbled chin with one hand as he thought. "It was a hell of a way to show it, but I love you, Shay."

Shay swallowed hard. She had really heard the words; this time she wasn't dreaming or so caught up in the throes of passion that she couldn't be sure she'd understood them correctly. She tried to speak and failed.

"You don't believe me?"

Shay swallowed again. "We haven't known each other very long, Mitch. Oth-other things are so good between us that—well, we could be confusing that with love, couldn't we?"

"Marry me," he said.

"No," she replied. "I can't."

"Why not?"

"Because."

"Oh, that's a great answer. God, I hate it when I ask someone a simple question and they say 'because'!"

Shay couldn't resist a smile, though it was a sad one. "I guess the day is over, huh?"

Mitch was glaring at her. "I guess it is. But we aren't over. Is that clear, Shay? You and I are not over."

"For a best-selling writer, you have terrible grammar. Speaking of that, how's the book going?"

"I'm halfway through the first draft," Mitch an-

swered in clipped and somewhat grudging tones.
"Why won't you marry me, Shay? Don't you love
me?"

"As crazy as it seems, I think I do love you. If I
didn't, I would have been on the main highway, trying to flag down a state patrolman."

"But?"

"But I've seen my mother fail at marriage over and
over. I've failed at it myself. I can't go through that
again, Mitch."

"If you need to prove that you can make it on your
own, well, it seems to me that you've already done
that."

"Have I, Mitch? Until you came along and offered
me a fat fee for my help in writing that book about
my mother, I was barely making it from one payday
to the next. I haven't proved anything; I've just been
lucky."

Mitch shook his head. "So now it's the catering
business. If you make that fly, you're a valid person.
Is that it, Shay?"

"I guess it is."

"Then I feel sorry for you."

The words came as a slap in the face to Shay; she
sat back on the narrow bench, her eyes wide, her
breath caught in her throat. "What?"

"You're in a trap, Shay. You're an intelligent
woman, so you must know that the value of a person

has nothing to do with what they prove or don't prove.''

Shay felt distinctly uncomfortable. Next he'd be saying that she was just using her need to succeed at something to avoid taking a chance on marriage. ''I suppose if we were married, you'd want me to give up the whole idea of starting a catering service.''

''On the contrary, Shay, I'd help you in any way I could.'' He looked grimly smug. ''Wriggle your way out of that one.''

Shay was stumped. ''Okay, so I'm afraid. It's human to be afraid when you've been hurt.''

''This conversation is getting us nowhere.'' Mitch stood up, took the keys to the RV from the pocket of his jeans. ''Can we at least agree that we'll give this relationship or whatever the hell it is a sporting chance?''

Shay could only nod.

''That's progress, at least. Let's go.''

They were both settled in the front seat and the RV was jolting up the narrow road to the highway before either of them spoke again.

''I want to read what you've written so far, Mitch. About Rosamond, I mean.''

Mitch did not take his eyes from the road. ''Buckle your seatbelt. You're free to read the manuscript whenever you want.''

Shay snapped the belt into place and sighed. ''Ivy

and Todd are coming over for pizza after I look at those properties. Why don't you join us?''

''Now that was an enthusiastic invitation if I've ever heard one. Are you afraid I'd end up staying the night?''

''I *know* you would end up staying the night.''

Mitch cast a sidelong look at her and shook his head. ''Woman, you defy logic. Caution is your middle name, and yet you seem to enjoy walking on thin ice.''

''I'm as confused as you are, if that helps,'' Shay admitted ruefully. ''Are you coming over for pizza or not?''

''I'm coming over for one hell of a lot more than pizza, lady, and you know it. Am I still invited?''

Shay thought for a long time. ''Yes,'' she finally answered. ''The invitation stands.''

Chapter 9

If Ivy and Todd were surprised when Shay arrived at Reese Motors promptly at five-thirty, they had the good grace not to show it. Freshly showered and made up, Shay went into her office long enough to check her telephone messages and align her work for the next day.

When she came out, her friends were waiting, Ivy wide-eyed and just a bit pale, Todd blithely unaware that anything was amiss.

Shay gave Ivy a scorching look that warned of an imminent confrontation and said, "Well, let's look at those buildings. We'll pick up the pizza on the way to my place, afterward."

Ivy swallowed visibly and croaked, "Okay."

Their first stop was the large Victorian house Todd had mentioned. It had been empty for a long time, but Shay could see vast potential in it; if she renovated the place, she would have room not only for her business, but for half a dozen small shops. She wouldn't run these herself, of course, but rent them to other people.

Todd assured her that the house was basically sound, though it needed a great deal of work. The plaster in most of the rooms was either stained or falling off the walls in hunks, and the ceilings sagged.

Shay liked the house; it had personality. The kitchen, while much in need of repair, was large enough to accommodate the needs of a catering service, and the spacious dining room could be converted to a reception area of sorts. The pantry, almost as big as Shay's kitchen in her rented house, would make a suitable private office.

"I have some rough estimates on the renovation, if you'd like to see them," Todd offered.

Shay was pleased by his thoroughness. Here was a man who would go far in the business world. She reviewed the estimates submitted by various construction companies as they drove to the other potential site. The amounts of money involved were staggering.

The second site was a small restaurant overlooking the water. The ceiling had fallen down, coming to rest across a counter still equipped with a cash register. Debris of every sort was scattered on the floor, seeming to pool around the bases of the tattered stools that lined the counter. The smell of mice was potent.

"It does look out over the water," Ivy ventured. She'd been very quiet all along.

"That's about all it has going for it," Shay replied. "If I were going to open a bistro or something, I might be interested, but I don't think a view is going to be any particular plus for a catering service."

Todd nodded his agreement.

Suddenly, Shay was very tired. After all, it had been a crazy day. "I'll need some time to think this over, Todd, but I'm interested in the other place. Do you think I could get back to you in a few days?"

Again, Todd nodded. "You might want to get some other estimates. The ones I gave you were meant to give an idea of what would be required."

Shay looked down at the sheaf of papers in her hand. "Do you recommend these people, Todd?"

He held the door open and Ivy sort of skulked through, just ahead of Shay. "I've dealt with all of them at one time or another and they do fine work. But you should still get other estimates, it's always good business."

They stopped at a pizza-to-go place and, as Shay waited at the counter for her order, she happened to glance through the front window. Ivy and Todd appeared to be having some kind of serious consultation in the car. Ivy's head was bent and Shay found her irritation with her friend fading away.

Ivy was a meddler extraordinaire, but she meant well. She was happy with Todd and she wanted everyone else she knew to be happy, too. Still, Shay thought the young woman deserved the lecture she was probably getting at that moment.

The pizza was ready and Shay was distracted from the scene in the car for a few moments. When she reached it, carrying the pizza, Ivy and Todd were sitting as far from each other as they possibly could. Shay let herself into the back seat, wrestling the huge pizza box as she did so and, of course, made no comment on the chill inside the car.

At Shay's house, a very subdued Ivy took over the making of the salad. When Mitch arrived she started and looked even more guilty and disconsolate than before.

Mitch gave Shay a quick kiss on the lips and turned to his sister, who tossed him a defiant look and made a face.

Mitch laughed and then reached out to rumple Ivy's gossamer hair, but he spoke to Shay. "Ivy didn't know why I wanted to rent that RV until it was too late."

Ivy startled everyone by bursting into tears and fleeing through the back door. Todd started to follow, but Shay stopped him with a gesture of one hand and a quiet "No. I'll talk to her."

She found Ivy sitting at the picnic table, her

head resting on her folded arms, her small shoulders shaking.

Shay laid a hand on her friend's quivering back and said, "Hey. It's all right, Ivy. I'm not mad at you."

"I could kill that brother of mine!" Ivy wailed, sniffling intermittently. "Oh, Shay, I never thought he'd do anything like that!"

Shay couldn't help smiling a little. "No harm was done. Let's forget it."

Ivy turned and flung herself into Shay's arms for a quick hug. After that, she recovered quickly.

During dinner, served on that same picnic table, the conversation centered mostly on the house Shay was thinking of taking for her catering business and her ideas about renting out the other rooms as small shops.

Mitch said very little, but the light in his brown eyes revealed a certain amused respect that told Shay he liked the idea. Ivy, of course, was bursting with suggestions: she knew a woman who made beautiful candles and would be overjoyed to be a part of such a project, was acquainted with another who had been wanting to import Christmas ornaments to sell to the tourists as souvenirs but had had no luck in finding a shop she could afford.

When the pizza and salad were gone and the paper plates had been thrown away, Ivy and Todd made an abrupt, if cheerful, exit.

"Was it something I said?" Shay said with a frown.

Mitch grinned. "Don't be naive," he replied.

While Mitch brewed a pot of coffee, seeming as at home in Shay's kitchen as if it had been his own, she settled onto the couch with the pages of his manuscript. She had never known a writer before, but she had expected a first draft to be a mass of scribbles and cross-outs and have scrawled notes in the margins. Mitch's pages were remarkably neat and there was something in his style that grabbed Shay's attention, made her read as someone who had never met Rosamond Dallas might.

Presently, Mitch set a steaming cup on the coffee table in front of her, but she didn't pause to reach for it. She was fascinated, seeing a side of Rosamond that she hadn't consciously noticed before.

By the time she'd raced through a hundred and fifty pages of concise, perceptive copy, her coffee was cold in the cup and her view of Rosamond—and Mitch himself—had been broadened by the length of a horizon.

"Wow," she said.

Mitch took away her coffee cup, refilled it and returned to the living room. "You approve, I take it?"

"I'm not sure if I approve or not, but I'm impressed. The writing is good, Mitch, really good. How could you have learned so much about Rosamond from a few pictures and scrapbooks and a couple of conversations with me?''

Mitch was settled into the overstuffed chair nearest the couch. "I did a lot of research, Shay. For instance, I talked to all six of her ex-husbands by phone. And your grandmother—"

"My grandmother?" Shay felt a quickening inside, one of mingled surprise and alarm. "I don't have a grandmother."

Mitch lowered his eyes to his coffee, taking a sip before he answered, "Yes, you do."

Shay set the pages of the manuscript aside, fearing that she would drop them if she didn't. "Speaking of things people don't bother to mention..."

Mitch set aside his cup and raised both hands in a gesture of peace. "I didn't find out about her until this afternoon, Shay, after I'd dropped you off here. One of my research people had tracked her down and they left her name and phone number on my answering machine."

Shay swallowed. "You called her?"

"Yes. Her name is Alice Bretton and she lives in Springfield, Missouri. Your father—"

"Is her son," Shay's voice was shaky.

"Was her son, I'm afraid. He was a navy pilot, Shay, and he was shot down over Hanoi in 1970." Mitch was sitting beside Shay on the couch now, holding her gently and not too tightly.

"They're sure? So many pilots were taken prisoner—"

"He's dead, Shay. He was positively identified."

An overwhelming feeling of betrayal and hurt washed over Shay. "I didn't even know him. Rosamond wouldn't tell me his name."

"His name was Robert Bretton."

"Tell me about him!"

Mitch sighed. "I don't know the whole story. He and Rosamond were 'going steady,' as they called it back then. When things went wrong, your mother bought a bus ticket to Hollywood and from what Mrs. Bretton told me, Robert finished college and then joined the navy."

Shay was dizzied by the sudden influx of information that had been denied her throughout her life, first by Rosamond's reluctance to talk, then by her illness. "There are so many things I want to know...."

"Why don't you get in touch with your grandmother tomorrow? She'll be able to tell you a lot more than I can."

"She might not want anything to do with me!"

Mitch shook his head. "She asked me a thousand questions about you, Shay." He pulled a wry face meant to lighten the mood. "Of course, I didn't tell her how you taste when you've just had a half ton of sugar dumped over your head."

Shay was making a sound, but she wasn't sure

whether she was laughing or crying or both. She gave Mitch a shove and then allowed her forehead to nestle into his broad shoulder.

"Make love to me, Mitch," she said after a very long time.

"Here?" he teased in a hoarse voice, but he picked Shay up in his arms and carried her into the room she pointed out to him. The night was a long one, full of tender abandon.

The pit of Shay's stomach quivered with nervousness as she dialed the number Mitch had given her. What, exactly, was she going to say to this grandmother she had never known, never heard a word about?

Mitch puttered around the kitchen, getting breakfast, while the call went through.

"Mrs. Bretton?" Shay's voice shook. "My name is Shay Kendall and—"

"Shay!" The name was a soft cry of joy, full of tears and laughter. "Is it really you?"

"It's really me," Shay answered, and she made a face at Mitch as he shoved a dishtowel into her hands. Then she dried her eyes with it. "T-tell me about my father. Please."

"There is so much to tell, darling, and so much to show. Could you possibly come to Springfield for a visit?"

Shay wanted to hop on the next plane, but she had

responsibilities to Marvin and Jeannie and she couldn't go away without letting Hank know. Suppose he got sick and Garrett brought him home and there was no one there to take care of him? "This is a bad time—my job—my son—"

"Then I'll come there!" Alice Bretton interrupted warmly. "Would that be all right, Shay? I could bring the photo albums and we could talk in person."

"I'd love to have you, Mrs. Bretton."

"In that case, I'll make arrangements and call you right back."

"That would be wonderful."

They said goodbye and Shay set the phone receiver back in its cradle as Mitch poured scrambled eggs into a pan of hash browns and chopped onions and bits of crisp bacon.

"I take it she's flying out for a visit?" Mitch asked moderately, looking back at Shay over one bare shoulder.

Shay nodded. "I can't make sense of what I feel, Mitch. I'm happy that I'm finally going to meet my grandmother and I'm sad because my father died and I'm furious with Rosamond! Here she is, this poor, sick, wretch of a woman, and I could cheerfully wring her neck!"

"That's normal, Shay. The important thing is that you wouldn't really do it."

"I want to thank you for this, Mitch. F-for my grandmother."

He turned from the stove, grinning, almost unbearably handsome in just his jeans. His hair was rumpled and his feet were bare and, as always, he needed to shave. "Don't be too hasty with your gratitude, kid," he warned. "For all you know, she's a bag lady with bad breath, bunions and bowling shoes."

"That was alliterative, in a tacky sort of way," Shay responded. She slid off the stool near the wall phone and put her arms around Mitch's lean waist.

He kissed the tip of her nose and gave her bottom a squeeze that brought back memories of the night before. Shay blushed to recall what a greedy wanton she'd been.

"I'm not sure whether you bring out the best in me, or the worst," she commented.

Mitch's eyebrows went into brief but rapid motion. "If that was your worst," he said in a Groucho Marx voice, "I'm all for it."

Shay tipped her head back and laughed. It was a throaty, gleeful sound, and it felt oh, so good. If she could be sure that life with Mitch Prescott would always be this way, she would have married him in a second. But in her deepest mind, marriage was linked with betrayal, with pain. She sobered, thinking of Eliott's desertion and the fickle vanity of her mother.

Mitch lifted his index fingers to the corners of Shay's mouth and stretched her lips into a semblance of a smile. "No sad faces allowed," he said.

He went to dish up the scrambled egg concoction

he'd made for their breakfast, and Shay sat down in a chair at the table. It was strange, having a man not only cook for her, but serve her as well. "I could get used to this," she said as he set a steaming, fragrant plate in front of her.

"Good. We'll get married and make it a ritual. I'll fix your breakfast every morning and then take you back to bed and make wild love to you."

Shay blushed again, but some vixen hiding deep inside her made her say, "Keep making threats like that, fella, and I'll accept your proposal."

Mitch's eyes were suddenly serious. "Eat," he ordered in a gruff tone, looking away.

Before Shay could say anything at all, the telephone rang. Alice Bretton had made her flight arrangements and she would be arriving in Seattle the following afternoon at two. Shay wrote down the name of the airline and the flight number and when she turned away from the phone, Mitch was disconsolately scraping their plates.

Standing behind him, Shay wrapped her arms around his middle and rubbed his stomach with tantalizing motions of both hands. "I seem to remember something about a threat," she said softly, her lips moving against the taut flesh of his back as she spoke.

Shay was late for work that morning.

Just talking to Alan Roget over the telephone gave Mitch a creepy feeling, as though a massive spiderweb had settled over him or something. He frowned as he listened to the first accounts of the murderer's childhood, entering notes on the screen of his computer throughout the conversation.

The night with Shay had been magical, and so had the morning. Life was so damned ironic: one minute, a man could be eating scrambled eggs or making love to a woman, the next, talking to someone who personified evil. Like most psychotics, Roget exhibited no remorse at all, from what Mitch could tell. He seemed to feel that civil and moral laws applied only to other people and not to him.

By the time Mitch hung up the telephone, he was a little sick. He immediately dialed Reba's number in California, and when she answered, he asked to talk to Kelly.

"You're in luck, big fella," Reba responded warmly. "The munchkin happens to be home from school today."

Mitch sat up a little straighter in his desk chair. "Is she sick?"

"Nothing serious," his ex-wife assured him promptly. "Just the sniffles. So, how have you been, Mitch?"

Mitch couldn't help smiling. Reba definitely wasn't your standard ex-wife. She was happy with her new husband and that happiness warmed her entire personality. "I'm in love," he confided, without really expecting to.

"Oh, Mitch, that's great!" Worry displaced a little of the buoyancy in her voice. "It *is* great, isn't it? Maybe great enough to keep you out of jungles and hotbeds of political unrest?"

"No more jungles, Reba," he said solemnly. He'd made changes in his life recently that he had refused to consider while he and Reba were married, and he wondered if she would resent that.

Not Reba. He should have known. "We'll all breathe a sigh of relief," she chimed. "On the count of three, now. One, two—"

Mitch laughed. He remembered the good times with Reba and, for a fleeting moment, mourned them.

When Kelly's piping voice came on the line, he forgot about Roget and all the other ugliness in the world. But the house seemed even bigger than it was after he'd talked to his daughter, and even emptier.

He threw himself into his work, concentrating on Rosamond Dallas and what had made her tick.

The need to throttle Rosamond was gone by the time Shay visited her that afternoon; in its place was a certain sad acceptance of the fact that mothers are women, human and fallible.

She approached her mother's chair, kissed her forehead. "How can I hate you?" she whispered.

Rosamond rocked and clutched the ever-present doll. It seemed to Shay that she was retreating deeper and deeper into herself and growing smaller with every passing day.

Tired because of a most delicious lack of sleep the night before, a day of work and telephone conversations with half a dozen contractors, Shay sighed and sank into the chair facing her mother's. "I'm going to meet my grandmother tomorrow," she said, hardly able to believe such a thing could be possible and expecting no reaction at all from Rosamond.

But the woman sat stiffly in her chair, her famous eyes widening.

Shay was incredulous. "Mother?"

The fleeting moment of lucidity was over. Rosamond stared blankly again, crooning a wordless song to her doll.

Shay looked at the doll and, for the first time ever, wondered if that raggedy lump of cloth and yarn could, in Rosamond's mind, represent herself as a baby. It was a jarring thought, but oddly comforting, too. Maybe, Shay thought, she loved me as well as she was able to love anyone. Maybe she did the best she could.

On her way home from the convalescent home, Shay stopped at the Skyler Beach mall and went into a bookstore, looking for the four titles Ivy had written down for her. Mitch's work was published under the odd code name of Zebulon, with no surname of any kind given and, of course, with no photograph on the back or inside flap of the book jackets.

Shay felt a little shiver of fear as she looked at the covers and thought of all the dangerous people who must hate Mitch Prescott enough to kill him. She was trembling a little as she laid the books on the counter and paid for them.

At home, she did housework, ate a light supper and took a bath, then curled up on the couch with one of Mitch's books. The one she'd selected to read first was an account of the capture of a famous Nazi war criminal, set mostly in Brazil. It was harrowing, reading that book, and yet Shay was riveted to it, turning page after page. In the morning, she awakened to find herself still on the couch, the open book under her cheek. Groaning, she raised herself to a sitting position and ran her fingers through her hair.

This was the day that she would meet Alice Bretton, her grandmother, for the first time. She was determined to think of that and not the horrors Mitch had to have faced in order to write that book.

After showering and dressing, she wolfed down a cup of coffee and half an English muffin and drove to work to find the usual chaos awaiting her. At least Richard Barrett wasn't around, wanting to film the last commercial. That was a comfort.

Shay delved into her work and the hours passed quickly. Soon it was time to drive to the airport and meet Mrs. Bretton's plane.

She wondered how she would recognize her grandmother and what she would say to her first. There were so many things to tell and so many questions to ask.

As it happened, it was Alice Bretton who recognized Shay. A tiny, Helen Hayes-type, with snow-white hair done up in a bun and quick, sparkling eyes, Mrs. Bretton came right up to her granddaughter and said, "Why, dear, you look just like Robert!"

Shay was inordinately glad that she resembled someone; Lord knew, she looked nothing like Rosamond and never had. It was that gladness that broke the ice and allowed her to hug the small woman standing before her. "I'm so happy to see you," she said, and then she had to laugh because, looking down through a mist of tears, she could see that Alice was wearing bowling shoes with her trim, tasteful suit.

"They're so comfortable, don't you know!" Alice cried in good-natured self-defense.

Shay looked forward to telling Mitch that Mrs. Bretton did indeed wear bowling shoes, though she obviously wasn't a bag lady and it was doubtful that she had bunions.

Talking with her grandmother proved remarkably easy, considering all the years and all the heartaches that might have separated them. The two women chattered nonstop all the way back to Skyler Beach, Shay asking questions, Alice answering them.

Shay's eyes were hazel because hazel eyes ran in the Bretton family, she was told, and yes, Robert had wanted to marry Rosamond, but she'd refused. He

had tried to see Shay many times, but she had always
been away in some school, out of his reach. Rosamond had never allowed any of his letters or phone
calls to Shay to get through.

Alice patted her sensible, high-quality purse. "But
I have most of those letters right here. When they
came back, Robert saved them."

Shay worked at keeping her mind on her driving,
and it was hard. She wanted to pull over to the side
of the freeway and read all of her father's letters, one
after another. "Why didn't Rosamond want him to
see me or even talk to me?"

Alice sighed, and if she bore Rosamond Dallas any
ill-will, it wasn't visible in the sweet lines of her face.
"Lord only knows. She wasn't very happy as a child,
you know, and I guess she didn't want anything to
do with anyone from Springfield. Not even her own
baby's father."

Rosamond had said very little about her life in
Springfield, only that her mother drank too much and
her father, a railroad worker, had died in an accident
when she was four years old. "Did you know Rosamond as a girl?"

Alice shook her head. "I only met her after she'd
started to date Robert. She was beautiful, but I—well,
I had my misgivings about her. She was rather wild,
you know."

Shay could imagine her mother as a young girl,
looking for approbation and love even in those pre-

fame days. It was strange that the search had never stopped, that Rosamond had gone from man to man all her life. "I wish I'd known about you and about my father."

Alice reached across the car seat to pat Shay's knee. "You'll know me, and I've brought along things to help you know your father, too." Suddenly the elderly woman looked alarmed. "I do hope I'm not keeping you from your work, dear!"

Shay thought of the commercials and the irate customers and the stacks of contracts and factory invoices she had left behind at Reese Motors. "My work will definitely keep until tomorrow. You can stay for a while, can't you?"

"Oh, yes. Nobody waiting at home but my parakeet, my cat and my bridge club. Now tell me all about this boy of yours. Hank, isn't it? You know, it's a funny thing, but your great-grandfather's name was Henry and they called him Hank, don't you know...."

Chapter 10

Shay bit her lower lip as the ringing began on the other end of the line. It was just plain unconscionable to awaken someone at that hour of the night, but after reading her father's gentle, innocuous letters, she felt a deep need to touch base.

On the third ring, Mitch answered with an unintelligible grumble.

"She wears bowling shoes," Shay said.

"You woke me up to tell me that?" He didn't sound angry, just baffled.

"I thought you'd want to know." She paused, drew a deep breath. "Oh, Mitch, Alice is a wonderful woman."

"She's your grandmother. What else could she be besides wonderful?"

"Flatterer."

"You love it."

I love you, Shay thought. "Good night, Mitch," she said.

He laughed, a wonderful rumbling, sleepy sound. "Good night, princess."

Shay was glad that no one could see her, there in the darkness of her kitchen. She kissed the telephone receiver before she put it back in place.

Alice was still sleeping the next morning when Shay left for work. Rather than disturb her grandmother, she scribbled a note that included her office telephone number and crept out. Alice had made it very clear, the night before, that she didn't want to disrupt Shay's life in any way.

On the way to Reese Motors, Shay marveled that life could follow the same dull and rocky road for so many years, and then suddenly take a series of crazy turns. She'd met Mitch, she'd found her grandmother, she was about to start the business she had only dreamed of—and all this had taken place in a period of a few weeks.

When Shay arrived at work, she found Richard waiting in her office with the fourth and final storyboard. She was relieved; after this, she would never have to make a fool of herself on camera again.

"It's a giant, hairy hand," Richard said with amazing enthusiasm.

"I can see that, Richard," Shay replied dryly,

frowning at the storyboard. "When are we filming this one?"

"Tomorrow, I hope. We had to special order that hand, you know."

Shay sighed inwardly. "It won't collapse or anything, will it?"

"Absolutely not. Would I risk your life that way?"

Shay shrugged philosophically. "I don't know, Richard. You almost smothered me in sugar the other day, so I thought I'd ask."

"Marvin's going to be pleased with these commercials, Shay," Richard said on an unexpectedly charitable note. "You've done a great job. The first spot aired late last night. You looked great, even in a bee suit."

Shay grinned, unable to resist saying, "I'll bet people are buzzing about it."

Richard laughed and left the office, taking the storyboard with him.

At noon, Alice arrived at Reese Motors by taxi, all dressed up for the lunch date she and Shay had made the night before. Shay proudly introduced her to Ivy, all the salesmen and even the mechanics in the repair section.

"I saw you on television today, dear," the elderly woman announced moderately over a chef's salad. "You were dressed as a bee, of all things." Alice looked puzzled, as though she thought Shay might say she was mistaken.

Briefly, Shay explained about Marvin's penchant for creative advertising.

"We have a car dealer like that in Springfield," Alice said seriously, and there was an endearing look of bafflement in her eyes. "He let a mouthful of water run down his chin and said he was liquidating last year's models."

"Oh, Lord," Shay groaned. "Do me a favor and don't mention that around Reese Motors. Marvin would probably get wind of it and come up with some version of his own."

"Is there a young man in your life, dear?"

The abrupt change in subject matter caught Shay off guard. "I—well—yes, sort of—"

Alice smiled. "Good. They're not all wasters like that Eliott person, you know."

Shay wondered what Alice would think of Mitch if she knew how he had hijacked her granddaughter to a private beach and made love to her in the sand. The memory of her own responses brought throbbing color to Shay's cheeks.

"What is his name, dear? What does he do?"

"His name is Mitch Prescott. He's the man who found you for me," Shay said, somewhat hesitantly.

Alice did not pursue the matter. "My, but you do look like your father," she said in a faraway voice.

That evening, after work, Shay drove to the Victorian house she hoped to restore and parked at the curb. The place was derelict, and yet, in her mind's eye, she could see so many possibilities for it. Suddenly she wanted that disreputable old white elephant with a consuming ache.

She drove home to find Alice happily cooking dinner and Mitch helping. The way the two of them were chattering, they might have known each other for ten years instead of ten minutes. It was crazy, but Shay was just a little jealous of both of them.

"Sit down, dear, sit down," Alice ordered, gesturing toward a chair at the kitchen table. "You look all worn out."

Over Alice's neatly coiffed and blue-rinsed head, Mitch gave Shay an evil wink.

Shay sighed and sat down, grateful for the coffee that was immediately set before her. "You two are going to spoil me if you keep this up. What will I do without you?"

The question, so innocently presented, caused a stiff silence. Mitch gazed off through the window over the sink, but Alice recovered quickly. "I was just telling your young man that I might sell my house and move out here for good. I could get a little apartment, don't you know."

Shay's eyes widened. "You would do that? You would actually move here, just to be near Hank and me?"

"You're my family," Alice said softly. "All I have in the world. Of course I'd move to be near you. That's if you'd want—if I wouldn't be in the way—"

"Never." Shay rose from her chair and embraced this woman who had come to mean so much to her in such a short time. "You could never be in the way."

"Our Mr. Prescott might have a thing or two to say about that," Alice pointed out with a misty wryness as she and Shay drew apart. "He has plans for you, you know."

Mitch was no longer looking out the window, and a grin tilted one side of his mouth and lit his eyes. His entire demeanor said that he did indeed have plans for Shay, and none of them could be mentioned in front of her grandmother.

Shay waited until Alice wasn't looking and gave Mitch a slow, saucy wink.

Color surged up from the neck of his dark blue T-shirt and he tossed Shay a mock scowl in return. "Actually," he said, "I think Shay needs a grandmother around to keep her in line. I've tried, but the job is too big for me."

Alice chuckled and gave him a slight shove. "Step aside, handsome," she said. "I've got to get these biscuits in the oven or they won't be ready in time for supper."

Mitch caught Shay by the hand as he passed her, pulling her out of her chair and into the living room, where he promptly drew her close and kissed her. It was a thorough kiss that left Shay unsteady on her feet and just a bit flushed in the face.

Holding her close, Mitch whispered against the bridge of her nose, "If your grandmother wasn't in the next room, lady..."

Shay trembled with the delicious feeling of wanting him. In a low, teasing voice, she retorted, "You shameless rascal, how can you say such a thing when you've been flirting with another woman under my very nose?"

Mitch grinned. "What can I say? I took one look at Alice and I was smitten."

"Smitten?"

He pulled her toward the couch, sat down, positioned her on his lap. His hand moved beneath her skirt to stroke her thigh. "Smitten," he confirmed.

Shay's breath had quickened and her blood felt warm enough to melt her veins. She slapped away his hand and it returned, unerringly, to create sweet havoc on the flesh of her upper leg.

"So," he said, as though he weren't driving her wild with the brazen motion of his fingers. "Have you decided whether or not to take the house Todd showed you?"

Shay could barely breathe. "I'm...waiting for... estimates."

"I see."

Again, Shay removed his hand; again it returned. "Rat," she muttered.

Alice was humming in the kitchen, happy in her work, probably pleased with herself for giving the young lovers some time alone. Mitch continued to caress Shay, slowly, rhythmically, skillfully.

She buried her mouth in the warmth of his neck to muffle the soft moan his attentions forced her to utter.

"You look a bit flushed, dear," Alice commented, minutes later, over a dinner of chicken, green beans and biscuits, her gentle eyes revealing worry. "I hope you aren't coming down with something."

"She's perfectly healthy," Mitch replied with an air of authority.

Beneath the surface of the table, Shay's foot moved and her heel made solid contact with Mitch's shin. He didn't even flinch.

After dinner, he and Shay did the dishes together while Alice rested on Hank's bed. She'd closed the door behind her, but Shay still felt compelled to keep her voice down.

"If you ever do a thing like that again, Mitch Prescott…"

He wrapped the dishtowel around Shay's waist, turned slightly and pulled her against him. "You can be sure that I'll do it again," he muttered. "And you'll react just the same way."

Shay knew that he was right and flushed, furious that he had such power over her and yet glad of it, too. Her body was still reverberating with the force of her response to those stolen moments of pleasure. "You are vain and arrogant!" she whispered.

He put one hand inside her blouse to cup her breast,

his thumb moving her bra out of place and then caressing her nipple. "I'm going to forget that copy of my manuscript when I leave here tonight," he said, his lips barely touching Shay's. "You, of course, will throw up your hands in dismay and tell your grandmother that you've got to return it to me immediately."

Shay shuddered with desire, still held close to solid proof of his masculinity by the dishtowel. His fingers were plucking gently at her nipple and she couldn't reason, let alone argue. "B-bastard," she said, and that was the extent of her rebellion.

Mitch slid the top of her blouse aside and bent his head to taste her now-throbbing nipple with an utterly brazen lack of haste. In fact, he satisfied himself at leisure before tugging her bra back into place and straightening her blouse. And then he left.

Shay finished the dishes and then, hating herself, tapped at the door of Hank's room. "Alice?"

The answer was a sleepy, "Yes, dear?"

"Mitch forgot something here, and I've got to take it to him. I'll be back soon."

Two hours later Shay returned, hair and clothes slightly rumpled, lips swollen with Mitch's kisses. Alice was knitting, the television tuned to a mystery program, and even in the dim light of the living room, Shay could see the sparkle in her grandmother's eyes. The lady was clearly nobody's fool.

"Did you have a nice time, dear?"

Every part of Shay was pulsing with the "nice time" she'd had in Mitch Prescott's arms. "Yes," she said, in classic understatement, and then she excused herself to take a bath and get ready for bed.

Because the last commercial was being taped the next morning and Alice wanted to watch, Shay arrived at work with her grandmother in tow.

The enormous hairy hand towered in the middle of the main showroom, and Shay shook her head as she looked at it. She was given a flowing white dress to put on in the rest room, and Richard's assistant applied her makeup.

At least the showroom had been closed for whatever length of time it would take to get the spot on videotape, Shay noted with relief. Using a stepladder, she climbed into the palm of that hand and stretched out on her side, trying to keep the dress from riding up. Richard followed her up and carefully closed the huge fingers of the hand around her.

Before going back down the stepladder he winked at Shay and told her again that Marvin was going to be proud of her.

"This is really the way Faye Raye got her start, huh?" Shay muttered, trying to be a good sport about the whole thing. After all, this was the last commercial she would ever appear in.

Looking down, Shay saw her grandmother talking with Ivy, but there was no sign of Mitch. Her feelings about that were mixed. On the one hand, she hated to have him see her in such a ridiculous position. On the other, it was always comforting to know that he was there somewhere.

This time the cameras were above her, on the mezzanine, along with an enormous fan. A microphone had been hidden in the neckline of Shay's chiffon dress.

"Ready?" Richard called from his place between the two cameramen.

Shay nodded; she was as ready as she was ever going to get.

The fan started up and Shay's dress and hair moved in the flow of air. She practiced her smile and mentally rehearsed her line as the cameras panned over the selection of cars available in the showroom. When she saw them swing in her direction, she beamed, even though the fan was buffeting the air from her lungs, and gasped, "You'll go ape when you see the deals we're making at Reese Motors! Come on down and talk to us at 6832 Discount Way, right here in Skyler Beach!"

"Perfect!" Richard exulted, and Shay's relief was such that for a moment she sank into the hollow of that giant ape hand and closed her eyes. One of the salesmen came to help her out from under the hairy fingers and down the ladder.

"You were magnificent!" Alice said when Shay came to stand before her, but there was an expression of profound relief in her eyes.

"I'm just glad it's over," Shay answered, wondering if Alice would tell her friends back home that her granddaughter earned her living by dressing up as a bee or lying in a huge and hairy hand.

"Well," Alice announced brightly, "I'm off to look at apartments with Ivy's young man. I may be late, so I took the liberty of setting out one of the casseroles you had in your freezer." The older woman's eyes shifted from Shay to Ivy, and they sparkled with pride. "My granddaughter is a very organized young woman, don't you know. She'll make a fine caterer."

The vote of confidence uplifted Shay; she said goodbye to Alice and went into the rest room to put on her normal clothes and redo her makeup. Within twenty minutes, she was so involved in her work that she'd forgotten all about her brief stint as the captive of a mythical ape.

After work, Shay met briefly with one of the contractors providing an estimate on the renovation of the old house. His bid was higher than the one Todd had gotten, but she reviewed it carefully anyway.

Over the next three days, the rest of the estimates came in, straggle fashion. Shay looked them all over and decided to go with Todd's original choices all the way down the line. She called her friend and, after taking one deep breath, told him that she would lease the house he'd shown her if the option to buy later still stood.

"You're certainly efficient, Todd," she said after the details had been discussed. "Alice loves that apartment you found for her. She's looking forward to becoming a 'beach bunny,' as she put it."

Todd laughed. "She's something else, isn't she? I'm glad you and Alice found each other, Shay."

Shay was glad, too, of course, for her own sake and for Hank's. What a surprise Alice would be to him when he came home from his trip! Even before her illness, Rosamond had never been very interested in the child, but now he would have someone besides Shay to claim as family.

For all these good things that were happening, there was one dark spot on Shay's horizon. "H-have you talked to Mitch in the last few days?"

There was intuitive understanding in Todd's voice as he replied, "He's working like a madman, Shay. I think he's got another project lined up for when he's done with Rosamond's book, and he's anxious to get to it."

Another project. Shay thought of Mitch's earlier books—she'd skimmed through all four of them during the past few days—and she was alarmed. Good God, did he mean to tangle with the Mafia again? With drug dealers and Nazis and militant members of the Klan? He'd be killed!

She said goodbye in the most moderate voice she could manage, then hung up the telephone with a bang and rushed out of her office, past Ivy's empty desk, through the deserted showroom downstairs and across the parking lot to her car.

Ten minutes later she was knocking on Mitch Prescott's front door.

His housekeeper, Mrs. Carraway, answered. "Hello, Mrs. Kendall," she said warmly. She probably knew a great deal about Shay's relationship with her employer, but Shay couldn't take the time to consider all the embarrassing ramifications of that now.

"Is Mr. Prescott at home? I really must see him as soon as possible."

Mrs. Carraway looked surprised. "Why, no, Mrs. Kendall. He's away on a research project or some such. I don't expect him back for nearly a week."

A week! Mitch was going to be gone for a whole week and he hadn't even bothered to say goodbye. Shay was devastated and she was angry and she was afraid. So afraid. Had he gone back to the jungles of Colombia, or perhaps to Beirut or Belfast or some other dangerous place? She swallowed her pride.

"Do you know if Mr. Prescott has left the United States?"

The housekeeper's face revealed something Shay found even harder to bear than surprise, and that was sympathy. "I really don't know, Mrs. Kendall. I'm sorry."

Shay muttered something polite and quite insensible and turned away. She should have known better than to get involved with a man who lived his life in the fast lane, she thought fiercely. She should have known better.

When Shay arrived home she found her grandmother packed to leave for Springfield on an early morning plane. Alice was eager to tie up the loose ends of her life in Missouri and get back to Skyler Beach.

Shay didn't want her to go, even for such a short time. Everyone she loved, it seemed, was either away or about to leave. "If you'd stay just a few more days, you could meet Hank—"

Alice left her packing to kiss Shay's cheek. "I'll be back soon, don't you worry. Besides, the boy will need his room."

"It isn't going to be the same without you," Shay said as Alice went back to the two suitcases propped on the living room sofa to arrange and rearrange their contents.

Alice went on working, but there was gentle understanding in the look she passed to Shay. "You think I'm going to get back there and change my mind, don't you?"

Shay sank into the easy chair nearest the couch. "Your friends are there. Your house, your memories."

The old woman gestured toward the stack of photo albums she'd brought with her. They constituted a loving chronicle of Robert Bretton's life, virtually from birth. "My memories are in my mind and my heart and in those albums over there. And my future is right here, in Skyler Beach. In fact, I'm thinking seriously of renting one of the shops in your building and opening a little yarn shop. I've always wanted to do something like that.''

Shay reached out and took one of the albums from the coffee table, opening it on her lap. Lord knew, she'd studied them all so many times that every last picture was permanently imprinted in her mind, but seeing her father's face, so like her own, was a comfort. ''A yarn shop?'' she echoed, not really absorbing what Alice had said.

''Robert's father provided very well for me,'' Alice reflected, ''and I've got no worries where money is concerned.'' She closed the suitcases and their fastenings clicked into place one by one. ''In my time, very few women had their own businesses, but I always dreamed of it.''

Shay looked up and closed the album. ''You could teach knitting classes, as well as sell yarn,'' she speculated, getting into the spirit of things.

Alice nodded. ''I've arranged for Ivy to come and pick me up, Shay. She's driving me to a hotel near the airport.''

Shay set the album aside, stung. ''I would have been glad to—''

''I know, dear. I know. You would have been glad to drive me to the airport tomorrow at the crack of dawn and interrupt your entire day, but I won't let you do it.''

"But—"

"No buts. My mind is made up. You've been running yourself ragged, what with our talks about your father and your job and those silly commercials, not to mention the catering service. I want you to eat a good supper, take a nice bath and go to bed early.''

Shay couldn't help smiling, though she felt sad. Mitch was gone, Hank was gone, and now Alice was going, too. ''Spoken like a true grandmother. Won't you at least let me drive you to your hotel?''

''Absolutely not. Ivy and her young man are taking me and that's final.'' Alice lowered her voice and bent toward Shay, her eyes sparkling: ''I do believe they're planning a rather romantic evening; though, of course, I'll never know.''

Shay laughed and shook her head, but inside she wished that she were looking forward to just such an evening with Mitch.

The call came within minutes of Alice's departure with Todd and Ivy. There would be no quiet dinner, no comforting bath, no going to bed early. Rosamond had taken an abrupt turn for the worse, the doctor told Shay, and the diagnosis was pneumonia. Rosamond was being taken by ambulance to the nearest hospital.

Shay raced to Skyler Beach's only hospital, driving so recklessly that it was a miracle she didn't have an accident and end up in the intensive care unit with her mother.

Rosamond had arrived several minutes before her daughter, but it was some time before Shay was permitted to see her. She looked small and incredibly emaciated, Rosamond did, lying there beneath an oxygen tent, and there were so many tubes and monitoring devices that it was difficult to get close to her.

Shay had expected this to happen, but now, standing beside her mother's hospital bed, she found that expecting something and being prepared for it are two very different things. She wept silently as she kept her vigil and, toward morning, when Rosamond passed away, there were no more tears to cry.

Shay walked out of the hospital room, down the hallway, into the elevator. She drove home in a stupor—there was a storm gathering in the sky—and somehow gathered the impetus to dial the telephone number Garrett had left for her. The first person to learn of Rosamond's death, besides Shay herself, had to be Riley.

After talking to a housekeeper and then a secretary, Shay was finally put through to Garrett, who told her that Hank and Riley were on another part of the ranch, participating in a roundup.

As the storm outside broke, flinging the rain and the wind at the walls of her tiny house, Shay sank onto her sofa, the telephone balanced on her knees. "Garrett, it's Rosamond. She—she—"

Garrett waited, probably guessing what was coming, for Shay to go on.

"She died early this morning. Pneumonia. Will you tell Riley for me?"

"Of course," Garrett answered gently. "I'm sorry, Amazon. I'm really sorry. Have any arrangements been made?"

"Not yet. I just—" Shay paused, pushing rain-dampened hair back from her forehead. She didn't remember getting wet. "I just got home."

"Are you all right?"

"I think so."

"Call someone. You shouldn't be alone."

No, I shouldn't, Shay thought without any particular emotion, but I am. "I think I'll be all right. You'll—you'll bring Hank home right away?"

"Right away, sweetheart. Hang tough; we're as good as on the road right now."

Shay mumbled a goodbye and hung up the telephone. Then she got up and made her way into her room. Clydesdale, her carousel horse, stood in one corner, his head high, his painted mane flowing.

Shay rested her forehead against his neck and this time she wept for all the happiness that might have been.

Chapter 11

Of all Rosamond's husbands, only Riley came to the funeral. A tall man with rough-hewn features and a deep melodic voice that echoed in the hearts of his hearers, he seemed, after all those years of fame, perpetually baffled by the attention paid him. Looking uncomfortable in his dark suit, he delivered a simple and touching eulogy to the remarkably small gathering. It seemed apt that the sky was dark and heavy with an impending storm.

Ivy and Todd were there to offer moral support, though neither of them had really known Rosamond at all. Marvin and Jeannie Reese, recently returned from their trip and still showing signs of jet lag, were present, too, also for Shay's sake. That left Riley,

Garrett and Shay herself as true mourners. Garrett's wife, Maggie, was looking after the children.

It wasn't much of a turnout, Shay thought, looking around her. Rosamond had made such a mark on the world, but it appeared that she had touched few individual lives in any lasting way. There was a lesson in that, but Shay was too distracted to make sense of it at the moment.

She wished for Mitch with a poignancy that came from the depths of her and when she turned away from the graveside, he was there. He took both her hands in his.

"I just heard," he said hoarsely. "Shay, I'm sorry."

Shay nodded, her throat thick with tears that made speech impossible.

It began to rain and the mourners dispersed, carrying black umbrellas, their heads down. Shay stood in the open, facing Mitch, wanting nothing so much as to be held by him. He took her arm and led her toward his sleek blue car, parked behind the somber trio of limousines.

After settling her in the passenger seat and closing the door against the drizzling rain, he approached Riley and Garrett. Shay watched through the droplets of water beading on the windshield as he offered his hand, probably in introduction, and said something. The two other men nodded in reply and then Mitch came back to the car.

Shay didn't ask what he'd told them; in essence, she didn't care. "You're here," she remarked. That, for the moment, was enough.

Mitch patted her arm and started up the powerful car. "I'll always be here," he said, and then they were leaving the cemetery behind.

They were almost to Mitch's house when Shay came to her senses. "I should go home. Hank is there, and—"

"Hank is all right."

Shay knew that was true. Hank was safe with Maggie. He'd barely known Rosamond anyway; her death had little meaning to him except as something that had upset his mother. "I didn't expect to grieve, you know," she said in a small voice. "Rosamond and I weren't close."

Mitch was concentrating on the sharp turn onto his property. "She was your mother," he answered, as though that made sense of everything. And in a way, Shay supposed, it did.

The rain was beating down by the time Mitch stopped the car in the driveway, and Mrs. Carraway stood holding the front door open as they dashed toward the house.

"I've made dinner," the housekeeper said in the entryway as Mitch began peeling Shay's sodden suit jacket from her shoulders. "I'll go home now, if that's all right."

"Be careful," Mitch said, without looking at the woman. "It's nasty out there."

Mrs. Carraway hesitated. "Mrs. Kendall?" she said, her eyes steady on Shay's face though it was clear that she would rather have looked away. "I'm truly sorry about your mother."

"Thank you," Shay answered. Her teeth began to chatter and she hugged herself, trying to get warm.

Mrs. Carraway went out and Mitch lifted Shay into his arms and carried her up the stairs and into his bedroom. The hot tub had been filled and the water steamed invitingly.

Mitch set Shay on her feet and, after flipping a switch that made the water in the tub churn and bubble, he gently removed the rest of her clothes. Then he lowered her into the wondrously warm, welcoming water.

Shay shuddered violently as her cold-numbed body adjusted itself to the change of temperature. "F-feels g-good," she said.

Mitch sat on his heels beside the tub and reached out to touch her hair. "You look like a lady in need of a glass of brandy and a good meal. Are you hungry?"

Shay felt guilty surprise. "Yes," she marveled. "That's awful, isn't it?"

"Awful? I don't follow your logic, princess." His hand lingered in her hair, and it felt as good to her as the surging warmth of the hot tub.

"I just left my mother's funeral. I shouldn't be here."

Mitch shook his head in exasperation, but his eyes were gentle and so was his voice. "Next you'll be asking for a hair shirt. You belong here, with me. Especially now."

"But Hank—"

"If you want Hank, I'll go and get him."

Shay bit her lower lip. "You'd do that?"

"Of course I would."

"I—I'd like to call him later, to make sure he's okay."

"Fine." Mitch bent, kissed her forehead and then left the room. He returned several minutes later carrying a tray of food, two crystal snifters and a bottle of brandy.

Shay ate without leaving the hot tub and then slid the tray away. Mitch was sitting on the tiled edge, wearing a blue terry-cloth bathrobe and dangling his hairy legs in the water.

Having finished her dinner and a hefty dose of brandy, the warm water soothing her further, Shay began to yawn. With a tender light in his dark eyes, Mitch helped her from the tub, dried her gently with a soft towel and bundled her into a bathrobe much like the one he was wearing. That done, he guided Shay to the bed and tucked her in.

He kissed her forehead and then turned away. Shay watched, half-awake, as he shed his blue bathrobe and flung it back toward the bed, just missing the target, and then lowered himself into the hot tub, his tanned and muscled body hidden from view.

Shay was disappointed. "Did you know that you're beautiful?" she yawned.

Mitch chuckled and braced himself against the edge of the tub, his arms folded on the tiles, his brandy glass in one hand. "Am I?"

"Ummm-hmmm."

"Sleep, princess."

Shay stretched, warm in Mitch's bathrobe and his bed, her mind floating. "I wished for you...and you were there...just like a prince in a fairy tale. You won't...you won't leave me, will you?"

"I won't leave you." The words were gruff, and they seemed to come from a great distance. "Go to sleep, my love."

"Come here. Hold me."

She heard a splashing sound as Mitch got out of the hot tub, and watched as he dried himself with a huge green towel. And then he was there, beside her, strong and warm, his flesh a hard wall that kept the rest of the world at bay.

They slept for a long time, and then awakened simultaneously to make love. The world was dark and the only sound Shay could hear, besides her own breathing and Mitch's, was the bubbling of the hot tub.

She crooned and stretched in luxurious abandon as

he kissed and tongued her breasts and her stomach, stroked her with his hands. Shay was seized by a keening tension as Mitch loved her and she clasped his shoulders in her hands. "Now, now," she breathed.

He parted her legs with a motion of one knee and took her in one swift, masterful stroke, filling her with himself, driving out all thoughts of death and sadness and loss.

With a cry, Shay arched against him, her body acting on its own, clutching at life, affirming life, demanding life. "Oh, God," she gasped, breathless. "Mitch, Mitch—"

He fit his hands beneath her quivering bottom and lifted her up, to possess her more fully, to be possessed by her. "It's all right," he said to that part of Shay that was ashamed to feel such primitive need. There were no words, however, as their bodies waged their tender and furious battle, rising and falling in a feverish search for fulfillment that ended in a hoarse shout for Mitch and a sob for Shay.

He held her, his chest heaving and damp beneath her cheek, as she cried.

"How could I—how could I do that? My mother—"

Mitch's hand smoothed her hair back from her face and then his arm tightened around her. "Shhh. You're alive, Shay. Your body was reminding you of that; it's an instinctive thing, so stop tormenting yourself."

"You're just trying to make me feel better!"

"Of course I am, I love you. But what I said was true, nevertheless. Any brush with death, direct or indirect, will produce that response in a healthy person."

He spoke with such authority. Shay thought of Mitch's encounters with death, all chronicled so forthrightly in his books, and wondered whom he'd been with afterward. Some Colombian señorita? "That lady pilot, in Chapter Six of *The Connection*—"

Mitch gave an exaggerated snore.

Shay jabbed him in the ribs and then, conversely, cuddled even closer. She fell asleep and dreamed that she and Mitch were making love on the lush floor of a Colombian jungle, vines and tropical plants and enormous, colorful flowers making a canopy for their bed.

Life went on, Shay discovered, and it carried her with it. She said goodbye to Riley and Garrett and Maggie, got Hank into school and gave two weeks' notice at her job.

"We'll be sorry to see you go," Marvin said quietly, sitting behind his broad, paper-littered desk. "But Jeannie and I both wish you the best of luck wth your business."

Shay let out a sigh of relief. Marvin was a reasonable man, but she had been worried that he'd think her ungrateful. "Thank you."

Behind his fashionable wire glasses, Marvin's eyes twinkled. "Those commercials you made were first-rate, Shay. I couldn't have done a better job myself."

Shay grinned. "It'll be years before I live those spots down," she answered. "Yesterday, in the supermarket, a little girl recognized me as the bee and called her mother over to meet me. It was half an hour before I could get back to my shopping. To make matters worse, Hank is selling my autograph for twenty-five cents a shot."

Marvin sat back in his chair, chuckling. His checkered jacket appeared capable of leaping into the conversation on its own, and Shay blinked as he replied, "Twenty-five cents, huh? That's definitely the big time."

Shay sighed philosophically. "Not really. He gets two-fifty for Riley's signature. The poor man must have written his name a hundred times while he was with Hank, just to keep the kid in spending money."

"Enterprising boy, that Hank," Marvin said with quiet pride. "Takes after his mother."

"That's a compliment, I hope."

"Absolutely. If you need help of any kind, Shay, you come to Jeannie and me."

Shay nodded and looked away, to hide the sudden tears that sprang to her eyes. "I'd better get back to work," she said softly, turning to go and then pausing at the door. "About my replacement—"

"I think Ivy can handle the job, don't you?"

Shay was delighted. She'd planned to suggest Ivy, but Marvin had saved her the trouble. "Yes."

"Get a new receptionist, then," Marvin said brusquely, tackling his paperwork with a flourish meant to hide emotions of his own. "Do it right away. Ivy will need to concentrate on learning your job and I want the transition to be made as smoothly as possible."

Shay saluted briskly, her lips twitching, and hurried out. Ivy was standing up at her computer terminal, at hopeful attention.

"The job is yours," Shay whispered.

"Ya-hoo!" Ivy shrieked.

Shay had obviously painted part of the old house herself, in a very light shade of blue and a pristine white. Both colors were well represented not only on the front of her coveralls but on her chin and her nose, too. Watching her, Mitch ached with the love of her, the need of her.

He'd been hard at work on Rosamond's book for several weeks and now it was done, ready for Shay's final approval. He cleared his throat and she lifted her eyes to his face, her conversation with a similarly clad Alice falling off in midsentence.

"Mitch," she said.

Alice rubbed her hands down the legs of her tiny coveralls and did a disappearing act.

"The book?" Shay whispered.

Mitch extended a fat manila envelope. "Here it is, princess. Photo layouts and all."

She approached him, took the envelope, but her wide eyes never left his face. "I'll read it tonight," she said.

"I've missed you," he replied.

"We've both been busy." Her eyes were averted now. "Y-you're starting a new book, aren't you?"

Mitch sighed. The Alan Roget project was something they hadn't discussed. "I've gathered some material, yes."

She paled. "I—I guess I'd better get back to work," she said.

Something in her manner panicked Mitch. He wanted to shout at her, grasp her arm, anything. Instead he simply said her name.

Shay turned away from him, holding the manuscript in both arms. "It's over now, I guess," she said distractedly. "You have your life and I have mine."

"Over?" Mitch was stunned. He reached out then and caught her arm in one hand and wrenched her around to face him. "What the hell are you talking about?"

"W-we'll both be so busy now—"

"Busy?"

There were tears gathering along her eyelashes and her lower lip was quivering. "Shall I call you if there are any changes to be made? In—in the book, I mean?"

Mitch looked around him then, at the beautifully restored walls and ceilings, and suddenly he thought he understood what was happening. He'd served his purpose and now there was no place in Shay's life for him. "Yeah," he bit out, letting go of her arm. "You do that." He turned and walked out, not daring to look back.

Shay sat down on the newspaper-covered floor and opened the packet containing Mitch's manuscript. She had to rub her eyes several times before the typewritten words would come into focus.

"Where's Mitch?" Alice asked innocently, holding out a cup of coffee to Shay and sipping at one of her own.

Shay felt hollow and broken. "He's gone."

Alice manuevered herself into a cross-legged position on the floor, facing her granddaughter. "Gone? I don't like the sound of that, Shay. It has a permanent ring."

"It is permanent," Shay confirmed sadly.

"Are you mad?" Alice asked in a low incredulous tone. "That man loves you, Shay, and you love him!"

"You don't understand. H-he's writing another book."

By now, Alice was a member of the necessarily small group of people who knew that Mitch Prescott and the mysterious "Zebulon" were one and the same person. She had read his books avidly, one after another, Shay knew, so she should have gotten the point. It was obvious from what she said next she hadn't. "Isn't that what writers do? Finish one book and start another?"

Shay was suddenly annoyed, and the sharpness of her tone reflected that, as did the hot color in her cheeks. "It isn't the writing that bothers me! It's the research! Alice, he could be killed, captured, tortured!"

"That's why you're throwing him over? Shay, I thought you were made of better stuff."

Alice's words, though moderately spoken, stung Shay. "I'd be sweating blood every time he left the house, Alice! I love him too much to—"

"On the contrary, dear," Alice broke in quietly. "It seems to me that you don't love him enough."

Shay leaped to her feet, insulted, and stomped out of the room, out of the house. Alice could get back to her apartment on her own, she knew; she had bought a small car from Marvin Reese and was already an expert at navigating every part of Skyler Beach. Shay got into her own car and drove away, going far too fast.

She got a speeding ticket before she had traveled four blocks, and the fact that she deserved it did nothing to temper her mood. By the time she got back to her house, she was a wreck.

When Hank came home from school, he took one look at his mother and asked if he could go over to his friend Louie's house to play until dinner. Feeling guilty, Shay smiled and ruffled his hair. "Have you got any homework?"

"They don't give homework in the first grade, Mom," he said indulgently.

"Oh."

Hank was perched on the arm of her chair, his eyes taking in the paint smudges on her face, her tangled hair, the coveralls. "Do you like your new job, Mom?"

"I haven't started it yet, but I'm sure I'll like it a lot."

"Will you have to dress like that?"

Shay laughed. "No. I painted my office today, that's all."

"I thought the contractors were supposed to do all that stuff."

"I wanted to do my office myself. And don't ask me why, tiger, because I don't know."

"Are we going to live over there, where your office is, I mean?"

Shay shook her head. "There won't be room, once all the other shops open. I rented the last one today."

"You didn't rent Grammie's knit shop out, did you?" Hank demanded. Rosamond had always been Rosamond to him, but Alice, who had won his affections instantly, was "Grammie."

"Of course I didn't," Shay said with a frown. "What made you ask a thing like that?"

Hank's thin shoulders moved in a shrug. "I was just wondering."

Shay didn't believe him. Somehow, in the uncanny way of a child, he'd sensed that she and Alice had had words. She felt ashamed of her outburst now and made a mental note to call Alice and apologize the moment Hank went outside to play. "Grammie's looking forward to having you help her at the shop."

Hank looked manfully apologetic. "I won't be able to go every day. I've got little-league practice and stuff like that."

"I'm sure Grammie will understand."

"And the guys might tease me if they see me messing around with yarn and junk."

Shay kept a straight face. "They might."

Hank brightened. "I'd better go and find Louie now. See ya."

"You be back here in half an hour, buddy," Shay warned. "Supper will be ready then."

"Okay, Mom," he called, the sound mingling with the slamming of the front door.

Shay got out of her chair, took a quick shower and put on her bathrobe and slippers. This was a night to be dissolute, she decided as she put hot dogs on to boil and opened a can of pork and beans to serve with them. After tearing the top off a bag of potato chips, she dialed Alice's number.

"I'm sorry," she said without preamble.

"Call Mitch Prescott and tell him the same thing," Alice immediately responded.

Shay stiffened. "I will not."

"You're a fool, then," Alice answered. "A man like that doesn't come around every few months, like quarterly taxes and the newest TV miniseries, you know."

"You're impossible!"

"Yes," Alice agreed. "But you love me."

Shay laughed in spite of herself. "That's true. I'll see you tomorrow, then?"

"Absolutely. My cash register and some of my yarn are supposed to be delivered."

Shay was hanging up the telephone just as Hank dashed in, flushed from some backyard game and ready for his supper. He ate and took his bath without complaint, then settled down to watch the one hour of television allowed him on a school night.

Shay settled into the easy chair in the living room and began reading Mitch's manuscript again. It was a great improvement over the first draft, which had been wonderful in its own right, and she again had the feeling that she was meeting Rosamond Dallas for the first time. She stopped long enough to see that Hank brushed his teeth and said his prayers, but the story of her mother's life drew her back.

She turned the last page at three-fourteen that morning, wide awake and awed by the quiet power of Mitch's writing. She had expected the book to need minor changes. But it was perfect as it was. Unfortunately. Revisions would have given her an excuse to work closely with Mitch again.

Stiff and sore, Shay set the manuscript carefully aside and rose from her chair. Working with Mitch would have been a foolish indulgence, considering her decision to end the relationship. No, it was better this way, she told herself—she would simply call him in the morning and tell him that she could see no problems with the book being published just as it was. Their association would then be officially ended, and Shay could go on with her life.

What kind of life was it going to be, without Mitch? The question chewed at Shay long after she'd fallen into bed. Sure, she had Hank and Alice and her business, but what was she going to do without those fevered bouts of lovemaking that always left her exhausted but strangely revitalized, too? What was she going to do without the laughter and the fights and the adventures?

Adventures. Shay sighed. That was the key word. She simply wasn't cut out to sit at home, chewing her fingernails, while the man she loved risked his life in order to research some new journalistic feat.

Alice's accusation came back to haunt her then, echoing in her mind. She did *too* love Mitch enough. She loved him, as she had maintained to Alice, too much. If she married Mitch and then he was killed, she would be devastated.

She sat up in bed with a jolt. Only in that moment did it occur to her that she would be just as devastated if he died without ever marrying her, ever touching her again. Why had she thought that separating herself from Mitch would save him?

The next morning was splashed in the singular glory of early October and Shay drove slowly up the hill to Mitch's house. The distant sound of a hammer made her walk around back instead of ringing the doorbell.

Mitch was kneeling on the roof of the playhouse, half a dozen nails jutting from his mouth, his tanned chest and shoulders bared to the crisp bite of the weather. Shay stood watching him for a moment, her heart caught in her throat.

He stopped swinging the hammer to look at her, and there was no welcome, no tenderness, in his eyes. "Well," he said.

Shay was careful not to reveal how much his coolness hurt her. "If you have a minute, I'd like to talk."

He began to drive another nail into another tiny shingle. "I'm busy."

Shay was shaken to her core, but she stood her ground. "I came to return the manuscript, Mitch," she lied. In truth, the book had been an afterthought, an excuse.

He went on working. "Leave it with Mrs. Carraway," he said brusquely.

"You aren't going to let me apologize, are you?" Shay reddened, embarrassed and hurt and yet unable to turn and walk away.

"Apologize all you want. I'm through playing the game, Shay."

"The game? What game?"

Now, Mitch set the hammer aside, but he remained on the roof of the playhouse and his manner was no friendlier. "You know what I'm talking about, Shay. You come to me when you need comfort or a roll in the hay, and then you run away again."

"A roll in the—my God, that's crude!"

The broad, sun-browned shoulders moved in a shrug cold enough to chill Shay. "Maybe so, but it's the truth. You want the fun, but you're too cowardly to make a real commitment, aren't you? Well, get yourself another flunky."

"You said you loved me!"

A small shingle splintered under the force of a blow from Mitch's hammer. "I do," he said, without looking at Shay. "But I don't want to play house anymore. I need the real thing."

Baffled and as broken as that shingle Mitch had just destroyed, Shay turned and hurried away.

Chapter 12

If there was one thing Shay learned in the coming weeks, it was how little she knew about the catering business. She made all the standard mistakes and a few new ones to boot. By the end of October her confidence was sorely shaken.

Alice lifted the furry Halloween costume she was making for Hank to her mouth and bit off a thread with her teeth. While her grandmother sewed at the kitchen table, Shay was frantically mixing the ingredients for enough lasagne to feed fifty people.

"You expected starting your own company to be easy, Shay?"

Shay sighed as she wrapped another panful of lasagne and put it into the freezer. "Of course I didn't. But I have to admit that I expected a lack of business to be the problem, not a surplus. I have four wedding receptions and people are already calling about Thanksgiving. Who ever heard of having Thanksgiving dinner catered, for heaven's sake?"

Alice chuckled. "The solution seems obvious. Hire some help."

Shay leaned back against the counter in a rare moment of indolence. "I hate to do that, Alice. If things slow down, I'd have to let people go."

"You'll just have to make it clear from the beginning that the work could be temporary."

"All right, fine. But how am I going to make the time to interview these people, let alone train them to cook?"

Alice let the costume rest in her lap. "Dear, dear, you are frazzled. You simply call the junior college. They have a Displaced Homemaker program, you know. Ask them to send over a few prospects. I'll do the interviewing for you, if you'd like, right in my shop. If any seem promising, I'll send them on to you."

"You're brilliant," Shay said, bending to plant a kiss on her grandmother's forehead. "How in the world did I ever get along without you?"

Alice chuckled and went back to her sewing. "What are you wearing to the Reeses' Halloween party?'' she asked over the whir of Shay's portable machine.

Shay was mixing tomato sauce to pour over a layer of ricotta cheese. "I'm not going."

The sewing machine stopped. "Not going? But it's going to be marvelous, with everyone in costume...."

"I plan to drop off the food and then leave, Alice, and that's that."

"You're no fun at all. Where's your spirit of adventure?"

Shay remembered a few of the "adventures" she'd had with Mitch Prescott and felt sad. "I've never been the adventurous type. Besides, I don't have a costume."

"You've got that bee suit. Wear that."

"Wear it? When I've been all this time trying to live it down? No way. I'll stay home and greet the trick-or-treaters, thank you very much."

"Party pooper."

Shay laughed. "What are you going to wear, by the way?"

The sewing machine was going again. "I'm dressing up as a punk rocker," Alice answered placidly. "Cyndi Lauper will have nothing on me."

Shay shook her head. It seemed odd that her grandmother was so full of life and she herself could think of nothing but work. She should wear the bee suit for Halloween after all, she thought. It was a costume that suited a drone.

* * *

Mitch was tired from the flight and sick to his stomach. Meetings with unrepentant serial killers tended to have that effect on him.

Mrs. Carraway was busy carving an enormous pumpkin at the kitchen table. "Hello, Mr. Prescott," she said, beaming. "Welcome back." She started to get up and Mitch gestured for her to stay put.

The last thing he wanted was food. He rummaged through a cupboard until he found a bottle of Scotch and poured himself a generous helping. "What are you doing?" he asked, frowning at the pile of pumpkin pulp and seeds on the table.

Mrs. Carraway arched an eyebrow, either at his drink or his question; Mitch didn't know which and didn't care. "Why, I'm making a jack-o'-lantern; it's Halloween."

Mitch lifted his glass in a silent salute to the holiday. He needed a shower and a shave and about eighteen hours of sleep and he'd just spent two days talking to a man who was a whole hell of a lot scarier than your run-of-the-mill hobgoblin. "How fitting," he said.

The housekeeper gave him a curious look, probably thinking that she'd signed on with a reprobate. "Are you all right, Mr. Prescott?"

He thought of Shay and how badly he needed her to hold him in her arms and remind him of all the things that made life good and wholesome and right.

"No," he answered, refilling his glass and starting toward the doorway. He paused. "The world can be a very ugly place, Mrs. Carraway. You see, for some people, every day is Halloween." He lifted the glass and took a burning gulp of Scotch. "The trouble is, they're bona fide ghouls and they don't wear costumes so that you can recognize them."

Mrs. Carraway looked really worried. "Won't you have something to eat, Mr. Prescott? It's almost suppertime."

"I may never eat again," Mitch answered, thinking of the things Alan Roget had confessed to him. He shook his head as he climbed the stairs, drink in hand. The tough journalist. He had walked out of that interview feeling as though he'd been exposed to some plague of the spirit and he'd been back in his hotel room all of five seconds before being violently ill.

Mitch entered his massive bedroom and it was empty, though specters of Shay were everywhere: lounging in the hot tub, kneeling on the bed, counting the extra toothbrushes he kept in the bathroom cabinet.

He drained the glass of Scotch and rubbed his eyes, tired to the very core of his being. "Shay," he said. "Shay."

Shay felt an intuitive pull toward Mitch's house; the sensation was so strong that it distracted her from the food she'd prepared for the Reeses' Halloween party. She hurried to finish packing the cheeseballs and puff pastries and then went into her office to dial the familiar number.

This is silly, she told herself as Mitch's phone began to ring.

"Prescott residence," Mrs. Carraway answered briskly.

Shay bit her lower lip. She should hang up. Calling Mitch was asking for rejection; he'd made his feelings perfectly clear that day when Shay had gone to him to apologize. "Th-this is Shay Kendall, Mrs. Carraway."

"Thank heaven," the housekeeper whispered, with a note of alarm in her voice that made Shay's backbone go rigid. "Oh, Mrs. Kendall, I have no right interfering like this—I'll probably be fired—but Mr. Prescott is in a terrible way."

"What do you mean? What's wrong?"

"He's been away on business for several days, and he just got home an hour or so ago. He said some very strange things, Mrs. Kendall, about every day being Halloween for some people."

Shay closed her eyes, thinking of the monsters that had populated Mitch's books. "Is he there now?"

Mrs. Carraway suddenly burst into tears. "Please come, Mrs. Kendall. Please. I don't know what to do!"

Shay looked down at her watch and bit her lower lip. She had to deliver the food to Jeannie and Marvin's town house, but after that the evening would be free. "I'll be there as soon as I can," she promised. "Don't worry. Everything will be all right."

Lofty words, Shay thought as she hung up the telephone in her office. Suppose everything wasn't all right? Suppose Mitch wouldn't even see her?

After loading the Reeses' hors d'oeuvres into her new station wagon, Shay went back inside her building to find Alice just closing up her yarn shop. "Something is wrong with Mitch," she told her grandmother bluntly. "I've got to go to him as soon as I deliver the Reeses' order. Hank is going trick-or-treating with his friend Louie at six, but if I'm late…"

Alice looked concerned. "Of course I'll look after him, my dear. You take all the time you need."

Shay kissed her grandmother's lovely crinkled cheek and hurried out to her car. She made the drive to Marvin and Jeannie's house in record time, and virtually shoved the boxes of carefully prepared cheeseballs and crab puffs and paté-spread crackers into the hands of a maid hired to serve that evening.

Everything within Shay was geared toward reaching Mitch at the soonest possible moment, but some niggling little instinct within argued that she needed a way to get past whatever defenses he might have erected against her. She stopped at her house for a few minutes and then went on to Mitch's.

Mrs. Carraway answered the doorbell almost before Shay had lowered her finger from the button. If

Mitch's housekeeper was surprised to find a velveteen bee standing on the doorstep, she didn't show it.

"Upstairs," she whispered. "In his room."

Shay made her cumbersome way up the stairs. This was no time to try to hide the fact that she knew the way to Mitch Prescott's bedroom.

She tapped at the closed door.

"Go away!" Mitch bellowed from within. His voice was thick. Was he drunk?

Shay drew a deep breath and knocked again, harder this time.

There was muffled swearing and then the door swung open. "Dammit, I said—" Mitch's voice fell away and his haunted eyes took in Shay's bee suit with disbelief.

"Trick or treat?" she chimed.

"Good God," Mitch replied, but he stepped back so that Shay could enter the room.

She immediately pulled off the hood with its bobbing antennae and tossed it aside. After that, she struggled out of the rest of the suit, too. Mitch looked a little disappointed when he saw that she was wearing jeans and a T-shirt underneath, but then he turned away from her, his broad shoulders tensed.

"What's wrong, Mitch?" she asked softly, afraid to touch him and yet drawn toward him at the same time. She stood close behind Mitch and wrapped her arms around his middle. "Tell me what's the matter."

He turned in her arms, and she saw hurt in his eyes,

terrible, jarring hurt, and disillusionment, too. "You don't want to know," he said hoarsely.

"Yes, I do, so start talking."

Remembering all the times when Mitch had been there for her, Shay took the glass from his hand—he'd clearly had too much to drink—and set it aside. She filled the empty hot tub with warm water and flicked the switch that activated the jets beneath the surface. She took Mitch's T-shirt off over his head and then removed his shoes and his jeans, too. He was still gaping at her when she began maneuvering him toward the bubbling hot tub.

"Get in, Prescott," she said in a tough, side-of-the-mouth voice, "or it won't be pretty!"

A grin broke through the despair in Mitch's face, though just briefly, and he slid into the tub. Shay kicked off her shoes, and then stripped completely, enjoying the amazement in his eyes.

She stepped into the tub, standing behind Mitch, working the awesome tension from his shoulders with her fingers. "Talk to me, Mitch."

Haltingly, he began to tell her about his interviews with Alan Roget. Shay had read about Roget, knew that he was a vicious killer with a penchant for calling attention to himself. She listened staunchly as Mitch poured out the ugly, inhumane things he'd be expected to write about.

When Mitch turned to her, there were tears on his beard-stubbled cheeks. Shay held him, her hands moving gently up and down his heaving back, her tears flowing as freely as his.

"How can I write about this bastard?" he demanded once, in raspy horror. "It makes me sick just to think about him!"

Shay caught Mitch's strong face in her hands and held it firmly. "You have to write about him, Mitch, because there are a lot of other psychos out there and if one woman recognizes the type and stays alive because of it—just *one woman*, Mitch—it will be worth all the pain!"

"I can't do it!" Mitch roared, and then a grating sob tore itself from the depths of him. He shuddered in Shay's arms. "Dammit, I can't do it anymore!"

"Yes you can, Mitch. I'll help you."

He drew back from her, studying her face with those tormented, fatigue-shadowed eyes. "You'll what?"

"I know you don't want a relationship with me," Shay said, wondering where she'd found the strength to admit to something that had been impossible to face only an hour before. "So there won't be any strings attached."

"Strings?"

"I love you, Mitch, regardless of how you feel about me. Tonight, I'm going to drag you back from everything that's ugly and base if I have to drive you out of your mind to do it."

She held her breath and plunged under the water

to pull the plug, and the water began to drain away, but neither she nor Mitch made any move to climb out of the tub. "Your therapy begins right now," Shay said.

Because of Shay, and only because of Shay, Mitch was able to fly back to Joliet for one final interview with Roget and then to return home and write about the man. It was hell, and he swore he'd never tackle a project like it again, but by Thanksgiving he'd roughed out the skeleton of a first draft.

Shay sat on her sofa with her feet tucked underneath her, reading the last chapter. The scent of the turkey Alice had cooked still hung in the air, mingling with the spicy aroma of the pumpkin pie that would be served later. Mitch tried not to watch Shay's every expression as she read, but his eyes strayed in her direction at regular intervals.

Hank, worn out by a day of celebrating, was asleep on the couch, his head resting on Shay's lap. Mitch grinned, remembering the game of Dungeons and Dragons he and the boy had played earlier.

To keep from looking at Shay again, he watched Alice, who was sitting in a rocking chair, knitting a bright red sweater. These two women and the boy made up a family Mitch wanted very much to be a part of, but he couldn't risk proposing to Shay again; their relationship was too delicate for that.

Sitting on the floor, Mitch cupped his hands behind

his head and leaned back against the chair he didn't feel like sitting in, grinning when Alice caught him staring at her and winking mischievously in response.

Shay finally finished reading and set the manuscript aside. Her eyes were averted and there was a slight flush in her cheeks and Mitch sat bolt upright.

"You don't like it," he said, hating his own vulnerability to this woman's opinion.

Shay met his gaze with a level stare of her own. "You detest this guy, Mitch. The other chapters were okay, but this one is a—a vendetta."

"Of course I detest Roget! He's a murderer!"

"Your emotions have no place in the book, Mitch. You're a journalist and you've got to be objective."

Hank stirred and muttered something and Mitch thrust himself to his feet, bending to gather the little boy up in his arms. "I'll put him to bed," he said through his teeth.

Shay smiled. "My, but you take criticism well, Mr. Prescott."

Mitch carried Hank into his room, helped him out of his clothes and into bed. "I wish you were around all the time," the child said with a yawn as Mitch tucked the blankets in around him. "It's almost like having a dad."

Mitch smiled and rumpled Hank's hair with one hand. "I'm doing my best, fella," he said quietly. "I'm doing my best."

"Are you going to marry my mom?"

Mitch thought for a moment, trying to find the right words. "I hope so," he finally said.

Hank snuggled down into the covers and yawned again, his eyes closed now. "I hope so, too," he answered.

When Mitch returned to the living room he was shocked to find Shay standing on the couch, holding out a chair, lion-tamer style, and pretending to brandish a whip with one hand. "Back, back!" she cried. To Alice, she said, "There's nothing more dangerous than a writer who's just been told that his last chapter stinks!"

Mitch was having a hard time keeping a straight face. "Oh, so now it stinks, does it?"

Shay clamped her nose with two fingers and Mitch was lost. He laughed, wrested the chair from her and pulled her down off the couch and into his arms.

"I think the pie's done," Alice chimed, beating a hasty retreat into the kitchen.

Mitch kissed the bridge of Shay's nose. "You wanna know what makes me maddest of all, lady? You're right about that last chapter. Still, you could have spared my feelings."

Impishly, she pinched him with the fingers of both hands. "I ask you, did you spare my feelings when my cheeseballs bombed at the mayor's party? No. You said you wouldn't feed them to a dog!"

"Actually, I may have spoken prematurely. I met a Doberman once, in Rio, who richly deserved one."

She laughed and the sound made a sweet, lonely ache inside Mitch. He'd never wanted anything as much as he wanted to marry this woman and share his life and his bed with her. As it was, they were together only when their schedules permitted, which wasn't often. "I love you," he said.

There was a puzzled look in her wide eyes for a moment, then she stood on tiptoe to kiss his chin. "Stay with me."

"I can't and you know it," Mitch snapped, irritated. "What would we tell Hank in the morning? That we're carrying on a cheap affair?"

Her lower lip jutted out. "Is that what you think this is, Mitch?"

He held Shay closer, desperate for the feel and scent and warmth of her. "You know damned well that that isn't what I think!"

She pinched him again, her eyes dancing with mischief. "Not even after what we did in my office yesterday?" she whispered.

Heat flowed up over Mitch's chest in a flood, surging along his neck and into his face. He swatted Shay's delectable rear end, hard, with both hands. "You little vamp, are you trying to drive me crazy or what?"

She wriggled against him. "Ooo-la-la!" she teased.

"Shay!"

She was running her hands up and down his hips and his sides. He remembered the episode she had mentioned a moment before, and Halloween night, when she'd saved him from demons that had nothing to do with the thirty-first of October. "Stay with me," she said again. "We'll set the alarm and you can leave before Hank gets up."

He set her away from him. "No, dammit. No."

Shay's eyes widened with confusion and hurt as he snatched up his jacket and the copy of the new book and started toward the door. "Mitch—?"

He paused, his hand on the knob. "I'll call you tomorrow," he said, and then he opened the door and went out.

She followed him down the walk, to the front gate and as he tried to outdistance her, she broke into a run. "What's wrong?" she asked, taking hold of his sleeve and stopping him. "Tell me what's wrong!"

"We're wrong, Shay. You and I."

"You don't mean that."

"Not the way you're taking it, no." Mitch sighed and scanned the cold November sky before forcing his eyes back to her face. "We should be able to share a bed without having to orchestrate it, Shay."

She receded. "You mean, we should be married."

"You said it, I didn't. Remember that." He opened the gate, went through it and got into his car.

Alice was in the kitchen dishing up pumpkin pie. Shay had baked so much of it for her Thanksgiving customers that she couldn't face the stuff, so she poured herself a cup of coffee and sat down at the table.

"Since nobody's volunteering anything, I'll butt my nose in and ask. What's the matter now?" Alice might have looked like a mild-mannered little old lady, but she was really a storm trooper, Shay had decided, undaunted by any assignment.

"Mitch wants to get married," Shay said despondently.

"Gee, that's terrible," came the sardonic response. "The man ought to be horsewhipped."

"It could be terrible," Shay insisted sadly. "I might be just like my mother and she was—you know how she was."

"Your great-uncle Edgar was a chicken thief, but I've yet to catch you in somebody else's coop."

Shay had to chuckle. Maybe she'd have a piece of pie after all. "Your point is well taken, but the fact remains that marriage scares me to death."

Alice refused to smile; she was clearly annoyed. "Mitch Prescott is a very fine man and you're going to fool around and lose him," she fretted.

"Have some pie," Shay said.

"I've lost my appetite," Alice snapped. "Good night and I'll see myself out."

Shay stood up. "Please, don't go."

"You should have said that to your man, Shay," Alice replied, and she walked stiffly out into the living room.

Shay followed, clenching and unclenching her hands, feeling like a miserable child. "I did. He wouldn't stay with me. He didn't want Hank to wake up and find him here."

"At least one of you has some sense." Alice murmured, her exasperation fading into tenderness. "If Mitch were your husband, there wouldn't be so many logistical problems, Shay."

"I can't marry him just so we won't have to explain going to bed!"

"You can't marry him because you're afraid, yet you love him, I know you do. And he loves you." Alice sighed, poised to leave. "Take a chance, Shay. Take a chance."

"I did that once before! And the man I loved ran off with a librarian!"

"It's a damned good thing that he did, kiddo, or you might never have found yourself. Look at you. You're in business for yourself. You're strong and you're smart and you're beautiful. What in Sam Hill do you want, a written guarantee from God?"

Shay just stared at her grandmother, stuck for an answer.

"That's what I thought. Well, you'd better not hold your breath, Shay, because we don't get any guarantees in this life." With that, Alice Bretton opened the door and walked out.

Shay went to the window and watched until her grandmother was safely in her car, then returned to the kitchen and sat staring at her half-eaten piece of pumpkin pie with its dollop of whipped cream. She stuck a finger into the topping and dolefully licked at it.

Some Thanksgiving this was. Hank was asleep and Alice had gone home in a huff and Mitch... She didn't even want to think about Mitch.

The next day she woke up with a chest cold and had to stay home, trusting Barbara and Louise, the two women she'd hired through the Displaced Homemaker program at the college, to run the business.

Half-buried in tissue boxes and decongestants of all sorts, Shay lay on her sofa, grimly watching game shows and soap operas and trying to be civil in the face of Hank's determined attempts to nurse her back to health.

By the time he finally gave up and went out to play with his friends, Shay was in a dreadful mood. The telephone began to ring and she made her way across the room, grumbling all the way.

"Hello," she said through her nose.

The response was a rich masculine chuckle. "Good Lord," Mitch marveled. "What's the matter with you?"

"I'm thick," Shay answered with dignity.

He laughed. "I would describe you as thin."

"Thick ath in not well," Shay labored to say.

"I'll be over in ten minutes."

Before Shay could protest that plan, Mitch had

hung up. Her head pounding, she stumbled back to the couch and huddled under the afghan she'd crocheted during her earth-mother phase. She coughed and pulled the cover up over her head.

It would save the paramedics the trouble.

Chapter 13

The two small shops on the first floor of Shay's building were all decorated for Christmas. She marveled at the industry of their proprietors; Jenna and Betty must have worked all of Thanksgiving weekend to assemble such grandeur, she thought.

Though her own office and kitchen were, of course, on the first floor, too, Shay climbed the stairs to see if Alice and the woman who owned the candle shop had followed suit. They had.

Shay crammed her hands into the pockets of her coat and went downstairs by the back way, feeling a little guilty because she hadn't put out so much as a sprig of holly.

Both Barbara and Louise were busy in the huge

kitchen, with its big tables and commercial refriger-
ators. Shay watched them for a few moments, unno-
ticed, trying to imagine what their lives had been like.

Barbara, a plump woman with beautifully coiffed
hair, was rolling out dough for an order of quiche.
She had signed up for the Displaced Homemaker program at the college after her husband of twenty-eight
years had divorced her for another woman. Louise, a
small and perpetually smiling blonde, had lost her
husband in a car accident a year before. She, like
Barbara, had never held a paying job in her life, and
yet she'd been faced with the prospect of earning a
living.

Inwardly, Shay sighed. These two women had
given their best to their marriages, and where had it
gotten them? They had been betrayed, abandoned.

At that moment Barbara spotted her and smiled.
"Good morning, Ms. Kendall. Feeling better?"

The inside of Shay's chest still felt raw and hollow,
while her sinuses were stuffed, but the worst was past.
Mitch had coddled her shamefully. "Yes," she said.
"Yes, I feel better."

"You look like you dragged yourself down here,"
Louise observed in her forthright way. "Why don't
you go home and rest? We can manage things on this
end."

Shay looked upon the two women with admiration.
Okay, so they were "displaced homemakers," but
they were also survivors. They had tallied what skills

they had—neither was a stranger to cooking for a crowd—and they'd gone out and found a market for what they knew. "I've got some book work to do in the office," she said in reply to Louise's well-meant suggestion. "But it probably would be better if you two handled the cooking today."

"I could make the deliveries, too," Barbara ventured.

I must look like I'm on my last legs, Shay thought. She nodded and went into her small office, closing the door behind her.

Her desk was piled with telephone messages, bills from food suppliers, catalogs offering fancy ice molds and serving dishes. She sighed as she sat down in her chair. She had her own business now, and she was keeping her head above water financially, which was something in the first year, so where was all the delight, all the fulfillment, all the pride of accomplishment?

Barbara and Louise were laughing in the kitchen, their voices ringing. They didn't sound very displaced to Shay. They sounded happy.

Shay opened a ledger and tried to concentrate on debits and credits, but her mind kept straying back to those two women in the kitchen. She had expected to pity them; instead she found herself envying them. Why was that?

She tapped the eraser end of her pencil against her chin. She guessed she'd qualified as a "displaced homemaker'' herself, after Eliott had left her, and she'd landed on her feet, like Barbara and Louise, but she didn't remember laughing the way they were laughing now. She remembered fear and uncertainty and a constant struggle, and she remembered leaving Hank with a baby-sitter on cold winter mornings when she would have given anything to stay home and take care of him herself.

Shay sighed again, laying down her pencil. That was it, that was what she envied. For all the heartache they'd suffered in recent months, Louise and Barbara had had their time with their children. They'd been there for the first giggle, the first step, the first word.

Resolutely, Shay took up her pencil again and forced her eyes to the neat columns written in the ledger. There was no point in bemoaning such things now; she was a career woman, whether she liked it or not. And on that cold, windy November day, she didn't like it very much.

At noon Alice breezed in with chicken sandwiches from the deli down the street, her cheeks pink from the cold weather. The two women chatted about inconsequential things as they ate, and then Alice went back to her yarn shop upstairs.

Shay marveled at the woman's energy, at the same time wondering what had happened to her own. She finished balancing the books and then went into the kitchen to help Louise and Barbara box fragrant crab quiche for delivery. Once the boxes had been loaded into the back of her new station wagon, Shay confessed that she didn't think she could make it through the rest of the day and her helpers promised to take up the slack.

She delivered the quiche to the home of a prominent surgeon and his wife and then drove around aimlessly, not wanting to work, not wanting to go back to her empty house. Finally, in desperation, she went to Reese Motors to say hello to Ivy.

The office was in an uproar. Marvin was about to make another commercial and Ivy was simultaneously going over an invoice with a salesman and sparring with Richard Barrett. It gave Shay a pang to see that she'd been so easily replaced.

She would have sneaked out without speaking to Ivy at all if her friend hadn't spotted her and called out, "Shay, wait. I need to talk to you about the wedding."

Ivy got rid of the salesman and Richard in record time and all but dragged Shay into her office. It was disturbingly neat, that office.

"How have you been, Shay? Good heavens, I haven't seen you in ages!"

"I've been…fine."

Ivy's gaze was level. "You don't look fine. Is everything okay?"

"Please don't start, Ivy. I get enough analysis from Mitch and Alice."

Ivy grinned and lifted both hands, palms out. "Say

no more.'' She sat down in the chair behind the desk and Shay took a seat on the sofa and it all seemed strange. It was amazing that a person could jog along in the same rut for six years and then suddenly find herself living a whole different life. ''When can you work in a fitting for your dress?''

Shay stared blankly for a moment and then realized that Ivy was talking about the gown she would wear as a bridesmaid in her friend's wedding. ''Flexibility is my middle name,'' she said awkwardly. ''Name a date.''

''How about tomorrow night, at my apartment? Bring Hank and Alice and we'll have supper after the sewing fairies close their little tufted boxes and steal away into the night.''

Shay smiled, hoping that she didn't look forlorn. ''I think I can collar Hank for the occasion, but Alice has a big date with a knitting-needle salesman.''

That brought a grin from Ivy, though her eyes were serious. It was obvious that she wanted to ask how things were going with Mitch. Shay was grateful that she didn't. ''How's the catering business?''

''Hectic,'' Shay replied without thinking. She felt foolish, sitting there in Ivy's office when she should have been in her own, working. ''Do you like your new job?''

Ivy smiled pensively. ''Most of the time, I thrive on it.''

''And the rest of the time?''

Ivy glanced toward the office door, as if to make certain that it was tightly closed, leaned forward and whispered, "Shay, I think—I think—"

"What, Ivy?"

"I think I'm pregnant," Ivy answered in a low rush of words, and it was impossible to tell whether she was happy or not.

Shay knew what *she* felt, and that was plain, old-fashioned envy. "Have you discussed this with Todd?"

Ivy nodded. "He's thrilled."

"Are you thrilled, Ivy?"

"Yes, but I'm not looking forward to telling my mother. She'll have a fit, because of the white dress and everything."

I should have such a problem, Shay thought. "Don't worry about your mother, Ivy. Just enjoy the wedding and take things as they come."

Ivy started to say something but the telephone on her desk began to buzz. Shay mouthed a goodbye and left, feeling even more bereft than she had before she'd arrived. Her life was in limbo and she didn't know which way to turn or how to go on. She wanted to go to Mitch, but that would have been a weak thing to do, so she drove around until it was time for Hank to get out of school.

She brightened as she drew the station wagon to a stop in front of her son's school. He'd be surprised to see her, and they'd go out for hamburgers and maybe an early movie, just the two of them. Shay had it all planned out.

Only Hank scowled at her and got into the car grudgingly, his eyes averted.

"I'm glad to see you, too," Shay said. "What's the problem, tiger?"

"Nothin'."

Shay shut off the car's engine and turned to her son. She moved to ruffle Hank's hair, but he pulled away. "You're mad at me, aren't you?"

He flung her a defiant look. "Yes. You found out about your dad, but you won't tell me anything about mine!"

Shay shrank back a bit, stunned by the force of the little boy's rage. "I didn't think you were ready," she said lamely.

"I wonder about him all the time and there's nobody to tell me! It isn't fair, Mom!"

Shay closed her eyes for a moment, trying to gather strength. Hank was right. Keeping him in the dark about Eliott had not been fair. Hadn't she been angry with Rosamond for not telling her about Robert Bretton? "I'll tell you everything you want to know."

Over take-out food and the few photographs Shay had kept of Eliott, she told Hank the whole story. She told him, as kindly as she could, about the stealing and about the librarian and she ached at the hurt she saw in her son's eyes.

Hank listened in stony silence and when Shay had

finished talking, he snatched up one of the snapshots of his father and went out into the backyard to sit disconsolately at the picnic table. It was cold out there, and windy, and Shay had all she could do not to go out and drag her son back inside.

Presently, he came in on his own, his small shoulders slumped, his eyes averted. Shay, conscious of his dignity, did not speak or move to touch him.

"I'll take my bath now, I guess," he said.

"Okay," Shay replied, looking out the window so that she could hide the expression on her face. The picture of Eliott was blowing across the surface of the picnic table in pieces.

At breakfast the next morning, Hank was in better spirits and Shay blessed the resiliency of children. In fact, she tried to emulate it.

She was humming when she got to the office and, just to give the day a little pizzazz, she went into the Christmas-ornament shop on the first floor and bought a fancy cornhusk wreath for the reception room. Clydesdale was positioned in the curve of the bay windows, and Shay hung the wreath on his head. "Hail, Caesar," she said, before going off to find a hammer and a nail.

The entire day went well and Shay was feeling better than she had in days when she got home. Hank was there, idly pounding one fist into his baseball glove and watching Sally, his baby-sitter, paint her toenails.

"Spruce up, fella," Shay said brightly. "We're due at Ivy's place for supper in an hour."

Hank's freckled face twisted into a grimace, then brightened. "Is Mitch going to be there?"

"I don't know. Why don't you call Ivy and ask her?"

The baby-sitter picked up a blow dryer, switched it on and aimed it at her toes. The roar drove Hank to make his call from the kitchen.

By the time Sally had dried her toenails and gone home, Shay was through with her shower and wrapped in her bathrobe, carefully applying fresh mascara. Sensing Hank's presence behind her, she asked, "Well? Is Mitch going to be there?"

Hank was silent for so long that Shay finally turned to look at him, mascara wand poised in midair. His lower lip was quivering and everything inside Shay leaped with alarm.

"He's bringing a stupid girl!" Hank wailed.

Shay swallowed. "A girl?"

Hank nodded. "I called him up and told him off! I told him *you* were supposed to be his girl!"

"Oh, Lord," Shay breathed, closing her eyes for a moment. "Hank, you shouldn't have done that. You had no right."

"I don't care!" Hank shouted. "He's just like my dad! He's a creep!"

"Hank!"

Hank stormed into his bedroom and slammed the

door and Shay knew it was useless to talk to him before he'd had a chance to calm down. She went into the living room and tried to make sense of what was happening.

Mitch and a girl? There had to be some misunderstanding. There had to be.

There was. Fifteen minutes after Hank's outburst, there came a knock at the door. Shay opened it to find Mitch standing on the porch, a small, brown-eyed girl huddling shyly against his side. "This," he said, "is the other woman."

Shay smiled and stepped back. She hoped her relief didn't show. "You must be Kelly," she said to the child, helping her out of her coat.

Kelly nodded solemnly. "I'm seven," she said.

"Where, may I ask," Mitch drawled, "is the staunch defender of your honor as a woman?"

"In his room," Shay answered, and as Mitch strode off to knock at Hank's door, she offered Kelly her hand. "Would you like a cup of cocoa?"

"Yes, please." Kelly's dark eyes made a stunning contrast to her pale hair and they moved from side to side as Shay led her toward the kitchen. "Daddy said you had a real carousel horse," she said. "I don't see him around, though."

Shay hid a smile. "I keep him at my office. We could stop there later, if you want."

"I'd like that, thank you." Kelly settled herself at the table and Shay felt a pang as she put milk on to heat for the cocoa. Her mother must be beautiful, she thought.

In a few minutes Mitch appeared in the doorway with a sheepish and somewhat sullen Hank at his side. "Another domestic crisis averted," muttered the man.

"I don't wanna go anywhere with any stupid girl," added the boy.

"I spoke too soon," Mitch said.

"Hank Kendall," Shay warned, "you go to your room, this instant!"

Kelly smoothed the skirts of her little dress. "I'm not a stupid girl," she threw out, just loud enough for a retreating Hank to hear.

"Is she always this good?" Shay whispered once Kelly had finished her cocoa and gone off to the living room to sit quietly on the couch and thumb through a copy of *House Beautiful*.

Mitch shook his head. "I'm still a novelty," he answered, trapping Shay neatly against the kitchen counter and bending to steal one mischievous kiss. "She's only staying a few days, Reba and her husband are attending some conference in Seattle." Liking the taste of the first kiss, he gave her another. "Hank's pretty upset, isn't he?"

Shay nodded. "I told him about Eliott."

Mitch's hand was in Shay's hair, his thumb tracing the rim of her ear. "You did the right thing, princess. He's going to need some time to come to terms with what happened, that's all."

"You were remarkably patient with him."

Mitch kissed her again. "I'm a remarkably patient man." His voice dropped to a whisper. "But I'd sure like to take you to bed right now, lady."

Shay trembled, needing Mitch and knowing that her need would have to be denied. "I'd sure like to go," she replied honestly.

Mitch laughed and nuzzled her neck once. "I'll try to arrange something," he said, and then they coaxed Hank out of his room and went to Ivy's apartment for the evening.

Mitch called Shay at the office first thing the next morning. "Keep the weekend open," he said. "I'm going to take you somewhere private and love you until you're crazy."

A hot, anticipatory shiver went through Shay. "What about the kids? Where would we—"

"Reba is picking Kelly up tomorrow night. Maybe Hank could stay with Alice."

"Well…"

"Ask her, Shay. You're talking to a desperate man, a man consumed with lust."

Shay laughed. "I'll check with Alice and call you back."

Alice asked no questions. She simply agreed to keep Hank for the weekend and returned to the group of knitters gathered at the back of the shop.

The rest of that week crept by, even though Shay

was busy day and night. She didn't see Mitch at all, but he managed to keep her blood at an embarrassing simmer by calling her at intervals and making scandalous promises.

Finally, Friday afternoon arrived. Shay left the office early, picked Hank up at school and brought him back to Alice's shop.

Alice immediately set him to work unpacking a new shipment of yarn. "You just go along, dear," she whispered, half pushing Shay out through the shop's open door and into the hallway. "Hank and I will be fine."

Shay pulled a crumpled piece of paper from her coat pocket and handed it to Alice. "This is a telephone number, where you can reach us, er, me."

Alice glanced at the number, which constituted the sum total of what Shay knew about where she would be that weekend, nodded her head and tucked the paper into the pocket of her apron. "Have a lovely time, dear," she said, dismissing Shay with a wave of one hand.

Because Shay had to leave the station wagon with Barbara and Louise so that they could make deliveries, Mitch picked her up in front of the building. She felt like a fool, standing there on the front steps with her suitcase at her feet.

"I didn't even know what clothes to pack!" she snapped once she'd gotten into Mitch's car and fastened her seatbelt.

"You probably won't need any," he replied.

Their destination turned out to be a log cabin in the foothills of the Olympics. There was smoke curling from the stone chimney and lights glowed at the windows. Pine trees towered behind the small house, scenting the crisp evening air, and among them were maples and elms, a few bright orange leaves still clinging to their branches.

Mitch took the box of supplies that he'd picked up at the store down the road, and carried it to the porch step, setting it down to unlock the door. Shay took as long as she could to get her suitcase and follow.

The inside of the cabin was simplicity at its finest. The wooden floors were bare, except for a few brightly colored scatter rugs, and polished to a high shine. A fire snapped and chattered on the hearth of the rustic rock fireplace, tossing darting crimson shadows onto the tweed sofa that faced it. There was a tiny bathroom and an even tinier kitchen, where Mitch immediately busied himself putting away the food.

"Whose place is this, anyway?" Shay asked, oddly nervous considering all the times she'd been intimate with Mitch.

Mitch closed the door of the smallest refrigerator Shay had ever seen and turned to unzip her jacket and slide it off her shoulders. "It belongs to a friend of Todd's," he answered, but his mind clearly wasn't on such details. His eyes were on the third button of

Shay's flannel shirt and it was a wonder that the little bit of plastic didn't melt under the heat.

"There isn't any phone. I gave Alice a number—"

"That number is for the store down the road. If anything happens, Alice will have no problem getting through to us."

Shay's arms were still in her jacket sleeves, the garment only half removed, when Mitch slipped out of his own coat and began unbuttoning her shirt. She quivered, unable to utter so much as a word of protest, as he undid the front fastening on her bra and bared her breasts.

When he touched her, with one tentative hand, she gasped with pleasure and let her head fall back, her eyes drifting shut. Mitch stroked her gently, shaping each of her breasts for his pleasure and her own, teasing her nipples until they tightened into pulsing little pebbles.

Finally he removed her jacket entirely, then her shirt and her already-dangling bra, her jeans and her shoes, her socks and, last of all, her panties. A low crooning sound came from Shay's throat as Mitch caressed every part of her with his hands, slowly, as if memorizing her shape, the texture of her flesh. One by one, he found and attended the spots where her pleasure was most easily roused.

After what seemed a dazzling eternity to Shay, he took off his clothes and they knelt, facing each other, before the fire. Now, while Mitch's hands brazenly cupped Shay's breasts, she used her own to explore him, learning each muscle in his powerful thighs with her fingers, each hollow and plane in his broad back and on his chest. At last she tangled her fingers in his hair and moved astraddle of him, catching his groan of surrender in her mouth as she kissed him and at the same time sheathing him in her warmth.

They moved slowly at first, their mouths still locked in that same kiss, their tongues mimicking the parries and thrusts of their hips.

But finally the need became too great and Shay leaned back in triumphant submission, bracing herself with her hands, her breasts swollen and heaving under the attentions of Mitch's fingers. She groaned with each slow thrust of his hips, pleaded senselessly at each lingering withdrawal.

He stopped plying her nipples with his fingers to suckle and tongue them instead and Shay was driven to madness. She threw her legs around Mitch and he shouted in a madness of his own, plunging deep.

Shay would not allow him to escape the velvety vengeance that cosseted him, rippled over him, sapped his strength. Her triumph was an elemental thing, and she shouted with the joy of it even as Mitch growled in a release of his own.

Once they'd recovered enough to rise from that rug in front of the fire, where they'd fallen in a tangle of perspiration and breathless laughter, they ate sand-

wiches and drank wine and then made the sofa out
into a bed and made love again.

In the darkest depths of the night Shay awakened
and lay listening, in perfect contentment, to the calls
of the owls and the cry of some lonely, faraway beast.
She felt her spirit, crumpled by the rigors of day-to-
day life, unfolding like a soft cloth. She snuggled
closer to Mitch and wished that they could stay there
in that cabin far longer than just a weekend.

The morning was cold and the sky was a brassy
blue, laced with gray clouds. Mitch and Shay consumed a hastily cooked breakfast of scrambled eggs
and toast and then went outside.

They found a silver ribbon of a creek, hidden away
among the trees and watched a deer dashing up a
hillside, white tail bobbing. It was all so beautiful that
Shay ached with the effort of trying to draw it all
inside herself, to keep.

Early in the afternoon snow began to fall, drifting
down in big, lazy flakes that seesawed their way to
the ground. Mitch built up the fire and then came to
stand behind Shay at the window, kneading her shoulders with his strong hands, his chin propped on the
top of her head.

"What are you thinking, princess?"

Shay knew there would be tears in her voice and
made no effort to hide them. "That two days isn't
going to be enough."

"Two centuries wouldn't be enough," he agreed quietly, and his arms slid around her and tightened.

They watched the snow for hours, it seemed, and then they went back to the bed. There was no love-making; they were too tired for that.

When Shay was prodded awake by hunger, she sat up in bed and yawned. It was dark outside and the fire was almost out. She squinted at her watch and was shocked at the time; it was after midnight!

She prodded Mitch with one hand. "Wake up!"

He stirred briefly and then rolled over, hauling most of the covers with him and burying his face in his pillow.

Shay swatted his backside. "I said, wake up!"

He muttered something and burrowed deeper.

Disgusted, Shay scrambled out of bed and hop-danced to the window because the floor was so cold under her bare feet. The snow was deep now and it glowed in the moonlight, so white and glittery that Shay's throat went tight as she looked at it.

Her stomach rumbled and she remembered that she was hungry. She found her robe and slippers and put them on, then began ransacking the kitchen, making as much noise as she possibly could.

Mitch woke up reluctantly, grumbling and groping for his jeans. "What the—"

Shay shoved a bacon, lettuce and tomato sandwich into his hands and began wolfing down one of her own. "I challenge you to a duel, my good man," she said, eating and putting on her clothes at the same time.

"Name your weapon," Mitch muttered with a disgraceful lack of enthusiasm.

Shay stepped outside the door for a moment, wincing at the cold, and then let him have it. "Snowballs!" she shouted as the first volley struck Mitch's bare chest.

Chapter 14

On Sunday morning the snow began to melt away, leaving only ragged patches of white here and there on the ground. In a like manner, Shay's dreams seemed to waste away, too. She had hoped that Mitch might propose to her again—she felt ready to accept now—but as the time for them to leave the cabin drew closer, his mood went from pensive to distant to downright sullen.

Shay watched him out of the corner of one eye as they drove past the small country store on the highway—the proprietor had been the one to build the fire and turn on the lights in the cabin before they arrived—but she didn't ask Mitch what was wrong because she thought she knew. He probably dreaded the inevitable return to the realities of the relationship as much as she did.

When Mitch reached out for the radio dial on the dashboard, Shay gently forestalled the motion.

"You've almost finished the Roget book," she threw out, to make conversation. "What's next?"

Mitch tossed one unreadable look in Shay's direction and his jawline tightened as he turned his attention back to the road. "I suppose Ivan will sift through the dregs of humanity until he finds some other scum for me to write about."

Shay stiffened. "Is that what my mother was, Mitch? The dregs of humanity?"

He cursed under his breath. "I was talking about Roget and you damned well know it. Don't bait me, Shay, because I'm not in the mood to play your games."

It was an uncomfortable reminder of the last time Mitch had accused her of playing games and Shay felt defensive. Still, she tried hard to keep her voice level. "Do you really think I want to argue with you, especially now? Especially after—"

"After what, Shay? Two days of reckless passion?" His tone was blade-sharp. Lethal. "That's our only real way of communicating, isn't it?" He paused, drew a deep, raspy breath. "I'll say one thing for us, love: we relate real well on a sexual level."

Shay was wounded and her voice sounded small

and shaky when she spoke. "If you feel that way, why did you ask me to marry you?"

The brown eyes swung to her, scoured her with their anger. "I guess I lost my head," he said bluntly. Brutally. "Rest easy, sugar plum. I won't risk it again."

"Risk—"

"If you want to marry me—and I don't think you have the guts to make that kind of commitment to any man—you'll have to do the proposing. Rejection hurts, Shay, and I'm not into pain."

Shay turned her head, and the tall pine trees along the roadside seemed to whiz past the car window in a blurry rush. The terrible hurt, the three-hundred-and-sixty degree turn in Mitch's attitude, all of it was proof that she'd been wrong to expect consistent, unwavering love from a man. Why hadn't she learned? She'd watched Rosamond enter into one disastrous relationship after another. She'd nearly been destroyed by a failed marriage herself. Why in God's name hadn't she learned?

"Shay?" Mitch's voice was softer now, even gentle. But it was too late for gentleness.

She let her forehead rest against the cool, moist glass of the window, trying to calm herself. "Leave me alone."

The sleek car swung suddenly to the side of the road and came to a stomach-wrenching stop. "Shay."

She shook his hand from her shoulder, keeping her face averted. "Don't touch me, Mitch. Don't touch me."

There was a blunt sound, probably his fist striking the steering wheel or the dashboard, followed by a grating sigh. "I'm sorry. It's just that I get so frustrated. Everything was so good between us and now it's all going to hell again and I can't handle that, Shay."

"That's obvious."

She heard him sigh again, felt a jarring motion as he shifted furiously in the car seat. "Don't give any ground here, dammit. Whatever you do, don't meet me halfway!"

Shay could look at Mitch now; in fact, her pain forced her to do that. She sat up very straight in her seat, heedless of her tousled hair and the tears on her cheeks. "I've met you more than halfway, Mitch. I came up on this damned mountain with you. I shared your bed. And you turned on me."

"I didn't turn on you, Shay. I got angry. There's a difference."

"Is there?"

"Yes, dammit, there is!"

"If you truly love somebody, you don't yell at them!"

Mitch's nose was within an inch of Shay's. "You're wrong, lady, because I love you and I'm yelling at you right now! And I'll keep yelling until you hear me! I LOVE YOU! Is that coming through?''

''No!'' Shay closed her eyes tightly. Memories of her mother filled her mind—Rosamond screaming, Rosamond throwing things, Rosamond driving away everyone who tried to love her. ''No!''

Mitch's hands were clasping her shoulders then. ''Open your eyes, Shay; look at me!''

Shay did open her eyes, but only as a reflex.

''I'm still here, aren't I? You can get mad at me, Shay, and I can get mad at you, and it's still all right. Don't you see that? It's all right.''

She fell against him, burying her face in his shoulder, clinging to him with her hands. She had always been afraid of anger, in other people, in herself. And she trembled in fear of it then, even as she began to realize that Mitch was right. Getting mad was okay, it was human. It didn't have to mean the end of something good.

Presently, Mitch cupped one hand under her chin and lifted, brushing her lips with his own.

''All weekend,'' he said, ''you've been telling me what your body wants, what it needs. Your mind and your spirit, Shay, what do they want?''

She sniffled. That one was easy. With her whole heart and soul she wanted Mitch Prescott. She wanted to laugh with him and bear his children and yes, fight with him, but she couldn't bring herself to say those things aloud. Not yet. She was still coming to terms with too many other emotions and her right to feel them.

Mitch overlooked her complete inability to answer and kissed the tip of her nose. "We'll get this right, Shay. Somehow, I'm going to get past all that pain and fear and make you trust me."

Shay swallowed hard. "I—I trust you."

He started the car again. "I'll believe that, my love, when you ask for my hand in marriage."

"It's supposed to be the other way around, isn't it?" Shay caught her breath as the car sped onto the highway again.

"Not in this case," Mitch answered, and the subject was closed.

The boxed manuscript landed in the middle of Ivan's desk with a solid, resounding thump.

Ivan looked at the box and then up at Mitch's unyielding face. "Good Lord," the older man muttered. "You're not serious!"

"I'm serious as hell, Ivan. I'm through writing this kind of book."

Ivan gestured toward one of several chairs facing his desk. "Sit down, sit down. Let's at least talk this over. You didn't fly three thousand miles just to throw a ream of paper in my face, did you?"

Mitch ignored the invitation to sit—he'd had enough of that flying from Seattle to New York—and paced the length of Ivan's sumptuous office, pausing at the window to look down on Fifth Avenue. He thought of Shay, back home in Skyler Beach and probably up to her eyes in cheeseballs, and smiled. "I flew three thousand miles, Ivan, to tell you face-to-face that you're going to have to get yourself another Indiana Jones."

"You're older now, more settled. I can see why you wouldn't want to do the kind of research your earlier books required, but your career has taken a different course anyway, between the Rosamond Dallas biography and the Roget case. What's the real problem, Mitch?"

"A woman."

Ivan sighed. "I should have known. Don't tell me the rest of the story, let me guess. She's laid down the law. No husband of hers is going to fly all over the country chasing down leads and interviewing murderers. Am I right?"

Mitch was standing at the window, still absorbed in Fifth Avenue's pre-Christmas splendor. "You couldn't be further off base, Ivan. If it hadn't been for Shay, I wouldn't have had the stomach to write about Alan Roget."

"So she's supportive. Three cheers for her. I still don't understand why a writer would turn his back on his craft, his readers, his publishers, his—"

"I never do anything halfway, Ivan," Mitch broke in patiently. "And right now holding that relationship together takes everything I've got."

"If it's that shaky, maybe it isn't worth the trouble."

"It's worth it, Ivan."

Ivan sat back in his swivel chair, his eyes on the manuscript box in front of him. "I almost dread reading this," he observed after several moments of reflective silence. "I suppose it's just as good as your other stuff?"

"Better," Mitch said with resignation rather than pride.

Ivan was, for all his professional tenacity, a good sport. And a good friend. "This lady of yours must be something. Once the dust settles and you want to write again, you give me a call."

Mitch grinned, already at the door of Ivan's office, ready to leave. "I expect her to propose any time now," he said, enjoying the look of surprise on his agent's face. "Goodbye, Ivan, and merry Christmas."

"Bah humbug," Ivan replied as Mitch closed the door behind him.

"Doesn't anybody cook their own Christmas turkey anymore?" Shay grumbled as she read over the work schedule Barbara had just brought into her office.

Barbara was wearing a bright red apron trimmed in white lace and there was a sprig of holly in her hair. Everybody seemed to have the Christmas spirit this year. Everybody, that is, except for Shay. "If you don't mind my saying so, Ms. Kendall, most people would be glad to have so much business."

Shay sighed. "I suppose you're right."

"You don't care much for all this, do you?"

The directness of Barbara's question set Shay back on her emotional heels. "I've dreamed of owning this catering business for years!"

Barbara was undaunted. "Sometimes, we dream of something and we work and sweat and pray to get it and, when we do, we find out that it wasn't what we really wanted after all. What is it that you really want, Ms. Kendall?"

Shay blushed. Damn the woman and her uncanny perception! "I'm almost embarrassed to admit to it, in this day and age, but I'd like to be married and have babies. I'd like to have the luxury of being weak sometimes, instead of always having to be strong. I'd like to be there when my son comes home from school and I'd like to watch soap operas and vacuum rugs." Shay caught herself. Barbara would be horrified. Any modern woman would be horrified. "Aren't you sorry you asked?"

Barbara chuckled. "I was married for a long, long time, Ms. Kendall, and those were some of the things I liked best about it."

"You're not shocked?"

"Of course I'm not. You're a young woman and it's natural for you to want a man and a home and babies."

Shay was gazing toward the window. There wasn't any snow and she wanted snow. She wanted to be alone in the mountains with Mitch again. "I'm not at all like my mother," she mused in a faraway voice threaded through with a strand of pure joy. "I'm myself and I can make my own choices."

Barbara must have slipped out. When Shay looked back, she was gone.

Shay propped her chin in her hands, running over her dreams, checking each one for soundness, finding them strong. All she had to do was find the courage to act on them.

Mitch wanted a marriage proposal, did he? Well, she'd give him one he'd never forget. She reached for the telephone book and leafed through the yellow pages until she found the listings she wanted. There was no way she could put her plan into action until after Christmas, what with the business and Ivy's wedding and the general uproar of the holiday itself, but it wouldn't hurt to make a few calls.

Kelly cast one questioning look up at her mother. Reba nodded, her eyes suspiciously bright, and the child scampered through the crowd of Christmas travelers and into Mitch's arms.

He lifted her, held her close. There was no time to tell Reba that he was grateful; he and Kelly had to catch a northbound plane within minutes. He nodded and Reba nodded back. A second later, she had disappeared into the crowd.

"Look, Daddy," Kelly chimed over the standard airport hubbub, pointing to a pin on her coat. "Mommy bought me this Santa and his nose lights up when you pull the string!"

Mitch chuckled hoarsely. "Your mommy is a pretty special lady. Shall we go catch our plane?"

Kelly nodded. "Mommy already checked my suitcase and I've got my ticket right here."

Minutes later they were settled in their seats on the crowded airplane and Mitch ventured, "I know this is the first Christmas you've ever been away from your mother...."

Kelly smiled and patted his hand as though Mitch were the child and she the adult. "Don't worry, Daddy. I won't cry or anything like that. It'll be fun to be with you and be in Aunt Ivy's wedding and, besides, I get a whole other Christmas when I get back here."

The plane was taxiing down the runway and Mitch checked Kelly's seatbelt.

"I'm kind of scared," she confessed.

He took her hand.

Shay dampened her fingers on her tongue and smoothed Hank's cowlick. "I want you to be nice to Kelly," she said as the arrival of Flight 703 was announced over the airport PA system.

Hank scooted away, his dignity ruffled. "Mom, don't spit on me anymore," he complained. "I look good enough already."

Shay laughed. "I'm soooooo sorry!"

The plane landed and, after several minutes, the passengers began to stream in through the gate, most carrying brightly wrapped packages and wearing home-for-the-holiday smiles. Mitch and Kelly appeared just when Shay was beginning to worry that they'd been left behind.

Kelly pulled at a little string and the Santa Claus face pinned to her coat glowed with light. "Look, Hank!"

Hank tried his best to be blasé, but he was obviously fascinated by the plastic Santa and its flashing red nose.

"I brought you one just like it," Kelly assured him.

Shay could feel Mitch's eyes on her face, but it was a moment before she'd shored up her knees enough to risk looking into them. She wondered what he'd say when he found out that he wasn't involved with a modern woman at all, but one who wanted a time-out, who would willingly trade her career for babies and Cub Scout meetings and love in the afternoon.

Maybe he wouldn't even want a woman like that. Maybe—

"Shay."

She realized that she'd been staring at Kelly's pin

and made herself meet Mitch's gaze. Her throat was constricted and though her lips moved, she couldn't make a sound.

"I know my nose doesn't light up," he said with a teasing note in his voice, "but surely I'm more interesting than a plastic Santa Claus."

Shay found her voice. It was deeper than usual and full of strange little catches. "You're definitely more interesting than a plastic Santa Claus," she agreed. "But we won't make any rash statements about the nose until after Marvin and Jeannie's Christmas party."

He laughed and kissed her hungrily, but then they both remembered the children and the airport full of people and they drew apart.

"Yuk," said Hank, but his protest lacked true conviction.

Ivy's face glowed as she turned, displaying her dress for Shay. It was a beautiful white gown with tiny crystal beads stitched to the full, flowing skirt and the fitted bodice. Because this was a Christmas wedding, the hem, neckline and cuffs boasted a snowy trimming of fur.

Shay's gown, like Kelly's, was of floor-length red velvet, also trimmed with fur. In lieu of flowers, the attendants would carry matching muffs with sprigs of holly attached.

"We look beautiful!" Kelly piped out, admiring

herself in the mirror of the little dressing room at the back of the church.

Ivy laughed and her joy brought a pretty apricot flush to her cheeks. "We do, don't we?"

There were still a few tinsel halos and shepherds' robes lying about from the Christmas program that had been held earlier and Shay gathered them up just for something to do to pass the time. It wasn't her wedding, but she was almost as excited and nervous as if it had been.

Ivy's mother, an attractive if somewhat icy woman, came in, followed closely by Mitch. It was obvious that Elizabeth was trying to ignore her stepson, but Shay couldn't. He looked so handsome in his dark tuxedo that she almost gasped.

He gave Shay a wink over Elizabeth's rigidly coiffed champagne-blond head and then turned his attention to Ivy. Elizabeth winced at his wolf-whistle, but Ivy glowed.

"We look beautiful, don't we, Daddy?"

Mitch crouched to look into Kelly's face. "Yes, indeed, you do."

"You shouldn't have just walked in here that way," Elizabeth fretted, speaking to Mitch but not looking at him. "They might have been dressing."

Mitch wagged a finger in her face. "Peace on earth, Elizabeth. Good will toward men."

To the surprise of everyone, Elizabeth permitted herself a faltering smile. "You are just like your father," she said. Shay hoped that Mitch had noticed the love in Elizabeth's face when she mentioned his father.

"Merry Christmas, Elizabeth," he said gently, and then he kissed Ivy's cheek and left the room.

There were tears glistening in Ivy's eyes as she looked at her mother. "Thank you, Mama," she said quietly.

"Pish-posh, all I did was speak to the man," Elizabeth replied, and then she was fussing with Ivy's skirts and straightening her veil.

Minutes later, Kelly led the way up the aisle of the candlelit church. Shay followed, smiling when she spotted Marvin and Jeannie. As she passed Alice, the old dickens winked at her.

There was a hush in the crowded sanctuary as Ivy appeared in the rear doorway, her face hidden by a veil that caught sparkles of candlelight. Mitch stood at her side, and he looked as comfortable in a tux as he did in the blue jeans and T-shirts he usually wore.

The organ struck the first chord of the wedding march and there was a rustling sound as the guests rose. Everyone else was looking at Ivy, of course, but Shay's eyes would not leave the man who would give away the bride.

For Shay, the ceremony passed in a shimmering haze. The holy words were spoken and Shay heard them in snatches, adding her own silent commentary. "For better or worse." *Let it be better.* "For richer or poorer." *No problem there. These two already have IRAs.* "In sickness and in health." *Please, they're both so beautiful.* "Till death do you part." *They'll grow old together—I want your word on that, God.* "I now pronounce you man and wife, you may kiss the bride." *My feet hurt. Is this thing almost over?*

It was over. Triumphant music filled the church and the bride and groom went down the aisle together, each with an arm around the other. Kelly followed, on cue, but the best man had to give Shay a little tug to get her in motion.

Snow was wafting slowly down from the night sky as Ivy and Todd got into their limousine and raced away toward the restaurant where their reception was being held.

Hank pulled at Shay's skirt. "Mom? If nobody's at home when Santa Claus gets there, will he still leave presents?"

Shay bent and kissed the top of his head. "Don't you worry, tiger. He'll definitely leave presents."

"That's easy for you to say," Mitch muttered into her ear. "Where did you say all that stuff was hidden?"

"On the big shelf over the cellar stairs," Shay whispered back.

"I'll meet you at the reception," Mitch said after he'd helped Shay and Alice into Shay's station wagon. Hank and Kelly were in the back seat giving voice to the visions that would later dance in their heads.

"He's tall for an elf," Alice commented as Mitch walked away and got into his own car.

A few hours later, when Hank and Kelly were both sound asleep on beds Mitch had improvised for them by putting chairs together, Ivy and Todd left the reception with the customary fanfare, the guests throwing rice, God throwing snow.

"Did you set the presents out?" Shay whispered to Mitch.

He touched the tip of her nose. "Yes. And I filled Hank's stocking."

The other wedding guests were all putting on their coats and the sight gave Shay a sad feeling. It was Christmas eve and she wished that she could share the last magical minutes of the night with Mitch. It would have been fun to set out presents and fill stockings together, talking in Santa Claus whispers....

"I'll see you tomorrow," Mitch said gently. It seemed that he had read her thoughts, that he shared them.

After dropping Alice off at her apartment—like Mitch and Kelly, she would spend Christmas day at Shay's house—Shay ushered her sleepy son out of the car and up the front walk to the door. The porch light was burning bright and she blessed Mitch for remembering to leave it on as she rummaged through her purse for her keys.

The tinsel on the Christmas tree shimmered in the dim light as Shay passed it, and snow still wafted past the windows. She put Hank to bed and returned to the living room, switching on the small lamp on the desk.

Hank's toys had been carefully arranged under the tree, his new skateboard, his electric train, his baseball glove. His stocking, resting on the sofa because there was no mantelpiece, bulged with candy canes and jacks, rubber balls and decks of cards. Shay had shopped for all these things herself, but it seemed to her that there were a few more packages than there should have been.

She took a closer look and found that four enormous presents, all tagged with Hank's name, had been added to the loot. Smiling to herself, she shut out the light and went into her room.

Santa had visited there, too, it seemed. Her bed was heaped with gifts wrapped in silver paper and tied with gossamer ribbons. Shay's heart beat a little faster as she crept closer to the bed, feeling the wonder, the magic, that is usually reserved for children.

Some of the packages were large, and some were small. Shay shook them, one by one, and the biggest one made a whispery sound inside its box. She lifted a corner of the foil lid but couldn't see a thing.

Should she or shouldn't she?

She tried to distract herself by stacking the gifts and carrying them out to the Christmas tree. She would open her presents in the morning, she decided firmly, when Hank opened his. When Mitch and Kelly and Alice were all there to share in the fun.

Resolutely, Shay washed her face, brushed her teeth and put on her warmest flannel nightgown. She tossed back the covers and started to get into bed, only to find a tiny red stocking lying on the sheet.

She upended it and a small, black velvet box tumbled out, along with a note. Shay's fingers trembled as she opened the paper and read, "I want your body. Love, Santa."

She was smiling and crying, both at once, as she opened the velvet box. Inside it was a beautiful sapphire ring, the stone encircled by diamonds.

On impulse, she grabbed for the phone on her beside table and punched out Mitch's number. He sounded wide awake when he answered.

"It's beautiful," she said.

There was a smile in his voice. "You're beautiful," he countered.

Shay willed him to say that the ring was an engagement ring, but he didn't. She wasn't going to get out of proposing, it appeared. "I left your present with Mrs. Carraway," she said, admiring the flash of the beautiful stones. "I asked her to put it in the library, on top of the TV."

"That's intriguing," Mitch answered. "I'll get it and call you back."

Shay's heart was in her throat. In order to withstand the wait, she scampered out to the living room and snatched up the big present that had made her so curious.

Chapter 15

The package was sitting on top of the TV set in the library. Mitch smiled as he picked it up and turned it over in his hands, savoring not the gift itself, but the thought of the woman who had given it. After some time, he tore away the wrapping; by the shape, he had expected a book, but he saw now that Shay's present was a videotape instead.

His lips curved into a grin. The woman was full of surprises.

He slid the tape into the videocassette recorder and pressed the proper buttons and, as he settled himself on the library couch, Shay's face loomed on the television screen. "Oh, Lord," she muttered, "I think it's going already."

Mitch chuckled.

The camera's shift from telephoto to wide angle was dizzying; Mitch felt as though he'd been flung backward through a tunnel. Shay was fully visible, standing in front of a gigantic cardboard rainbow and looking very nervous.

"I love you," Mitch mumbled to her image.

The cardboard rainbow toppled over, and Shay blushed as she bent to pick it up. "You'll have to be patient," said the screen Shay. "I rented this camera and I don't know how to work it."

He heard Alice say, off-camera, "I'll be going now. Good luck, dear." A door clicked shut.

The rainbow threatened to fall again and Shay steadied it before going on. The pace of her living room production picked up speed.

"Mitch Prescott!" she crowed so suddenly and so volubly that he started. "Do I have a deal for you!"

Mitch leaned forward on the couch because the picture on the screen seemed blurry. He told himself that the video camera must have been out of focus.

"We all know that rainbows are a symbol of hope," Shay went on with an enthusiasm that would have put Marvin Reese to shame. She thumped the rainbow in question and it toppled to the floor again; part of Shay's TV set and the end of her sofa came into view. Resolutely she wrestled the prop back into place. "But rainbows can get a bit ragged, can't they?"

Mitch almost expected a toll-free number to appear on the screen, along with an order to have his credit card information ready. He grinned and rubbed his eyes with a thumb and forefinger.

"I'm offering you a brand-new rainbow, Mitch Prescott," Shay went on, in a gentle voice. Then, suddenly, she made him jump again. "But wait!" she cried. "There's still more!"

Mitch leaned forward.

"With this rainbow—" this time she held onto it with one hand while thumping it for emphasis with the other "—you get one wife, guaranteed to love you always. Yes, that's right! Even if you get bored and go back to doing dangerous things and writing books about nasty people, this wife will still love you. She'll laugh with you, she'll cry with you, and if worse comes to worst, she'll even fold your socks. Call now, because a woman this good won't last long! She's ready to deal!"

Shay left the rainbow to its own devices and came closer to the camera, peering into the lens. "You wanted a proposal and this is it. Will you marry me, Mitch?"

Mitch was overwhelmed with a crazy tangle of emotions; one by one, he unwound them, defined them. There was love, of course; he felt a tenderness so deep that it was almost wounding. There was admiration, there was humor, there was gratitude. He knew, perhaps better than anyone else could have, what it had cost Shay to lay all her emotional cards on the table.

The screen was blank now, buzzing with static. He left the couch, pressed the rewind button on the recorder and watched the tape again, this time standing, his arms folded across his chest as if to brace himself against some tidal wave of emotion.

Shay felt downright dissolute, waking up in a mink coat, curled up around the telephone as though it were a teddy bear.

Mitch hadn't called. Surely he'd seen the tape by now, but he hadn't called.

Shay sat up and squinted at the clock on her bedside table. It was five-fifteen. No point in going back to sleep; Hank would be up and ready to rip into the presents at any moment.

She lay back on her pillows, setting the phone away from her. Her hands came to rest in the deep, lush fur of the coat and tears smarted in her eyes. Maybe Mitch didn't see her as wife material after all. Maybe she was more of a kept woman, a bird in a gilded cage.

Shay bounded off the bed, tore off the fur coat and flung it across the room. Then, in just her flannel nightgown, she padded out into the living room to turn up the thermostat and light the tree. She had just turned away from the coffeemaker when she heard Hank's first squeal of delight.

GET 2

HOW TO GET YOUR
2 FREE BOOKS AND FREE GIFT!

1. Peel off the MIRA® sticker on the front cover. Place it in the space provided at right. This automatically entitles you to receive two free books and an exciting surprise gift.

2. Send back this card and you'll get 2 "The Best of the Best™" books. These books have a combined cover price of $11.98 or more in the U.S. and $13.98 or more in Canada, but they are yours to keep absolutely FREE!

3. There's no catch. You're under no obligation to buy anything. We charge nothing – ZERO – for your first shipment. And you don't have to make any minimum number of purchases – not even one!

4. We call this line "The Best of the Best" because each month you'll receive the best books by some of today's most popular authors. These authors show up time and time again on all the major bestseller lists and their books sell out as soon as they hit the stores. You'll like the convenience of getting them delivered to your home at our special discount prices . . . and you'll love your *Heart to Heart* subscriber newsletter featuring author news, horoscopes, recipes, book reviews and much more!

5. We hope that after receiving your free books you'll want to remain a subscriber. But the choice is yours – to continue or cancel, anytime at all! So why not take us up on our invitation, with no risk of any kind. You'll be glad you did!

6. And remember...we'll send you a surprise gift ABSOLUTELY FREE just for giving THE BEST OF THE BEST a try.

SPECIAL FREE GIFT!
We'll send you a fabulous surprise gift, absolutely FREE, simply for accepting our no-risk offer!

Visit us online at
www.mirabooks.com

® and TM are registered trademark of Harlequin Enterprises Limited.

BOOKS FREE!

Hurry!

Return this card promptly to GET 2 FREE BOOKS & A FREE GIFT!

The Best of the Best™

Affix peel-off MIRA sticker here

YES! Please send me the 2 FREE "The Best of the Best" books and FREE gift for which I qualify. I understand that I am under no obligation to purchase anything further, as explained on the back and on the opposite page.

385 MDL DRTA   185 MDL DR59

FIRST NAME	LAST NAME

ADDRESS

APT.#	CITY

STATE/PROV.	ZIP/POSTAL CODE

THE BEST OF THE BEST™ — Here's How it Works:

Accepting your 2 free books and gift places you under no obligation to buy anything. You may keep the books and gift and return the shipping statement marked "cancel." If you do not cancel, about a month later we will send you 4 additional books and bill you just $4.74 each in the U.S., or $5.24 each in Canada, plus 25¢ shipping & handling per book and applicable taxes if ^ny.* That's the complete price and — compared to cover prices starting from $5.99 each in the U.S. and $6.99 each in Canada — it's quite a bargain! You may cancel at any time, but if you choose to continue, every month we'll send you 4 more books, which you may either purchase at the discount price or return to us and cancel your subscription.

*Terms and prices subject to change without notice. Sales tax applicable in N.Y. Canadian residents will be charged applicable provincial taxes and GST. Credit or Debit balances in a customer's account(s) may be offset by any other outstanding balance owed by or to the customer.

If offer card is missing write to: The Best of the Best, 3010 Walden Ave., P.O. Box 1867, Buffalo, NY 14240-1867

BUSINESS REPLY MAIL
FIRST-CLASS MAIL   PERMIT NO. 717-003   BUFFALO, NY

POSTAGE WILL BE PAID BY ADDRESSEE

THE BEST OF THE BEST
3010 WALDEN AVE
PO BOX 1867
BUFFALO NY 14240-9952

NO POSTAGE
NECESSARY
IF MAILED
IN THE
UNITED STATES

When Shay reached the living room, her son was whizzing over the linoleum on his new skateboard. She couldn't help smiling. "Hank Kendall, get off that thing!" she ordered, a mother to the end.

"I suppose we can't open presents until Grammie gets here," he threw out as he came to a crashing stop against the far wall.

"You suppose right, fella."

Hank was beaming as he left the skateboard behind to crouch in front of the tree and examine his electric train. "This is going to be a great Christmas, Mom!"

Shay leaned against the jamb of the kitchen doorway, her smile a bit shaky now. She'd bared her soul to Mitch Prescott, like a fool, and he hadn't even bothered to call. Sure, it was going to be a great Christmas. "I'll get breakfast started." She waggled a motherly finger at her son. "You content yourself with the Santa Claus things and whatever might be in your stocking, young man. No present-peeking allowed!"

The doorbell rang fifteen minutes later and Shay greeted a package-laden Alice.

"Look, Grammie!" Hank crowed, delighted, as his electric train raced around its track, whistle tooting. "Look!"

Alice laughed and rumpled her great-grandson's red-brown hair, but it was obvious that she had noticed Shay's mood. She placed her packages under the tree, took off her coat and bright blue knitted hat and joined Shay in the kitchen.

Shay was thumping dishes and pans around as she set the table for breakfast.

"What's the matter, Shay?" Alice asked. The look in her eyes indicated that she already knew the answer.

"He gave me a mink coat!" Shay exclaimed, slamming down a platter of sausage links.

"I always said that man was a waster," Alice mocked in a wry whisper.

Shay was not about to be amused. "It's some kind of sick game. I made an absolute fool of myself proposing to him—"

"I take it he's had an opportunity to watch the commercial?"

"He's had all night!" Suddenly tears began to stream down Shay's cheeks. "Oh, Alice, he's going to say no!"

Alice shook her head. "I doubt that very much, Shay. Mitch loves you."

"Then why hasn't he called? Why isn't he here?"

"He probably wants to accept in person, Shay." At the protest brewing on Shay's lips, Alice raised both hands in a command of silence. "The man has a little girl, and it *is* six o'clock on Christmas morning, you know. Give him a chance to wade through the wrapping paper, at least!"

Shay was comforted, if grudgingly so. "I still think he should have called," she muttered.

"Let Mitch have this time with his daughter, Shay," Alice said gently. "It's probably the first Christmas he's spent with Kelly since the divorce."

Chagrined, Shay nodded. "Breakfast is ready," she said.

Except for the stack of gifts Mitch had left, Santa Claus-style, on Shay's bed the night before, all the presents had been opened. The living room looked like the landscape of some strange wrapping-paper planet.

Shay was gathering up the papers and stuffing them into a garbage bag when the doorbell rang. A sense of sweet alarm surged through her as Hank left his electric train to answer.

"That stuff you gave me was really neat!" the little boy whooped, and his face glowed as Mitch lifted him up into his arms and ruffled his hair.

"I'm glad you liked it," was the quiet answer.

Kelly came shyly past her father, holding the doll that had been her gift from Shay. A beautiful, delicate fairy, complete with silvery wings and wand, the doll was well suited to its ladylike owner. "Thank you very much," the little girl said, looking up at Shay with Mitch's eyes.

Shay forgot her own nervousness and smiled at Kelly. "You're welcome, sweetheart."

Alice, who had been quietly reading a book she had received as a gift, suddenly leaped out of her rocking chair, the warmth of her smile taking in both Kelly and Hank.

"Let's go and see how that turkey of ours is coming along, shall we?"

The children followed Alice into the kitchen.

"Crafty old dickens," Mitch muttered, watching Alice's spry departing figure with a smile in his eyes.

Shay suddenly felt shy, like a teenager who has just asked a boy to a Sadie Hawkins dance. She just stood there, in the middle of a mountain range of Christmas paper, the garbage bag in one hand, stricken to silence.

Mitch seemed similarly afflicted.

Alice finally intervened. "Get on with it," she coaxed from the kitchen doorway. "I can't keep these kids interested in a turkey forever, you know!"

The spell was broken. Mitch laughed and so did Shay, but her nervousness drove her back to her paper gathering.

Mitch waded through the stuff to stop her by gripping both her wrists in his hands. "Shay."

She looked up into his face, her chin quivering, and thought that if he turned down her proposal, she'd die. She'd surely die.

"Where did you get that rainbow?" he asked softly.

Shay was incensed that he could ask such a stupid

question when she was standing there in terrible suspense. "I made it myself," she finally replied through tight lips.

He pried the garbage bag from one of her hands and a wad of paper from the other. "I love you," he said.

Shay thought of the mink coat lying on her bedroom floor, the sapphire ring on her finger, the stack of elegantly wrapped gifts tucked beneath the Christmas tree. "I will not be your mistress, Mitch Prescott," she said in a firm whisper.

Puzzlement darkened his eyes to a deeper shade of brown. "My what?"

"You heard me. If we're going to be together at all, we're going to be married."

One of his hands rose to cup her face. His skin was cold from the crisp Christmas-morning weather outside, and yet his touch was unbelievably warm. "I'm ready to deal," he said, and the light in his eyes was mischievous.

Shay's heart was hammering against her rib cage. "Are you saying yes, or what?"

"Of course I'm saying yes."

Shay's relief was of such intensity that it embarrassed her, coloring her cheeks. Her eyes snapped. "It so happens, Mr. Prescott, that there are a few conditions."

"Such as?" he crooned the words, his thumb mov-

ing along Shay's jawline and setting waves of heat
rolling beneath her skin.

Shay swallowed hard. "I feel so foolish."

He kissed her, just nibbling at her lips, at once
calming her and exciting her in a very devastating
way. "You, the rainbow mender? Foolish? Never."

"I worked very hard to start my catering business," she blurted out. There was more to say, but
Shay's courage failed her.

"I understand."

Shay forced herself to go on. "I don't think you
do, Mitch. I—I thought it was what I wanted, but—"

Mitch arched one eyebrow. "But?"

"But it isn't. Not for now, anyway. Mitch, I want
to take a time-out. I want to let Barbara and Louise
run the business for a while. For now, I'd just like to
be your wife and Hank's mother."

His lips twitched slightly. "Why was that so hard
to say?" he asked, and he was holding Shay close
now, so close that she could feel the beat of his heart
through his coat.

"I guess I thought you were going to be horrified,
or something," Shay mused aloud. "Most women of
today…"

"You are not 'most women,' Shay." He cupped
his hand under her chin and made her look at him.
"I hope you kept that cardboard rainbow."

Shay was puzzled. "It's in the utility room. Why
would you want a paper rainbow?"

Mitch ran a finger along her jawline again, setting her aquiver. "For the rainy days, Shay. There will be a few of those, you know."

She understood then, and she smiled. "We'll have our quarrels, I suppose."

"Quarrels? We'll have wars, Shay." The brown eyes twinkled. "But we'll have a good time negotiating the peace treaties."

Shay laughed and snuggled closer to him. "Ummm. I like the sound of that."

He swatted her bottom with one hand. "You would, you shameless vixen!" His whisper sent an aching heat all through her, and so did his gentle nip at her earlobe.

The tropical sun was hot, shimmering on the white sands of the secluded Mexican beach, dancing golden on water of so keen a blue that just looking at it made Shay's breath catch in her throat.

"Mitch?"

He was sitting on the small terrace outside their hotel room, his feet up on the railing, a man with five long minutes of marriage behind him. He looked back over one shoulder and laughed. "It's a little warm for that, isn't it?"

Shay ran her hands down the front of the mink coat he'd given her for Christmas. "It's New Year's day," she answered. "That means it's cold at home."

"Your logic, once again, escapes me."

Gulls and other seabirds squawked in the silence; it was the time of siesta and most of Mexico seemed to be asleep. Shay yawned and opened her coat.

Mitch, the sophisticate, the man of adventure, actually gasped. His eyes moved over Shay's naked body with quiet hunger, leaving a fever in their wake. He rose slowly from his chair and came toward her, pressing her back into the shadowy coolness of their room. "Mrs. Prescott," he muttered. "You are about to have the loving of your life."

She slid the coat back from her shoulders, allowed it to slip sensuously down her back and arms to the floor, where it lay in a lush, sumptuous pool. "Call now," she purred. "A wife this good can't last long."

As if bewitched, Mitch stepped closer. His throat moved, but he seemed incapable of anything more than the guttural growl he gave when she began unbuttoning his shirt.

Shay undressed her husband very slowly, pausing now and then to touch a taut masculine nipple with the tip of her tongue or tangle a finger in the hair on his chest. His groans of pleasure excited her to greater devilment.

Mitch bore her mischief as long as he could, then, with gentle force, he pressed her to the bed. He lay beside her for a time, caressing her breasts, her stomach, her thighs and even the backs of her knees. And when he had set her afire, he began kissing all those same places.

Shay's triumph became need; she twisted and tossed on the satin comforter that covered their marriage bed, she whimpered as he loved her, tasted her, tormented her.

Only when she pleaded did he take her.

Nine months and ten minutes later, as Mitch liked to say, Robert Mitchell Prescott was born.

Epilogue

It had been one hell of a fight; the rafters were still shaking.

Glumly, Mitch climbed the steps leading to the attic and opened the door. He flipped a switch and the huge room was bathed in light.

There were cobwebs everywhere and for a moment Mitch hesitated, then grew angry all over again.

It wasn't as though he intended to do anything really dangerous, after all. He wouldn't be tangling with Nazis or Klan members or hit men. This book was about racecar drivers, dammit!

He sat down on the top step, his chin in his hands. Okay, so he'd told Shay that he was through writing adventure books and now he was about to go back on his word, however indirectly. Hadn't she told him herself that she'd love him even if he did that?

Mitch gave a long sigh. He loved Shay, needed her, depended on her in more ways than he dared to admit. And yet he'd just spent half an hour hollering at her, and she'd hollered back, with typical spirit.

Mitch was glad that Hank and the baby were with Alice that day. The uproar might have traumatized them both.

After a long time, he stood up and went into the attic.

Shay sat in one corner of the library sofa, her eyes puffy from crying, her throat raw. She couldn't believe that she'd yelled those awful things at Mitch. He was her husband, the father of her son, and she loved him more than she had on her wedding day, more with every passing minute.

She hugged herself. She'd known that Mitch would eventually want to write again, once the scars on his spirit had had time to heal. She'd known it, even without being warned by both Alice and Ivan, Mitch's agent.

Shay snatched a tissue from the box on her lap and blew her nose. Loudly. She supposed she should be grateful that Mitch was only planning to drive race-cars; knowing him, he might have parachuted into Central America or slipped past the Iron Curtain into some country where women wore frumpy scarves and men talked in Slavic grunts.

She rested her hands on her still-flat stomach, where a new baby was growing. She'd wanted to tell Mitch, use it to hold him to a quiet life of building condominiums with Todd Simmons, but that wouldn't have been fair. She sniffled again and reached for another tissue.

If she insisted that Mitch stay, he would give in. Shay knew that. But he would be miserable and there would be more fights. Gradually the great love they shared would be worn away.

The telephone rang and, because it was Mrs. Carraway's day off, Shay answered. The voice on the other end of the line was Garrett's.

"Hi'ya, Amazon," he said.

Shay burst into tears.

"What is it?" Garrett asked softly when the spate of grief was over.

Feeling like an absolute fool, Shay explained. The book about Rosamond had been published under Mitch's real name, so that much of his career was no longer a secret.

Garrett waited until Shay had told him all her fears of seeing Mitch crash in a burning racecar on some faraway track and there was a gentle reprimand in his voice when he spoke. "If you wanted to go back to your catering business, you'd do it, wouldn't you, even if it made Mitch mad?"

"That's hardly the same thing! I made cheeseballs, Garrett. I didn't race around some speedway, taking my life in my hands!"

"It *is* the same thing, Shay."

Shay dabbed at her face with a wad of tissue. "I know, I know. But I love him, Garrett."

"Enough to let him be himself?"

"Yes," Shay answered after a long time. "But that doesn't mean I have to like it."

Garrett chuckled. "I guess I called at a bad time. I'll get back to you later, sweetheart. Keep the faith."

Shay might have protested, but for the strange bumping-and-thumping sound coming from the stairway. "If you were calling about this year's camping trip, Hank is all for it."

Garrett promised to call again and hung up.

"Shay?"

She turned on the sofa to see Mitch leaning against one side of the library doorway. Despite his attempt at nonchalance, he looked wan and haggard and Shay felt a painful tightening in her heart. But fear for him made her voice cool. "Yes?"

"I won't go if it's that important to you. I'll write a novel or something."

Shay felt all broken and raw inside. "You'll only be racing for two or three weeks, won't you? Actually driving the cars, I mean?"

She thought she saw hope leap in the depths of his

dark, dark eyes. "Three weeks at the most," he promised hoarsely.

"I'll hate every minute of it. I love you, Mitch."

He disappeared around the corner, came back in a moment dragging a very large and very dusty cardboard rainbow. A shower of glued-on glitter fell from the colorful arch as Mitch pulled it across the room and propped it against his desk.

"I think this is one of those rainy days we talked about," he said.

Shay felt tears sting her eyes. It was late July and the sun was shining, but Mitch was right. She held out her arms to him and he came to her, drawing her close, burying his face in the warm curve of her neck.

"I love you," he said.

Shay tangled the fingers of one hand in his hair. It was dusty from his foraging expedition in the attic. "And I love you. Too much to keep you here if that's not what you want."

"You could go with me." His hand was working its way under her sweater, cupping one breast, not to give passion but to take comfort.

"Of course I'll go."

Mitch lifted his face from her neck, let his forehead rest against hers. His fingers continued to caress her breast, after dislodging her bra. "Thank you," he said.

"I'd better get at least a dedication out of this," Shay warned. "I don't exactly enjoy standing around racetracks with my heart stuffed into my sinuses, you know.''

Mitch had found her nipple and his fingers shaped it gently. ''My other books were dedicated to you. Why would this one be different?''

Shay was kneeling on the sofa now, her forehead still touching Mitch's. He had dedicated her mother's book to her, and the one about Alan Roget, too. She couldn't for the life of her remember what he'd said in those dedications, though. She groaned softly with the pleasure he could so easily arouse in her. ''Is this the part where we work out a treaty?''

Mitch chuckled. ''Yes.'' Deftly, he unfastened the catch of her bra, freeing her breasts, catching first one and then the other in the warm, teasing strength of his hand. With his other hand, he caressed her.

''Clearly, sir,'' she managed to say. ''It isn't a treaty you want, but a full surrender.''

He lifted her sweater high enough to bare one of her breasts and bent to take a tantalizing nip at its throbbing peak. ''How astute you are,'' he muttered, his breath warm against her flesh.

Shay trembled. They were, after all, in the library. It was the middle of the day and anyone could walk in. ''Mitch,'' she protested. ''Alice—the kids—''

Mitch circled her nipple with the tip of his tongue, then got up to close and lock the library doors.

SOMETHING TO HIDE

Laurie Paige

For Wendy and Sayde and Stacey and Josie...
with apologies for the name switch!
Love, Aunt L.

Dear Reader,

Living less than a hundred miles from the Pacific Ocean, I have to head east to get to most places, such as Kentucky for a family reunion, or Colorado for the Romance Writers of America conference. I view all trips as wonderful opportunities to explore places for romantic stories. My husband is used to my adding hundreds of miles to a journey because a name on a map caught my eye. While he fishes for trout, I look for angles and hooks to catch a love story.

I discovered the Seven Devils Mountains on such an excursion. Who could resist He Devil and She Devil mountains? As we traveled through the region, and both sides of Hells Canyon—it was a lo-o-ong way down!—stories began to buzz through my head. When visiting old churches and graveyards, or stopping by the local Forestry Service offices, I always find a gold mine of information on families, legends, plants and geology.

Uncle Nick is my idea of everyone's favorite uncle and a loose composite of three longtime residents of one of the many towns tucked away into those devilish hills. They were having morning coffee in a tiny diner where we stopped for breakfast. After listening to their conversation (okay, I admit it; I'm an inveterate eavesdropper), I soon joined in and asked about a million questions. That people answer them always amazes my hubby. But not me. I find wonderful folks wherever we go.

Well, I have to pack. It's off to Kentucky, but first there's this place in Montana, near the Canadian border, that I'd like to explore....

Laurie Paige

Chapter 1

A stranger in a small town was always cause for curiosity and speculation among the local population. A lone female hiking in the Seven Devils Mountains of Idaho, some of the roughest backcountry in the U.S., was an anomaly not to be ignored.

From his mining site, Travis Dalton observed the woman through the powerful lens of his binoculars as she stopped, consulted a map, gazed in the direction of He-Devil Mountain, then set out along the trail she was following, which was hardly more than a rabbit track.

She was either lost or stupid to be wandering alone through the mountains with nothing but the map, a light jacket tied around her waist and a bottle of water hooked to the waistband of her jeans. He opted for lost *and* stupid.

After a couple of minutes, he decided her goal was to get to the top of the limestone ridge. If she crossed it, she would be in the watershed of Hells Canyon, the deepest gorge in the continental U.S., cut by the Snake River as it plunged along the border separating Oregon and Idaho.

Why the devil would she be heading into the hills?

It was none of his business, and frankly, he didn't give a damn, as someone had once said. He wasn't Sir Galahad, out to rescue some female from her own folly.

But she was encroaching on his territory and he resented the hell out of that.

Okay, so she was on national forestland, not the ranch, but nobody in her right mind wandered through the region as if on a field trip. This was wilderness. Deep wilderness. Puma country. Bears, too.

In fact, he'd thought it might be the big mama cat on the prowl when he'd spotted movement a couple of times on the upland trail. That's when he'd gotten out the binoculars. It didn't pay to let down your guard, not if a person wanted to survive out here.

The woman stopped again and rubbed a hand across her forehead, a gesture conveying fatigue and worry.

Uneasiness ruffled the abyss of calm inside him. With a muttered curse, he reminded himself he came to the mountains to get away from people. This was his time to be alone, to escape his family's concern and their everlasting prying into his emotions.

The chasm stilled, becoming one with the endless darkness that was his soul. He preferred it that way. Two years had passed since he'd had any feelings. He'd buried those along with his wife and unborn child.

Grimly he watched the woman as she checked the map once more, his mind automatically recording a description as if he might have to write up a police report later or describe her to his brother, who was with the sheriff's department.

Mid to late twenties. Five feet six inches. Hundred and twenty pounds. Light-brown to dark-blond hair. Gray or green eyes?

She glanced behind her, then all around. She looked directly his way, startling him as her eyes seemed to meet his through the spy-glass lens, an expression of despair in the smoky-green depths.

As if in sympathy with the woman's troubles, the darkness stirred again, burning him in its fiery void, the *nothingness* that could only be kept at bay through hard work or a resolute anger.

He focused on the intruder once more. In addition to the despair, he picked up more than a hint of determination in her manner. The question was: what the heck was she determined to do? It was suicide to be up here with no supplies.

A harsh ripple of anguish tore through him at the thought, reminding him of a time when he'd thought life wasn't worth the effort of living. Sometimes he still felt that way; however, the woman didn't seem bent on self-destruction.

She folded the map and stuffed it into her pocket. He noted she didn't have a compass or one of the global positioning system devices all the yuppies carried these days. At least with a GPS, she could have punched in location coordinates so she could find her way back to wherever she came from.

His mood went from black to blacker, and he considered getting back to work. She seemed to know what she was doing.

At that moment, a breeze stirred the new spring growth on the trees above her and a ray of sunlight flooded her in an aura of brightness, freezing him in place.

It was as if she'd been gilded. Her hair shimmered with golden highlights, a secret treasure hidden among the shining waves. Her skin became alabaster, so translucent it seemed as if the light came from within, as if she were made of some magical substance containing only sunshine and fairy dust in equal portions.

He reached out instinctively to touch her, to gather a handful of the magic for himself. She heaved a visible sigh, then moved on. He lowered the binoculars and realized his hands were trembling.

Turning abruptly, he stored the mattock and spade in the shallow cave where he was working a thin vein of gold and replaced the binoculars in the case. He'd known from the moment he'd spotted her that he would have to check out the situation. Even he couldn't leave a woman to become crow bait in the wilderness.

So he'd have to see if he could help her out, but he didn't have to like it.

After a quick glance at the slant of the late-afternoon sun, he figured he wouldn't get back to the mine that day. He hoisted the day pack. It was better to have emergency equipment on hand than to wish for it a mile up the trail.

Settling the pack and the rifle over his shoulders, he started out, aware of the fading light and knowing there was no way to rescue the woman before dark. He would have to take her to his base camp for the night. Beyond that, he didn't want to think.

Muttering a curse, he quickened his pace. Where the devil did the woman think she was going, heading up an old game trail that eventually petered out deep in the Payette National Forest?

She was almost five miles from the logging road, at least forty miles from town. Since she was above him on the trail with a good quarter-mile lead, he'd be lucky if they made it back to camp and didn't have to sleep in the shelter of a tree. He preferred the relative comfort of his tent.

While the days had been warm and sunny for a week, the night temperature could drop into the freezing range. May was as unpredictable as any month during the spring or fall when the weather patterns were changing.

The anger flared. He needed this time alone, pitting his strength against the mountain until he was too tired to lift the pick. The fatigue erased the memories.

Forcing himself to the present, shaking his head at the human capacity for stupidity, he followed the woman. He was more and more puzzled by her actions as she picked her way farther into the mountains. She didn't act lost. She acted like a person with a mission.

Several possibilities came to mind. As a volunteer deputy, he'd agreed to keep an eye out for some squatters. The local ranchers were complaining about cattle being slaughtered in the field, most of the meat left to rot while steaks and roasts were removed from the carcass. His task was to gather information and/or evidence of such a group actually being in the area.

There were also paramilitarists who occasionally invaded the hills. They played war games with paint balls, but they might use bullets if they wanted a fresh beefsteak for dinner one night.

Keeping tabs on the wilderness wasn't as difficult as most people thought. There was only one main road into the mountains, plus a few nearly impassable logging cuts. Hiking trails followed the winding paths of the local wildlife along creeks. There weren't many of those, either.

Was this woman one of the squatters or with a gang? If so, it was the first time he'd seen her.

Instead of a rescue, maybe he'd better see where she was going and if anyone was meeting her. He slowed his pace a bit. Wearing an old camouflage shirt, he had only to stand still and most people wouldn't notice him if they gave a quick glance over their shoulder. She'd done that a couple of times already, as if she sensed trouble.

His mood darkened even more. He didn't want to involve himself in another's problems, and it was obvious the woman was worried about something.

Suicide? A lovers' meeting? Some clandestine plan that he couldn't begin to imagine? The scenarios raced through his mind. He had a gut feeling that nothing good would come of this encounter.

It never paid to give in to desperation, Alison Harvey reminded herself sternly. She was tired. She was hungry. And she might also be lost.

No. She wasn't lost. She had only to follow the faint trail back to the place where the little stream cut across it, then down the stream to her car hidden behind some trees in a rocky clearing off the gravel road.

For some reason she'd thought this would be easy. Finding her sister when she obviously didn't want to be found was proving difficult and exasperating. Janis had told her, on one of her infrequent calls, that she was visiting friends at a ranch in this area.

"Not to worry," the younger sibling had said with her usual disregard of any but her own desires.

One of the advantages to managing her father's local senate office was that one learned how to get information. Alison had checked the county records for the location of the ranch where her sister was staying. Getting there without local knowledge was another story.

Spying a sturdy boulder close by, she perched on it and removed her hiking shoe. After shaking out the tiny pebble that had embedded itself in her sock under her right heel, she replaced the shoe, took a drink, eyed the water left in the bottle and decided that maybe she should go to plan B.

Too bad she didn't have one.

Find her sister and get her home. That was her goal—and her promise to her mother—and why she was running around in the hills like some modern-day Annie Oakley, only without the gun. However, she did have a can of pepper spray in case she ran into a bear.

She managed a weak smile at the thought of facing down a black bear, or worse, a grizzly. On the other hand, she was adept at handling irate constituents, politicians and lobbyists. A bear might be a piece of cake compared to some of those people.

Spotting movement along the sharp bend in the trail below her, she stiffened and stared intently.

Nothing moved.

She was pretty sure she'd seen something. Perhaps it had been a deer moving through the brush. Or a bear.

Ha-ha, she cynically responded to the suggestion of lurking danger. She hadn't seen a living thing since she'd started out…was it only that morning? It seemed she'd been hiking for days rather than hours.

Checking her watch, she saw today was still Wednesday, the fifteenth of May. She wondered if the ides of May would be as dangerous for her as the ides of March had been for Julius Caesar. Very funny. She forced her mind past the morbid thought.

It was getting late. Time to be heading back to the Lost Valley B&B where she'd checked in last night. She'd taken longer than she'd intended, but who was to know the road would end at a creek filled with boulders bigger than the tires on her car?

The map from the forestry station showed a road going all the way to the private ranch—resort—whatever the place was where Janis was visiting. So much for accuracy.

The comforting bulge of the cell phone in her jacket pocket reassured her. Apparently there was no telephone at the ranch or anywhere else in this back-of-beyond wilderness. With the cell phone, she remained connected to civilization, even if only in a technological way.

A wave of loneliness washed over her. It was a rare feeling, brought on by the very real isolation of these mountains. She folded her arms across her waist as if to protect herself from danger and her own emotions. She wasn't a despairing type of person. Really, she wasn't.

On the western side of the Seven Devils Mountain range was Hells Canyon, a 5,500-foot trench cut into the rocky terrain by the Snake River and described as "one hell after another" by a long-ago mountain man.

Most of the roads in the area were shown as dotted lines on the map, meaning they were dirt tracks and one needed four-wheel-drive vehicles to navigate them.

Ha. A horse would have a hard time in this place.

She should get back to her car before dark, but what if she was close to the ranch house?

It could be over the next ridge and all her time would be wasted if she gave up now. Besides, she'd just have to do it all over tomorrow. But with food. Ignoring her grumbling stomach, she pushed on.

Only to the top of the ridge, she reminded the part of her that didn't want to give up. If she didn't see anything that looked like a ranch from there, she was definitely heading down the mountain for the night.

Giving vent to frustration and other emotions in a

heavy sigh, she put her misgivings aside. As she stood, she again noticed something out of the corner of her eye. She hesitated, then went on up the trail. Approaching a tree at a bend in the path, she made a plan.

After rounding the turn, she stepped to the side and out of sight. Pressing her shoulder against the trunk of a mountain maple, she peered through the new spring leaves on the lower branches.

Nothing.

From this vantage point, she got a glimpse of Lost Valley and the tiny town of the same name tucked in close to the reservoir. The valley was five thousand feet above sea level. He-Devil Mountain to the north was listed as 9,393 feet in elevation on the map. She was someplace between the two and still climbing. Between the devil and the deep blue sky? She managed a silent laugh at her thoughts.

A shiver chased down her back. The day was warm, in the sixties, but nights were cold in the mountains. Could a person freeze overnight? Refusing to give in to ridiculous fears, she trudged onward and upward.

At last she came to the ridge. Intense disappointment hit her. No road. No fences. No ranch house to welcome the chance visitor with its friendly, twinkling lights. Nothing but trees and more peaks as far as the eye could see.

Where were those dashing cowboys when a damsel needed rescuing?

Ah, well. Defeating the oddest urge to sit down and cry her heart out, she pivoted for the return trip.

As she turned, she spotted something moving through the trees that partially blocked the path from view. She'd been right. There was someone on the trail.

A man in green cammies, looking like a soldier on jungle patrol, paused and bent forward to study the trail.

She watched intently, then realized he was probably looking at her footprints. Her heart seized up.

Don't be silly, she sternly advised her imagination. He wasn't following her. Dressed as he was in camouflage clothing and with a gun slung over his shoulder, he was most likely a hunter. After all, mad murderers didn't search for victims in a forest.

But what if he had followed her from town and was toying with her until he decided to finish...

No, surely she was being melodramatic.

Calming down, she stepped off the trail, then watched as he proceeded. He appeared to be around her age, which was twenty-eight, and had a clean-cut, all-American look in spite of his outfit. His hair was short under his billed cap. He had a firm jaw and a decisive way of moving. She detected a strong sense of purpose in him.

She didn't really feel in any danger—she'd never

had any reason to be scared of people and it wasn't in her nature to be a coward—however, she wasn't ignorant of the bad people in the world.

What she really needed at the present was that elusive plan B. Should she stay hidden until he went on up the trail, then follow him? Should she wait for him on the path and ask if he happened to be going to the ranch?

Hide, then head back to the car, she decided. That was the safest course.

She'd make inquiries in town tomorrow, then start out fresh when she knew more about where she was going. She slipped deeper into a willow thicket behind some fir trees and crouched down to wait.

The minutes ticked off. One, two…five, six…nine, then ten…

Where was the man? Had he passed by so silently she hadn't heard one crackle of a twig under his foot?

She didn't dare look. Since movement had caught her attention, she was astute enough to know it would catch his.

A chill swept over her. She felt danger now. Like a bunny sitting as still as possible but knowing the predator was near—

"How long are you planning on sitting there?" A male voice spoke behind her with more than a little exasperation.

"*Aaaiii.*" She leaped to her feet, spun around and

shrieked all at the same time, surprising herself as well as him. She was not usually a screamer.

"Be quiet," he ordered.

"You startled me, sneaking up behind me like that." She flashed him a chiding glance to show she was not intimidated by a strange man silently walking up on her in an isolated mountain setting. The fact that he hadn't grabbed her or made any threatening move with the gun helped.

Her heart gave a funny lurch. He was good-looking. *Really* good-looking. His hair was dark, his eyes the bluest she'd ever seen. He stood a couple of inches over six feet and had brawny shoulders, sinewy arms—revealed by shirtsleeves rolled up nearly to his elbows—and a stare like honed steel.

"Who are you?" he asked at the same time she did.

In the silence, they watched each other warily. Alison was aware of the pulsing of blood through her body, of the quiet of the forest, of the loneliness that had assailed her earlier and was now made sharper by another's presence.

"I asked first," he informed her, a frown indenting a crease between his black eyebrows.

She shook her head. "I did."

He cocked his head slightly to one side as he studied her through narrowed eyes as if assessing her mental and physical abilities. "I could find out," he said softly, a threat veiled in the smooth velvet baritone.

Worry and fatigue dissolved into the sharp relief of anger. She'd learned long ago not to be intimidated by bullies or irate citizens. *Don't be a victim* was the first rule of self-defense. "I think not."

Those midnight-blue eyes sized her up. To her surprise, he smiled. It didn't brighten his eyes, it didn't come from the heart, but it was a reprieve from the frown.

"You're right. Uncle Nick doesn't allow us boys to rough up girls."

She recognized a wry resignation in his tone. He didn't want to fool with her, but he'd been raised to be a responsible person. She relaxed and even managed a true smile. "Uncle Nick is a wise man."

"But I do need to see an ID," he added with a hardening of his lean features.

His teeth were very white against the tan of his face, his lips thin but expressive. His eyes were deepset, causing intriguing shadows that obscured his thoughts. There was a seriousness about him that was reassuring. There was also anger. She supposed she'd interrupted his plans, whatever they might be.

She considered. Her purpose in being there was supposed to be a secret. A politician's career could be ruined by hints of health problems. "I'm just a tourist."

He flicked her a glance that would have cut through stainless steel. "Name?"

"Alison…" No one would believe a last name like Smith or Jones. "Alison," she repeated firmly, determined not to give away more than she had to. "And you?" she challenged, directing the inquisition to him.

He fished out his wallet and flashed an ID at her. It was imprinted with the sheriff's department decal.

"Travis E. Dalton," she read aloud. Dalton was a well-known name in the state's history, first family and all that. "You're a lawman?"

"Volunteer deputy." He put the wallet away. "What are you doing here?"

She decided the truth was the only way. "Looking for someone. My sister," she added at his skeptical stare. "She's needed at home. A family crisis."

"She's in the mountains?"

"She's supposed to be visiting some ranch near here. I didn't realize the road would be impassable."

"What road?" the man asked, showing the first sign of real amusement and more than a hint of irony.

She smiled and relaxed somewhat. A person with a sense of humor couldn't be all bad.

"Put your bear spray away," he advised, "and we'll try to figure out what to do with you. There's a storm coming."

She glanced at the can of pepper stray she'd gotten out just in case she needed protection and slipped it back on her belt loop, then surveyed the clear blue sky.

"What storm?" she asked in the same tone he'd used about the road.

"It'll be here long before you can get back to…" His voice trailed off in question.

"Lost Valley B&B. My car is on the other side of the creek. Where the road ended."

He nodded. "People used to be able to ford there, but some boulders got washed down in the spring thaw." He frowned again and looked resigned to a fate worse than death. "It'll be dark before you get down the trail. Too dangerous. You'll have to stay at my camp."

"That's perfectly all right. I'm sure—"

"You'll stay put until I say it's safe to go down," he interrupted. "Besides, you might be under arrest."

"Arrest! Whatever for?"

"Vagrancy." He gestured toward the pepper spray. "Pulling a weapon on an officer of the law. Resisting arrest. Lying under interrogation. Pick one."

"What part do you consider lying?" she asked, curious.

"The part you're leaving out. There's no active ranch near here. Why is your sister up here in the wilderness?"

She considered how much to tell the man. Her mother had sworn her to secrecy, and a deputy, even a volunteer one, might make the connection to the senator's family. If her impetuous sister had gotten herself into trouble, there could be a scandal. That put her between a rock and a hard place, so to speak.

"Let's go," he said impatiently.

"Mr. Dalton—" She began and stopped, not at all pleased with the uncertainty she felt.

"Travis," he said curtly.

"Travis," she repeated. She surveyed the deepening shadows, considered the situation and admitted she was probably being foolish to even hesitate. "I accept your kind invitation of hospitality," she said in a light manner, although the urge to weep surrounded her like a persistent swarm of gnats.

She was simply tired and worried about her sister. Her father had revealed his goals recently. He intended to run for governor of the state and wanted his family's support for his ambitions. If he became governor, Alison suspected he would run for president next. She'd been delegated to bring her sister back into the fold.

More seriously, her mother had told her that her father had a small tumor at the base of his skull. He'd refused to have it removed until his other daughter was home, safe and sound. That was the real reason Alison was here in the woods. Her father might have cancer. He needed his family with him. Besides, Janis was his favorite. She could always make him laugh.

Lengthening her stride, she hurried to keep up with

the part-time lawman, who had apparently taken her into protective custody or something like that.

Dalton was an old pioneer name. Was he from that hardy stock who had come West after the Civil War? Another branch had been outlaws, she recalled, a murderous gang from the Wild West days of long ago. Her spirits dipped again.

Over an hour later, her guide stopped. Alison blinked in surprise when she realized they had arrived at a camp that was remarkably well hidden.

A tent was placed to advantage under some pine trees. Splotched with green and tan and nearly covered by cleverly placed branches, it blended perfectly with the trees and brush and was almost impossible to see.

She saw no fire ring of stones and wondered if he cooked anything or ate only cold food. Her stomach growled at the thought of dinner.

"Sit," he ordered.

Like a well-trained pet, she did.

Perched on the boulder he pointed out, she glanced at her watch. After seven. The sun had dipped behind the hills west of them. She realized that while some light might linger until nine o'clock, the high peaks cast deep shadows into their area long before that.

"You were right," she told him. "I wouldn't have made it back to my car before nightfall."

His answer was an affirmative grunt as he busied himself about the site. First he let a bag down to the ground from high overhead. It had been suspended from a tree branch higher than any bear or other animal could have reached. The bag was also in camouflage green. The cord that held it was black. She hadn't noticed either one when she'd looked around.

"Here," he said after rummaging around in the bag. He handed her half an apple and half of a square of cheese, keeping the other halves for himself after cutting them with one of those multipurpose knives loved by men.

Murmuring thanks, she downed her share.

He removed dried pouches of food and a can of coffee from the pack. From another hidden cache, he retrieved a tiny stove, along with stacked pans, and started water from the nearby creek to boiling. She wondered if this was the creek that led to the ford and her car. And how long it would take her to follow it there.

"Don't even think about trying to make it," he said as if reading her mind.

She flushed guiltily. "How did you know what I was thinking?"

"Prisoners always think alike."

"I am not a prisoner," she informed him. "I'm familiar with the law. You have no grounds to hold me."

He looked up from his tasks with a stare that froze the blood in her veins. She had never realized how revealing eyes could be, and what she saw was neither kind nor friendly. His show of courtesy was a facade.

He blinked and the dark mood—anger? resentment?—disappeared, leaving a stern, expressionless mask in its wake. That she wasn't welcome in his camp became clear, but he was determined to do his duty by her.

She sighed. Duty was something she understood.

While he finished cooking their meal, she sat in wary silence, misery slicing hot and quick inside her, bringing on that odd need to weep.

Her host was handsome and competent. There was something solid and definite about him. They were alone in a wilderness. For all she knew, they might never get out. She wished they could be friends.

Ah, well, that wasn't in the cards. Her mission was to hunt down her errant sister. Recalling her parents' ambitions, she felt a cage closing about her as she thought of the future and their political plans. Her mother had said they were depending on her. And she always came through. She had to.

Breathing deeply of the rapidly cooling mountain air, she experienced an odd, painful impulse to run and keep running until she reached the point where the earth joined the sky, a place where she could be free—

''Here,'' he said, breaking into her introspection to hand her a metal plate.

Within thirty minutes of arriving at the camp, they

were eating their dinner. He gave her a fork while he used a spoon. She wolfed down as much of the beef and noodle dish as he did. For dessert, he handed her half a candy bar.

"I'm using up your food," she said in apology.

"I'll get more when we go to town tomorrow."

Now that she'd had food, her determination to finish the mission was stronger. Rested and refreshed, in the morning she could surely make it to the ranch. "Uh, I can find my way alone if you'll take me back to the trail I was following."

He shook his head. "I'll have to check out your credentials," he said cryptically.

Just what she needed—every law agency in the state knowing where she was. "Why?"

"I want to know who you are and why you're wandering around in the wilderness on your own."

"Why are you here?" she challenged.

"Business."

"Personal or official?" she retorted.

He hesitated. "Some of both." His glare dared her to question him more. "You were heading deeper into national forestland. Just where is it that you think you're going?"

"The Towbridge ranch."

"Dennis Towbridge has been dead for years. No one lives on his place anymore."

"I'm sure you're mistaken. My sister is visiting friends at their ranch."

He eyed her as if assessing her honesty. "The area is dangerous for a hiker. Local ranchers have had their cattle and sheep butchered recently. They think paramilitarists or squatters have taken up residence in the woods."

A chill settled in her chest. She'd seen reports on the military groups. They could be extremely dangerous, often led by someone with delusions of grandeur. Surely her sister wasn't mixed up with them.

"Is your sister among either group?"

"No. I don't know," she admitted, pulling her jacket over her shoulders as the air cooled.

Her sister had turned twenty-one a few weeks ago. She'd taken off on her own a day later. Their parents were understandably upset.

Janis had another year of college to go, then Father wanted her to work as part of his campaign staff. She was so naturally outgoing, people gravitated toward her charm. She was also something of a free spirit, rebellious when she was thwarted, but usually able to wrap everyone she met around her little finger.

Alison pressed her fingertips over her mouth to stop the disloyal thoughts. She was tired and sometimes it seemed she did everything her family wanted with no concessions for her own wishes and hopes and desires.

However, her father did important work, work she believed in, for the good of the country. She must remember that. Janis was needed at home.

Their father's operation would be carried out in utmost secrecy. If the news was leaked, the press would forever be questioning his health when he announced he was running for president, as she was sure he would.

She sighed at the machinations that formed the core of her existence. Life was very complicated.

Looking at the rugged terrain, breathing the crystal-clear air, she wondered why it had to be. Here in the mountains, things seemed simple. One had to survive, of course, but there was also something more here, something she sensed deep in her heart.

She listened to the quiet. It was peaceful. Yes, that was it. It was peaceful here.

Her host caught her in the act of smiling to herself. When she widened the smile to include him, he frowned and grimly went about the business of cleaning up the dishes.

Obviously he didn't feel the same soulful contentment. Just as obviously, he didn't want to be within a hundred miles of her. Travis Dalton was a recluse and a loner.

She held the smile with an effort and assumed a cheerful manner. Miss Congeniality. Yeah, that was her.

Chapter 2

The temperature grew progressively colder. Alison huddled in her nylon jacket, aware that she'd been ignorant to come into the mountains with so little gear for survival.

Her companion sat silently over his coffee, his face nearly hidden by shadows. She shivered uncontrollably and wished for a cheery fire. There was plenty of dead wood on the ground. Should she suggest it?

"Sorry," he said mysteriously.

He went to the tent and returned with a down parka, also in cammie green, and tossed it to her. She put it on after she saw he had a sweater and a jacket. Snuggled into the fluffy parka, her hands in the pockets, she felt his gaze on her.

"I'm really sorry to be a pest," she said. "It was stupid to head into the unknown with so little preparation. I assure you I'm not usually like this. It was just…"

"A family crisis," he supplied.

"Yes."

"Do you have some ID on you?"

After handing over her driver's license, she waited tensely for his next pronouncement.

"Alison Harvey. You were born the same year I was." He studied her for a sec as if to judge whether he agreed with the information. His eyes narrowed. "Harvey, as in the esteemed U.S. senator from Idaho?"

"A—a relative," she admitted, hoping he wouldn't catch the hesitation as she replied truthfully but evasively.

He shrugged and handed the ID back. "Your sister may be mixed up with a bad bunch."

"I'm sure it's a mistake. Janis would never do anything illegal." She mentally crossed her fingers, suddenly not sure at all.

This trip, the long day, the man's unrelenting gaze, as if he could sort truth from lies with just a glance, wore on her. It struck her as absurd, being out in a wilderness looking for her prodigal sister. But someone had to do it. If not her, then who?

No one else came to mind, a depressing realization. It always seemed to be her job to smooth out problems in the family. For a second, she felt trapped by that expectation, then she pushed the odd thought aside.

"Why the secrecy?"

"I don't know what you mean," she said coolly, putting on a polite mask that revealed nothing.

"You didn't want me to know who you were."

She tensed. While he didn't give much away about himself, he seemed to be unusually perceptive where she was concerned. She should have had a plan, except she hadn't expected to meet up with a handsome volunteer deputy out in the middle of nowhere.

Candor was often disarming. She decided to try it. "My family doesn't want anyone to know we're looking for my sister. It, uh, might sound as if there's a problem when there isn't. There *is* a complication."

"Such as?"

Could she trust him with the truth? People were wary when it came to illness and the presidency. Not that her father was going to die, but still... "My father has a slight medical situation."

"What kind of situation?"

Alison glared at her inquisitor. "He has a small tumor at the base of his skull. Father doesn't want anyone to know. Like so many men, he thinks illness of any kind is a weakness. My mother told me, and asked that I bring Janis home for the surgery. I promised that I would."

There was a subtle difference in the man's expression. She thought she saw sympathy, perhaps sadness, flash through his eyes. This gave her an inordinate sense of hope that she was doing the right thing.

"I see," he said in a musing tone. "That's tough."

Alison nodded. "So you see, I have to make it to the ranch and talk to Janis. She'll come home once I explain things to her."

"Put a guilt trip on her," the man corrected. "The same as your mother did to you." He shook his head. "Sending an inexperienced female into the mountains. That was smart."

The forlorn hope went up in a puff of smoke. She didn't need his approval anyway. Clenching her hands in the warm jacket pockets, she didn't bother to respond. She'd learned that was the best way to handle remarks about her family.

Travis noted the way Alison clammed up at any criticism of her family. She was protective of them.

Brave, too, to venture into the hills like this, he grudgingly admitted, but ignorant of the dangers. However, neither her courage nor her family loyalty meant a flaming thing to him, other than the nuisance factor.

At nine, he suggested it was time to go to bed. That visibly got her attention. She sat up straight and stared at him. "Where shall I sleep?"

"In the tent."

"Where will you be?"

He spoke slowly and patiently. "It's a two-man,

uh, -person, tent. There are two sleeping bags. Sometimes it gets chilly—or I meet up with a lost hiker.''

''Oh.'' She took a minute to consider, then nodded.

As if they had any other choice.

He heated water in a pan. ''You can wash up behind those bushes over there. Toss the water on the ground, not into the creek. Don't stray off.''

She rose and looked around, then headed toward the thicket across the slope from the camp. While she prepared for bed, he closed the bear bag and pulled it high into the air, the nylon cord suspended over a tree branch at least twenty feet from the ground.

Bears were getting smarter, he mused while he waited for his guest to reappear. Some of them had learned they only needed to follow the rope to its end, break it and food would fall to the ground like manna from heaven. He used a black rope, which was harder to see, and ran it through some brush to further disguise it, then secured it to a tree.

Glancing at the luminous dial of his watch, he decided she'd had enough time. He rose and strode toward the bushes. ''Yo,'' he called out. ''About finished?''

''Yes,'' she said, returning to camp.

The relief surprised him. He'd half expected her to try to escape in the dark. She was smarter than that, thank heavens. There were other things he'd noticed about her. The fact that she was putting up a cheerful front was one.

Her lips, a soft pink without lipstick, had trembled ever so slightly at times. When she thought he wasn't looking, the despair returned. In spite of the smiles, he detected a delicate vulnerability in the smoky-green eyes.

It wasn't a fact he wanted to know. He didn't give a damn what her problems were. He closed his eyes for a second. Couldn't a man just be left alone?

Leaning on the anger that had gotten him through the blackest days of his life, he grabbed his kit, brushed his teeth and prepared for bed. After that, he stored the stove and pans in their bag and pulled them back into the air.

Slowly, reluctantly, he went to the tent. It would be tight quarters in there. He hadn't been that close to a woman in two years.

Women had tried to comfort him, but he hadn't wanted them. He hadn't wanted the passion. Passion brought memories and memories brought pain. He willed the abyss into stillness as he opened the nylon flap and ducked inside.

She was tucked safely in one of the down bags, her back to him. Her hair was a pool of shadowy waves against the material. He knew it would be warm if he ran his fingers into it. And in the sunlight, it gleamed like gold.

A spasm rippled through him, a strong, undefined emotion that took him by surprise. Odder still was the fatalistic notion that he wouldn't make it through the night if he slept in here.

He considered taking his down bag outside and sleeping under a tree, but the temperature was dropping fast.

Don't be stupid, he ordered. He could handle one night. It wasn't as if it meant anything. Nothing had impinged on his heart or his soul for a long time. Nothing ever would again, if he had any say about it.

After removing his shoes, he stored them under the rain fly, zipped the door flap and scooted into the sleeping bag.

A spark shot up his leg as his foot brushed against hers, causing heat to spear through his gut. Memories, too painful to bear, stirred at the accidental touch.

Two years ago, he'd been awakened by his wife's moans. She'd been in labor. He'd gotten her to the hospital, but it had been too late, too late for Julie and too late for their unborn son. With all the modern miracles of medicine, the doctors hadn't been able to revive that which was gone.

"Don't grieve," she'd said during that grim trip to town that had ended in hell for him. "I'll love you forever. I'll always be with you."

Julie, ever the optimist. For them, forever had been their three years of marriage. She'd died that night.

He willed the memory and the agony into the pit of oblivion where he'd consigned all his dreams and hopes.

Finally he was able to see a certain irony in the present situation. Not wanting to be close to anyone, here he was, sleeping with a woman, one who was a relative of the state's most popular senator.

Wait a minute. The senator had two daughters. The older one worked in his Boise office. He recalled seeing her on television a couple of times, always discreetly in the background when her father was announcing his campaign for office or making a statement to the press.

This woman had to be one and the same. She was prettier and more approachable than he'd thought. Up close, there was something valiant about her, but also something fragile. She'd been ethereal standing in the pool of sunlight on the trail, as if only her will kept her pinned to earth.

He cursed silently, not wanting to know these things about her. *Live and let live;* that was his motto.

Pushing the sleeping bag down to his waist, he put his arms behind his head for a pillow and stared into the darkness of the tent. From over the near peaks, he heard the rumble of a building storm. He doubted it would rain much, so they should get out without difficulty tomorrow.

Alison stirred and turned toward him, snuggling her nose into his armpit. A bolt of hunger went through him like summer lightning.

Stunned and rock-hard with needs he didn't want, he thought this chance encounter with the senator's daughter just might be the death of him. He hoped it came soon.

She moved closer. Her hair tickled his chin. He smoothed it down, unable to stop his fingers from running through its softness. It was like warm, spun gold.

He tensed for the pain he knew would follow.

Instead, an odd sensation, like the gentle caress of a breeze, flowed over him. He thought of things he'd left behind years ago—the comforting touch of his mother as she tucked him into bed, his father's rough but careful hands as he lifted him high off the ground, gave him a mighty toss, then caught him, the older man's laughter blending with his shouts of glee. Later, there had been Julie, his friend, his lover, his beloved. That's what happiness had been. Once.

Old wounds ripped open. He held on until the old dreams faded. He would never allow himself to be that vulnerable again. It wasn't a vow, only a certainty embedded in the granite that enclosed his heart.

Turning his back on the sleeping woman, he welcomed the darkness.

Alison woke with a groan. Her companion pushed the sleeping bag aside. She realized it had been his stirring that had awakened her.

"The ground makes for a hard mattress," he said. "Even with pine straw under the tent."

"I noticed." She peered at the faint light in the clearing through the mosquito net. "What time is it?"

"Time to get going. Around five," he added when she frowned at him. "I want to get to town before noon."

"Why?"

"So I can get back before dark."

It came to her that he would rather walk across burning coals than have to deal with her. So much for femme fatale. "You wouldn't be going to town if it weren't for me."

"True."

"So, take me back to the trail."

"No."

The flat refusal told her he would do his duty as he saw it no matter what she wanted. She was silent while he put on his shoes, then left the tent. Combing her fingers through her hair, she watched him let down the bear bag and start water to boiling.

"Coffee?" he called.

"Please."

"You take anything in it?"

"Nothing, thanks." She cautiously pushed the covers down, hating to leave the coziness of the sleeping bag for the great outdoors, which was decidedly cold.

"Stay put. I'll bring it to you."

To her amazement, he did just that. While she sipped the wonderfully warm brew, he fried bacon, prepared scrambled eggs and toasted bread slices on a fork. Again he told her to sit still and served her in the tent.

"I thought campers weren't supposed to have food in their sleeping quarters."

"That's right. I'm making an exception for you."

"Why?"

"It's about thirty-six degrees this morning," he told her. "I don't want you taking a chill before I get you off the mountain. My camp doesn't extend to nursing facilities."

Grim Reality 101. He was truthful if nothing else.

Watching him while she ate, she decided he might act contrary, he might not want to deal with her, but he was really very nurturing, even though he didn't like her for some reason. She refused to let herself be hurt by this insight.

After eating, she set her plate outside, donned her hiking boots, then joined him in the clearing, the warm parka fastened up to her neck. She handed her plate and fork over when he held out a soapy hand. In a few minutes, he had the bags stored in the air again.

"Ready?"

She nodded, touching her hair self-consciously when she saw his glance on it. Her comb was in her purse, which was in the trunk of her car. She'd only carried her wallet and cell phone with her.

He turned abruptly and headed down the mountain

via a different route from the one she'd hiked yesterday. She followed silently, aware of the wall of dislike he'd erected between them.

In much less time than it had taken her to go up the mountain yesterday, they arrived at the creek ford. He went at once to her car as if he'd parked it himself.

"How did you know my car was here?"

He waited while she dug her keys out of her jeans pocket. "I saw the sunlight glinting off the bumper."

Once she was inside, he leaned down to her window. "I'll follow you into town."

"On foot?"

"In my truck."

To her astonishment, he disappeared behind some brush, tossed a bush aside, then backed a pickup into the clearing. She hadn't seen his vehicle at all.

At his gesture, she started her midsize luxury sedan, a graduation present from her parents six years ago. Where had the time gone? Where had her dreams gone?

She headed down the bumpy road to the county highway. An hour later, they passed the small lake formed by a dam and arrived in Lost Valley, a bustling community that served the ranchers and tourists who drove through the valley on their way to Yellowstone or Hells Canyon in the summer.

In the winter, she imagined the place must go into hibernation. The snow would be deep at five thousand feet and last all season. She shivered, imagining it.

Parking at the Lost Valley B&B, she mused on what it would be like, being snowed in for days. Her gaze was drawn to Travis as they stood on the gravel parking apron in front of the old Victorian house.

"Stay out of the woods," he advised without preamble. "I'll look for your sister. Are you going home?"

"I'll stay. I have to talk to Janis." She retrieved her purse from the trunk of the car.

He nodded. His thick black hair blew across his forehead in attractive disarray. For some reason, she thought of the crisp, woodsy scent that had surrounded her like a warm cocoon during the night. She realized it had come from him.

"I'll bring her to town." He gazed down the street. "I'll have to tell the sheriff that you two are in the area. Don't worry. He can keep a secret."

At his sardonic tone, her whole endeavor suddenly seemed foolish. Stiffly, she thanked him for his help. When he returned to his truck, she called, "Mr. Dalton...Travis. Don't tell Janis why I'm here. Please."

He nodded, then climbed into the pickup and left.

Alison went inside. Amelia Miller, the amiable owner of the place, greeted her. "Are you okay? I was worried when I didn't see you come in last night. Not that I keep tabs on my guests, but..." Her voice trailed off. "Well, anyway, I'm glad you made it back."

"I'm fine. I was hiking and it got late."

Amelia nodded. "So you spent the night at the Dalton place," she concluded. "I saw Travis outside with you. I didn't realize you had friends here."

Alison debated about telling the truth. She hated to lie, but neither did she feel like explaining. "More like acquaintances," she said.

Amelia's gray eyes took on a speculative aspect. "All the girls in town have been in love with one of the Daltons at some point in their lives. Some people say Seven Devils Mountains were named after the Dalton bunch, but there're only five boys. And one girl."

"Plus Uncle Nick," Alison added, recalling the name.

"Yes, that does make seven, doesn't it? I understand the uncle and his two brothers—they were also twins—were hellions in their younger days, too."

"Too?" Alison asked. She defended her interest in the Daltons as natural after her encounter.

"Travis and his twin, Trevor, were pretty wild in school, not mean or dangerous, but fun and totally fearless. All the Daltons are known for their courage." She mentioned others in the family, including a doctor, lawyer and deputy sheriff. "The youngest cousin is the girl," Amelia finished.

Alison's mind reeled. Twins. Brothers. Cousins. So many Daltons. If they were anything like Travis, meeting them would be daunting.

She rushed up the broad, curving staircase before

Amelia could ask her anything about the Dalton family and she had to confess she knew nothing of them.

In her room she locked the door, then took a shower and changed to fresh slacks and a knit top. She hesitated, then picked up the phone and dialed her mother's personal number. The older woman answered right away.

"Mother, it's Alison."

"Oh, good. Do you have any news of Janis?"

For the briefest instant, Alison wondered why her mother couldn't have asked after her health first. However, no one knew of her strange night, so it was unfair to expect concern where there was no cause.

"Not yet. I'm still looking. The ranch she told me about is in a remote location. The road is washed out, so I'll have to hike in."

"How long do you think it will take?"

Alison heard the anxiety in her mother's voice. "I'm not sure. A couple of days, I should think. I'll hurry, but the mountain trail is steep and rough."

"Thank you, darling. I know you'll find Janis and convince her to come home at once."

Alison wished she felt as certain. "How's Father?"

"Oh, you know him. Stubborn as ever." Her mother lowered her voice. "He refuses to even consider surgery at present."

Until the beloved but prodigal daughter was back in the fold, Alison interpreted. "I'll do the best I can."

"Of course," her mother said.

After they hung up, Alison sat in the white wicker chair and contemplated her life. A smile tugged at her lips as she thought about Travis Dalton and his wild relatives. It would have been fun to grow up with them, to have known them when she was young.

Twenty-eight wasn't *that* old. However, at times she did feel ancient. Seven years older than her sibling, it seemed she'd always had to baby-sit while her parents went to political and social functions. She'd felt responsible for Janis and her behavior.

She wondered why.

It was such an odd thought she forgot to dry her hair as she sat and tried to figure out why the last two days seemed so momentous, as if she'd gone through one of those life-changing epiphanies she'd read about.

Funny.

"Hey, bro," Trevor yelled across the street.

Travis swung around to face his twin. He cursed. Trevor could be a pain. He waited for the other to cross the busy street and catch up with him.

"Where you headed?" Trevor wanted to know, falling into step with him.

"The café."

"Great. You can treat your favorite brother to lunch just to show everyone what a good guy you are," Trevor said.

"They already know I'm a good guy. It's you who are questionable."

"Yeah, but what about that blonde I saw you talking to over at the B&B?" Trevor poked him in the ribs with an elbow.

"Business," was his terse reply.

"Right," Trevor declared, his blue eyes alight with mischief. "I like that kind of business. So she helped out while you were digging for gold up in the woods?"

Travis gave his twin a warning glance. He was in no mood for nonsense this morning. "How the hell do you know about that?"

"I saw you on the highway and followed when I realized you were following another car. Who is she?"

Travis entered the café, his brother hot on his heels. He chose a table where he could see the street in the direction of the B&B where he'd left Alison two hours ago. He needed to eat, pick up supplies and head back to the hills. After a restless night, he wanted the solitude.

"How's Uncle Nick?" he asked after they'd ordered.

"Mean as a snake and twice as ugly," Trevor said. "You better plan on being home for his birthday or the old boy will come after you with his six-shooter."

"I'll be there."

Their uncle had taken in the whole brood of Daltons after the deaths of his two brothers twenty-two years ago. That the cousins would do anything in the world for him was a given.

"Bring the blonde," Trevor suggested. "What did you say her name was?"

"I didn't."

The twins flashed identical smiles, one guarded, the other devilish.

"I'll find out," Trevor promised.

"Leave her alone," Travis said in a serious tone. "She's looking for someone."

Trevor was immediately intrigued. "Who?"

"Her sister, she says." He shrugged to indicate he didn't know if that was true or not.

"You mean there's another like her?" His twin waggled his eyebrows. "Hey, this is sounding more interesting. Where did you meet her?"

"In the woods."

That piqued his twin's curiosity, but Travis wouldn't tell him another thing. After making Trev chip in his share of the meal, he left his sibling devising various ways to meet the stranger and her sister. Travis wondered if he should warn Alison about his devil-may-care bro, then decided she could watch out for herself.

Another complication had arisen. The sheriff had suggested using her as bait to infiltrate the group, either squatters or paramilitarists, up in the hills, assuming her sister was mixed up with them. After he'd explained the probable connection to the senator, both had agreed it was wiser to get the two women out of the area ASAP.

Sunlight glinted off mica in the sidewalk outside the window, little sparkles of brilliance that reminded him of the woman he'd found in the woods.

A sensation like the heat lightning that had zigzagged across the night sky ran over him. Alison Harvey had opened a door inside him that he wanted to stay closed.

Grimly he reviewed the unexpected passion. He didn't want hunger or need. He didn't want involvement of any kind. He simply wanted to be left alone.

Was that too much to ask?

He would bring her sister to town so the two of them could leave. Then he'd head back to the mine and the solitude he craved. End of episode.

Chapter 3

Alison handed over her credit card. The clerk didn't notice the name or make any connection to her family. She signed the credit slip and eyed her purchases.

"I'll make two trips," she said.

The teenager behind the counter gave her a cheery smile. "I'll help."

Living in a small town had its advantages. No one in the city would have considered leaving the store to help a person carry her shopping bags to the car. Of course, the environment was different there, not so trusting.

The young man hoisted the backpack onto one shoulder, then grabbed two bags. She picked up the last one and directed him to her vehicle. They stored the items in the back seat. Before she could decide whether to tip him or not, he gave her a friendly salute and headed back into the sporting-goods store.

She tossed her purse into the car, intending to head to the B&B, sort through her purchases and pack for the trip. Just then, she spotted a familiar figure coming toward her.

With his masculine physique, dark hair and startling blue eyes, wearing a cowboy hat pushed back on his forehead, tight jeans and a chambray shirt, he looked the archetypal cowboy, at home in this rugged country.

Her heart clenched into a knot that swelled until it crowded her lungs to the point where she couldn't breathe. There was something about Travis Dalton that unraveled her usual composure.

She waited warily, then was surprised at his smile—a real smile, relaxed and pleasant and cheery. She glanced away, feeling unsure and sort of achy inside. This wasn't good, not at all. She met his eyes when he stopped.

"Hi, there," he said. "I'm not Travis."

She sorted through the greeting and came to a logical conclusion. "Then you must be the twin."

"Right. I'm Trevor, the handsome, friendly one. Travis is the ugly, mean twin. I'm also older by twenty minutes…in case you like older men." He tipped his hat to her.

Her heart eased. "I'm glad to meet you."

"I saw you at Amelia's place with Travis this morning."

"I'm staying there." She noted the speculation in his eyes. Did he know she'd spent the night in the mountains with his twin?

He eyed the sporting-goods store, her purchases so clearly visible in the car, then her. "You going on a backpacking trip?"

"No," she said quickly.

He looked skeptical.

"Not exactly," she amended. She considered, then, figuring he'd learn the facts from his twin, decided to take him into her confidence. "Actually, I'm looking for someone. My sister is visiting a ranch north of here, near He-Devil Mountain. The Towbridge place. Perhaps you could direct me on getting there?"

"You don't want to go up there," Trevor said, his expression becoming dead serious. "It could be dangerous, especially for a lone hiker."

"Travis warned me of the paramilitary gang and the squatters. I intend to avoid them. Is there a road to the ranch house, perhaps from the northern approach?"

Trevor shook his head. "Only one way in and that's by an old gravel road. It may not be passable."

"It isn't. The ford has boulders washed across it. A car can't make it." She sighed and gave him her best big-eyed, helpless look, something she despised when other women used it. Desperate times called for desperate measures. She had come up with an idea. "Is there a guide I could hire? With horses, it should be an easy trip."

She hoped he would volunteer.

"Not around here. You'll have to go to Council. That's the county seat. But I doubt the fishing guides know the mountains well enough to get you in and out safely. Travis is your best bet. He's prospected all over the hills, looking for gold. Too bad he won't take you," Trevor told her, certainty in his voice.

Curiosity got the better of her. "Why won't he?"

After the briefest hesitation, the brother said, "It's not his thing. He's sort of a loner."

This information wasn't news. Travis had made it clear he was an unwilling rescuer. "Well, thanks for your help."

"Travis isn't going to like it when he hears you're heading out by yourself," Trevor said.

"How will he know?" she challenged.

"Well, I'll have to tell him." His eyes flashed with wicked delight.

"This is really none of your business. Nor your brother's. I have business at the ranch, urgent family business, and no one can stop me from crossing public land to get there."

Trevor snorted at her declaration. "You a lawyer?"

"No."

"Why don't you come out to the ranch and talk to

Trav before you take off?'' the twin invited. "Uncle Nick would like to meet you."

Alison was wary of the sudden change in subject. "Why would Uncle Nick want to meet me?"

"Well, you spent the night on the mountain with his nephew, for one thing."

"How did you know about that?" she demanded, furious that Travis would tell his family about her foolish trip.

The twin chuckled. Alison realized he'd been fishing for information. And had gotten it.

"I saw him follow you to Amelia's place this morning," he explained smoothly.

"So you decided to hang around and accost me?" she asked with an acid sting in her tone, angry that she'd been tricked into confirming his suspicions. She was better at handling people than that. Usually.

"Sorry. I didn't mean to upset you," Trevor said in a consoling manner.

"I'm not upset." She spoke through gritted teeth.

Her eyes met pure blue ones. His grin was so good-natured and understanding, she couldn't help the smile that sprang to her lips at the blatant lie.

"Come out to the ranch and talk to Travis. He's staying there until tomorrow," Trevor urged. "You can have supper with us. Uncle Nick is a great cook."

Alison shook her head. She wanted nothing more to do with Travis Dalton. He stirred something inside her that she didn't like. Or maybe she liked it too much.

Anyway, he confused her, and she had no time for personal qualms. She had a job to do.

Travis stepped off the porch of the double-winged ranch house that had originally been a log cabin. Trevor had returned with the pickup piled high with bags of feed for the horses. Restless, he went to help unload.

Hefting a fifty-pound bag, Trevor grinned at him as if he had a secret.

"What?" Travis demanded, grabbing another bag.

"I met your girlfriend," his twin said as they entered the storage shed. "The one you spent the night with up on the mountain." He heaved the bag onto the shelf.

Travis didn't fall for the attempt to weasel information out of him. He tossed his bag on top of the other with a grunt. "Yeah? Did she tell you all about it?"

"Uh-huh. She said she was looking for her long-lost sister and ran into you. What I want to know is— did she sleep in your tent alone, or were you there with her?"

For a split second, Travis was dumbfounded... which was just long enough for his brother to know he'd hit upon the truth. Trevor broke into guffaws.

"Okay, so you know the whole story," Travis admitted, feeling defensive. "Keep it quiet, will you?"

"Uncle Nick would find it very interesting that the elusive Travis Dalton holed up in the hills with a woman. A real pretty one," Trevor added. "By the way, she's heading into the hills again."

Travis was sure he'd misunderstood. "What?"

The mischievous light faded from Trevor's eyes, and he became serious. "It's true. She bought a backpack and camping gear at the sporting goods store. The owner's son was working the counter. He says she prepared for a long hiking trip with a supply of freeze-dried food packets, plus lots of jerky and chocolate and coffee."

"That little fool. Somebody needs to pound some sense into her head." It wouldn't be him. He'd warned her about the dangers of the mountains. If she got into trouble this time, it was on her head, not his.

"You probably ought to talk to her," Trevor suggested.

"I told her to stay put at Amelia's."

"Well, I don't think she listened. She's definitely heading out, probably at first light."

Travis shrugged and tried not to recall a shimmering spotlight of gold. Or the fragile tremble of soft lips. Or smoky-green eyes filled with despair. "Not my problem."

"She mentioned hiring a guide. Maybe you should take her to her sister if you know where she is."

"The Towbridge ranch." He'd known, watching her through the binoculars, that he should have stuck with his business and left her to hers. He'd known she was going to be trouble with a capital *T*. This merely confirmed it. "Why don't you take her there, since you're so damn concerned?"

Trevor shot him a hard glance. "You're the one who found her. I figure she's your responsibility."

"I don't." A ripple of emotion flowed over the smooth surface of the abyss, stirring the depths he didn't want disturbed. His responsibility? Huh. Let some other fool jump in and be the hero. He wouldn't.

"Man, you have changed," his twin said slowly. "I thought you were okay now, but I guess when you lost your wife, you lost touch with the human race."

"Shut up," he said, no emotion, no heat, just a deadly warning in the two words.

Trevor stuck his chin out. "Make me."

For half a second, Travis considered doing it. Giving vent to the anger inside would be a relief. Temporarily. He went to the truck and hoisted another fifty-pounder, Trevor following, his gaze mocking.

"It isn't worth the effort," he said.

Trevor lifted the feed sack to his shoulder. "What is?" he asked softly. "What's worth anything to you these days, little brother?"

The black surface roiled, filling him with hot bitterness that wanted to erupt. He forced it at bay. "Not a thing," he said just as softly. "Not a damn thing."

Silence followed at their heels as they completed their work, then Trevor stalked off without a backward glance.

Travis stood at the paddock and patted an inquisitive mare's neck. Sunlight cast red highlights into the light-brown hide. The mare murmured low in her throat and nudged his hand when he stopped.

He thought of the woman who had snuggled against him, seeking warmth, of soft hair laced with gold, warm under his hand, of courage, foolish as it was, that had kept her going when she trembled with weariness.

Even while he fought with his conscience, he knew he was on the losing end of the rope. A sense of self-preservation urged him to simply call and warn her off, but he went to his pickup and grimly cranked the engine.

His twin was wrong. He hadn't lost all sense of human kindness, but life would be easier if he did.

Alison's car was gone when he pulled up in front of the B&B. Frowning, he went inside. Amelia was on the phone. He waited while she wrote down a reservation, then hung up.

"Travis, hello. What can I do for you?" she asked, obviously curious.

"Uh, I need to see one of your guests."

"Miss Harvey is gone."

"What do you mean—gone?"

"She left this afternoon. She'll be back day after

tomorrow. That'll be Saturday. Today is Thursday.''
Amelia offered the reminder when he didn't say anything.

''I *know* what day it is,'' he said. Yeah, trouble
with a capital *T*. He'd known it from the first glance.
''What time did she leave?''

''Midafternoon. Around two. She's visiting relatives in the area. That's what she said,'' Amelia added
defensively.

Travis calculated the time element. Alison had
nearly a three-hour jump on him. It would have taken
her at least an hour to get to the creek. From there,
she would have to hike. She'd planned for a two-night
trip, so maybe she'd stay in her car tonight and take
off at first light, figuring an overnight stay when she
found her sister, then hiking out Saturday and returning to the B&B.

Satisfied that he understood the plan, he thanked
Amelia and left. He'd head Alison off at the ford.

Alison let the backpack slip to the ground. She
hadn't done this kind of thing since the last time she'd
gone to camp fifteen years ago. Whew, she obviously
wasn't in the same shape now as she'd been as a
teenager.

She sat on a log and wiped her face before taking
a drink of water. Nibbling on trail mix, she rested for
ten minutes. While some part of her urged that she

hurry, she knew a break every hour or so was a more efficient way of traveling in the mountains.

Leaning against the stump of a tree, she let the quiet run through her like a life-giving stream. Her days were always filled with duties, appointments and crises, it seemed. She never had time to simply relax—

"Where the hell do you think you're going?" a coldly furious male voice interrupted her musings.

Alison jerked around in shock. "You!"

"Yeah. Me. If I'd been a grizz, you would already be dinner."

She tried to quell his temper with sarcasm. "That's rather dramatic, don't you think?"

"I've been thinking a lot the last three and a half hours, mostly about what I'd like to do when I caught up with you. The possibilities were endless."

"I'm glad you were entertained," she said just as coolly. "You needn't have followed. I'm not a teenager out past curfew, in case you haven't noticed."

His gaze ran over her so hotly she was surprised she didn't melt on the spot. "Pick up your gear," he ordered. "We're heading back."

She decided humor was the better part of valor. "Sorry, I can't. I have a job to complete. Neither hail, nor snow, nor dark of night, also irate ranchers, prospectors and volunteer deputies, shall stop me from doing it."

"Very funny. You may be interfering with an on-going investigation. I can arrest you for that."

"I'm not, and you can't." She pushed her fingers through her hair in frustration and tilted her head to frown at him. "You bring out the worst in me."

His harsh expression didn't alter. They were silent for a long minute, locked in an impasse. Regret and longing mingled. Sensing the unexplained hostility in him, she watched his eyes for a clue to his next action.

"I told you I'd bring your sister to you," he finally said. "I generally keep my word."

"I don't think she'll come with a stranger." She observed the deepening of the frown line over the bridge of his nose. His eyes were hard and opaque, as if his thoughts had disappeared behind granite.

"Then I'll just have to tie her up and force her off the mountain." He glanced around. "Were you planning on pitching camp or walking all night?"

"I thought I'd follow the stream up to your camp, stay there for the night and start out early in the morning. I brought an alarm clock so I can get up at the crack of dawn." She gave him a bright smile.

"Okay," he said, giving in so easily she was startled and more wary of him than ever. "Let's go."

"Is this some kind of trick?" she asked. "Because if it is, let me remind you that my father wields some power in this state—oh!" She realized she'd given herself away.

"Watch it, the politician's daughter is showing through your meek facade."

So he'd already figured it out. She shrugged. "You'd be surprised at the number of people who fall for that line."

He didn't crack a smile. "Yeah, right. Let's head for camp. It'll be dark within an hour."

This time he put her in front and kept an eye on her the whole way as they followed the stream upward, ever upward, into the Seven Devils Mountains.

"Whoa," he said just as she was beginning to wonder if they were lost.

She looked around and realized she'd nearly walked past the place. If she'd done that while on her own...well, someone would surely have found her before she starved to death wandering around in circles.

"Where shall I pitch my tent?" she asked.

"Wherever you decide," he said in a snarl.

While he let the bear bags slip to the ground, she searched out the best place for her tent. Naturally he'd chosen the perfect spot, a level section with a layer of pine needles for extra padding.

A site near the creek looked inviting. Except she might not hear a bear if it approached her tent during the night due to the burbling of the stream. She explored another on the opposite side of the clearing, but there was a boulder in the middle of it. After a couple of attempts to dislodge it, she gave up.

On the other side of his tent was a nice location.

It was rock-free, littered with pine straw...and close to him in case she needed his help during the night.

Several scenarios played out in her mind in quick order, all of them ending with her in *his* tent again.

Cheeks flushed, she extended her search among the adjacent trees. All day, visions of the previous night had run like a continuous film through her head. Travis had been the most thoughtful of hosts, a true gentleman in all ways.

Her heart catapulted around like a jumping bean.

Startled, she pressed a hand to her chest. Of all the men she had ever met, none had given her that sense of...of peace and security she'd experienced with him.

"You having a heart attack or something?" he asked in his usual caustic manner.

"No. I was just trying to decide where to put the tent." She gave him a mock frown. "You have the best place."

He gave an impatient snort. "Put your tent on that level spot right behind mine."

Her heart jumped and beat in her throat. She nodded and took her bundle to the site. Opening the compact bag, she removed the set of hollow plastic sticks with the stretchable cord running through them and put them together the way the teenager had shown her so that they formed one long pole.

There were three of these devices, two going one way and one running opposite, thus forming the supports of the tent. She removed the tent and tried to figure out which flap to run the first support through. She learned that one demonstration did not constitute expertise.

"Lay the tent out flat and square it up," Travis advised. "Then you'll see the shape of it and the guides for the supports." He picked up a pine branch from the ground and returned to his tasks.

Following his directions, she found it was easy to see how the tent worked once it was neatly laid out. She quickly ran the supports through the guides, then inserted each end through a loop. The tent popped upright into a dome shape. She grinned as if she'd won a blue ribbon.

She remembered to stake each side so the wind wouldn't blow the tent, her in it, down the mountain. Finished, she grabbed the wool sweater and jacket from her pack, then returned to the clearing. Supper bubbled in a pot over the tiny gas stove and a fire crackled in a shallow pit.

"Oh, wonderful," she murmured, sitting on a log that Travis had pulled into position in front of the fire and putting on the outerwear. "Aren't you afraid someone will see the fire and come investigate?"

"No."

She studied his lean face in the leaping shadows created by the fire. "You're angry," she concluded.

"Damn right."

"Why?"

He paused in stirring the pot and directed a cutting stare her way. His eyes were dark in the firelight.

Mysterious. Dangerous. Exciting.

Something ancient and primitive stirred within her. A part of her seemed to have awakened from a deep sleep.

Right. Sleeping Beauty and all that.

"What have I done to earn your animosity?" she asked, determined to get to the root of his problem.

"This isn't a safe place for anyone, man or woman, to be running around alone. A greenhorn like you shouldn't be allowed out without a nanny."

At his scorn, her spirits dropped several notches. "I have to see my sister."

She spoke quietly, convincingly. Travis had to give her an A for determination. "I said I would bring her to you."

Her eyes were fathoms deep, glowing with rich lights from the reflection of the fire. He had a sudden vision of simply picking her up and taking her to his tent, there to have his way with her the whole night through.

His heart did some strange, painful things. Okay, so there was a sexual attraction. He stared at her hair, the way the firelight shot sparks into it. He forced himself to look away.

"I know. I appreciate that, really I do," she insisted when he glanced at her again. "But I gave my word."

He sensed the struggle inside her as she tried to explain, but he understood perfectly. Like honor and duty, a person's word was sacred. He'd once given his word to cherish and protect, but he'd failed.

With a silent curse, he spurned the memory. The past was gone, and nothing he could ever do would change it.

"Supper," he said more gruffly than he meant.

He held out a plate and fork, ignoring the air of vulnerability that surrounded her slender form as she sat perfectly still for an instant.

Then, "I have my own things," she told him.

She dashed to her backpack and returned with a fork. Smiling brilliantly—as if she'd thought of everything—she took the plate and sat on the log, moving over so he, too, could use it. Not once did she look at him.

Fine. Let her keep her distance. He intended to. But first, he had to get past an odd knot that had formed right under his breastbone as she smiled and ate and murmured over how good the food was.

So her eyes looked sad and uncertain as she hunched over the plate, the delicate line of her head and neck and spine in one gentle curve of hidden anxiety. So what?

He chose to sit on the ground and use the log for a backrest. He stretched his legs out along one side of the fire. In a minute she did the same.

After eating and cleaning their dishes, he made

them each a cup of spiced cider from a mix. Slowly a sense of contentment stole over him. It felt so odd he couldn't identify the condition at first.

"It's so peaceful here," she murmured, picking up the thought. "I had no idea. I now understand why people like to get away by going to the wilderness. Life can be such a treadmill at times…"

Her voice trailed into silence. The refined planes of her face took on a pensive mood as she gazed into the fire. When she met his eyes, she seemed troubled, but again she smiled. He was beginning to dislike that fake cheer.

Not that it was his business. Whatever her problems, she would have to work them out, he reminded himself savagely. At the moment, he didn't have a care in the world. He wanted to keep it that way.

He yawned as the fire burnt down to embers. "I'm heading for bed," he told her.

"Me, too."

He secured the campsite, stirring the embers and drowning them completely. After making sure the supply bags were suspended, he recalled her backpack.

"Did you bring any rope?" he asked.

"Yes."

"Get it and we'll hang your pack up in case the local wildlife decides to poach. The ground squirrels have been known to chew a hole right through the material."

He showed her how to tie a rock on the end of the rope, toss it over a high branch, then tie her pack to the line and haul it up into the air.

Her hands on the rope brushed his as they worked together. He was aware of her body and its slender agility, of her determination to show him she could do a good job, of something in her that was soft, as soft as the pale pink lips that trembled ever so slightly at the corners when she didn't keep her guard up.

Hell. He didn't want the awareness. Moving away, he tied the rope around a handy tree trunk.

When she told him good-night and disappeared inside her dome tent, he experienced a return of the more primitive urges that had plagued him since spying her through the binoculars yesterday.

Maybe he was low on the milk of human kindness, but he was lush with other human traits, like the need to crush those soft lips under his.

Not that he would. The abyss churned painfully. His twin was dead wrong, he decided. This woman was not his responsibility. He'd never take another's love or happiness in his hands again or depend on someone else for his. He'd learned that lesson early on.

Shortly before his seventh birthday, his parents, plus his father's twin and another woman, had died in a freak storm while visiting the family homestead. Uncle Nick, the oldest of the three original Dalton brothers, and Aunt Milly had been saddled with six kids to raise in addition to their own daughter. Less than two years later, that daughter disappeared from the site of a tragic accident that had claimed her mother's life and hadn't been seen since.

A fierceness ripped through Travis. Uncle Nick had sacrificed to provide a home for the orphaned youngsters. He'd never expressed a single regret for taking them in. How had he stood it after losing his own wife and child?

The sound of a zipper being closed reminded him that morning would arrive all too soon. Then he'd have to do something about his stubborn guest. He checked the perimeter of the camp, then went to his tent.

Yeah, trouble, he thought when he was inside. Written in all caps.

Don't!

Alison woke to the sound of her own panicky voice. She felt as if she was being smothered. She pushed against the material that covered her face. Sobbing, she tried to fight clear, but she was hopelessly bound in something. Finally she managed to sit up. The sleeping bag fell to her waist.

A shadow, large and menacing, brushed by the tent. A bear! She yelled to make it go away.

"Hey, hey, take it easy," a masculine voice spoke from the darkness.

The zipper slid open and strong arms enclosed her in warmth and safety.

"I thought there was a bear," she murmured, trying to still her pounding heart. She was embarrassed as reality rushed in. "I was dreaming."

"You scared the pants off me when you yelled."

Alison rested against him, needing his strength for a moment. "The sleeping bag was over my face. It became part of my dream. There was danger all around, and I was alone."

"It's okay," he said. "You're safe."

Inhaling deeply, she caught the scent of him and lemon-fresh clothing, then more subtly, the faint aroma of aftershave lotion and talc, and fainter still, the masculine essence of him and his warmth.

Against her ear, she heard the steady pound of his heart as he held her close. She felt the strength of his enclosing embrace. Under her palm, she caressed the smoothness of bare flesh. She explored further and discovered wiry hairs in a rough diamond across his chest.

"Aren't you cold?" she asked in a near whisper.

"No."

Slowly, as if still in a dream, she tilted her head against his arm.

His face was a lighter shadow against the deeper one of the tent. The sudden tension between them made the air grow thicker and more difficult to breathe.

"Travis," she said, the name falling experimentally from her lips, as if it was an exotic word, foreign to her.

She heard him exhale, a slight hissing sound between his teeth, and felt the quick rise of his chest against hers as he inhaled. The movement of his head gave warning a second before his lips met hers.

Sound rose to her throat—a protest, a demand, she wasn't sure which—and she clung to him as if he was her anchor to sanity as a matrix of wildness stirred to life deep inside. It was like being caught in a whirlwind.

Sensation poured over her. The firmness of his lips against hers. The hard pound of his heart, echoing the beat of her own. The intimate mingling as his tongue sought hers and she opened to him, seeking the honey of his mouth as he did hers.

Softness washed over her, making her boneless and pliable. They slid downward until the sleeping bag puffed gently around her. His arm cradled her head, and his long frame partially covered her body.

The kiss deepened, becoming almost unbearable as pleasure rushed through her, wave upon wave of it, lifting her to heights she'd only read about. She felt his hand at her side, then the soft rasp of the zipper. He pulled the sleeping bag from between them. She found he was wearing thermal knit underwear that covered his lower body like skin, smooth and luxuriant to the touch.

His hand skimmed down her side and paused at her waist. With a gentle squeezing motion, he kneaded desire into her until flames seemed to spiral from his fingers right to her innermost being.

She kissed him just as fiercely, letting her hands roam his back and explore the solid muscles there. She trailed her fingers along his lean hips.

With a gasp, he moved against her, making her as aware of his passion as she was of her own. To her shock, she found she wanted to explore this tumult of sensation to the final reaches of desire.

When she writhed against him, he slid his hand upward until he cupped her breast. She felt the beading of her nipple as an intense pleasure. He murmured against her skin as he trailed kisses along her neck.

"What?" she asked. "What did you say?" She found she wanted words, sweet words, magic words, promises…

Lifting his head, he stared down at her. "What are we doing? Just what the hell are we doing?" he said in a voice filled with self-loathing.

The magic vanished. Sanity returned with a jolt Alison felt all the way to her soul. She scrambled away. He said a distinct curse, backed from the tent and zipped her inside once more.

"I'm sorry," she heard him say from outside, his tone rough with anger and regret.

"Don't be," she said, chilled to the bone. "It was only…only a kiss."

Chapter 4

Alison woke to luxurious warmth. The sun was shining on the tent, making it toasty warm. Dressing hastily, she crawled from the nylon dome and found Travis sitting beside the fire, a coffee cup cradled in his big hands. Gentle hands, she recalled.

A flush spread throughout her body. Last night, after regaining his sanity and apologizing for the kiss, he'd rekindled the fire, his movements restless and angry.

She wondered if he'd sat up all night, tortured by the brief passion they'd shared. Why did he resent it so?

"Good morning," she murmured when she took a seat close to the crackling fire. "The sun feels good, doesn't it?"

He nodded. "Breakfast is in the skillet."

She helped herself to bacon and eggs and a sourdough roll. Using her own fork, she ate, then cleaned the dishes.

"I'll take you back to town," he told her.

"I need my car."

He scowled impatiently. "I'll take you to your car, then escort you back to town."

"I'll go without an escort. How long do you think it will take you to find Janis?"

"That might be according to whether she wants to be found. A couple of days at most," he added when she started to protest the flippant reply.

"It's Friday, so I should hear from you on Sunday?"

He finished off his coffee, then stood. "You are the most persistent female I've ever met."

It wasn't a compliment.

She drained her cup, then rinsed and stored it in her backpack, now leaning against a tree. She packed the tent, which took as much effort as setting the thing up. Every item had to be folded and rolled to its minimum size in order to fit back in the nylon bag. It took two tries to achieve this feat.

Travis replaced the circle of soil and thin grass over the fire hole after drowning the embers. Alison realized that the casual observer wouldn't even notice the spot.

"Ready?" he asked.

With a sense of déjà vu, she nodded and fell into step behind him on the faint trail that led downward. For a second, her gaze lingered on the little campsite as if to memorize the setting.

Nostalgia settled over her, and she experienced an intense longing for something undefined but very, very real.

Sighing, she admitted she didn't understand herself anymore.

Once more at the B&B, Alison promised Travis that she would stay put this time. "Until Sunday," she pledged. "If you…if Janis isn't here by then, I'm leaving."

"For home?" he asked hopefully.

"No, to find her."

"That's what I figured. Stay off the mountain, or I'll report you to the sheriff," he warned in a harsher tone than any he'd used previously with her.

"I don't respond to threats," she felt compelled to inform him, hearing the haughtiness in her tone.

"You're on my turf here. You'll do well to remember that."

Alison realized they were on the verge of a quarrel. From the front desk, she saw Amelia flick an inquiring, speculative glance their way, a smile at the corners of her mouth. The B&B owner probably thought they were having a lovers' spat.

Memories of last night's kisses flooded Alison

without notice. Her eyes were irresistibly drawn to his lips, now compressed into a thin line of disapproval. Last night they had been mobile and sensuous, enticing her to follow his lead into passionate play.

Hunger swept through her, flooding her with needs stronger than she'd ever known. This fierce mountain man had opened up a void inside her, one she hadn't been fully aware of until two days ago. It was very disturbing.

"Well?" he demanded.

"I'm sorry. What did you say?"

He looked as if he could grind glass with his teeth. "I want your word that you'll do as I request."

For once.

The words were almost audible although he refrained from saying them. She couldn't help it; she smiled.

"What?" he demanded.

"It's just that we're so intense with each other. I mean…"

"I know what you mean."

His reply was spoken grudgingly. His eyes, locked on hers, admitted there was something different between them, something neither had encountered before. They blazed with blue fire, igniting the ready embers in her.

Her breath fluttered to her throat and seemed to die. She couldn't breathe, couldn't look away…

"What is this?" he demanded in a low tone only she could hear. "What the hell *is* this?"

She had no answer.

Without another word, he strode out, the door closing decisively behind him.

Amelia smiled and nodded to Alison as she passed the desk on the way to her room. The landlady wisely didn't comment on anything she'd seen or heard between the couple.

Suppressing a sneeze, Alison dropped her backpack inside the door and headed for the shower. She had a headache, and she needed to think. She did her best thinking under a stream of cleansing water.

On Monday, Travis photographed two beef carcasses for evidence, then left them to the buzzards. The birds pranced, wings spread, several feet away, impatient for him to be gone. Returning to the pickup, he tossed the camera into the glove box and headed for town.

He was tired, irritated and felt worse than death warmed over, as Uncle Nick would say. He sneezed four times in succession. A cold. Just what he needed.

After reporting the slaughter to the sheriff's office, he stopped by the B&B and discovered Alison had gone to lunch. Ignoring the amused gleam in Amelia's eyes, he asked her to have Alison call him at the ranch when she returned.

Outside, he decided to walk down to the local

diner. Since there were only five places in town to eat, he could surely find her at one of them. Unless she'd gone shopping.

He suddenly recalled his mother had loved to shop, not to buy anything, but to look at the possibilities.

"When we get our mansion, we'll have one of those," she would say, pointing to a hot tub that cost five thousand dollars.

"Two," his dad would chime in. "One for the kids and one for us."

"I want one big enough to swim in," Travis had once told them.

"Well, of course, a heated pool, the very thing," his mom had agreed.

His parents had been dreamers, but they'd had so much fun as a family. A lump clogged his throat. What the devil had brought those old memories on?

"Hey, Travis," a rancher called out when he entered the small café that had served the town for over fifty years.

"Elmer," he acknowledged, stopping by the table where two longtime ranchers sat. "Hello, George," he said to the second man. The men were as grayheaded as Uncle Nick and as cantankerous.

"Any news on that riffraff hiding out in the woods?" Elmer wanted to know.

"Not a trace. They seem to be keeping to their end of the county."

"I found one of my bulls shot through the head

two days ago," the rancher said. "Whoever did it took the haunches and left the rest. I filed a report over at the sheriff's office."

Travis spotted Alison at a table by a window. "Uh, good. I have a report, too. Two of your neighbor's cows were slaughtered up near She-Devil Mountain."

The ranchers cursed. George told him, "Those guys come on my land, they're going to regret it. I'm keeping a loaded shotgun close to hand."

Travis was sympathetic. "I know how you feel, but don't take the law into your own hands. You could get yourself killed. I've been tracking the men. They're staying on public land. See that your cattle don't stray."

The ranchers grudgingly promised to check their fences. Travis told them to enjoy their meal and headed toward Alison's table. She watched him approach and take a seat, her mouth pursed into disapproving lines.

"You didn't find Janis," she concluded when he didn't speak at once.

"I had other fish to fry. There are paramilitarists in the area. They seem to have divided into two groups. From the paint-ball splatters, I'd say they are playing war games. The ranch has registered a business license for a game camp—"

"What does that mean?" she interrupted.

"That Keith Towbridge, the grandson who inherited the land, intends to use the place as a vacation resort for war games and such. It's legal.''

''I see.'' She gazed out the window.

Travis noticed the way the sunlight, filtered through a light layer of clouds, hit her eyes, showing up the green outer circle and the smoky-gray flecks around the iris. He detected worry in their depths. What else was new?

''Personally, I don't see that your sister is in any kind of trouble. Other than some poaching of cattle—and we don't know who's doing that—I can't find anything illegal in this operation.''

''That isn't the issue.''

''I know. You need to find her because of your family concerns.''

''If the ranchers and the pretend soldiers get in a shoot-out over some dead cows, people could get hurt. My sister, an innocent bystander, could end up dead.''

''Not as long as they use paint balls for ammo.''

''Those two ranchers you talked to won't be using fake bullets.''

He had to give her credit for logic. ''The military group is staying strictly in the mountains. They haven't been on any land but the Towbridge ranch or national forest. Your sister isn't involved in poaching.''

She visibly relaxed. ''That's good to know.''

Travis yanked out a handkerchief and covered a sneeze. "Sorry. I've caught a cold."

She gave him a wry glance. "I have one, too. Those two nights in the woods must have done it."

Her words, spoken in a light, teasing voice, surprised him into recalling the moments of passion they had shared. He gazed into her eyes and saw an acknowledgment of the hot current that surged between them.

"I don't want this," he muttered in savage anger. "I can't go into my tent now without remembering—" He broke off, images of her snuggled up close to him, taunting him with her soft, feminine scent, coming to vivid life.

"I didn't know it would happen. I had the nightmare, then you were there, safe and comforting that second night. You came to my tent."

"We could have gone farther, much farther."

"We didn't."

The waitress brought him a menu and glass of water. He took a drink to relieve the tightness in his throat. That wasn't the only part of him that had reacted to the thought of them alone together up in the mountains.

"But we could have," he said when they were alone again. "I don't recall you telling me to stop. I'm not even sure why we had to."

"Because it wasn't wise," she told him, holding

his gaze without backing down. "There was no point in it."

"Right," he agreed. "No point at all."

Except they had been a man and a woman intensely aware of each other, alone and filled with needs that refused to be suppressed. Why the waking of desire now? Why this woman?

"I heard you say cattle had been slaughtered. If not the paramilitarists, then who did it?"

He shrugged. "I found two sets of footprints at the site. Probably hikers who passed through the area and decided they needed fresh meat."

"That's a relief. Maybe Janis isn't involved in anything that could embarrass our father—"

Alison stopped, but the words had already fallen from her lips. She saw no surprise in Travis's eyes.

"That is," she began, trying to recover. She had never been so indiscreet in dealing with anyone before.

"I think I know how it is."

His voice was hard, but it seemed as soothing as hot cocoa on a cold morning, deep and rich and comforting.

Sometimes she felt as if she needed comforting. She couldn't figure out why.

Travis Dalton was a very attractive, masculine person. He was strong, at times gruff, but he had an innate sense of honesty and fairness. A man one could depend on.

She didn't know why that thought should console her. It wasn't as if *she* depended on him.

Travis rummaged through the kitchen cabinet where Uncle Nick kept the medicines. Finding the bottle of cold tablets, he shook two into his hand and swallowed them down. He felt miserable all over.

"Hey, bro," Trevor said upon entering the house. He spotted the pill bottle. "There's no medicine for a broken heart."

Travis groaned at the quip. He didn't feel up to dealing with his twin at present. He could see Zack outside, tossing a stick for one of the three dogs who lived on the ranch. The older brother lived in town, but came out to the ranch to work with the horses he raised when he wasn't chasing crooks for the sheriff.

"My heart is fine," he told his obnoxious sibling, deciding to leave as soon as his clothes came out of the dryer. He sneezed three times.

Trevor grinned. "I saw your girlfriend in town this morning. Funny, she was in the drugstore, stocking up on cold remedies. You sure nothing went on in that tent—"

Travis was in the twin's face in an instant. "Shut up about Alison."

Trevor held up his hands in mock surrender. "Please, don't shoot. I was only asking."

The quips made Travis see red. With supreme effort, he controlled the impulse to sock Trevor in the mouth.

"The only thing between her and me is concern for her sister's safety."

Trevor removed a bottle of medicine from the fridge. "Yeah?" He headed for the door. "Then we won't hear the patter of little feet around here next February? Too bad. I like kids."

The door banged shut.

Travis took a deep breath, then another, but it did no good. Following on his brother's heels, he caught up with him at the stable door. "You've stepped over the line," he warned, the fury a hot, welcome escape from his thoughts.

Trevor set the medicine bottle on top of a post. "You have got it bad," he said. "Hey, Zack, ol' Travis is in love."

That's when Travis took a swing at him.

However, his brother ducked to the side and Travis swiped thin air. Zack came over to watch. Travis feinted with his right, then hooked with his left and got in a glancing blow.

Trevor put up his fists. "You'll pay for that, little brother," he warned with a careless grin.

"You boys want a hiding?" Uncle Nick demanded, coming out of the stable. "Trevor, where's that medicine you were supposed to bring out?"

"On the post—"

Travis tackled his brother and they rolled across

the ground. He felt like a good fight. He'd been wanting to pummel something for days. He realized he was taking his frustrations out on Trevor. Damn. He got to his feet and helped his twin up.

"Sorry, Trev," he began, then got socked in the eye. So much for apologizing. He tried for a headlock.

"Stop them," Uncle Nick ordered.

Travis felt hands grab him. His cousin Beau, coming out of the stable behind Uncle Nick, pinned his arm high on his back with a thumb hold. Zack did the same with Trevor.

"I don't know what's wrong with you two, fighting like a couple of kids." Uncle Nick glared at them. Plainly disgusted, he said, "Last time you fought, it was over a girl Trevor took to the senior dance. What is it this time?"

Travis gave Trevor a threatening stare.

"A girl," Uncle Nick concluded as silence ensued. "Aren't you boys ever going to grow up?"

"I was trying to apologize," Travis muttered, "and got a poke in the eye for my efforts."

Trevor appeared contrite. "Sorry about that, bro. I didn't realize that things were serious between you and—"

"Nothing is serious," Travis immediately denied.

"Enough!" Uncle Nick roared. His eyes, true Dalton blue, raked over all four nephews. "If you need something to do, I can find a few chores to keep you busy."

Uncle Nick could assign enough work to wear the soles off a new pair of boots.

"Uh, I'm going to check on my mare," Zack said.

"Yeah, we need to give that horse her medicine," Trevor agreed. He and Zack ducked inside the stable.

"I've got to head back to the clinic for afternoon rounds," Beau, the doctor, stated, backing toward his pickup in the driveway.

"I'd better see about packing my clothes." Travis headed for the utility room next to the kitchen.

Within thirty minutes, he was on his way back to his hidden camp in the hills. He was going to get Janis Harvey to town if he had to kidnap the girl. Having seen the younger sister on TV a couple of times, Travis knew she resembled Alison in coloring and facial features, so he wasn't worried about identifying her. He just hoped she wasn't as stubborn as her older sister.

He sneezed, blew his nose, then gingerly felt the soft tissue around his eye. He was glad he would be out of town and out of sight for the next few days so he wouldn't have to take any guff about a black eye. Upon consideration, he decided he would also be glad when the Harvey sisters were out of his hair.

The hollow blackness within stirred painfully. The world seemed to be shifting, so that up was down and down was up. He couldn't figure out what was happening to him.

* * *

Alison picked up a sandwich and carton of milk at the local deli and ate in her room. When Amelia invited her to join her for a glass of wine, she went willingly, needing to get away from her own thoughts.

Other guests were gathered in the large front room of the B&B where wine and snacks were served each evening. Amelia called out a greeting when she entered.

"Be with you in a minute," she said, placing a tray of hot hors d'oeuvres on a table. To Alison's surprise, the owner then led the way into a private area of the house. "Red, rose or white wine?"

"The cabernet will be fine." Alison looked around the sitting room. A place of wicker and chintz and colorful pillows, it was more casual than the lobby-reception area. Greenery lined the windowsills. African violets bloomed in many pots.

"You have a green thumb," Alison mentioned, indicating the flowers. "I can kill a silk plant."

Amelia laughed. "My grandmother showed me how to care for violets, so those are my one and only claim to gardening fame."

Alison sat in a comfy rocking chair and sipped the wine. Amelia served a tray of poppers and cheese sticks along with slices of Asian pear and kiwi fruit. The poppers, hot peppers filled with cheese, then battered and baked or fried, were the best Alison had ever eaten.

"Delicious," she told her hostess.

"From the frozen-food section at the grocery," Amelia said with a grin. "I do everything the easy way."

Alison nodded. "Good thinking."

"So how's your search coming along?"

"Search?"

Amelia shot her a rueful glance. "A lone female doesn't wander off into the hills unless she's very, uh, outdoorsy, which you're not, or on a mission. You being the senator's daughter would indicate the latter."

Alison sighed. She had always tried to maintain a low profile. "You knew who I was all the time?"

"Actually, I wasn't positive, but the last name was the same and I saw you on TV during the election. Plus, you have your father's eyes and light hair."

"You didn't say anything."

"Well, I figure, whatever you're doing here, it's your business." She grinned. "What *are* you doing in these parts?"

"Looking for my sister. She's on vacation at some ranch in the mountains, which I can't find."

"So Travis is helping," her hostess concluded. "Don't worry. If anyone can find your sister, Travis will. The Daltons know these hills better than anyone. They've hunted every inch of land in the Seven Devils range."

"Legally?" Alison asked, unable to hide her interest in the Dalton clan.

Amelia shrugged. "They've never gotten into trouble with the law that I know of."

"Do all six of the cousins live at the ranch?"

"No. Three are in Boise. Zack is a deputy sheriff for the county and has a room here at the B&B. The twins are the ranchers and they do some prospecting, I think. They're both volunteer deputies, too."

She tried to sound casual. "Are any of them married?"

Amelia shook her head. "Travis was, but his wife died in childbirth, along with the baby."

Alison was so shocked she couldn't speak for a moment. "How terrible for him," she said at last. The air about her became fragile, so that she had to breathe carefully to keep it from shattering.

"Julie was his childhood sweetheart. I think they fell in love in first grade. He changed after her death. He's tasted sadness. His brothers and cousins haven't, not in that sense. Well, except when their parents died."

Unable to stop, Alison probed and discovered that the cousins' parents had died while home on a visit. A heavy wet snow laid down over a light fluffy one had resulted in an avalanche, which swept their vehicle away like a cork caught in a tidal wave. A house-size boulder had crushed the pickup they were in.

"That's how all of them came to live with their

uncle. He added more rooms to the original cabin on the ranch and kept all of them.''

"Uncle Nick must be a saint."

Amelia laughed outright at this. "If he is, he's an odd one. He's sort of crotchety and very plainspoken. He loved the ranch and settled on it while his brothers went off to make their fortunes following the rodeos. Unfortunately, there wasn't the money in them then as there is today."

"So they never struck it rich?" Alison asked.

"Right. The uncle shouldered all the financial problems of raising six additional kids as well as the emotional ones, in spite of his own tragedy shortly after that. Did you know his wife died in a car wreck and his daughter disappeared at the same time? She was only three or four."

"What happened to the daughter?"

"No one knows. The sheriff thought she'd been kidnapped at the accident site. She was never seen again. They found footprints next to hers, but no one knew whose they were. It's been an unsolved mystery for over twenty years."

Alison was silent for a minute as she absorbed this information. "Travis and his twin turned out all right, so their uncle must have done a good job with the orphans in spite of his own losses."

"They kept each other in line. If one misbehaved, the other five beat him up."

"Five? Did the sister join in?"

"Whatever the Daltons did, they did together."

Alison managed to laugh, not without a little envy of the close-knit family. "The Daltons of Seven Devils Mountains. Sounds like an old Western movie."

"Yes, but are they the good guys or the outlaws? The local folks have often wondered about this, especially at Halloween when the boys used to pull a wagon across the roof beam of a barn if the ranchers were so foolish as to leave their equipment outside."

Again Alison felt the twinge of envy. Not that she hadn't had fun in her life, too, but a politician's child had to think of the consequences of foolish acts. She and Janis had been taught early to be aware of their duties in that regard.

For a moment, she envisioned how life might be if one were free to sample all the possibilities. To laugh with abandon. Maybe to go a little wild and not have to worry about what people would say. To fall in love without having to justify one's choice.

Not that she was in love, she quickly amended, but to be free to love whom she wished seemed a wonderful luxury.

Her mother pushed the young lawyers and aides in her father's Washington, D.C., office in her direction, but she'd never fallen in love with any of them.

She'd had a high school steady but that hadn't worked out. Later, another man had said he loved her, but she'd soon realized he was more interested in her father's position and achieving his own ambitions than he was in love with her.

She'd even considered marrying him, but some remnant of a long-ago dream had held her back. She'd stopped believing in fairy-tale romances before that, but there had been a faint hesitation, as if she knew she would forever lose something precious if she took that final step.

Observing the stars as they gathered in the night sky, she wondered if she hadn't already lost that part of herself.

Thinking of Travis's loss, she asked, "When did Travis lose his wife and baby?"

"It was two years ago. Two years this month."

Alison considered the darkness inside him and the anger he used to cover it. Travis had fallen in love, married and fathered a child. And had lost them.

The fragile air broke apart in her lungs, sending shards of pain through her chest.

"Excuse me," she said and went to her room as darkness fell across the wild beautiful land.

Chapter 5

Alison hit the off button on the alarm clock. Five o'clock wasn't her favorite time of day. Gritting her teeth, she rolled out of the warm bed and headed for the shower.

Today was Tuesday.

She'd warned Travis that she intended to go look for her sister if he hadn't found Janis by now. Actually she'd given him until Sunday and then had waited all day yesterday, an extra day, for word from him.

So why this niggling sense of guilt?

Stopping by the front desk, she left an envelope addressed to Travis, advising him of her intentions, which assuaged the guilt that ate at her. She couldn't wait around here forever.

Thirty minutes later, she slipped out to her car and crept out of town like an escaping criminal. When she'd arrived last Tuesday—had it really been a week ago?—she'd figured on finding Janis on Wednesday and heading home on Thursday. She *hadn't* counted on a run-in with Travis Dalton, rancher, prospector and volunteer deputy, or that her younger sibling would hide out in the wilderness.

Everything she'd learned since arriving in Lost Valley had reinforced her fears that Janis was mixed up in something not quite legit. What it was, she couldn't begin to imagine, but she had a bad feeling about it.

At the end of the road, she checked her gear and food supplies, then donned the backpack and headed up the tiny creek that flowed by Travis's camp. The trail she wanted to travel was closer that way than by following the road and taking the other trail farther north of here.

Finding Travis's camp was no problem for her this time. She was becoming an adept mountain woman.

Resting on the log Travis had provided, she ate a handful of trail mix, her thoughts going to the two nights she'd spent here with her reluctant rescuer.

A fist squeezed her heart as she gazed at the camouflaged tent under the pine boughs. Travis might act gruff, but there had been gentleness in him when he'd comforted her after the nightmare. For those few moments, it had been wonderful to lean against him and feel his strength and innate kindness.

The passion had been a surprise, for him as much as her. His lips had been warm and supple, moving against her mouth, hesitantly at first, then firmer as the hunger seized them both. It had been a long time since she'd been so attracted to a man. She'd wanted to forget everything and simply let the desire take them where it would.

Fortunately it hadn't, not quite. As her mother had reminded her last night, she was a practical, level-headed person. Family obligations were her first concern.

Funny, only Travis had ever made her forget duty completely. Those moments in his arms had been the sweetest interlude, the haunting notes of an all-too-brief melody heard from a distance.

An odd, nostalgic sadness engulfed her.

A minute later, a birdcall reminded her she must be on her way. She sighed as she rose and headed for the northern trail by the path she and Travis had followed. It wasn't a well-defined track, but she found, by careful observation, it was fairly easy to detect.

She had to smile at this new sense of accomplishment. Travis would surely have been impressed.

Right after he got over being furious.

The sun was inching toward a western peak when Alison finally reached the crest of the mountain, stopped and gasped. The view was spectacular.

The land dropped away in jagged ridges into a gorge. Hells Canyon—a place of ancient myths and timeless dreams, of glacier-scoured cirques and arêtes—an area as unforgiving as Everest in its indifference to humans.

Gazing at the ruggedly beautiful scene, she experienced an excruciating yearning to embrace the land and its vastness. Its lonely beauty weighed heavily in her breast, reminding her that once she'd been young and full of dreams.

Where had those dreams gone?

"I don't know," she said to the wind as it rose from the gorge and tousled her hair.

The words were whipped away into the mournful silence. She frowned, then smiled. She wasn't ancient, but she was old enough to know where dreams belonged.

Reality was a rocky trail and long hours of hiking. She'd better get with it rather than standing there on a lonely crest mooning over fantasies better forgotten. She pushed on.

Sometime later, she took a long break, shrugging out of the backpack and propping it against a sturdy tree. After drinking deeply from her canteen, she selected a seat on a log in a shady spot and rested her back against the tree.

Munching on trail mix, she mused on a trip through the mountains with a special person. Right, Annie

Oakley meets Frank Butler in the Great Outdoors and lives happily ever after. Ha.

After checking the topography maps, she decided she was on the right track to intersect the ranch house that was supposed to be in the next valley to the north. If she ever got that far.

A sound came to her on the breeze, that of a voice speaking irritably. She listened intently. Someone was on the trail and coming her way.

She crouched under a low-hanging fir branch where she could see the trail clearly. Her heart quickened as the men came closer. There were two of them, both middle-aged, both panting from the climb. They didn't appear to be locals.

"There's nobody on the trail," one man griped.

"I saw something from below," his companion replied. "Let's go to the top of the ridge before turning back."

She heard them coming closer, then the footsteps stopped. A chill raced along her spine. She waited, not sure what to do. "Well, what have we here?" one man said.

Alison realized she'd been spotted. She rose. The two men gaped at her, their faces identical with comical surprise. "You're not the commandos," the bald one stated.

She assumed an air of confidence. "No, I'm not. I'm on my way to the Towbridge ranch."

"Who are you?" the taller of the two wanted to know. He shifted his position, blocking her on one side.

She stepped back. "Alison Harvey. I'm trying to get to the ranch. My sister is there."

"What's your sister's name?"

Alison hesitated, then told them. "Janis."

The man with the receding hairline nodded. "She's the cook."

Cook? Janis? Alison didn't have the foggiest idea what this meant, but she decided it was better to act as if she understood. "Then this is the correct trail to the ranch?"

"Yep, just follow it down to the camp. Keep going north when the trail forks."

"It's time we were getting back," the other man remarked. "You can come with us," he told Alison.

She wondered if she should. The men seemed harmless, but looks could be deceiving. Remembering her mission, Alison gripped the bear-spray can and nodded. "Would you mind introducing yourselves?" she asked pleasantly.

"I'm Merv," the taller man said. "This is Harry."

"Glad to meet you. Are you with a paramilitary group?"

Merv snorted. "We're playing at being soldiers, but we're just a bunch of overweight businessmen up here on a retreat. The company thinks this will teach us to be resourceful, think out of the box and improve our teamwork.''

Harry, the balding one, nodded. ''So far, all I've gotten is blisters from these hiking boots.''

Alison relaxed as they laughed ruefully. She fell into step between the men when Merv indicated she and Harry should go first. As they marched along, she planned the coming meeting with her sister and how she should present the facts concerning their father. The simple truth was the best way, she decided.

''Almost there,'' Harry said after a half-hour walk.

Anxiety rippled through her as they left the trees and entered a small plateau tucked up against a high ridge of layered rock. A picnic table with a camp stove on it stood next to a cooking pot hung over a fire pit. Short sections of logs supplied the seats. A cabin stood to one side of the clearing.

A woman, dressed in denim coveralls and a man's plaid shirt, sat at the table. Her hair was pulled back with a blue scrunchy. She looked like a country girl, fresh-faced and wholesome. She was smiling as she turned toward them. The smile froze on her face.

''Janis!'' Alison said and rushed forward, relief at finding her sibling bringing her close to tears.

''How did you get here?'' Janis demanded, disbelief and anger flashing into her eyes.

''What do you mean, gone?'' Travis demanded. He looked from Alison's ridiculous note to the B&B owner.

Amelia shrugged. "As in, she left early this morning. With her backpack. I saw her from my bedroom window when she got in her car around five-thirty."

"Both of you were up that early?" he asked, hoping this was a joke. He felt dangerous, on the brink of an explosion he was so furious with Alison and her stubborn dedication to her task.

"I always get up at five-thirty," Amelia said defensively. "I have work to do."

"Sorry, I didn't mean to sound like a bear, it's just…" He couldn't say exactly what was eating at him. "It's stupid for someone to go off into the hills alone and without a clue about the danger. Hypothermia kills more hikers a year than grizzlies have in the last hundred."

At Amelia's assessing stare, he shut up. A flush warmed his neck and ears. His glare dared her to make a smart remark. "I suppose I'll have to go find her," he said.

"Yes, I suppose you will," she said, a gleam dancing in her eyes.

Cursing silently, he thanked Amelia and left the B&B. He'd planned on returning to the gold mine. The vein was small and wouldn't take long to pan out. Now he'd have to track into the mountains before Alison got herself into real trouble.

His heart pounded all of a sudden, startling him. Thinking of the politician's daughter and the passion she'd induced got his insides all twisted. She was everything he knew to stay away from in a woman, but the hunger lingered, taunting him at odd moments.

For a second he considered an affair with her. It would be brief and hot, then she'd go back to the city and he'd head for the hills again. However, passion could lead to complications, and he didn't need those.

He found her car exactly where he'd expected. After hiding his truck, he donned his gear and started out. When he caught up with her, she was going to be in big trouble.

Hopping across the creek from boulder to boulder, he searched for her tracks on the other side. No new ones. He used his flashlight to highlight the trail. Nothing.

Cursing, he returned to her car. There he picked up her fresh footprints and carefully followed every move she made. To his surprise, she'd gone up the creek.

An hour later, Travis approached his campsite silently. He wanted to catch her off guard and thus teach her a lesson on forest safety. She deserved to have the pants scared off her. When the camp was in full sight, he stopped and observed the area. Where the hell was she?

Giving her five minutes in case she'd heeded nature's call, he leaned a shoulder against a tree and waited. Within a minute, he knew she wasn't in the vicinity. He could feel the emptiness of the place.

Checking the campsite, he saw she'd eaten something, probably trail mix. He studied the raisin on the ground beside the log as if it could give him a clue to her perverse female mind.

Yanking a candy bar out of his pocket, he ate it as he picked up her path, this time heading up the obscure game trail that would take her farther into the wilderness. He followed her footprints without a problem.

Finally he breached the crest of the trail and started down. He paused and surveyed the crenellated valley far below. Other valleys veered off the main one as far as the eye could see. This was the Nez Perce National Wilderness, which was part of the Payette National Forest.

Thousands of acres of mountains, valleys and trees spread out before him, covering the copper-rich deposits the area was known for. Glacier-gouged lakes abounded—Black, Emerald and Baldy being the best known.

He'd search every damn inch if he had to.

Going a few steps, he stopped abruptly, then bent forward and studied the rocky, slightly wider place in the trail. Two sets of footprints had joined Alison's, one on each side of her.

She'd been waylaid by two guys wearing heavy-tread boots. The prints told him the whole story.

She'd tried to back up, but the men had her trapped. The three had headed downhill, single file with her in the middle.

Something akin to panic bit deep into his gut. An urge to run down the dangerous slope as fast as possible fought against the self-control he'd learned at a young age.

Hell, there wasn't a body lying in the trail, so why was he getting himself tied into a knot? There wasn't even signs of a struggle.

Travis studied the men's prints so he could easily recognize them. Hiking and combat boots, most likely purchased at an army-navy store, he concluded. Pretend soldiers. Just what the world needed more of.

He checked his weapons, made sure they were fully loaded although he didn't chamber a shell, and hooked a spare can of pepper spray on his belt. He had a full stash of ammo in his backpack. Moving fast but carefully, he pushed deeper into the wilderness.

A coldness entered his blood, chilling his thinking processes until every one of his five senses were as sharp and clear as ice crystals. He forged ahead, his eyes constantly on the alert for danger.

When it was too dark to risk a mishap on the steep, downward grade, he tossed a tarp over some pine boughs, slid into his sleeping bag after eating a helping of trail mix and bedded down.

Before going to sleep, he thought of other nights

spent in the mountains. The emptiness of his life over the past two years seemed to expand until it filled the vast darkness of the night sky. He was no stranger to loneliness, but tonight it seemed more profound....

"Why did you come?" Janis continued.

Merv and Harry glanced at the two women, then muttered about having something to do and moved to the far side of the clearing, giving the sisters some privacy.

Alison dropped her backpack and rushed around the table. Janis held both hands up, palms out, when Alison would have dropped to her knees to hug her.

The action, coming on top of the difficult hike and the week of worry, cut deeply. Alison retreated to the other side of the hewn-log table. She felt discouraged and unsure about why this trip had seemed so important, why she'd been so driven to find this cool stranger whose welcome was anything but friendly.

"Everyone was worried about you," she said, finding it difficult to speak. "Your cell phone stopped working."

"I had it turned off. It was too expensive."

"I'm sure Father would take care—"

"There was no one I wanted to talk to," Janis interrupted. Her eyes, usually a warm, lively gray with a green outer edge, were mutinous.

Alison fought to not be offended. She was used to her sister's defiant ways.

"You're needed at home," she said in a calm, soft voice that wouldn't carry to the men. "Father is ill."

The anger disappeared. "Ill? With what?"

Alison explained quickly. "He has a tumor at the base of his skull. He refuses to have it removed until you're home. You must come," she finished.

Janis hesitated, then said, "This is a trick to get me to go back, isn't it? I don't believe Father has any such thing. Who told you about it?"

"Mother. No one else knows."

"Ah, yes," Janis said as if it all became clear.

She seemed older and sadder, too, in a way Alison had never noticed. With something like shock, she saw her sister as a person separate from the family, one determined to have a life apart from them.

"Father isn't a fool," Janis continued in a low voice. "He has access to the best medical advice in the world. If he were really ill, he'd have already had it taken care of. You've wasted your time coming here. Tell Mother that when you see her."

Alison hadn't expected this to be easy. Dealing with her family never was. She would simply have to convince Janis to do the right thing.

"I want you to leave," Janis said.

Alison blinked. When she spoke, it was in her most reasoned manner. "I can't return today. It's too late."

Janis's lips thinned in anger, but before she could speak, a male voice chimed in. "She's right."

A man Alison had never seen entered the clearing

from a path through the trees. He was young, no more than twenty-five or so. He wore jeans and a T-shirt with boots and a cowboy hat. His hair was medium brown with sun streaks. His eyes were brown and had an earnest expression as he glanced from her to Janis.

He stopped beside Janis and laid a hand on her shoulder. "She'll have to spend the night," he said.

Janis swung her legs around the seat and pushed herself to her feet. "I don't want her here."

Alison didn't react to the last statement. Instead, she gasped aloud, her eyes glued to her sister's abdomen.

"Yes, I'm pregnant," Janis said, her chin tilted at a proud angle. She slipped an arm around the man and leaned against him. He held her close in a protective embrace.

For once, words failed her. Finally she asked, "Are you...you two are married?"

The man answered. "We're committed to each other. I'm Keith Towbridge. You must be Alison."

She nodded.

He smiled rather solemnly. "I'm glad to meet you."

Her sister spoke. "Well, now that the truth is out, I suppose you can't wait to call Mom and Dad and spread the word."

"Don't you want them to know?" Alison couldn't fathom leaving one's family out of such important news. Slowly she gathered her composure. "You surely didn't think you could hide your condition forever.''

Janis shrugged indifferently.

"When are you due?'' Alison asked.

"July. The twenty-ninth,'' Keith answered after a short silence.

Two and a half months to go. *A baby. Dear God.* "Have you seen a doctor?'' she asked Janis.

"It's none of your business.'' At a glance from Keith, she added impatiently, "Yes, and I'm fine.''

Alison stood rooted to the spot while Janis went to the fire pit. She removed the lid from a kettle and stirred a big pot of stew. The hearty aroma reminded Alison that she'd only had trail mix in the last several hours. She started to offer her help, but thought better of it.

Slowly she sank to the rough log stool. There was so much to think about—the baby, her parents' shock when they found out, her own sense of responsibility, as if she'd somehow failed her little sister by not seeing this disaster coming and averting it.

A baby. She would be an aunt. Janny, little Janny, a mother. Her baby sister.

Somehow she had to think this through, figure it out and... What to do? They had to do something...

The irony of the situation hit home. This was life as usual in the Harvey family. Janis resented any interference while Alison tried to keep the peace between the family members.

A baby. This was more than youthful rebellion.

She stared at the couple. Keith had moved over beside Janis, his stance cautious, his eyes wary, his every gesture protective of the woman who stirred the cook pot.

Turning toward the deepening twilight and last glory of the sunset fading beyond the far horizon, Alison suddenly wished she could walk away and never, never look back.

"Dinner is ready. Did you meet our guests?" Keith asked her politely.

"Two of them. They found me on the trail and showed me the way here. They said they were on a company retreat."

Keith nodded. "We teach strategy and teamwork, then have war games with two armies to develop skills. I'm in charge of operations on this end."

"I see."

"You don't approve," Janis stated, reading more in her stiff posture than was there. "Women don't, but it's a guy thing." She shrugged.

"Do you have a place to sleep?" Alison asked, looking around the sparse encampment, seeking practical matters to occupy her mind until she could think more clearly.

A baby. She couldn't think of a thing to do about that.

Janis eyed her backpack. "Didn't you bring a tent?"

"We'll put her in the cabin," Keith told Janis in a firm tone. "We have a house," he said to Alison. "You can stay with us. This way."

Grabbing her pack, he led the way to an old ranch house. Behind it, the overhang of a gigantic cliff offered protection from the north wind. She heard water rushing over stones and realized a creek must be close.

"An underground spring runs at the back of a cave in the rocks. We're in the watershed of the Snake River. You can hear the roar of the rapids if you listen. The Salmon runs into the Snake north of here."

A shiver rushed over her. The Salmon River was also known as the River of No Return because it was so rough and dangerous. Once down it, there was no way to go back upriver. The mountain men had returned on a southerly route.

"Why did you bring Janis here?" Alison asked, her gesture indicating the camp and all it represented.

"We want to revive the ranch. No one has lived here for over twenty years, but I remember visiting when my granddad was alive. It's a good place to raise a family. The retreat was a friend's idea to provide cash flow while we get started. We're working on the house."

Alison recognized the glow of a long-held dream as he recounted the plan. Her sister had evidently bought into it, too. Saying nothing, she followed him inside.

The house was four small rooms, all connected by doors leading from one to the other. The first one was the living room. The kitchen was right behind that. The other two were bedrooms, used mostly for storage.

"I'll clear a place in here for you." He went into the bedroom immediately to the right of the living room.

Following, she saw stacked bunk beds against one wall. He put her backpack down and removed some boxes and blankets from the lower bunk, placing the items in chairs that were already piled high with household things.

"There's electricity," he said and flipped the switch.

A light fixture mounted on the ceiling came on. "Thank you." Alison managed a smile. "This will do nicely. I thought I would have to sleep in a tent tonight."

"I'd better help with dinner. There's a bathroom beyond the other bedroom. Uh, the well isn't hooked up yet, but there's water in a bucket. Join us when you're ready."

Alison explored the house after he left. The kitchen was being remodeled. A new stove and dishwasher waited to be installed. The wall had been repaired where the old stove had stood. New cabinets were already in place.

While this work showed promise, it was still a

small, rather primitive abode. She couldn't imagine her sister living here for very long. With a baby to care for, it would be even harder. She hurriedly washed up, using water from the bucket, then returned to the picnic table.

Janis was alone. She gave Alison a wary glance, then set plates and forks on the table. After a few minutes of silence, she spoke. "Go ahead and yell at me before you explode," she advised sarcastically.

Alison inhaled slowly. "Why?" she asked. "Why go off without a word to anyone? Surely you knew we would worry."

"I wanted to be with Keith."

"You only have another year of college. Couldn't you have waited until you graduated to start the pioneer life?"

Janis grimaced. "I'd flunked economics—"

"Oh, Janny."

Her glance was scalding. "I never wanted to take it in the first place. That was Dad's idea."

Alison nodded. There'd been many quarrels over school and grades and spending money. Father would yell, Mother would retreat to her room with a headache, Janis would threaten to leave home forever. Alison would sweep up the pieces of family life and put them together again.

"Anyway, I met Keith. He was working in construction and saving his money to start the ranch. We realized we didn't want to be apart, so I came with him.''

Alison stared at her sister's enlarged body. ''Without a word to the parents,'' she reminded the younger woman.

''I called you a couple of times.'' She flicked Alison an angry glance before stirring the stew again. ''You could have told me you were coming.''

''How? You said there was no phone at the ranch. You turned your cell-phone service off.''

''We're on a tight budget.''

''Can you afford the baby?''

Janis laughed. ''Well, he's on the way, no matter what.''

''He?''

''It's a boy.''

''Do you need money for the doctor?''

The aloof coldness returned. ''Keith will help me with the delivery.''

This took a moment to sink in. ''You're going to have the baby at home?''

''Don't look so shocked. Babies were born for thousands of years without hospitals and doctors and modern medicine.''

''A lot of them didn't make it through the first year, either,'' Alison retorted and was immediately ashamed. ''I'm sorry. I didn't mean—''

''I'm not worried. I'll have Keith. He loves me, and he's all I need.'' Janis shot Alison a proud glance.

"We have checked with a doctor in town. Everything looks fine. His nurse is a midwife. She'll come when it's time."

Alison refrained from asking how they planned on contacting the midwife. She felt disoriented, as if she'd stepped into another time, another place. She no longer recognized her sister in this very pregnant young woman who cooked over an open fire.

Where was the Janis who'd never learned to boil water, as far as Alison could recall?

"This is all very romantic and pioneering," Alison said, smiling in sudden understanding.

Janis whirled around. "Don't," she said. "Don't make fun of it. This is Keith's and my dream, to make a go of this place that no one in his family wanted to keep but him. We can build a life here. And we will!"

"I wasn't going to ridicule your ideas. I'm just worried about you and the baby," Alison murmured.

"Don't be. I want to do this. For once, I want to do something without worrying about Father's career. I'm so *tired* of his damn career."

Keith appeared with a bucket of water and placed it on the table. He put an arm around Janis when she leaned against him and rested her head against his shoulder.

Alison thought of arms that had enclosed her when she'd had the nightmare. She wished someone was there to offer her comfort now as Keith did for Janis.

An image came to her—dark hair and eyes as blue as the sky, someone like her, who'd lost his dreams... his wife...his child...

A baby. Oh, dear Lord.

Chapter 6

Breakfast came early the next morning. Keith did the cooking on a camp stove set up on the end of the picnic table. Alison joined him and the other two men in the chilly dawn light. Her sister didn't appear.

They had all gone to bed shortly after dark the previous night. Through the thin walls of the cabin, Alison had listened to the whispered conversation between Keith and Janis, unable to understand the words but recognizing her sister's stubborn anger as the couple argued.

Over her being there, she'd presumed.

She inhaled deeply and tried to ignore the ache, both physical and mental, that had stayed with her during the night. She'd never felt so unwanted and unnecessary and unsure about what she should do.

Before she began the long hike out, she decided she would talk to Keith about a phone, and the future. There were a couple of questions she wanted to put to him.

Finished with the meal, she helped clean up while the company men drank their coffee. Both were quiet. Harry carved on a cedar stick while Merv puffed on a cigarette.

This was the peaceful scene that greeted Travis when he strode into camp. He cast an assessing glance over the four people at the table. "This certainly looks cozy," he said.

He couldn't decide if Alison was surprised to see him or not. He gave her a mock-menacing scowl. "I thought I told you to stay put, that I'd find your sister." Including the men in an exasperated grin, he added, "Women, they never do what they're told."

The youngest of the three men rose and held out a hand. "I'm Keith Towbridge. You know Alison and Janis?"

"Travis Dalton," he said, shaking hands. "I know Alison. The Seven Devils Ranch, over the ridge in the next valley, is our spread. I didn't know anyone was living over here until Alison came looking for her sister."

"Janis and I are rebuilding—"

Before he could say more, all hell broke loose. Several men, whooping like banshees, dashed into the clearing from the trees, surrounding the area. They wore cammies and had black streaks on their faces. All of them toted rifles.

During the first moments of confusion, Travis shoved Alison under the table. He shielded her with his body while he pulled a .38 semiautomatic from a belt holster.

She laid her hand over his. "War games, I think."

"Don't move or you're dead," one of the men shouted.

Travis lifted his head above the edge of the table in order to take a quick count of the enemy. A shot rang out and almost immediately a stinging sensation hit his side. He glanced down at the spot and saw a blob of yellow start to drip down on his pants leg.

"Drop your weapon," the leader of the group told him. He chuckled gleefully. "We got the whole bunch."

Travis holstered the gun, helped Alison to her feet and turned on the leader of the pretend soldiers. "Don't you know better than to raid a camp when women and strangers are present? I could have shot all of you. And my bullets are real." He swiped the paint off with a paper towel.

"Uh, at ease, men," the leader said. "We're Commando Unit Alpha. I thought we were supposed to capture you guys."

Keith spoke up. "You got us fair and square. I didn't think you'd be able to find our camp so soon."

Travis nodded to the commandos as Keith introduced them. "Travis here is a neighboring rancher. We didn't get a chance to tell him about a possible raid."

The new men settled on stumps and logs with fresh mugs of coffee and related their adventures of the past three days. It had taken them that long to track their comrades through two miles of wilderness and find their camp.

Travis was aware of Alison sitting beside him, a pleasant, attentive expression on her face as she listened to the tale of adventure in the wilderness. He knew on some basic level that it was a facade.

There was weariness in her pale face, as if she'd taken a serious blow and it was only a matter of time before it became a mortal one.

Someone had hurt her. He knew it on an instinctive level that had no bearing to reason and logic.

Big deal, he scoffed as some softheaded part of him wanted to take her in his arms and offer comfort. Live long enough and pain was inevitable. The fates loved to whack people down when they least expected it. Apparently Alison was just learning this lesson. If so, she'd had an easy life as far as he was concerned.

Where was the other Harvey girl? He had an impression of a spoiled brat in the younger sister, but what did he know? It wasn't as if his opinion meant a thing in the grand scheme of things. If he were wise, he'd keep his thoughts to himself and far from the

woman who silently observed, her eyes deep pools of
fortitude laced with profound worry.

She stirred beside him. "More coffee?" she asked.

He nodded and moved slightly to let her fill his
cup, then her own. The heat from her body caressed
his side as she stood close, her attention focused on
the task.

A sudden, fierce need came over him. He didn't
understand where it came from, only that it reminded
him of the pain from the past and he didn't like it.
Walking a few steps away, he swallowed a gulp of
the strong, boiled cowboy coffee and surveyed the
camp.

Earlier, he'd realized Alison wasn't in danger as
he'd observed their morning meal—that's why he'd
walked calmly into the clearing with the three men
present—but he'd known there was a problem from
the tension in her.

Eyeing the encampment, he wondered if the kid
sister was in the old ranch house nestled in the trees.
The two weekend warriors had been in the other cabin
when he'd first arrived and scouted the place. Alison
and Towbridge had been preparing breakfast.

When he'd walked into their midst, he'd seen a
flash of welcome in her eyes, as if she'd been glad to
see a friend. As if she'd needed one.

Not him, a part of him advised. He wasn't anyone's
friend. He considered gathering his gear and heading
for his own camp, far from the troubles of others.

"Have you had breakfast?" Alison asked.

"Not yet."

Indicating that he should sit in her place, she prepared scrambled eggs with quiet efficiency on the camp stove. Travis figured that was the way she did everything—with simple competence and no expectations of praise. She did her job, no fuss, no muss.

She toasted bread over the burner, then set the meal before him and asked if anyone wanted more coffee.

"Sure," Merv said. He pulled out a cigarette pack, peered inside, then sighed and put it away. "I'm supposed to quit these. My wife keeps a spray bottle handy. If she catches me smoking, she squirts water on me."

"A woman after my own heart," Alison said with a true smile that brightened the worry in her eyes.

"You gals are hard-hearted," Merv lamented.

Janis appeared while they were laughing. "What's so funny?" she asked.

Her grouchy tone put a pall over the table. Travis understood at once what Alison's problem was. The younger sister was in a delicate condition…and an embarrassing one for the senator. There was no ring on her finger to go with the bulge of her tummy.

Trouble with a capital *T.* Yeah. Thank heaven it wasn't his problem this time. He wondered how Alison was going to handle this "situation," as she diplomatically termed her family's crises.

"Feeling bad this morning?" Keith asked, giving Janis his stool.

"Just tired." Janis smiled at him before turning a hard gaze on Alison.

Alison was aware of Travis's comprehensive glance at the couple, then at her. Lifting her chin, she dared him to say anything. He merely raised his eyebrows as if asking what she was going to do now.

Well, she still hadn't come up with plan B, although she'd fretted about it the whole night. She intended to call and let the parents know she'd found Janis. She'd decided to let Janis explain her condition.

"I suppose we should start home soon," she said to Travis. "I'd like to get back to town before dark."

No one, including her sister, responded.

Alison felt a wrenching sense of personal failure. She felt burdened by it all—the difficult search for her sister, the expectations of her family that she would find Janis and somehow talk her into coming home, the ambitions of her father that drove them all.

Well, she had failed on the second part. During the night, she'd realized there was no way she could make the younger girl do anything. Perhaps she should wait until she was at the B&B to call her parents. That would give her time to think of what to say.

Travis shook his head. "We may as well rest for a day before starting back over that ridge. It's going to be a hard day's hike."

"I'm fine, if you're concerned about my making it."

His gaze ran over her, assessing her condition. While he concealed it better than her sister, Alison knew he didn't want her around, either. She stared into the steaming mug until pride could drive the sting of tears away.

"I want to scout out the area first," he continued.

"Because?"

"There might be an easier trail than over the ridge. I can see a saddle farther down the mountain. See that dip in the tree line over there?"

She followed his line of sight. "Yes."

"There used to be a logging road around the flank of the mountain and over that saddle. I have topography maps of the area. I'll study those and the lay of the land, then we'll decide."

Feeling her sister's hostile gaze, Alison cleared her throat and said, "I would rather go today."

Keith spoke to the other men. "If you men are ready, it's time you were starting back to the main camp."

"How did you get them in?" Travis asked.

Keith explained he had a partner and they had cleared and repaired an old road from the highway to a lodge they were building on the front side of the property.

"Shouldn't you take Janis over there? She's getting close to time, isn't she?" Travis asked.

"The lodge is only a foundation so far. There's no place for her to sleep. I'm fixing up the old ranch house. It'll be done before winter."

Travis frowned. "In that case, I'll get some help and clear the ford at the creek so you can get out that way."

Janis scowled at their helpful neighbor. "We don't need a road. I'm going to have the baby here."

Alison could have strangled her sister. She saw Travis's knuckles turn white as he gripped the mug. Memory washed through his eyes like a spring downpour, and she saw everything he'd once been in a glance—the loving husband, the delighted father-to-be, the man who had cared so much for his little family.

Overlaying all that was the man he'd become—the one filled with black desolation, his soul a wasteland that rejected anyone who came close. Now he had her problems to deal with.

Oh, Travis, I'm so sorry.

He shrugged. "It's your life."

"I wish others would remember that." Janis looked directly at Alison.

Alison kept her face expressionless as she returned the glare. In the silence that followed, the other guests recalled they were leaving. Merv and Harry said their farewells, gathered their backpacks from the cabin and took off a few minutes later with their commando buddies. Keith advised them on the correct trail to follow.

Janis went to the house while Alison volunteered to wash up the few dishes that remained. Travis brought out the topo maps. He and Keith studied them, then decided Travis should scout out the old road and see if it was passable.

Left alone, Alison finished her task, then explored the cliff area behind the house. She found the spring bubbling out of the rock at the back of a shallow cave.

Following its course as it became a creek meandering toward the river in the distance, she spotted a flint arrowhead among some rocky debris. She held it up to the sun and admired its translucent edges, carved by some skillful warrior long ago.

A yearning for another time welled up inside her. She longed for something she'd never known—a purpose, a sense of destiny, something, anything. Her breath tangled in a knot and she ceased to breathe as she waited, poised on the brink of a great discovery...

Finally she had to exhale, then she laughed softly, regretfully, at how absurd she was to stand there in the middle of a wilderness and expect a grand revelation. She walked on.

Travis scouted the area south of the camp most of the day. He found the remnants of the logging cut he sought. It was riddled with rocks, trees had sprouted down the middle, but with a little bulldozing, it could be made passable. It was also an easier walk to the ranch.

Hiking back to the old ranch quarters, his thoughts reverted to Alison's sister. Pregnant. Determined to deliver her baby at home. Stupid, stupid, stupid.

He clenched his fists as the worrisome thoughts chased themselves around and around his mind like a dog chasing its tail. It wasn't his problem, he added into the mix.

Dammit, it wasn't.

It was almost dark when he returned to camp. Alison rose and dished up a plate of fish and chips. "Keith gave me some tackle and showed me his favorite fishing hole. I caught three trout."

"You can fish?"

She nodded, a shyness in her smile as she explained that a gardener who had been with the family forever had taught her and Janis when they were little.

His stomach rumbled. "Looks great."

The food tasted as good as it looked. Watching Alison, seated across the table from him, he experienced a shift in the dark center at his core. Her quiet distress was not his doing. It was none of his business. This time, a woman's pain wasn't his fault.

"Where are your sister and Keith?" he asked over a cup of boiled coffee.

"Her back has been hurting today, so she stayed in the house. Keith has the water hooked up and was working on the new kitchen he's putting in."

Travis nodded. "I thought I'd see about helping him with the back road into this place from ours. Trevor and I can clear it with the tractor and lay down a bed of gravel from a bar along the creek."

A glow ignited in Alison. "Would you?" she asked. "I've been so worried. That would be such a help. With a good road, they can get to town in a hurry in case...in case they need to."

She realized where her tongue was taking her in time to change the words, but she saw the darkness in his eyes before they became expressionless once more. She'd been about to say, "in case something happens with the baby." He'd known what she was thinking.

Impulsively she leaned across the table and laid her hand over his. "Thank you, Travis. Thank you for all your help."

He nodded, then moved his hand away to lift the mug to his lips, his eyes as blue and cold as mountain glaciers.

The last of the light faded while they sat at the table. Suddenly a shadow swooped around her head, startling her. She batted at it.

"Don't," he said. "Sit still. They won't hurt you."

Bats dipped and darted all around them, grabbing insects in midair, their needle-sharp teeth ominous, but never once brushing against the two humans who watched, spellbound, as they worked.

It wasn't until the little creatures flew off that she

spoke again. "I'm going to bed." She hesitated, then nodded toward the newly constructed cabin. "I moved my things there this afternoon so that Janis and Keith can have privacy. The cabin has bunk beds, four of them. It's okay, I mean, I don't mind if you share it."

"Thanks."

She couldn't tell anything from his tone. She hurried off without looking back. The idea of being alone with him didn't worry her nearly as much as the animosity she felt in the other house.

Better the devil you know...

She managed a mocking smile. Travis Dalton didn't want her any more than her sister did.

Chapter 7

It was well after dark before Travis decided he should go to bed. At the cabin, he knocked, announced himself and entered when she called it was okay for him to come inside. The interior was dark as a tomb.

Using his flashlight, he checked the place out. In the soft light, he saw Alison's clothing neatly folded and laid atop her hiking boots beside a bunk bed. From the bunk, she watched him with eyes that were shadowed with concern.

Not his problem, he reminded his conscience.

Sitting on the opposite bunk, he removed his boots and rubbed his tired feet. After turning off the flashlight and placing it under his pillow, he slipped off his outer clothing, leaving in place the thermal underwear he wore in the mountains. He heard a sigh.

Across from him, she was a slender outline within the sleeping bag. In the spill of moonlight through the windows, he saw her eyes on him, felt their pull, the magnetism that arced between them, knew her thoughts.

Heat rampaged through him. Hunger jumped on his flagging conscience and beat it into submission. He fought it, then crossed the few feet of space between them.

She was ready when he got to her. Her arms slipped from the cover and closed around him. Her mouth met his. No coy denial. No subterfuge. Just sweet, sweet hunger. Mutual hunger.

He tried to touch her all over, all at once, moving his hands here and there, exploring the womanly curves, reveling in the warmth that grew between them, becoming fiery as the need increased.

Pushing the zipper down, he slipped into her sleeping bag, tucking his thigh between hers, experiencing the full impact of her as he pressed closer, then eased.

"I could take you right here," he murmured, "and to hell with the consequences, I want you that much."

"I know." She kissed him all over his face, skimming his eyes, his nose, his lips, making him fiercely hungry for all of her. "But you don't want to."

Her honesty stilled his hands for a moment. "No," he whispered. "I don't want to. I don't want passion and need and wanting.'' He exhaled in defeat. ''But I want *you*.''

Under his hands, her thermals were silky smooth and fit her curves like skin. He stroked her back, her sides, her belly. He captured her small but perfect breasts and exhaled sharply as her nipples beaded under his caress and she pushed upward to meet his touch.

Sliding over her, feeling her legs open then close over his hips, he pressed into that enticing notch and heard her moan sweet and low with pleasure. He took the kiss deeper.

Wildly, they moved as one, sensation strong in spite of the clothing that kept them from complete contact.

At last he eased the kiss, that cautious, unwilling part of him knowing it was time to stop while they still had some control. Sex with this woman wouldn't be merely sex. He couldn't, wouldn't, make it more.

So, it had to stop. But gently. He'd started this. He had to end it without hurting her.

He kissed her in several gentle forays and let them come down from the peak. For a minute there was no sound but that of their labored breathing. Then he shifted to the side and rose. Guilt ate at him as he slid the cover over her heated body.

''I'm sorry. That was a…'' He tried to think of a word.

''Mistake,'' she supplied.

That honesty again. She was a woman who could face facts. "A mistake," he agreed, aware of the sexual gruffness in his tone that spoke of needs not quite met. He resented those needs. "Sleep. Tomorrow will be a long day."

To his surprise, she smiled. "I know."

He was once again aware of the courage in her, the sense of duty that drove her and the weary concern within her that was as haunting as the whispers of a lonely ghost.

Something shifted in him, a balance beam of emotion that had held steady for him these past two years. Grimly he settled in his bunk. He hadn't asked for this.

Alison woke before first light. Listening but not moving, she heard the woodstove door being opened and logs added. She peeked over the edge of her sleeping bag.

Travis was up.

Staring at his broad back, she relived the excitement of being in his arms. Then she remembered all the problems that awaited her with the coming of day. Fatigue assailed her, a weariness of mind more than body.

"Is it time to go?"

He swung around, his eyes catching the embers and the flames that had begun to leap along the fresh logs.

"Not yet. We'll eat, then head out when the sun is up." He left the cabin.

Swinging her legs into the chilly morning air, she rose and dressed, then packed up. Keith invited them to the ranch house. Janis had breakfast ready when they arrived.

"Are you leaving today?" she asked when the four were seated at an oak table that was carved and scrolled by an expert craftsman from long ago.

Alison met her sister's eyes, which were very much like her own. The wrench in her heart was painful, a reminder of the closeness that had once existed between them.

During the night, she'd said goodbye to the children they had been. Janis was a woman, intent on living her own life and capable of making her own decisions.

Alison thanked the couple for their hospitality. She offered to leave her cell phone with them.

"I'll have the phone line in before the end of the month," Keith assured her when Janis indicated she wouldn't accept the offer.

"I'll see that the ford at the creek is cleared," Travis promised. "If the logging road is good all the way to our place, that would be a shorter drive to the highway, in case you need to get to town."

"Thank you," Janis said, sounding sincere. "I'm sure we'll be fine."

Keith didn't look quite so certain. Alison saw him

exchange a glance with Travis, a telling communication between the two men that indicated an unspoken but shared thread of concern.

At last it was time to go. Donning her backpack when Travis did, Alison hesitated, then hugged her sister. Janis was stiff for a second, then she returned the hug.

"I'll be all right," she said.

"Shall I tell the parents of the situation?" Alison was compelled to ask.

"I'll call them," Janis said. "I promise. As soon as the phone line is installed."

Keith touched Alison's shoulder. "I'll see that she does."

Relieved, she nodded. "If you need anything, anything at all, please call. Janis has my cell-phone number."

"Ready?" Travis asked, standing apart from the tense family scene.

She fell into step behind him and only once did she look back. Janis and Keith walked them to the clearing, then stood arm in arm and watched as they left. There was a naturalness about the couple, as if they belonged to the rugged land and to each other.

Alison swallowed hard and faced the trail. She and her reluctant escort had miles to go before the day ended. He was keeping his distance from her. She could almost hear the buzz of an electric fence surrounding him.

Last night he'd overstepped his set boundaries. Today he was determined it wouldn't happen again. At least he didn't seem to blame her for the passion. Both knew it was a mutual thing. Her heart hammered as she recalled their kisses, then ached as she remembered his rejection.

For the next hour, they hiked steadily, down the smaller valley and into the larger one. The land began to rise as they hiked southward. To the west, she could hear the faint roar of the rapids as the Snake River plunged through the treacherous twists of the mountains on its journey to the ocean.

"We'll rest here," he said when they came to a fork in the path. "Eat some trail mix. You'll need the energy."

She propped her pack against a boulder, then sat on another one. She gazed at the scenery as she munched on the snack and tried not to worry about the future.

"Ready?" he asked.

"Yes." She slipped her arms through the straps on her pack and stood. "Didn't we miss the trail?" she wanted to know, gazing at the ridge high above them.

"No. This one joins the road that goes over the saddle and connects to our ranch. I think we can clear the weeds and get a pickup over to the Towbridge spread if we need to."

The worry returned. "I hate to leave."

He didn't reply.

"She could die, having a baby out here."

He ignored her concern.

"She's only twenty-one. Her life is just beginning."

"You're twenty-eight," he said. "Isn't it time you started living your own?"

At the harshness of his tone, she went totally still for a second, then she calmly agreed with him. When he indicated she should follow the ruts of an old logging road, she resumed the hike, her pace much faster.

"Steady," he said behind her.

She slowed somewhat, setting an even pace she could sustain. Another hour sped by. When he called for a second rest stop, she was grateful. Although this path was much easier than going over the ridge, it wasn't a stroll through the park, either. Sinking to a handy rock, she didn't remove her pack. She was too tired.

Travis handed her his water bottle. She gulped several swallows. He gave her a bag of trail mix, then drank deeply himself. The rest wasn't nearly long enough.

"Let's go," he said after five minutes.

She started uphill. When the trail flattened out at the top of the saddle, she spoke her thoughts aloud. "I don't know her anymore. I've fed her and diapered her and even spanked her once, but my little sister is gone. It's as if I've lost some part of myself when I wasn't looking."

Travis gave her an unreadable perusal when she glanced over her shoulder. "Maybe she just grew up."

She nodded and pressed forward. The road was clearer now, less overgrown with weeds down the center. A little later, it smoothed out into a one-lane track that had been surfaced with gravel. Travis moved up beside her.

"This is Seven Devils Ranch land," he said.

She heard the note of pride in his voice. "Your land?"

"Mostly my uncle's. My brother and I are buying into it. We own almost half now."

Forty minutes later, they rounded a bend and stood on a small rise. A lovely green valley spread before them like a feast. She could see a ranch house and outbuildings, pastures and enclosures. Cattle and horses grazed in the fields. The scene was so peaceful, it seemed surreal.

"Paradise," she murmured, the ache of an unknown grief returning briefly to haunt her.

"Home," he corrected.

Another part of her that she'd been totally sure about seemed to fall away as she followed him the last mile to the charming ranch set in the pristine meadow.

Travis knew he was in for trouble when he spotted the gleam in Uncle Nick's eyes. The old man ambled off the porch where he'd been reading the paper and met them in the center of the quadrangle that separated the house from the barn and stables. "Well, who have we here?" he asked.

"Uncle Nick, this is Alison Harvey." Travis made the introductions reluctantly, the darkness shifting inside while his mood became dangerous. "My uncle," he told Alison.

"Welcome to Seven Devils Ranch," Uncle Nick said, his gallantry putting Travis's teeth on edge. The old man still had an eye for the ladies.

He let himself look at his companion. The sun found the gold in her hair, the alabaster in her skin. Her smile was charming as she shook hands with his uncle. It didn't quite reach the depths of her eyes, though.

"Alison Harvey," Uncle Nick repeated. "Come sit on the porch. Would you like some coffee? Travis, take her backpack. We'll put her in the Rose Room."

Alison shot an alarmed glance in his direction.

"She's not staying," he told his bossy uncle.

Uncle Nick was having none of that. "Of course she is," he insisted. "Can't you see she's tired?" He chuckled as he guided Alison to the porch and nearly pushed her into a chair. "Here." He thrust her pack at Travis, then pulled another chair close and sat down.

Travis shrugged, then went inside, leaving her pack in the Rose Room that was reserved for guests and his own in his room located in the opposite wing of the house. Through the open windows, he could hear Alison speaking.

"The ranch is lovely," she was saying. "So peaceful."

"This is its best time of the year," Uncle Nick said with modest pride. "The grass is green and the trees are budding out. See those dogwoods and redbuds over there? Planted them myself more than thirty years ago."

"They're truly beautiful."

Travis had to give her credit. She sounded totally sincere with his uncle.

"So you're here to find your sister," Uncle Nick continued, changing the subject. "Did you succeed?"

Travis hurried to the rescue before his uncle could grill her in depth. "Janis is at the Towbridge place," he said, going onto the porch and closing the screen door behind him without letting it bang against the house. "The grandson, Keith Towbridge, is rebuilding the ranch."

He detailed the operation as told to him by Keith, including the war games and businessmen.

"Keith and his partner need cash flow," Alison added. "We didn't meet the partner. He's working on a lodge while Keith remodels the old ranch house."

"Which reminds me, I need Trevor to help me remove the boulders at the creek ford, then I thought we would open the back road between the two places,'' Travis finished the tale.

Uncle Nick gave him a shrewd glance. "Why?"

Travis tossed the conversational ball to Alison with a glance. She shook her head slightly. He raised his eyebrows at her, questioning her reticence.

"Why?" Uncle Nick repeated, his eyes on Alison.

Travis was surprised when she answered without evasion.

"My sister is living there. With Keith. She's seven months pregnant. There's no phone, no road to the house."

Uncle Nick looked shocked. "What's that young man thinking, taking his wife—"

"They aren't married," Alison interrupted. She spread her hands in a helpless gesture. "People don't think it's necessary these days."

"That's foolish," Uncle Nick said sternly. "Children need the sanctity of marriage. A family needs to be legal so everyone knows where they stand. These young people," he muttered in disgust, "they don't think about the future."

Travis had once believed that. Observing Alison nod in response to his uncle's declarations, he realized she still believed it. She wouldn't go for a casual affair.

Not that he wanted one, either. He wanted nothing to do with the woman who politely agreed with Uncle

Nick as he went on and on about the importance of marriage and stability within a family.

Travis had heard this lecture. He'd been spared the details after he and Julie had married. After her death, his uncle had never brought the subject up to him again, although his brothers and cousins still got their share of advice. For all his gruffness, Uncle Nick was a dreamer. He believed in "happily ever after."

Restless, Travis rose and headed across to the stable. "Is Trev out there?"

Uncle Nick nodded. "Dinner in about an hour. Don't go off," he ordered. "That's lunch to you city folk," he told Alison with a grin.

Travis didn't find his twin. The gelding they'd recently agreed to train as a riding horse for a neighbor was gone from the paddock. Fresh tracks indicated his twin had taken the horse out on the trail. Travis hesitated, then followed the path into the trees.

When he came to the unfinished house, set in its own woodsy clearing, he stopped. Slowly he crossed the new grass that had grown among the yellowed blades of last year's unmown lawn. Up the steps. Across the porch.

At the door, he willed the abyss to stillness as he turned the knob. The door swung open. The cold air rushed out to enclose him in a miasma of regret and grief.

He'd never understood why she'd been taken from

him, how one moment could be filled with happiness and the next…with nothing.

A faint echo of laughter stirred from the blackness as fate mocked the questions that had haunted him for two years. There were no answers, just life with all its cruelties as people went through meaningless rites.

Marriage. A demand of society. Birth. A demand of nature. He wanted nothing to do with either. Reaching inside the frigid-as-a-tomb house without stepping across the threshold, he closed the door and turned his back on all that it once had meant to him.

He hadn't cleared the steps when he heard hoof-beats on the trail. Trevor and the gelding loped into view. He pulled up. "Hey, bro," he called, his glance taking in the house.

Travis leaped from the porch and crossed the small yard. "How's he doing?"

Trevor patted the horse's neck. "Super. He's a natural. He'll make a great birthday present for the guy's wife. You want to try him out?"

"Not now. I, uh, need your help with something."

Trevor swung down from the saddle. "Shoot," he said.

"Alison Harvey is at the house—"

"Here?"

"Yeah."

"You found her sister?"

Travis nodded impatiently. "She's about seven months pregnant—"

"The sister?"

"Yes, the sister. Will you listen?" He explained about the Towbridge ranch and Keith's plans, including Janis's determination to have the baby at home. He ignored the quiet flash of sympathy in his twin's eyes at the mention of a baby. It wasn't something he was going to discuss. "Anyway, we need to make sure the ford at the creek is clear. Also, the back road could be fixed with a little grading and some gravel in the low spots in case the creek floods and makes the other road impassable."

"We'd better get on it," Trevor agreed. "I don't imagine Alison is very happy about the situation."

"She's worried, but short of kidnapping her sister, there's nothing she can do."

The helplessness. That had been the worst thing. Waiting in the hospital corridor while the doctors worked on his wife and knowing there was nothing he could do. He shoved the memory into the abyss.

"So you'll help with the road?" he finished.

"Sure. So will the rest of the family. And we can ask some guys from the neighboring ranches. Heck, we can put in a trestle bridge. Let's make a weekend out of it. Throw a big feed in, add Uncle Nick's cakes, and people will show up in droves."

He hadn't planned on anything that big, but Trevor was right. They could clear the ford in no time with help. The back road could be done in their spare time.

"Here. Ride back to the stable and see what you think of him," Trevor invited, holding out the reins.

Travis took him up on the offer. Mounted on the tall gelding, riding through the trees, he felt a return of the uncertain peace he maintained with an effort. He'd tell Alison the plans about the road. That would wipe the worry out of her eyes. She could return to her home. Then all would be well.

"Have you known my nephew long?"

Alison shook her head. Travis's uncle had been fishing for information from the moment the nephew had left them.

"He and I met last week rather unexpectedly." She explained her various attempts to get to the Towbridge ranch, making light of her forays into the wilderness, and was rewarded with chuckles from the old man.

"Here, pour up this pot of peas in that bowl and put it on the table," he said when she finished.

They were in the kitchen now, busy with the noon meal. The uncle had no qualms about putting her to work. She was grateful for the chores. It kept her from dwelling on her own problems.

"Travis is a good man," the uncle told her, giving her a shrewd glance from those heavenly blue eyes. "He's a little gun-shy with women. He's had heartbreak in his life, but he's steady as a rock."

She felt the need to clear up any question about Travis and herself. "Mr. Dalton—"

"Uncle Nick," he corrected. "Here."

When he thrust a wooden bowl filled with dinner rolls into her hands, she dutifully carried them to the table and returned. "Uncle Nick," she repeated. "Travis has been very kind in helping me find my sister, but I don't want you to…to think there's anything more."

"Don't you like him?"

"Well, yes. Of course. But—"

"You're the first woman he's looked at since his wife died. Actually the only one he's ever noticed since Julie. They were childhood sweethearts, you know. The boy's faithful. Once he gives his heart, it's forever."

"And now it's buried," she said softly, trying to be gentle because it was obvious the uncle cared deeply for the orphans who had been left in his charge.

The old man removed a roast from the oven and set it on top of the stove. "A part of him will always belong to her," he acknowledged. "He loved her with a boy's love. The man will learn to love in a different way. There'll be memories, but reality will fade until only a pleasant glow remains, the same way we recall our childhood delights."

"Can the present, with its day-to-day irritations, ever compete with those memories?" she questioned.

"Can an apple stay green and remain on the tree forever?" he retorted. "It isn't nature's way."

Giving her a disappointed frown, he moved the roast and potatoes to a huge platter and indicated she should take it to the table. She did so, beating a hasty retreat from his steely glare. Footsteps sounded on the porch. She heard Travis talking, then other voices joining in.

"Seduce him," the uncle advised as four men entered the living room and headed their way.

A jolt of shock sped along Alison's nerves. Upon meeting Travis's eyes, blood rushed to her head, making her dizzy.

Seduce him? This man who wanted nothing to do with her? This man who had resented her very presence in his mountain retreat? This man who had already loved and lost everything?

"Did you boys wash your hands?"

With nearly identical smiles—all filled with devilish amusement—the men lined up and held out their hands.

"Huh," their uncle snorted. "Travis, introduce your guest to the others, then take her to the table."

Alison resorted to the cordial smile of a politician's daughter, one that disclosed nothing of the turmoil inside.

"I'm happy to meet you," she said after Travis sorted out his twin, his older brother and his cousin

for her. "You're the deputy sheriff?" she said
to Zack.

He nodded.

"And you're the doctor?" she said to Beau.

"At your service." He executed a little bow and
held a chair out for her at the long dining-room table.

Uncle Nick sat at the end. She was on his right
with Travis beside her. Trevor, Zack and Beau sat
opposite them.

"Seth sits on the other side of Travis," Trevor explained, seeing her glance at the two empty chairs.
"Roni, our girl cousin, usually sits where you are."
She and Seth lived in Boise and usually came up on
weekends.

That left the end chair opposite their uncle unused,
she noted. She thought of Uncle Nick's wife, who had
died in a tragic accident, and their daughter, who was
lost.

"My wife sat there," Uncle Nick said, as if reading
her mind. "Tink was still in a high chair."

"I see," she murmured.

"Travis told us about your sister. We're going to
fix the washout at the ford first," Trevor told her.
"I'll call everyone and invite them out tomorrow to
help, then we'll have a cookout."

"You don't have to do that," she said. "I can arrange…that is, it's a county road—"

"Her father is the senator," Travis interrupted, his

tone cool and without inflection. "She can get things done."

A beat of silence followed.

"Yeah, but that would take forever. Besides, we want to do it," Trevor announced, putting an end to her protests.

Alison knew when to shut up. "That's very kind of you. I'll feel much better, knowing the road is open."

"Yeah," Trevor agreed. "With your sister expecting, it needs to be done."

"Right," the other two Daltons chimed in.

Alison cast a startled glance at Travis.

"I told them." He shrugged.

The five males didn't seem at all embarrassed by her sister's condition. Alison took a deep breath. The pregnancy was a fact of life, and therefore had to be dealt with.

Grim Reality 101. She would have to tell the parents right away…before they heard it on the evening news.

"Everything is fine, Mother." Alison put as much assurance into her tone as she possibly could. "No, Janis is fine. There's a slight problem with the phone line at the ranch. As soon as it's fixed, I'm sure she'll contact you. She seems to be enjoying ranch life."

No phone line at all was a slight problem? She

hoped her mother didn't question the evasions. She hated to outright lie about the situation.

Not mentioning the pregnancy was lying by omission, her conscience reminded her.

She ignored it.

"It's been well over a week since you left," her mother interrupted her worried thoughts.

Anger, quick and surprising, surfaced at her mother's impatience and implied criticism. Alison bit back a retort. "Yes, well, Janis prefers to stay at the ranch for now. Do you recall the Towbridge family?"

"There was a Dennis Towbridge who confronted your father in his early days in the senate about cattle prices."

"It's probably the same man. Keith is his grandson. He inherited the ranch and has decided to live there. Janis met him at college."

Okay, so she was putting a spin on how and where her sister and Keith met. She figured Janis needed all the help she could get.

"Is there something serious between Janis and the grandson?" her mother immediately asked.

"Only Janis can answer that," Alison said, respecting her sister's right to tell the parents whatever she wanted them to know. "How is Dad doing?"

"He's fine. He has a doctor's appointment Monday. Tell Janis to call as soon as possible. I have to run. Another boring luncheon of some committee."

Alison managed a sympathetic chuckle as she said

goodbye, then clicked off the cell phone and put it in her backpack. She knew her mother loved being part of the ''bigger picture,'' as she sometimes put it. Alison tried to see herself in that snapshot but couldn't.

She was suddenly tired of it all, tired and drained and infinitely sad.

Well, she had a right to be tired. She'd hiked more during the past ten days than she had the past ten years.

Sitting on the rose-patterned coverlet of the bed, she surveyed the pretty bedroom with its old-fashioned charm. Entering it had been like stepping into another era.

For a moment she sat there, her mind curiously blank, as if it, too, was tired of planning and scheming and always, *always,* considering the consequences.

A knock on the door sent her heart to her throat.

Chapter 8

"Uncle Nick says I'm to take you on a tour of the place," Trevor said when Alison opened the bedroom door. His grin was infectious.

She relaxed. "Did you draw straws and you lost?" she asked with mock sympathy.

"Heck, no. I had to arm wrestle Trav and Beau for the honor." He placed a hand over his heart to avow the truth of his statement. "Do you want to go or not?"

"That would be nice," she replied with grave formality.

Outnumbered by the Dalton gang during lunch, she'd agreed to spend the weekend at the ranch. Uncle Nick needed her help with the big cookout tomorrow night after the road repairs. Or so he said.

The final argument had been Trevor's promise that he and Travis would get with Keith and restring the telephone wires that had broken in a long-ago storm after Dennis Towbridge had died. Alison wanted to be sure the phone service was connected before she left the area.

She knew one person who would be glad to see her gone, she mused as she and Trevor ambled outside.

Travis had clammed up as the weekend plans had unfolded. If not for her duty to her family, she would have insisted on going back to the B&B that day.

She stole a glance at her handsome, easygoing companion as they walked down the front sidewalk to the road, then to the paddock where two horses chased each other along the fence. Had Travis once been as lighthearted as his twin?

Putting the question aside, she surveyed the ranch. A grand entrance formed the east side of the quadrangle defined by the ranch house, the barn and outbuildings and, to the west, an orchard enclosed in a white rail fence.

The entrance was outlined by a huge log that rested on two equally large ones. Carved into the wood was the name of the place and a date. Seven Devils Ranch, 1865. Nearby was a rail where cowboys had once tied up their horses.

Trevor leaned his arms on the top rail of the horse paddock. Alison followed suit.

"Your family has owned the ranch since 1865?" she asked, patting one of the horses who came to the fence to check them over.

"Yeah. They came West after the Civil War."

"From where?"

"Tennessee. There wasn't a ranch here then. It was all wilderness. The first Dalton had to cut a road and build a house. The living room and kitchen are part of that original home. It burned one time, but they were able to save most of the logs and repair it."

She gazed at the one-story ranch house that had a front porch and central section made of logs. Wings extended to either side of the log part. Limestone steps that looked as if they'd been there since Stonehenge days gave access to the porch and formed the threshold under the front door.

Alison stifled the envy that rose inside her. "It's nice to know your roots," she said sincerely.

"I figure your family goes back to the Pilgrims."

She laughed. "We mostly came from starving Irish immigrants, with an Italian farmer and an indentured servant thrown into the pot."

"Was it hard growing up as a senator's daughter?"

"Not really. Sometimes it was confusing to know which home my parents meant when they talked about going home. As a child, I lived most of the year in D.C., but spent holidays and summers with my grandparents when they were alive. Later, Janis and I stayed at the family home with the housekeeper and gardener when my parents had to stay at the capital.''

Beau came out of the house, waved to them, then drove off in an old pickup that had seen better days. An SUV with a sheriff's decal on the side was parked in the shade of an oak tree. Zack left in it a few minutes later.

Travis came out on the porch.

''I'm glad you came along,'' Trevor murmured. ''My brother needs to come out of his shell. He's grieved long enough.''

''You're mistaken if you think that has anything to do with me.''

''Don't let him scare you away.'' Trevor started for the stable. ''I have work to do. Get old Trav to take you for a ride up to the ridge. It's a great day for it.''

The twin walked off and left her standing by the paddock. She felt like a rabbit caught too far from its bolt-hole as Travis's laser gaze settled on her. She saw his chest lift and drop as if in a resigned sigh, then he strode purposefully across the distance between them.

''You want to go for a ride?'' he asked without cracking a smile.

Something perverse in her reared its head. ''I'd love it,'' she said in the same hard tone.

He saddled up the two horses in the paddock and they rode up a limestone ridge that overlooked the snug valley. A huge rock perched on top of the bluff, looking like a table for a giant. Another rock formed a stool beside it.

"The Devil's Dining Room," Travis told her. "That's what we named these two rocks when we first came here."

"It fits, but there's only one seat. Where will the He-devil sit?"

"You're assuming the She-devil gets the stool, but I've always thought of this as his favorite place."

His eyes followed the valley from mountain peak to mountain peak, his love of the ranch reflected in the azure depths. This was his solace, she realized. The ranch and the mountains gave him whatever peace he could find.

Odd, but it did the same for her. They finished the short ride in silence, then Travis left her at the house while he went to help with the chores.

"How come her folks sent a lone female to chase after her sister?" Uncle Nick wanted to know that evening.

Travis finished setting the table. "I suppose it was because they don't have any boys."

"Seems careless of them to me."

"Yeah."

"She's a pretty little thing, but kind of quiet."

Uncle Nick, Travis recalled, had been taciturn once, but with six kids asking "why this" and "why that'' during their first years on the ranch, he'd become more and more talkative. Now it was hard to shut him up when he was digging for something. Travis knew what the something was.

''She's not a candidate for marriage,'' he said bluntly.

''Huh. Who said she was? It would be more than any woman wanted to do to take on the likes of you boys.''

Uncle Nick figured the Dalton boys had let him down in the marrying-and-having-kids department. Maybe Seth would fulfill the old man's hopes in that direction since he was the oldest of the orphans.

''How old do you think Alison is?''

''She's my age. Table's ready,'' he said to distract the other man.

''You can't live in grief forever,'' Uncle Nick said, determined to have his say.

Travis held emotion at bay while the abyss roiled within him. He was done with male-female stuff, with loving and longing and thinking life was his to command. ''I'm not.''

''When a man is offered a second chance, he ought to grab it with both hands.'' Uncle Nick removed rolls from the oven and put them in a wooden bowl lined with a napkin.

''Right,'' Travis said with savage control. ''The way you did after Aunt Milly died.''

His uncle paused, his eyes on the distant peaks visible from the window. "Love came late in life for me. It was a lovely gift, totally unexpected. For some, lightning doesn't strike twice."

Travis ignored the pain in the old man's voice even as its echo reverberated through the lonely corridors of his soul. Love was a gift made all the more cruel by being taken away. He sought the bitterness that made the loss bearable.

"It's a lonely life for a man without a woman by his side. You'll regret it when you get to be my age."

He gave his uncle a cold stare. "More than you regret the loss of your wife and child?"

"No," the older man murmured, "that's the worst pain, but a man regrets the things he didn't do, not the things he did, especially those that brought him happiness. You and Julie were happy, weren't you?"

Blue eyes met blue eyes. Travis saw the challenge in his uncle's unrelenting gaze. "You know we were," he said, his voice going hoarse, desperate as the old anguish rose once again and pressed hard against his breastbone. He didn't want to talk about this.

"Life does go on," Uncle Nick said as if to console him for all that had been taken away.

"Yeah. Tell me about it," Travis replied.

From the living room came a burst of laughter. Trevor and Alison played a battle-strategy game. Apparently she was winning.

"Tell them supper is ready," his uncle said, heading for the table with the last items.

Travis went into the living room and paused at the doorway to observe the couple who were having so much fun. He couldn't remember the last time he'd laughed like that with another person. As a memory surfaced, he quickly suppressed it. The remembrance of happy times hurt worst of all.

"She's an expert at this," Trevor grumbled, seeing him standing there watching them. He hunched over the board and concentrated on his next move.

"Dinner is ready," Travis told them. He'd heard Alison laugh several times during the game with his twin. Their merriment irritated him, and he considered punching out his brother for no reason other than his own grouchiness.

"Your house is wonderful," Alison told Uncle Nick after the four of them were seated at the table.

"The boys built most of it," his uncle said with obvious pride. "I added a couple of bedrooms when they first came here, but they redid the kitchen and the master bedroom, then added a new wing a few years ago. The living room used to be four rooms, but they took the walls out and put in bookcases and a TV. Paid for it themselves."

"I suspect Seth paid for most of it," Trevor put in. "He's the only male in this family who can hang on to a dollar long enough to get it to the bank."

"I read an article on how many people are in the

stock market these days," Alison mentioned. "You'd think everyone was a billionaire, but most of them have less than ten thousand dollars invested."

"Hey, you know a lot about finance?" the twin asked.

Alison shook her head. "Actually, I have a teaching degree for business and accounting. Of course, I only taught a year before my father asked me to run his local office while he and Mother were in Washington. He found it impossible to get someone he could trust, he said."

She stopped as she realized this sounded as if she was bragging. People who showed off were annoying.

"A family ought to help each other," Uncle Nick said in approving tones.

Alison relaxed under the old man's watchful eye as he urged her to eat up and put some meat on her bones. The food was plentiful and delicious. A plate of hot corn bread completed the meal.

After offering to help with the dishes and being told it was Trevor's turn to clean up, she went into the living room where Travis flicked through the news channels.

Sitting in a leather chair with a crocheted afghan folded neatly across its back, she imagined a fire in the huge fireplace and snow outside. The family would gather here and read or play games. The television—there was one on a shelf of the built-in bookcases—would be tuned in to a football game, but the sound would be muted.

"It's peaceful here," she began, then stopped.

Was she implying her home wasn't peaceful? She lived alone most of the time in the house her parents maintained in the state. Naturally. They had to stay in Washington.

The housekeeper and her husband, the gardener, lived above the garage, though, so it wasn't as if she were completely alone.

There were always social functions to attend, too. And fund-raisers. She was often asked to give speeches for her father, to women's groups usually. It was a full life.

Travis glanced her way, but didn't comment.

Flames leaped in her, but his eyes were the color of distant glaciers. "All of you have the bluest eyes," she murmured, hardly aware of speaking.

Trevor entered the room. "A family trait in all the Daltons, except Seth. His mother was Native American and he got her brown eyes. Our father and uncle, another set of twins, had blue eyes. They were six years younger than Uncle Nick."

"You were lucky to have him when...when you needed someone."

Trevor nodded. "He'll soon be seventy, but I'd swear he's as strong as he was at fifty. However, he had a heart attack a few weeks ago. He's supposed to take care of himself, but he worries about us. He thinks it's his job to get us married off before he kicks the bucket.''

His soft laughter touched a chord inside her and set it to vibrating. Her life had been too busy to consider marriage very often.

Doing what?

Working. Planning dinners and fund drives, answering questions and solving problems for constituents. Important things. Truly, they were. They just seemed rather distant because of other, more pressing problems at the moment.

Sighing, she let the peace of the ranch steal over her spirits. She and Trevor played two more games before bedtime while the other two men watched a documentary about water shortages in California and Florida.

Going to the pretty Rose Room, her mind filled with scenes of family life, idealistic, romantic pictures right out of Currier and Ives, with her as the centerpiece.

Right. The perfect calendar heroine, that was her.

Saturday dawned bright and sunny. The morning was spent in chores on the ranch, but after a quick lunch, Alison and the twins headed for the ford where the road was washed out and where her car was parked. It hadn't once occurred to her that it might be stolen.

Her faith was justified. The car was still there,

along with Travis's truck. Four other men, ranging in age from an eighteen-year-old to his father, who was in his forties, to two old school chums of the twins, were there.

They discussed the job, then unloaded a small tractor from the trailer behind the father's truck. With the backhoe, they stacked earth and boulders securely on each side of the creek, forming a foundation.

To her surprise, a county truck appeared at midafternoon. The driver delivered two long trestles that fit perfectly on the foundation piers. "The boss says thanks for taking care of the ford. It was on our list but we had several washouts this year."

"No problem," Trevor assured the man. He explained that the Towbridge ranch had people living there again and that the road was needed. After the driver left, the workers took a break. Uncle Nick had sent cookies and sodas for them.

"Now," Trevor informed her, "if Zack will get here with the lumber, we'll have this job done."

They had hardly finished eating the last of the homemade cookies when an SUV belonging to the sheriff's department arrived. This time the driver was Zack.

"Hey, looks as if you guys need wood. The sheriff says he doesn't know anything about a delivery of lumber in a department vehicle and he doesn't want to." The older Dalton brother gave them a big grin.

"He won't hear it from me," Trevor vowed, hand

on his heart. "Let's get on with it. Uncle Nick said the steaks would be ready at seven sharp."

After the cruiser was unloaded, the deputy left. With renewed energy, the men anchored the trestles, built access ramps at either end, again of packed earth and stone, then nailed two-by-four boards across the trestles.

Alison was relieved at this latter work. She'd been worried that Janis and Keith would have to drive across the trestles, keeping the tires centered on the twelve-inch-wide square logs. With the cross planks, they wouldn't have to be so precise in guiding the vehicle.

Shadows were beginning to grow long when they finished the last boards, the two work crews meeting in the middle of the bridge. Alison stretched her back. She and the older man had kept busy supplying boards to the men.

"Here," Travis said, nearly his first words of the afternoon. He handed his hammer to her. "You can nail the last one in place."

She whacked the thick nails until they were securely seated in the wood. "I feel like a VIP driving the last spike in the cross-country railroad."

"Only it was gold." Travis stored the hammer in a toolbox in the back of the ranch truck. "I think we're ready to head in."

They loaded the tractor, then formed a caravan with Trevor leading the way, her second in her car, Travis next and the neighboring ranchers last. They arrived at the Dalton place right on time. True to his word, Uncle Nick had the steaks ready when they arrived. A table on the porch was loaded with chips, baked beans, potato salad and every kind of pickle and pepper she could imagine.

Zack drove up fifteen minutes later. "Look who I found on the side of the road," he called.

With him was an older woman with ash-blond hair who turned out to be a rancher's wife and mother to the young man who had helped build the bridge. Connie Steadman also taught at the county high school.

"Uncle Nick left a message that I was to come over and have supper. I had a flat tire less than fifty feet from the house, so I called the sheriff's department to see where Zack was," Connie said, taking a seat beside her at the table. "I'm happy to meet you, Alison. Did the men get all the work done today?"

"We did," Trevor declared. "We're thinking of starting our own construction company."

"Dream on," Connie told them. "A few days of laying a road in ninety-degree heat will cure that notion. Thank goodness, we didn't go to that year-round school plan the board was considering. I want my summers free."

Alison liked the down-to-earth teacher. "I have my teaching credentials," she confided. "I only did it for a year but thought it was fun and fulfilling."

Connie's eyes lit up. "What subjects?"

"English and business."

"They need teachers at the high school. You should apply now for next year. With your credentials, you could teach accounting or any business course."

"Oh, well, I really can't. I have a job." She explained about managing her father's Boise office.

"That must be exciting," Connie said, a thoughtful look in her eyes.

"It's…" She stopped before she said "difficult." She didn't want to sound like a whiner. "It has its moments," she finished with a smile.

The meal was a happy, boisterous occasion filled with teasing remarks about the workday. Trevor sat on the other side of Alison and kept her entertained.

She was completely at ease with him and delighted in his tales of woe, mostly caused by Connie and her fellow teachers, to hear him tell it.

Once, laughing, her eyes met those of Travis. They observed each other for a minute. Her heart began a slow, heavy beat and she was overcome with longing so intense it was painful. In that instant she knew what she wanted.

Him. As a lover. As her love.

His eyes darkened to smoldering indigo as if he read her deepest thoughts, as if he could see the longing and with it, the desire that burned bright as a new star within her. She blinked and looked away, the odd loneliness of late gathering and dimming the pleasant ambience of the cookout.

Travis Dalton wasn't for her. His heart was locked in stone as hard as the rock that formed He-Devil Mountain.

After the neighbors left, with many expressions of gratitude on her part for their help, Alison helped with the dishes. Zack headed back to town. Trevor also left to meet a couple of friends. Uncle Nick went to his room for some peace and quiet shortly after. She and Travis were left to themselves. He turned on the TV and channel surfed.

"I didn't realize a bridge could be built so fast," she said during a commercial. "Is it temporary or will it hold up to the weather for a long time?"

"It'll hold. That's why we brought the tractor out to pack the base. If the creek floods, Keith might have to make repairs. If he pursues the dude ranch idea, he may have to get the county to put in a steel frame someday."

"I see." She drummed her fingers on the chair arm. "With the phone line in, they'll be all set."

"Yeah." He flicked her a glance, then went back to surfing. "You can write up a report for your folks, then stop worrying."

"Except for the baby."

A subtle change came over him, a hardening of his features that indicated he wasn't going to discuss the child and any problems associated with it.

"It's a boy," she continued. "It seems so odd, Janny having a baby—"

He rose, spun on one foot and, bending, laid his hands on the leather arms of the chair. Surrounded by his male aura, aware of the fury in him, she waited in silence for him to speak.

"I don't want to hear about your sister and her baby," he said in a low, grating voice. "It's their problem, hers and Keith's. Let them deal with it. If they're stupid enough to live in a wilderness—"

He stopped abruptly.

"Sorry, it's none of my business," he finally muttered. Spinning about, he walked out of the house, the door slamming softly but solidly behind him.

Alison released the breath she held and with it, the pity she couldn't express. The young couple and the baby reminded him of all he'd lost. Two years ago he must have been a lot like them, sure of his life and the future.

After switching off the television, she went to the bedroom and looked through a photo album before turning out the light and settling down to sleep. The wind whispered mournfully around the house. She didn't hear Travis return before drifting off.

Chapter 9

Alison was alone in the house when she awoke. A note in the kitchen informed her that Uncle Nick and Trevor had gone to church. She wondered where Travis was. After eating a bowl of cereal, she donned her jacket and went outside.

Travis was in the paddock, riding the gelding she'd seen the previous day. From the porch, she watched him put the horse through its paces with a calm, sure touch. He didn't glance her way. When he dismounted and led the gelding into the stable, she headed toward an opening through the woods.

Yesterday she'd spied a roof among the trees. She ambled along the shaded path. Birds chirruped in happy voices all around her. Like Keith and Janis, they were busy with nests, preparing for their new broods.

She felt left out, as if all the magic of nature had passed her by. Travis Dalton wasn't *her* Prince Charming, so there would be no rites of spring for them. She managed a smile and refused to feel sorry for herself even as the intense longing surged through her.

Coming into a clearing, she stopped to peruse the house she found there. It was obviously a home, unfinished and unoccupied. She knew instinctively whose it was.

For a long time, she studied the structure, noting its clean architectural lines, the native stone on the bottom half, the cedar shingles on the top. A massive stone chimney anchored it to the ground. There were lots of windows to let in the light and frame the breathtaking views of the mountains and the sweep of the valley.

Without conscious direction, she walked across the new spring grass of the unkempt lawn and onto the porch. At the door, she paused with her hand on the knob. She feared to enter, but she knew she was going to, no matter how much it hurt to see the house Travis had built for his beloved.

With a slow turn of her wrist, the door opened and swung back on its hinges. A chill rushed out to greet her, as if the house had stored the frigid air for a long time and was eager to expel it.

With silent steps, she entered as one enters an ancient tomb, sensing its mystery deep in her bones. She could almost hear the laughter of happier days echoing through the great room and kitchen, the four bedrooms. The house had been planned for a family.

In her mind's eye, she could see them—blue-eyed boys and girls, towheaded when young as the pictures in the family album showed, their hair darkening as they grew up to take their place in the Dalton clan.

In the large kitchen, she leaned against the counter and gazed out the window at the perfect picture of woods and mountains. One by one, she erased the scenes of family life from her inner vision.

This would never be her home. Her husband would never burst through that door and swing her off her feet and kiss her breathless. She would never know the bliss of complete love and happiness acted out within these walls.

The laughter of imagined children slowly faded until there was no sound but the buzzing of a fly beating itself senseless against the window.

Those children would never be born. They wouldn't be Travis's children. His children would never be hers.

She didn't turn when footsteps sounded on the wood flooring and stopped at the archway into the kitchen.

"You here for the grand tour?" a familiar male

baritone inquired, his tone shaded with sarcasm, anger and other emotions she couldn't read.

With masochistic calm, she asked, "This was the house you were building for Julie and your child?"

"Yes."

"It has the makings of a lovely home. She must have loved watching it take shape under your hands."

He made her nervous, standing there without moving, his eyes like a void, as if his soul had gone away to a place neither he nor she could reach.

"I'm sorry for invading your space," she told him. "I saw the roof from the ridge earlier and wondered about it."

The hopelessness of loving one such as him rose starkly to taunt her. But it was too late. She'd already fallen.

"Have you seen all of it?" he asked, so polite it set her teeth on edge.

"No," she lied.

He gestured for her to come with him. He then proceeded to take her from room to room, explaining the function of each as they entered, giving her an overview of the house.

"The firewood will be stored here." Travis opened a metal door next to the fireplace in the living room. "Outside, there are other doors so you can clean out ashes or replenish the logs from the storage shed I'd planned to build when the house was done."

"I see."

She was uneasy. He could tell that by her silence and the self-contained way she followed him. He didn't care. He wanted her to be apprehensive, to pay for her meddling.

He hadn't been inside this house for two years. It was the symbol of his failure as a husband. Alison should suffer for forcing him to it. He led her through the house with calculated coldness, refusing to feel anything.

"The mantel was rescued from an old house being demolished in town to make way for the new grocery. Julie liked old things like that. She refinished it, crafting the moldings with wood putty where they were broken or missing."

Alison admired the work. "She must have been very good with her hands."

"Yes, she was." He remembered soft, feminine hands touching him, stroking and exploring with an eagerness that filled him with the sweetest longing and an exquisite gentleness—

Alison pushed a tendril of hair behind her ear, and he realized he'd been staring at her hands, that it was her touch he was recalling. He blinked in confusion, then doggedly continued with the tour from hell.

Taking her arm, he led the way down the hall. "The master bedroom is back here, near the other bedrooms so we could hear the children if they woke during the night."

He was pleased at the passivity of his voice. He

could almost believe he felt nothing. Stopping in the master bedroom, he pointed out the bathroom, the closets, the window seat with the built-in bookcases. The skeletal walls—wood frames without the wall-board—didn't bother him at all.

"The bedroom is on the east," he continued. "Julie wanted the light. She was a morning person and loved to watch the dawn brighten the sky."

His guest nodded. "So do I," she said.

Some part of him that watched them from a distance noted the slight quiver in her voice. He hardened himself against it. He cared for nothing.

Guiding her through the other bedrooms, the office where he'd planned to put all the ranch records on computer and the mudroom off the kitchen, which included the laundry, he told her every plan for every room, every dream he and Julie had constructed as they put each beam into place.

Finally it was done. He led the way outside through the mudroom door and around the house to the front.

"This was to be the rose garden," he added. "Julie loved roses—"

Alison rounded on him. "Stop it! Just stop it!" she said, then put her hands over her face and turned her back to him.

He stood there, unable to move. "It's just a house," he told her, edgy now that he'd pushed her beyond the brittle composure she was so good at. He realized he'd wanted to do that from the moment he'd seen the open door and realized she was inside. He'd wanted her to hurt… God, what was wrong with him?

"A house built of dreams," she murmured, her voice husky in a way that sent ripples along his spine.

"Dreams only half realized before they were destroyed." He laughed cynically. "The house is wood and stone. Whatever it represented at one time no longer exists."

He thrust his hand into his pocket before he did something really stupid like reach for Alison. For some reason, the visions kept getting all mixed up between the past and the present.

The sun, filtered through a hazy cloud, came out full force. Standing in the overgrown grass, looking like a wildflower in tan slacks, a pink T-shirt and nylon jacket, his companion rubbed her hands over her face, sniffed, then faced him.

He didn't like the ravaged despair he saw in her gaze or the effort it took for her to meet his eyes. He didn't like himself very much, either.

"It's okay to grieve," she told him. "It's not okay to pretend dreams don't matter."

She bent and picked the flower from a columbine, studying it as if looking for clues to one of the great mysteries of nature. The sun spun gold into her blond-brown hair as the breeze tossed it this way and that. The hunger, ever present of late, filled him with needs long denied.

"Julie wouldn't like that," she finished softly.

The abyss plunged and heaved. A wave of blackness rose from it, choking him with its bitterness, flaming like brimstone straight from the hell that consumed him.

With two steps, he was by her side. He grasped her shoulders, forcing his hands to a gentleness he was far from feeling. He wanted to hurt, to strike back. "What do you, the remote, always calculating politician's daughter, know of someone like Julie?"

Her gaze was steady. "Nothing. Why don't you tell me."

The wind gusted around them and golden strands of hair blew across her face. For a second, for a terrible, terrible instant between two heartbeats, he saw another face, another pair of eyes, watching him with gentle pity—

Hearing a rustle in the clearing, he jerked his head toward the sound. A deer stood at attention at the edge of the woods, her gaze on them as if she'd just noticed the humans in her domain. Her ears twitched once, then she bounded away and out of sight.

Alison studied him, and her eyes were like those of the doe, big and soft. Sorrowful. Hurting. For him. And because of him. He didn't like causing that look. He didn't like the guilt he felt over it, either.

"Damn you," he muttered. "Why did you ever have to show up here?"

"My family," Alison began, then faltered as his touch changed, becoming gentler although he hadn't hurt her when he'd clasped her arms. His thumbs stroked her skin through the nylon jacket in an unconscious caress.

Or maybe it wasn't unconscious. A shaky breath escaped from her parted lips. His eyes went to her mouth. She almost moaned aloud when he moistened his lips.

A sense of danger became interwoven with the excitement of being near him. Her body responded eagerly, wantonly. She wanted him, desperately wanted him. It was a passion unlike any she'd ever felt.

She suddenly didn't care what was right or wrong, if they were being foolish or not. She was tired of trying to always do the right thing, of being responsible and sensible, hemmed in by loyalty and duties she resented. Yes, she resented them, she admitted, and it was like a weight being tossed aside.

Like his house, her dreams were only half-finished. She now knew what she needed to complete them.

Him.

"Alison," he said, just her name.

He said it in a raspy, shaken voice that brought all her senses to an acute edge. Tremors formed, eddied, rushed away to some far haven inside her soul.

Her name, not Julie's.

"Kiss me," she whispered, needing that from him.

He did. Thoroughly, but not gently this time. Wildly, but not callously. A shudder went through him, then he drew her closer until they touched everywhere.

There was no resisting the temptation. In his embrace she discovered the fulfillment of all her hopes.

When he slipped his hands under her T-shirt, it seemed natural to do the same to him. She loved the smooth feel of his flesh—the warmth and strength of sinewy muscles that flexed under his skin. She loved the way his taller, broader frame seemed to shelter her.

''Need to see you,'' he muttered, desperation in the words as anger faded and desire took its place.

She nodded, unable to resist the passion that raged between them. He carried her to the porch and peeled the jacket, then the top from her. Bending, he gathered her close and laid a trail of kisses down her chest to her modest white bra.

She wished she wore lace, then realized it made no difference. She'd never felt so feminine, so desirable, as she did at this moment.

He nibbled the tip of her breast, visible as a hard pebble of desire under the material.

Laying her cheek on his head, she inhaled the shampoo cleanliness of his hair and the aftershave he'd splashed on that morning. She thought of their nights together in the woods and marveled that they hadn't made love.

''I've never known passion could be like this,'' she

told him, burying her fingers in the neatly cut strands. "It almost hurts."

"Yes." He drew back, his eyes so dark, they reminded her of blue-black ink. "The call of nature is strong."

"Overpowering." She wondered if she should confess that much. "Very close to it," she amended.

"I wanted you from the first day I saw you hiking up the mountain. The mysterious lady of the woods," he named her, reminding her of their first meeting.

"Not that first day," she protested breathlessly.

"Yes. You tempt me more than any woman I've ever met. Why?"

It wasn't a question she could answer. His gaze roamed moodily over her as he caressed her breasts, cupping them and rubbing the sensitive tips. Little electrical currents spiraled down inside her, joining the other feelings that he incited with his masterful touch.

She wished she could have been his first love, that they could be starting on this wonderful adventure now, with no past. But that could never be.

Never, echoed the wind as it blew across them.

"You're so gentle," she murmured, pressing her hands over his and fighting the sadness that haunted her.

"I don't want to hurt you." He brushed a kiss over her lips. "But it could happen. I can be...cruel."

He sighed, stirring the hair at her temple. She wished he would kiss her again.

"You confuse me. With you, I think of things I put aside long ago."

"What things?"

"Impossible ones." His smile was harsh. "Things that can never be. But I want them. And I want *you*."

"Yes," she whispered. "You're the one thing I needed. I didn't understand before, didn't know what it was."

She now knew why she hadn't been able to marry her high-school steady or the ambitious young lawyer. It wasn't their love that was at fault. It was her own. She'd never felt the emotion for anyone else that she now experienced for this man, this one person who spoke to her heart.

"You make me weak," he said, stroking along her throat. "You're like alabaster and stardust, radiant from within, and I have to touch you."

He ran his hands over her sides and down to her waist. He stroked her thighs and parted them. Stepping forward, he thrust gently against her. With a groan, he stripped his shirt and her bra away, so they could touch flesh to flesh.

When he pressed, she lay back on the warm planks of the porch, his body melded with hers as they half lay there in the sun. He began a slow, rhythmic movement.

Fire flowed through her veins, and she no longer

was made of flesh and blood, but only of something not of this earth. As in a magical dance, she moved with him, her hips rising to the fall of his, meeting each sensual demand. The need for fulfillment made her cry out.

"Take it," he said in a ragged tone. "Take all you want. I want to feel you shake...the way I'm shaking."

She rubbed down his back and slipped her hands under his waistband until she could feel the straining muscles there as he thrust again and again. "Please. Oh, please."

Raspy cries escaped her as he took them higher and higher on passion's wings. His lips devoured hers for endless moments, then he moved to her breasts and suckled until she writhed in helpless wonder.

"It's never been like this. I've never wanted to beg," she told him desperately. "But I want more."

"Good, darling. I'll see that it's there for you."

He moved away enough to unfasten her slacks. When he stroked her intimately, every muscle in her body clenched as ecstasy rolled over her, wave after wave of pure ecstasy.

She tugged at his jeans. "Come to me."

"Can't," he said, panting heavily now. "I don't have protection."

A moan of frustration slipped from her. Then she caught her breath as he moved against her again, harder, faster, pushing her on...and on...

"But we can have this," he murmured and took her mouth in a raging kiss as their bodies strained and tensed and flexed with increasing need.

"Ohh," she cried as sweet fulfillment crashed over her. "Travis, oh, darling, yes. Yes. Yes. Yes."

He brought one thigh up over hers and pressed hard, barely moving now. She felt the ripple of his body, heard him stop breathing for a minute, then felt the long, shuddering release of his breath just before he relaxed against her.

She stroked his back and once again felt the wash of sunlight over them and heard the wind ruffling the trees.

A faint drone reached her through the wonderful lethargy. He tilted his head, listening.

"Someone's coming," he told her and pushed himself upright. He slipped his shirt on.

His eyes were dark with thoughts and feelings she couldn't read. He found her bra and quickly fastened it around her, then helped her with her T-shirt.

"I'm sorry," he began, then hesitated. "I didn't mean to do that, to go that far."

She felt the terrible hopelessness of a love that could not thrive. He wanted her, he would share his body, but his heart wasn't part of the bargain.

Tears rose from some deep well of grief, but she forced them aside. She hadn't come to the mountains expecting to find happiness, so there was no need to cry over what wasn't to be. She brushed his hair into order with fingers that trembled. "There," she said.

From the ranch house, the wind carried voices to them. Uncle Nick and Trevor had returned.

"Travis," his twin called.

"Yo," he answered. He sighed, then left her after one more searching glance.

After smoothing her hair and giving herself a second to completely regain her composure, she joined the men at the other house. They were already planning the task of checking and repairing the telephone wire to the Towbridge place.

"Why didn't the phone company repair it when it broke?" she asked.

"Ranchers have to string their own lines when they live off the public road or pay someone to do it," Trevor explained. "We have a spare reel on hand to make repairs, so we should be able to handle it."

"I can arrange for someone to come out," she told him. "You're taking time away from your ranch chores."

"Neighbors help out," Uncle Nick said firmly.

That ended her argument, although she was still concerned at involving them in her problems. "Thank you," she said warmly. "Since there seems to be nothing further I can do, I thought I should start home. To Boise. I can be there in a couple of hours if I leave now."

No one said anything for a moment, then Uncle Nick nodded. "If you need to go, then you should."

"I really do. I've been gone long enough."

Long enough to lose her heart, long enough to be hurt by an apology he felt he had to give. For the rest of the time she was there, she smiled and smiled until her face hurt with the effort.

Miss Braveheart. She should get a medal.

"But you'll come back for my birthday, won't you?" Uncle Nick asked. "It's on a Saturday. June eighth."

Alison didn't make any promises. It was time to go home and take up where she'd left off before that hurried trip to the Seven Devils Mountains.

"Goodbye," she said to the twins after giving the older man a hug. To Travis, she added, "Thanks for your help in locating my errant sister." She didn't look into his eyes.

"Rescuing fair damsels is our greatest calling," Trevor grandly informed her when Travis only nodded.

"Take care," Travis said, surprising her.

"Yes. Yes, I will." She hoped the other two didn't notice how flustered she became at his slight smile and the regret in his eyes, as if he apologized again for the way things were between them and the fact that he didn't, couldn't, love her.

The three men walked her outside and saw her off. She looked back and waved just before the ranch house was out of sight. Turning toward the open road, she let her gaze sweep over the soaring peaks around them. Her days of roaming through the hills and learning to be a mountain woman were at an end. She would always remember it.

However, she was returning to her rightful place, and it wasn't in this valley…or his arms.

She'd known that fact since the first night she'd slept, safe and secure, in his tent. The emptiness she'd felt of late returned with a *thud*.

Back to Grim Reality 101. Travis, while attracted to her, would never risk his heart again. He'd been too much in love the first time, too hurt by that loss.

Besides, he thought she didn't belong here. She forced herself to accept that he was probably right. It was just that she didn't feel she belonged anywhere.

Yeah, right. Poor little orphan.

She swallowed hard when she passed the city limits sign of the little town. The ache she felt was inside her. With time, she assured herself, it would heal. She turned south on Highway 55, which would take her home.

Today was Sunday, the twenty-sixth. Nearly two weeks ago, she'd arrived in town intending to find her sister and bring her home. She'd expected to be there for two days, three at the most. Instead, she'd stayed twelve.

A lot could happen to a person in that length of

time. One could meet new people. Make friends. Fall in love. Be wild and foolish and miserable and happy.

One could live a lifetime, all in the space of a heartbeat.

As she'd expected, Alison found her parents in residence at their family home when she arrived.

"Finally you're home," her mother said, returning her hug. "I'm disappointed that Janis didn't come with you."

The familiar undertone of censure grated on Alison's nerves. She went to her father. "How are you?" she asked, worried that he was worse than he appeared.

"Fine, sweetheart. How was your trip?"

"Fine." She realized how silly that sounded in light of all that had happened.

"Your mother and I are eager to hear the details."

Alison told them of the charming town and Amelia at the bed-and-breakfast inn, about the mountain treks she'd attempted and the rescues. She described the Dalton ranch and finished with Uncle Nick and his heroic efforts to raise six kids on his own.

She added her adventure with Merv and Harry and the war games. Finally she explained about Keith's plans for his grandfather's ranch. "Janis is helping. She was actually cooking over an open fire when I arrived."

Alison saw her parents exchange glances. Nothing

would please them more than for their children to settle down with a young man from a good family. She wondered if Keith would qualify, although he didn't take part in politics.

Biting off the cynical thought, she ended the tale with a description of the Towbridge place and the repair of the creek ford by the Daltons, plus their intention of helping with the telephone line.

"They're good neighbors," her father said in approval.

"Janis promised to call as soon as the phone is working," Alison told them.

Her mother huffed in annoyance. "What happened to her cell phone?"

"Uh, she felt it was too much of an expense."

"What about college? When is she going back? She'll have to catch up on her work—"

"She isn't going back," Alison interrupted, feeling defensive on her sister's behalf. "She and Keith are, uh, in love. I think they might marry soon."

There was a beat of silence.

"What?" her mother snapped.

"She'll tell you all about it when she calls." Alison turned to her father. "When do you go to the hospital?"

He was plainly puzzled. "For what?"

"For the surgery."

"It can be done as an outpatient procedure," her mother said.

Alison was astounded. "A tumor at the base of the skull can be done without a stay in the hospital?"

"What are you talking about?" her father asked.

"The tumor," Alison said. "The one at the base of your skull. Isn't it being removed Friday?"

The elder Harvey appeared puzzled. "I'm having a mole taken off the back of my neck Friday. In the doctor's office. I won't be put to sleep or anything like that. It isn't even surgery. He'll zap it with a laser, and I'll be out in fifteen minutes."

"Oh." Alison looked at her mother.

"It could have been serious," the older woman said.

The senator chuckled. "Was that the story you used to bring Janis home? Nothing stops her once she's set on having her way."

Alison felt the sharp nip of betrayal as she realized their mother had exaggerated the situation for her own reasons, laying a guilt trip on the siblings, as Janis had guessed. Her father, blind to his wife's machinations, thought it amusing. She didn't.

Something that had been brewing in her—for a long time, she now realized—burst forth. "I have some news, too," she said, speaking to her father. "I'm resigning as your office manager. You have three other people there, any one of whom can run the place effectively."

"You can't do that," her mother protested. "Your father needs you. You know our plans for the future."

"Your plans," Alison said softly. "Your future. They aren't mine. I'm sorry, Father, but I don't want to be involved in your campaigns and political life."

The senator, looking concerned, motioned his wife to silence. "What are your plans? Do you want to go back to teaching?"

"Maybe," she said. "Maybe I'll travel for a while. Or move to California."

This last statement was a ploy to throw her family off track. She honestly didn't know at the moment where her future might lie, but a name pinged in her heart. *Seven Devils,* it whispered mischievously to her.

Her father peered at her intently. "Did something else happen on this trip that we haven't heard about?"

Alison wondered what they would say if she told them she'd fallen in love with a rancher, one who would have agreed with them about where her place was.

"This is ridiculous," her mother declared. "You can't leave when your father needs you the most."

The senator held up a hand. "Wait a minute, Virginia." He looked at Alison. "You've thought this through? You're sure this is what you want?"

She shrugged, then smiled. "I don't know what I want, only what I *don't* want. I think it's time I explored the possibilities a bit more."

Thinking of those possibilities brought a surge of

trepidation…and excitement. Suddenly a whole future of possible scenarios rushed through her mind.

"Then it's settled," her father said.

"This…this delayed rebellion is irresponsible in the extreme," her mother declared indignantly.

"It's time," Alison said quietly. "Janis and I have our own dreams to fulfill."

Alison smiled at the sense of unity with her sibling. She realized her little sister didn't need her to watch out for her anymore. Alison had tried to be the family she'd thought a child needed, but Janis was on her own now, so *she* was free to go, too.

It was an odd sensation, like dropping fast in a freight elevator. For a few seconds, she was weightless and giddy with relief.

Coming back to earth, she acknowledged she would have to think carefully about where she went from here.

Uncle Nick's birthday was coming up. Maybe that would be the first stop on her journey to self-discovery.

Chapter 10

Travis sat with one hip propped on the railing of the porch and watched the sky deepen into twilight. A restless hunger ate at him. Maybe he should have gone to town with his twin. Yeah, big Friday night out—shooting pool with guys he'd known all his life.

His older brother, Zack, came out of the stable where he'd been rubbing down the gelding's sore knee. The smooth riding horse had pulled up lame that morning, but it was a simple strain, nothing serious.

Zack settled on the porch railing. "Why don't you call?"

"Who?" Travis asked, deliberately obtuse as all his defenses slammed into place.

"Alison."

The sound of her name stirred the blackness of the abyss, shifting things better left undisturbed. For a second, in the fiery red and gold of the sunset, he saw the outline of a woman, shimmering in the radiance of the sun, foolish but determined, ridiculously courageous in her quest for her sister.

A wise person looked out only for himself or herself. Maybe she would learn that someday.

"Why?" he asked, putting indifference in the word.

Zack was silent for a minute. "You could ask how her father's surgery came out."

"I already know. Someone leaked the story to the press, so it was on the six o'clock news. A mole was removed from his neck. The biopsy indicated it was benign."

"So ask about *her* health."

Travis snorted at the suggestion. There was no reason for him to contact her. She was in the setting where a politician's daughter belonged.

"If you love her, don't let her go without a fight. At least make sure she knows how you feel."

His brother's remark produced a zigzag of white-hot lightning down his backbone. He quickly checked the barriers that blocked the stupid, useless emotions and found them intact. He'd failed one woman. He wouldn't do it again.

"I don't feel anything. There was an attraction, but that's as far as it went," he admitted.

He sounded amused, casual, as if nothing mattered. It didn't. Not to him. Alison, with her worried eyes, hadn't yet learned to let go. She took on a load of responsibility and what did it get her? Certainly not gratitude from her sister or even the thanks of her parents.

Zack didn't say a word.

"Besides, she doesn't belong here," Travis added, blocking the vision of green eyes with flecks of silver and pools of despair. She'd been tired at the time, that day he'd discovered her hiking up the mountain.

But she'd kept going, some part of him added.

And there had been that sunbeam radiance, reaching out to him, warming that cold place inside. Sunshine and fairy dust. Stuff to be admired, but not clutched to the heart and kept for all time. Nothing was forever.

"So? You're good with computers. Maybe you could find a job in the city." Without waiting for an answer, Zack ambled down the steps and over to his truck, heading for Lost Valley.

Travis waited until the blackness settled. Move to the city? He'd never considered it. He didn't now. His roots were sunk deep into the mountains. His life force, what there was of it, came from them. He'd go insane in a city.

Inside the house, the telephone rang.

Travis tensed as Uncle Nick answered. The old man talked cheerfully, chuckling and obviously enjoying himself, then he hung up. After another minute, Travis went inside.

"Anything good on TV?" he asked.

"A game show. I could've won. I knew the answer to almost every question," his uncle reported.

Uncle Nick labored over the questions as if he were the contestant with a million dollars on the line.

"Yeah, they're pretty easy," Travis agreed.

"Not all that easy."

"Who called?" The question was casual, as if he was barely interested in the answer.

"Alison."

"How was her father? Did the news get it right?"

"About the mole? Actually it was precancerous, but the doc got it in plenty of time, she said."

"That's good," Travis said, and meant it. That was one less worry for her. If ever there was a person who worried too much about others, it was her.

"She's lonely," Uncle Nick stated.

First Zack, then Uncle Nick. Travis was surrounded by worrywarts, all concerned about Alison. "Yeah? What makes you think that?"

His uncle shrugged, then surfed through the TV channels and paused at the weather. "She's given notice to quit her job managing the senator's office and is thinking about moving. She mentioned California. I don't know why she would go there."

Travis paced to the window, the restlessness hovering on a dangerous edge. Why California? Maybe she knew someone there, an old friend. Or an old lover.

"However," Uncle Nick continued, "she says she needs to find something more fulfilling. I told her there was nothing better for a person than a home and family and honest work."

"Yeah, so you've told us for years."

"And rightly so," the old man retorted. "A family represents the future."

Not always. Sometimes it represented failure and anguish so raw it shredded the soul. Promises made, but not kept. He walked out of the living room, heading for his bedroom and solitude.

An elusive golden brightness seemed to dance down the hall in front of him, always out of reach. He realized it was moonlight shining in the far window.

"Something needs to be done," he heard his uncle mutter before he closed the door.

Lying on the bed, his thoughts went to Alison and her courage, her deep loyalty, which he doubted her family deserved, and her sense of duty. She'd been annoying, she'd driven him mad with her persistence, but she hadn't flinched or wavered in her goal.

Yeah, and she'd been hurt for her efforts, first by her sister's angry reception and then by her parents' careless manipulation when she'd realized they'd sent her on a wild-goose chase under the pretense of serious illness.

No one deserved to be used like that. The anger churned in him as he imagined her glow diminished, her smile subdued but bravely in place as her sharp mind put all the pieces together. Alison, who'd believed everyone was as honorable as she was, had apparently had the scales stripped from her eyes, thus her decision to find a new life.

Something in him twisted painfully. He shoved the pity under the inky surface. Live long enough and everyone learned that life was treacherous. A person had to be on guard every moment.

After a while, he rose and prepared for bed. He'd had a long day and tomorrow would be no different. Slipping between the cool sheets, he tried to relax and induce sleep. Instead, he recalled sleeping in a tent with a woman nestled against his side as she sought his warmth.

Her hair, even in the darkness, had shimmered like spun gold, and he hadn't been able to resist touching it…touching her. She'd been silk and honey in his arms, the embodiment of fantasies he'd thought long dead and buried in the black chasm that was his soul.

Not again, he vowed. He wasn't sure what he felt for Alison, but he wouldn't be sucked into the happily-ever-after thing. Love? Yeah, he'd been there. It was the closest thing to hell he'd ever known.

The void roiled and split apart, spewing a lava flow

of need and desire throughout his body. Gritting his teeth, he wondered what sins, from what past lives, he was now paying for.

Alison signed her name to the last form. She placed it on top of the other forms and slid them into the waiting envelope. There. Finished.

It was Friday, June the seventh. Now she only had to wait about six weeks to see if she had a job replacing a pregnant teacher who wouldn't return come autumn.

Fear nibbled at her. She paused, her hand hovering over the trash can. The teaching job was at the county high school twenty-five miles from Lost Valley.

What would Travis think if she moved there?

Some philosopher had once said people wouldn't worry nearly so much about what other people thought of them if they realized how seldom others did.

She'd been home almost two weeks and hadn't heard a word from anyone on the Dalton ranch, except for last week when she'd taken her courage in hand and called. Then she'd spoken to Uncle Nick and told him about her father and, very briefly, about her plans to go back into teaching, maybe with a move to California thrown in.

Uncle Nick had informed her they needed teachers in the county, his manner sharp with disapproval that she would consider leaving the state. He'd also been disappointed when she'd explained she had work to do and wouldn't be coming up for his birthday party. She'd mailed him a present earlier in the week.

Affection for the old man soothed her unruly emotions. She sighed again, irritated with herself for the unsettled feelings that plagued her. She wasn't one of those females who reacted hysterically to every little thing. She was cool and in control, a thinking person.

As if to give lie to her self-discipline, she fought the need to put her head down on her desk and cry…just cry. But of course she didn't.

She placed stamps on the manila envelope and put it in the mail bin.

It was late afternoon and she was alone in the office. She'd agreed to continue to work for her father until she got a new job. Her mother was angry with her, her father absentminded about her resignation, as if it hadn't yet impinged on his conscious mind.

Her sister had called and managed to win forgiveness for her disappearance. No mention had been made of the coming baby. No promises had been given to return home.

Alison wondered if they were a strange family or basically like the rest of the world. Hearing footsteps in the hall, she stopped the morose musing and got busy.

Retrieving her purse and suit jacket, she locked the office and headed for the elevator. A man stepped from an adjoining corridor, blocking her way. Her heart knocked against her ribs.

Beau took her arm. "This is an abduction," he told her. "Will you come peacefully or do I have to use force?" He gave her a reassuring grin.

"I hope you're talking about dinner," she told him, calming down. "I haven't eaten in hours."

"Well, no," he said, his manner serious and a bit worried. "I'm talking about a trip."

Worry set in. "Where?"

"Home."

"Home?" she asked, confused.

"Consider this a vacation. Hurry," he advised. "It's getting late."

The Dalton cousin ushered her into his old pickup.

"I shouldn't do this," she said as they left town.

"You have no choice. Besides, it would hurt Uncle Nick's feelings if you missed his birthday party."

She told him the reasons she couldn't go to the ranch. He listened and nodded and kept driving.

After two hours on the road and a quick meal, she was surprised again when they turned off a side road before reaching the ranch house. She heard the soft whickers of horses as Beau stopped, and surmised they were heading for a more remote area.

There could only be one reason for this absurd abduction. Her heart drew into a knot as she thought of what it could be.

"Trev?" Beau called.

"Here," a masculine voice answered.

Beau opened the camper on the back of his pickup and pulled out a nylon bag. "You might want to change into something more comfortable."

"What is this?" she demanded, finding new jeans, two T-shirts, pajamas and toiletries inside.

"Clothes. So you can ride."

There were also socks and sneakers in the duffel bag. She put on the shoes after slipping into casual clothing and tying her jacket around her waist.

Her heart began a tom-tom beat. She'd planned on returning to Lost Valley if the teaching job came through. However, she wasn't sure her courage was up to facing anyone tonight.

Dressed, she called to the cousins. "I'm ready."

Trevor was already mounted when she stepped from behind the truck. Beau gave her a leg up on a tall gelding, then handed the duffel to his cousin.

"Any trouble?" he asked.

"No," Trevor said. "Everything's ready. Come with me," he told her. With a wave to Beau, the twin escorted her up a winding trail and down a sharp ridge.

Twenty minutes later, he announced, "This is it." He gestured in front of them and moved aside to let her see.

The sun was setting beyond a spectacular view of the peaks to the west, bathing the remote cabin in golden light.

On a rise to the southeast, she recognized the outcropping the Daltons called the Devil's Dining Room. The logging road she and Travis had hiked from the Towbridge ranch was nearby. They were no more than an hour or so from the Dalton house by foot, she realized.

"I can't believe you're doing this," Alison said for the tenth or twentieth time.

When she'd realized Beau really intended to take her to the mountains, her heart had flipped several times in dread, anticipation and so many other emotions that she'd lost count. All her arguments about why she couldn't go on this wild-goose chase had fallen on deaf ears. Beau had assured her it was "all planned."

"Dismount," Trevor ordered.

He slid off his horse and reached for her. Alison pulled free of the stirrups and let him help her down. Taking the gelding's reins, Trevor mounted again and turned back toward the trail. He dropped the duffel at her feet.

"Wait!" she cried. "When will you be back?"

"Tomorrow," Trevor said. "That should be enough time."

"Enough time for what?" she asked to detain him. She knew this was a kind but foolish idea on his part.

"Go to the cabin," Trevor advised. "There's food and, um, other things for you there."

He rode off, leaving her standing in the soft hues

of twilight. Little bolts of lightning ran over her nerves as she slowly turned and stared at the wooden cabin. She had to go in sometime. Picking up the luggage and pushing her purse strap back on her shoulder, she headed for the shelter.

The door had a padlock on it, the key in the lock, but she found it wasn't snapped closed. She removed the padlock from the hasp and turned the rusty knob. The door swung open on squeaky hinges.

"Ohhh," she said in alarm as a tall muscled figure leaped from the dark interior.

The flying tackle took them both to the ground, then the world spun in confusion as they rolled, ending with her on top of a lanky, tough body primed for a fight.

"Travis," she murmured.

"Are you okay?" he asked in a near growl. "I thought Trevor had returned. I was going to kill him."

"He left. How long have you been locked in?"

"Long enough to contemplate murder."

She nodded. "Beau kidnapped me when I left the office after work."

"Beau was in on it?" He cursed, then seemed to notice their position. "Would you mind moving? There's a rock digging into the middle of my back."

Hastily she moved off the warm masculine body cushioning her from the ground and gathered the duffel, purse and jacket that had fallen during the brief tussle.

With an angry glance in the direction she had come, Travis bowed from the waist and gestured at the door of the cabin. "Welcome to my humble abode."

She went inside. A single twin bed, with a pillow and sheet already on the mattress and several blankets folded at the end, graced one wall. A woodstove stood near the other. In the middle was a card table and four chairs of the foldable variety.

Shelves were stocked with cereal, powdered-milk boxes, oatmeal, canned vegetables, meats and stews. There were fresh five-pound bags of flour and sugar, a big can of coffee and a loaf of bread along with two mesh bags, one of oranges, one of apples. A case of bottled water, a box of breakfast tea and a bag of energy bars finished off the loot. A lantern had been provided, along with plenty of fuel, matches and firewood.

The place had electricity. A single light with a dingy shade was attached to one wall.

"All the comforts of home," she said after a quick glance around. "What is this place?"

"An emergency cabin in case someone's caught in a storm. Did my cork-brained brother happen to mention how long he planned to keep us here?" Travis asked, disgust rampant in his tone, fury in his stance.

"Uh, overnight, I believe. Uncle Nick's birthday dinner is tomorrow."

Travis cursed expressively but with less descriptive

terms than if she hadn't been present, she suspected. She couldn't help it. She smiled.

Travis's fury dried up like a puddle in sunlight. Alison's smile was a beacon on a dark shore, steady and bright. But then, he'd known she was like that, always ready to make the best of a bad situation.

"You don't seem upset," he said. "Were you in on the plot with them?"

She shook her head. "I'm merely stunned."

"This is so typically Trevor." His snort of laughter wasn't amused. "The whole bunch think they know what's best for me."

He stood at the open door and studied the terrain. The mountain air was cooling rapidly as the day faded into the purple shades of evening.

Alison suppressed a shiver and let her eyes roam over him, taking in the attractive masculinity, the strength she recalled each night in her dreams.

The slam of the door brought her back to reality. "There's a storm brewing," he said. "We'll have to stay put tonight."

It hadn't occurred to her that they would try to leave. "Yes, I thought so."

He checked the woodstove. Finding starter, kindling and logs already laid, he put a match to it. In a few minutes, the cabin began to warm. He added water to the teakettle and put it on the stove.

"Have you eaten?" he asked.

"Uh, yes. We stopped on the road."

He studied the pantry shelves. He went still, then cursed again under his breath. Finally he opened a can of beef stew and one of vegetable soup, mixed them in a pan and set it next to the kettle. When the food was ready, he poured up a bowl, glanced at her, then fixed another.

"Join me. This will warm you up."

She went to the table while he set out a tin of crackers. The meal passed in complete silence.

"Thank you," she said. "I do feel better. Warmer," she added at his quick glance.

He washed the dishes in a pan of soapy water. She dried and put them away. She made two cups of hot tea and handed him one, then pulled a chair close to the stove. He added several logs and joined her.

And there they sat while the wind whispered outside the cabin and the tension built inside. She'd never felt so awkward and uncertain. The barrier around him sizzled like a high-voltage fence.

But when she met his eyes, she knew it wasn't an impenetrable wall. Passion had already breached his defenses. A sensation like lightning zigzagged through her, hot and wildly out of control. She looked away, but the feeling didn't fade. It grew with each moment until she thought she would burst with longing.

"We need to get some sleep if we're going to get out of here early in the morning," he announced in a flat voice. "You can have the bunk. I'll take the floor."

"Oh, no, I couldn't," she protested. "I don't mind sleeping on the floor. I—I like a hard bed."

He laughed at her stumbling lie. From a chest under the shelves, he removed two more blankets, spread one on the floor between the stove and back wall, then removed his boots and stretched out with the other blanket over him.

Rolling over so his back was to the room, he said, "Turn out the light when you're ready."

After brushing her teeth using only half a glass of water and turning out the light, she went to the bed and slipped out of her shoes, then glanced at her jeans and shirt. She'd sleep in those. With two blankets over her—there was only a bottom sheet—she snuggled down to wait out the long night. She wondered if she should warn Travis that she talked in her sleep. Oh, but he knew that.

The wind picked up, then the rain started. At first the storm was full of lightning and thunder, then it gentled into the patter of raindrops on the metal roof. The sound lulled her into sleep.

"Wake up. Alison, wake up. You're dreaming."

She sat up abruptly, smacking her head on Travis's chin. His hand slipped from her shoulder and bumped against her breast. Her nipple peaked at once.

They both froze, then jerked back at the same time.

"I must have been talking in my sleep." She laughed nervously, aware of his nearness in every fiber.

"You sounded distressed," he told her, his voice low, a lullaby that calmed the fears of the dream.

"I was lost in the mountains," she explained. "And I was expecting. Twins, I think. I needed a safe place. There was a cave but I was afraid to go in. It was the only refuge from the storm. I knew there was great danger in there, but I didn't know what it was, and I didn't know what else to do. It was so real."

In the faint light from the stove, she saw his chest lift and fall in a deep breath. The rain continued outside. She noticed the temperature had dropped.

He moved away without saying anything. Pulling the blankets up to her chin, she watched as he built the fire back up. Instead of lying down, he wrapped a blanket around his shoulders and settled in a chair.

He looked so very alone.

"I'm sorry I woke you," she said hoarsely. She cleared her throat.

He turned his head until he could see her. She couldn't turn away, although she knew she should. She should pretend to sleep until this moment passed. She didn't.

They continued to observe each other as the wind whispered seductively around the cabin and the rain pattered on the roof. The glow from the fire glimmered through the isinglass window of the stove, casting a rich warm ambience about the room.

He rose. The blanket fell to the chair.

Her breath knotted in her throat and she didn't take another until he stood by the bed again.

''Tell me no,'' he said, the words raw as if it hurt to say them.

Chapter 11

Alison propped herself on an elbow. "No," she said, but it was a denial of the request, not the person, and they both knew it.

When he bent to her, she met him halfway. Closing her arms around his shoulders, she clung to him as the last terrifying shreds of her dream faded.

Safe, she thought. Safe at last. In his arms she'd found her haven. She knew it was temporary.

He sat beside her and lifted her to his lap. With his back braced against the wall, he cradled her against him, just holding her, as if reluctant to take the next step.

"Your touch is gentle, cherishing," she whispered.

He bent close. "I don't feel that way. I want to ravish you right here, right now."

The words were savage, filled with rage and a haunting despair, but she wasn't afraid, not of him. Maybe herself, though. "I want you, too."

Desperately. Wildly.

"Like this?" He grabbed a handful of her hair, closing his fist on it and squeezing hard, but careful not to pull. "Like I want you? The demand of the body? A physical thing?"

"Yes." That wasn't all she wanted from him, but she couldn't tell him that. He wasn't ready for confessions of undying love, not while every muscle in his body screamed with tension that said he wanted to resist the need and hunger that arced between them. "I'm sorry," she whispered. "I'm sorry you were hurt."

A breath hissed between his teeth. He closed his eyes as if in pain. She hurt, too, with longings so strong she knew she wouldn't deny them tonight.

A clap of thunder directly over the cabin made her jump. She wondered what had been hit. Maybe her. Maybe her heart had been struck and was lying in pieces inside her.

"It's only thunder," he said, running soothing hands over her arms. "A summer storm in the mountains."

"In me, too," she admitted. "A storm in me."

He studied her for a long second, then, "And me," he murmured. "Everywhere."

Resting an arm over her drawn-up knees, Travis

leaned forward and touched her mouth with his, a glancing kiss, not nearly enough to satisfy.

"I'm not this way," she said suddenly. "I'm always in control. I never get rattled. Or do foolish things."

He moved, sliding his hands up her sides until his thumbs rested under her breasts. He could feel her heart beating in rhythm with his, sense the worry in her. She always worried. "Until now."

Leaning his head against hers, he tried to still the pound of hot blood through his body. He wasn't convinced she was ready for this…for sex, nothing more.

She moved, then her hands caressed his shoulders and down his chest, bringing a gasp that shuddered all the way through him. Her touch was bliss. Too much bliss. He had to be careful. A man always had to be careful.

When she lowered her knees and slid down on the bunk, he followed so that they lay side by side, touching lips and bellies and thighs, arms and legs all entangled. The hunger increased to a roar that drowned the storm.

"You're like silk and velvet, the finest things I can imagine," he said as he caressed under the shirt she wore. Her skin was warm and he remembered the radiance that seemed to come from inside her. He needed that…no, it was a physical thing. That's all he wanted.

Her smile erased the worry in her eyes. "You, too,

but solid. Like earth. Like rocks and trees and wild things.''

''I'm wild for you,'' he said, ''but you can tell that.''

Those words were okay. He wasn't making promises. He didn't have to cherish or protect, except for one thing. His twin had thoughtfully included protection in the supplies, so they were okay there.

Pulling his head to hers, Alison kissed him with all the longing that had stayed hidden inside her, with the thirst of unquenched passion and the sweetness of dreams she'd thought were lost.

She was trembling.

So was he.

He branded her with kisses.

She gave each one back and with them, the pieces of her heart, one at a time until he possessed the whole.

Like metal to magnet, he lowered his head and touched her mouth. And then she was lost, truly lost.

Reason dissolved like snowflakes in the heat of their passion. His kisses drove her beyond thinking. For once in her life, she felt this was truly her.

Vaguely she realized the feelings had been there a long time, but like Sleeping Beauty, desire had lain dormant until the right prince came along.

But maybe he wasn't her prince. He had made it clear she wasn't his princess. She shoved the thought aside as despair dimmed the moment.

She said his name. There was more she wanted to say, but a lifetime of repressing her deepest longings came to her aid. She wouldn't burden the magical moment with demands, wouldn't ask for more than the moment.

He shifted slightly so that their bodies meshed chest to chest, thigh merged to thigh. She found it wasn't enough.

Stretching upward, she arched into his strong, masculine frame and felt the kick of his heart against her breast. Her pulse pounded, too.

"Easy," he murmured, kissing her ear, her throat. "There's time, all the time we want."

"I need you...your strength, your tenderness."

Cupping her face in his big hands, he gazed deeply into her eyes. "With you, I want to be as gentle as possible. But I feel fierce inside. Like a warrior. I want to conquer, to claim the prize—you."

"It's the same with me," she admitted.

Burning with needs she barely understood, she ran her hands along his back and under his shirt so she could touch his warm, living flesh. It seemed so natural to press against him and let her body experience the feel of his.

When his hands moved between them, she closed her eyes and leaned her head against the pillow.

"You are incredibly beautiful," he whispered, lifting her shirt and pushing the material up her chest. "Like sunlight. Like fairy dust."

She saw that, in the firelight, their bodies indeed glowed like molten gold.

In a second, he had the bra unfastened and pushed upward. He took her breasts into his hands and pressed his face between them, turning so that he could kiss one then the other. Flames erupted at each spot he touched.

She caressed his hair, his neck, the long line of his spine, the slender length of his hips and thighs. Finally, emboldened by passion, she touched the front of his jeans.

He sucked in a harsh breath.

Leaning her head back, she stared into his eyes, not bothering to hide the hunger as she rubbed slowly up and down his body. He opened her jeans and hooked his thumbs under the waistband.

Travis waited for her to come to her senses and refuse further involvement. He steeled himself for it, to let her go as he knew he should.

But there was no denial in the smile that lifted the corners of her mouth or in the darkness of her eyes, dilated with the passion they couldn't deny.

"Yes," she said, barely audible.

His heart nearly leaped out of his chest. Tomorrow, either or both of them might regret this moment, but for now…for now…

When he sat up and began removing his clothing, she did the same. When she pushed his shirt off his shoulders, he did the same with hers.

"Have to touch you," he said, drawing her close. "You make me ache in ways I've never ached before."

"I know. It's the same for me. I don't understand why or how."

"It just is," he whispered against her lips, nipping at them in tender forays. "Like needing air and water and food. Like living. You bring me to life."

Alison closed her eyes as desire ricocheted through her, mixed with the pain of future loss. "The time passes so fast."

"Too fast," he agreed, leaving wildfires on her skin as he kissed along her neck and collarbone.

Then he wrapped her close and settled against the blankets, his body stretched out, partially covering hers. She opened her thighs and he slid one leg between them. Outside, the storm flashed and roared; inside, the heat of a thousand suns burned between them.

Aeons later, she slipped her hands between them and stroked him intimately. He lifted his head and watched her for a solemn minute. "More?" he questioned.

"More."

He bent and kissed her mouth with such tenderness she nearly wept. She trembled uncontrollably.

"I won't hurt you," he assured her when she stared at his beautiful masculine body, fascinated by the differences between them.

"I know. I'm not worried." She was breathless. "It's just that I want you so." She broke off, not sure she wanted to disclose this much.

He expelled a harsh breath. "Maybe you shouldn't be so honest."

Travis gazed into her eyes and had a sudden insight into a life crammed with appointments, of every moment scheduled and accounted for, of duty beyond her years.

"When did you have time to dream?" he asked, sorry for that young girl, and didn't give her time to answer.

He explored every nook and cranny of her exquisitely feminine body. She wasn't inhibited, he discovered. Instead, she followed his lead, intensely interested in every sensation and caress they could share. After thirty minutes of such exploration, he was near bursting.

"Ready for more?" he asked, his lips against her ear.

"Y-yes."

He didn't miss the slight quaver. Extricating himself from their embrace, he retrieved a condom from the box on the shelf. Her eyes widened slightly.

"Trev thought of everything."

"I'm glad. I don't want to wait. I don't think I could stand another night without you, without knowing—"

"How it could be between us," he ended the thought for her. "I've thought about it, too."

He finished his task, then kissed her again, his tongue enticing her into honeyed play with his. Then his hands roamed slowly down, past her waist, circling her belly button and settling intimately at the juncture of her legs.

Alison tried to relax but she was acutely aware of every place he caressed as he made his way down her body. She clutched his hips as he swung over her, both his legs now between hers. Like a full-body massage, he caressed all of her by sliding his body up and down hers. It was wildly satisfying and pleasing.

"More," she said as tension rose even higher.

"Anything the lady wants," he told her, his tone passionate and thrilling to her ears. "I would do anything to please you."

"You do please me…when you touch me…when we kiss. It's so perfect."

He gazed at her breasts. "You're perfect, the most perfect woman I've ever seen."

Then he joined them into one.

His pleasure increased hers in ways she'd never imagined. She'd never shared such heated kisses, never given this much of herself, never taken so much delight in simply touching. When he caressed her intimately, she writhed against him, wanting fulfillment.

"When you touch me…" She didn't know how to say all he made her feel.

"Me, too," he whispered. "It's the same when you touch me. I lose my mind."

"Yes. Oh, yes." Then she laughed because she wanted the insanity and the mindless joy of the moment. She wanted this man and no other. And in that moment of crushing happiness, while stars burst around and within her, she knew she wanted him forever, even if it could never be.

Travis was aware of Alison in a way he'd never been aware of another person. He knew where she was in her passion and how close she was to the edge. He moved against her, letting her experience the full caress of his body on hers. She went very still, then she trembled all over and held on to him as she cried out softly again and again.

He couldn't wait another second. He claimed the prize he'd wanted nearly from the moment he'd spotted her on the mountain trail. Triumph burst through him in a bright rainbow of color as he closed his eyes and let the hunger take him until he was completely sated.

"Ahh," he said on a low moan as he sank against her, unable to move at that moment.

When she opened her eyes, the radiance was there, a gentle sun pouring forth from her inner self.

Alarm spread through him. Fate had a way of extinguishing the brightest flame, and he wanted no part in that. He didn't want to be around when that shimmering brightness dimmed and flickered out.

He rolled to the side. She closed her eyes and soon fell asleep. Lying beside her, he breathed deeply, pulling her sweet scent inside him like a balm. Staring through the rafters to the slanted angle of the roof, he remembered something Uncle Nick had once said.

"A man must build his home big enough and strong enough to hold all the treasures the woman will bring to it," the wise old uncle had told his wards.

For the first time, Travis understood what that meant. Holding Alison in his arms, he'd caught a glimpse of the bounty that a woman could bring to a man. He wondered what a man who had nothing inside to give could bring to a woman.

Still pondering this odd question, he fell asleep, his body cupped around hers, his slumber deep and quiet and content for the first time in two years.

Travis woke Alison at first light. "All good things come to an end," he said, trying for a light note. "It's almost dawn. We'd better go."

The fire had gone out, so they ate a cold breakfast and decided to forgo coffee. Travis gave her a bottle of water and an energy bar and kept the same for himself. He tied a rope through the handles on her duffel and attached it to the day pack he'd brought, then slipped the straps of the pack over his shoulders. "Let's go."

Outside, he found the wooden shutters had been nailed closed, which was why he hadn't been able to open them from the inside. A hammer had thoughtfully been left on a stump below one of them.

The freshly stocked pantry should have been his first clue to his twin's intent. He'd been furious when he realized he'd been tricked into going to the cabin for a supposed fishing trip. Trevor had planned this to the last detail, including securing the windows before locking him inside…and the box of condoms he spotted while he prepared their supper.

The fury was gone, along with the mindless passion. Now he felt only a bone-deep weariness, as if he'd fought his way through a dangerous quagmire during the dark hours. Glancing at his companion, he noted her composure. It was the face she showed the world, not that of the woman he'd held last night.

From the trees came the sleepy calling of birds as they woke to the new morn. He studied the clouds to the south of them. That was a worry. A new squall was heading their way.

Indicating she was to follow, he started out. She fell into step behind him without a murmur.

He tried not to recall the passion of the night. Trevor and Beau had meant for him and Alison to spend the night at the cabin. They would be elated that their plan worked. But what now?

Glancing over his shoulder, he was rewarded with a smile from her, this golden woman with the sun-kissed radiance that upset the safety of the darkness inside him, making him want to reach out and grasp that warmth.

It wasn't going to happen. He had nothing of value to offer someone like her. He knew that even if she didn't. She deserved the best…a first love…an intact heart, not pieces…a future…

"I'll shoot my brother on sight," he promised grimly.

"Uncle Nick wouldn't permit it."

Her manner was amused, but he detected the quietness beneath the calm she projected. The abyss bubbled and boiled as he sensed things between them better left alone.

"You're right. I'll have to beat him up when I catch him alone. You can help," he responded flippantly.

Her soft laughter winged its way right down to the innermost part of him. There were no recriminations in either her eyes or her smile.

He could offer her his body. The passion was enough for him, but someplace inside her were dreams that needed to be fulfilled. He couldn't do that for her.

"I'm sorry about all this. I don't know what Trevor was thinking, but Beau usually has better sense."

"It was rather fun, being kidnapped and abandoned in the wilderness. I feel like a real mountain woman."

The stoic cheer caused an ache inside him. He examined his feelings—the odd tenderness, induced by her humor at the situation; the hunger that wasn't yet appeased; the ache beneath his breastbone, caused by her shimmering warmth and undaunted valor. This wasn't good.

They fell into a rhythm, him ahead, her behind and matching his stride with three steps to his two. The climb to the logging road wasn't long, but it was steep. He heard her panting when they stepped onto the gravel. "We'll take a breather."

"The road has been graded," she noted, scuffing a toe over the fresh surface.

"Yeah. Trev and I worked on it and added gravel. Keith can get to the county road from two directions." He paused, then asked, "Did your sister call?"

"Yes, however she didn't mention the baby." She sighed, then added, "Thank you for all your help."

"It was nothing one neighbor wouldn't do for another," he said before she could go all gushy with gratitude the way women did. He hurried on, walking beside her.

They proceeded up the road that climbed a long ridge bordered by trees on one side and a cliff on the other. He slowed his pace when he heard her breathing in quick gasps.

Peering at the darkening sky, he could see more clouds blowing up rapidly toward them.

"You have a jacket?" he asked.

"Yes, in the duffel."

He stopped and retrieved both their jackets. "New clouds are moving up from the south."

A moment ago, he'd heard the rumble of thunder and felt the first chill breeze from the new squall caress his face.

"It's going to pour," he warned. "Do you have your cell phone?"

"Yes, in my purse."

"We'll try the house from here. If we can reach Uncle Nick, he'll come pick us up." He tried the call but got nowhere. "Too many mountains," he grumbled, handing the phone back.

For a second their eyes held as memories of their previous nights in the mountains arced between them.

Then it was back to hiking. He went faster as the thunder rumbled again and again, closer and closer. He thought of chills, pneumonia, human frailty.

A light rain started a couple of minutes later. He checked his watch. Probably another forty minutes of hard walking before they reached the ranch house.

The little creek beside the road rushed downward with increasing volume. Travis studied it. Heavy rain was falling on the higher elevations and heading their way. The jackets offered minimal protection.

"Is something wrong?" she asked.

He didn't want her to worry, but he had to tell her the truth. "The storm is growing worse. The only shelter between here and the ranch is a tree. We'd better keep moving."

A flash lit the sky, and a finger of lightning hit a dead tree on the ridge high above them. The tree sizzled brightly for a minute, then the flames were extinguished by the rain. Travis blinked, dazzled by the brilliant display.

"I'm glad we aren't on the ridge trail," Alison said.

"Yeah. We'd be barbecue about now."

Her smile flashed. He wished she would complain. Somehow it would make things easier, if only she wasn't so damn stoic. But she was, and he had to live with it.

"Let's go." He headed on up the road at a brisk pace, slowing only when he heard her running to catch up. "After the next hill, we'll be on the downward slope."

"Good."

Head down against the wind, they kept going as the rain became a downpour. "We should have stayed at the cabin," he said at one point.

"We couldn't."

"Why not?" He didn't mean to snarl, but he did.

She glanced once at him, then away. "Because we would have made love again, and you don't want that."

It took him a second to collect his thoughts after that bombshell. "Do you?" he demanded savagely, his heart thumping while the void inside whirled and heaved.

"Well, yes, I think I do." She held up a hand as if to forestall his anger. "I know you don't want involvement and that you wish I'd never shown up here, but life happens. I can't change that."

He cursed silently, but it did no good. He stopped. So did she. "Sometimes you drive me crazy," he muttered, then he reached for her.

Her lips were sweet and supple against his. She wrapped her arms around him, returning his embrace with a show of open desire that burned clear through him.

Standing there in the rain, a chill wind blowing down his collar, he was suddenly warm, as if he held the radiant heat of summer in his arms. What did the future matter when he could have this moment, when they could share the most elemental of human needs.

Moving her head, she murmured something.

"What?" he said, letting his lips roam over her damp face until he found the protected place beneath her ear where her skin was dry and her perfume lingered in an enticing whiff of floral nectar.

"I think someone is coming," she repeated.

He paused, then the words sank in. Glancing down the road, he saw twin lights stabbing through the dim morning light, coming at a pace that was just short of dangerous.

"Something's wrong," she said.

He'd just reached the same conclusion. He shuddered as a trickle of cold rain seeped down his neck.

Chapter 12

Travis waved at the approaching vehicle. Alison was relieved when the SUV stopped, blinding her in the glare of its headlights.

"Dalton?" Keith Towbridge called out.

"Yeah, Travis," her companion said, automatically supplying his name so the neighbor would know which twin he was. "Let's get inside," he said to her.

Guiding her in front of him, he opened the SUV's front passenger door and lifted her into the seat, then he got into the back seat and slammed the door against the rain.

"Thank God," Keith said. "I was on my way to your place. We need help."

"What kind of he—" Travis began.

A moan sounded from the rear of the vehicle. Alison jerked around, her heart lodging in her throat. She knew instinctively who was in pain...and why.

"Janis," she said. "She's in labor?"

"Yes," Keith told them grimly. "I don't think we're going to make it. Her water broke. It happened all of a sudden. We're supposed to start classes next week," he finished, as if this fact would delay the inevitable.

"Ali?" came a faint call from the back.

Alison climbed over the front seat and peered into the cargo space. In the pale light, she saw Janis lying on a sleeping bag, her hands clenched in its folds. A pillow and blanket lay close by and towels were placed under her.

For a second, Alison felt faint. She turned to Travis, hating to ask but having no choice. "Do you know anything about delivering a baby?"

The bones seemed to stand out against his skin, giving him a harsh, foreboding countenance as he hesitated, then he nodded. "I've had some training." He removed the wet jacket and rolled up his sleeves.

She did the same.

"You'll have to assist," he told her. "Do you have any disinfectant in your duffel?"

"Uh, I have mouthwash, but not much. It's travel-size."

"We'll wash our hands in it. Give me something clean to dry off on."

She dug through her duffel for the items, poured some of the mouthwash in his cupped hands when she found the plastic container, then gave him a towel to dry on. She washed and dried her hands, too.

"Help her remove the slacks," he ordered, motioning for her to climb over the back seat.

Her heart pounded. She forced herself to breathe deeply as she knelt beside her sister. "Let's get these off," she said, eyeing the loose maternity pants.

"I'm...sorry." Janis clutched both of Alison's hands as a contraction started. When it was over, she continued, "I'm sorry for being so hateful to you. I was afraid you'd talk me into going back. I love Keith. I want to stay with him and...make a new life. Please understand. Ohh..."

The next contraction was longer, harder. Alison held Janis's hands. "I understand. It's all right."

Travis knelt next to Janis. "Let's see where we are."

Alison was grateful for his competent manner and calm tone. Looking at his drawn face, she knew—oh, yes, she knew!—how much this was going to cost. She could see the barriers slamming into place, hiding the vulnerability.

As soon as the contraction eased, she helped get the maternity pants and undergarments off. Travis told Janis to prop her knees up. He asked Alison to hold the flashlight.

"It's crowning," he murmured.

"What does that mean?" Alison asked.

"Ready or not, this baby is coming." He bent toward Janis. "Now we're going to have to work some. When I tell you to push, I want you to hold your breath, grasp the back of your knees and push like crazy. Think you can do that?"

Janis nodded. "I think…so."

"Should I stop?" Keith asked.

Even in the dim light, Alison could see the worry in his eyes and his fear for Janis, but she had no assurances that all would be well. For once, she didn't have any ideas on what to do.

"No," Travis said. "We need to get to the house. Beau should be there."

Relief surged through Alison at the mention of the doctor but not for long. Janis doubled up and cried out as the next contraction began.

"Put that pillow and blanket behind her," Travis ordered Alison. He smiled at Janis. "Okay, it's time to push. Grab your knees and bear down as hard as you can."

"What's happening?" Keith asked, risking a quick glance over his shoulder. "Is she okay?"

Holding the flashlight as steady as possible, Alison described what was happening as Travis worked with Janis. She was vaguely aware of heat flushing through her body and a sheen of perspiration breaking out all over her.

"Rest now," Travis said. He swiped over Janis's

face, then his own, with a T-shirt. "Prepare something for the baby," he said to Alison.

She selected her nightshirt, not sure what she was preparing for.

"Okay," he murmured. "Big push. Take a deep breath. Grab those knees. Push."

Alison held her breath, too. A low, keening sound issued from Janis, then a cry as the baby came in a gush of effort and released breath.

"What was that?" Keith demanded, sounding frantic. "Is she okay?"

Travis ran a finger inside the baby's mouth, then flipped the baby over and swatted his rear. The infant gave a strangled snort, then his chest lifted in his first gulp of air and he let out a cry of indignation.

"You have a son," Alison said to Keith, tears burning her eyes. She blinked them away.

"Dental floss," Travis said. "You have some?"

Her fingers visibly shook as she got the floss out of her toiletry kit and handed it over.

"Mouthwash."

She poured some into his hand and over the floss. When she set the container aside, he held the baby out to her.

"Wipe him down with the T-shirt," he ordered.

While he tied off the umbilical cord and tidied up the birth scene, she dried the protesting infant on her nightshirt, then tucked another T-shirt around him for a diaper, then finally wrapped him in a fleece vest.

"Here, Mom," she said to Janis. "Meet your new son. Have you picked out a name yet?"

Janis's smile was wobbly. She cradled the baby in her arms. "Keith Jr."

"There's the ranch house," Keith announced. "We're almost there."

The relief was palpable in the truck. Alison smiled and blinked rapidly as her eyes misted over again. Her gaze was drawn to Travis. "Thank you," she whispered. "You were wonderful...*wonderful.*"

She'd never felt such a tide of love as she felt now. Sensitive to his every nuance, she was also aware of the darkness in his eyes and the way the skin stretched over his bones and the tic of a muscle in his jaw as he rolled the used towel and clothing up and stored them in a plastic bag he found by the rear door.

She laid a hand on his arm in apology. Somehow she felt responsible, as if she'd been the one to drag him into the drama of the birth scene.

He returned her gaze impassively, and she knew he'd withdrawn far into himself where he allowed no emotion and rejected any connection to what had just taken place. She removed her hand.

Keith had to stop at a gate. He jumped out, opened it and was back before Alison could volunteer.

"Leave it," Travis said when the younger man would have closed the gate behind them.

Keith drove to the lighted house. The rain had settled to a steady drizzle when Travis lifted Janis from the SUV and took her into the warm house. Alison followed with the baby, Keith right behind.

"What the—" Uncle Nick began.

"Beau!" Travis yelled.

"In the kitchen," the cousin replied.

"Janis had her baby in the car," Travis explained as Beau and Trevor appeared in the kitchen doorway, each holding a plate of toast and eggs.

Beau became all business. He thrust the plate at Trevor. "Put her in the Rose Room. I'll get my bag."

Alison trailed after Travis and Keith. Trevor, after putting the plates on a counter, followed behind her, then pulled the covers back when Travis paused beside the bed.

Beau entered with the black doctor's bag and several towels. "Thanks," he said to Travis. "You men can go. Uh, the father can stay. Alison, let me see the baby."

Travis and Trevor beat a fast retreat and closed the door after them. Beau checked the baby, who was now nodding off to sleep. He listened to the infant's heart and told her to wrap him back up. Then he turned to Janis.

After several minutes, he finished the medical exam and pronounced mother and son fit, then asked the parents about the Rh factor. "No problem there," he said upon finding Janis and Keith were both positives. "We can call an ambulance and have you taken to the hospital at the county seat, if you'd feel more comfortable there.''

"Can't I stay here?" Janis asked in a teary voice.

Beau nodded. ''It would take an ambulance an hour to get here and another hour to get back. Since you're doing fine, I don't see any reason to get out in the weather again.'' He spoke to Alison, who sat in a rocker. "Bring that boy over and let's see if he wants to eat.''

Under Beau's coaching, Janis fed the baby his first meal. Next, Beau showed Keith how to burp the infant. The baby fell asleep against his father's shoulder.

Beau left and returned in a moment with a laundry basket lined with a blanket. ''Here's his first bed.''

Alison slipped from the room while they tucked the newcomer in. She paused in the hallway and pressed her hands over her eyes until she was sure of her composure, then she joined the men in the living room.

Trevor was in one chair, Uncle Nick in another. Travis wasn't with them.

"He went out," Trevor answered her unspoken question.

"He was marvelous. I don't know what Keith and Janis would have done without him."

"I think he needs to be alone just now," Uncle Nick said quietly. "He'll return when he's ready."

Glancing out the front window, she realized his

truck was gone. She understood at once that he'd headed for the mountains and that he wouldn't be back, not for a while at any rate. He needed to let the old wounds rest.

She'd leaned on him many times since coming to the Seven Devils area. Closing her eyes for a second, she relived his strength, his innate gentleness that a woman could depend on. She wished he could have turned to her, but she hadn't expected it. Travis was too used to turning his anguish inward. He refused to need anyone.

"I'm sorry," she said, "but is there a place I can wash up? I need to shower and change into dry clothing."

Trevor was on his feet with an apology in an instant. "This way. I left your bag in here." He led her to a pretty bedroom along the same hallway as the Rose Room where Janis was. "The bathroom is across the hall. Uh, I'd better tell Keith he can use the other bedroom."

Alison closed the door and sank onto a chair at a pine desk. She didn't think Janis would need her, not with Keith and Beau taking care of her and the baby. She needed time alone.

After a hot shower, she did feel better. Dressed in clean clothing, she patted back a yawn, realized it was still early and decided to rest for an hour.

Hearing a muted cry next door, she smiled as a soft glow brightened her spirits. A baby. Little Janny's baby. She was an aunt. Wouldn't the folks be surprised to learn they were grandparents!

But that was Janis's story. She'd let her little sister tell it.

" 'Happy birthday, Uncle Ni-ick, happy birthday to you.' "

Alison joined the Daltons in singing the traditional song that evening, Uncle Nick blew out the one big candle on his cake, then they all clapped. Veronica Dalton, called Roni by her family, cut the first slice and presented it to the old man.

Glancing around the dining-room table, Alison perused each person. Today she'd met the entire Dalton gang when they'd arrived for the birthday celebration.

Seth, the oldest, was odd man out in this family of blue-eyed, pale-skinned siblings and cousins. He was dark-eyed with black hair and swarthy skin. Zack was next in age, then Beau and the twins, while the lone girl cousin was the youngest at twenty-five.

Janis and Keith took part from the living room where the new mother rested on the sofa, her attentive husband beside her. The baby was asleep in the Rose Room.

The little family had gone into town with Beau for a more thorough checkup in his office that morning. All were fine. Uncle Nick had suggested they stay at his place until tomorrow in case they needed to ask

Beau's advice. The couple had accepted the invitation gratefully.

After everyone had a slice of cake and ice cream and were seated in the living room, Uncle Nick spoke, "A man's family means a lot to him on special days like this. I'm glad you could all make it." He smiled at Janis. "It's especially nice to welcome a new life into the world. The boy and I share the same birthday so we'll have to celebrate together every year."

A murmur of laughter passed over the room. Uncle Nick thanked them for his gifts. Alison had given him a cookbook that had recipes for using wild plants that grew in the area, while his kin had given him clothing and personal items.

Only Travis was absent from the happy scene.

Night fell softly on the land. Seth and Roni left for Boise, deciding to return that night due to the additional guests in the house. Zack went to his place in town. After Keith and Janis retired to the Rose Room, Alison watched the TV news with Trevor, Beau and Uncle Nick.

It was only after the old man went to bed that Trevor spoke to her. "Why don't you go to him?"

She didn't pretend to misunderstand. "I don't think he wants anyone right now."

"He's hurting," Beau said.

She nodded. She'd seen his eyes before he'd disappeared from the house. The birth had brought back memories of all he'd lost. He would have to come to terms with the grief—and his guilt—by himself.

Trevor spoke again. "He's probably gone to the cabin since it's stocked and closer than any other place."

She inhaled slowly, carefully. "Wherever he is, he'll have to get over his grief alone. No one can do it for him."

"But you could remind him of all that he's giving up by staying locked in the past," Beau suggested.

"He isn't locked in the past. He simply doesn't want a future. Maybe he never will. Or maybe he hasn't met the woman who will reawaken his dreams."

She wasn't that woman. Last night had given her false hopes, but the morning had dispelled such foolishness.

"You're as stubborn as he said," Trevor muttered. "Both of you are. Kidnapping again?" he asked his cousin.

Beau thought it over. "How about it?" he asked her. "Are you afraid to give it another try?"

Her heart set up a harsh beat that echoed through her like a danger signal. She shook her head.

"Good. Let's go." Trevor grabbed a raincoat from the front closet and glanced at her as if assessing the size.

"No, no," she protested. "I'm not going to him."

The twin looked disappointed. He put the raincoat

away. Beau announced he was going to bed and left them. Lights flashed outside.

"Little brother has returned," Trevor told her.

With a grin, he crossed the room and plopped down beside her on the sofa. Before Alison could figure out his intent, he put an arm around her and hauled her close.

"Don't," she said, startled by his action but not alarmed. There was too much friendly mischief in his eyes.

"This worked once before. Trav and Julie had a fight, the only one I ever knew them to have. I took her to the senior prom. That woke him up."

"It won't work this time," she managed to say just as Trevor kissed her.

Cold air swirled around them as the door opened. Trevor lifted his head and frowned at his twin. "Bad timing, bro," he complained lightly.

"Sorry," Travis said. "I'm just passing through."

He didn't glance her way, but walked past them, down the hall and into his bedroom. The door closed.

Trevor cursed softly. "It's worse than I thought."

She pulled away and stood. "I know you're concerned about him, but please leave me out of it."

For once there was no merriment in Trevor's eyes. "Maybe you're right. Maybe no one can reach him now. I don't know…the way he looked at you when you held the baby…I thought…but maybe not."

He was still trying to figure it out when she retreated to her room. Through the wall, she heard the faint cry of the baby. Little Keith's first day had been exciting.

She sensed the passing of time as the fall of sand through an hourglass. Sometimes it seemed fast, sometimes slow. The years passed. Before she knew it, she would be middle-aged, then old. Last night had taught her something—she didn't want to spend her life alone.

"She has a slight fever," Beau announced, putting the thermometer and blood pressure cuff away. "I think you'd better stay here for a couple of days," he told Janis.

"We have several new horses to see to," she protested.

"I'll go to the ranch and take care of them," Keith told her. He appealed to Alison. "Can you stay with her?"

"Yes, Alison must stay," Janis at once agreed. She pressed her lips together, then gazed at Alison, who was in the rocking chair with the baby. "Would you?" she asked with surprising humbleness, her smile hesitant.

Alison smiled at her sister. "Of course. I want more time with this little darling."

"Good." Beau took a throat swab to culture in case of strep throat, which had plagued Janis as a child. "I'll call when I have the results."

Sunday afternoon passed quietly after that. Alison and Janis had a long talk after Beau and Keith left. Janis shared her dream of making a successful ranch with Keith. Alison mentioned her desire to go back into teaching.

"Do it," Janis urged. "I dare you!"

Alison wandered outside after Janis and little Keith fell asleep. The weather had cleared on Saturday afternoon and today was as beautiful as polished crystal.

On an impulse, she walked through the woods to the unfinished house. Instead of going inside, she sat on the porch and let the quiet seep into her soul.

The past two days had been tumultuous, filled with fears for her sister and the child. The sweet tenderness between Keith and Janis as they cared for their son, as well as his concern at her illness, tugged at her heart. She observed the bonds growing moment by moment between the young couple as they shared life.

Love could be a beautiful thing.

Janis had finally called home with no urging from her big sister. The parents had naturally been astounded, but Janis had made the delivery in the truck into an adventure and her failure to tell them of the pregnancy a surprise she'd planned from the beginning.

A rustle in the grass drew her attention to the sunlit clearing. Travis crossed the springy turf and took a seat on the steps, keeping a couple of feet between them.

"Beau says your sister is running a fever," he said.

"Yes. He put her on antibiotics."

"Good."

She saw him inhale deeply and release the breath as if relieved. "I'm sorry we're imposing on your family," she said. "Beau suggested we not move Janis yet."

"It's okay." He gripped the edge of the porch.

"You were wonderful during the birth," she continued, needing to thank him, but not sure if he would let her.

"I took classes…we did, Julie and I."

She nodded. "I assumed you did."

His smile was beautiful, and so sad it shattered her heart. She looked away.

After a pause, he continued, "We went to Council once a week—Beau insisted—and learned to breathe and watched some videos. At first I didn't think I could go through with it, but then I looked at the other men and realized we were all scared out of our boots over assisting in birth."

His laughter was brief, painful in its irony. She held her smile in place with an effort. Not for anything would she let him see her pity.

"But we had been in on the conception, so it was only fair that we follow through on the rest." He paused and his smile became real. "My grandmother told me the first Dalton here had to help his wife. There wasn't anyone else.''

She nodded, envisioning the ranch house, which had been a log cabin then, seeing the couple struggle to make a living from the rugged land and bringing their children, literally, into the world by their own efforts. It all seemed so endearing.

Travis continued, ''So we waited for the birth of our son and built the house. Our plan was to have it done before the baby came.''

''But it didn't work out that way.''

''No,'' he said quietly. ''It didn't work out that way.''

She waited, wanting him to go on, but not pushing. This was his story. She'd let him tell it in his own way, just as she'd learned she must do with her little sister.

Perhaps she was growing up, too.

Finally he finished in a deadpan voice. ''She woke me one night, moaning and in pain. I thought she was having a nightmare at first. She was, only it was real. I called ahead and started for the hospital, but I knew…before we got there…that we weren't going to make it.''

A jay scolded another from the cedar tree at the edge of the clearing. The breeze rippled across the long blades of grass, forming it into waves as if it were a green sea.

"I'm sorry," Alison said. There were no other words.

"Yeah, so was I. It didn't help. She was dead and I was the one who did it."

Pity wrung her heart. "No, you didn't. It was a tragedy, but it wasn't your fault."

"Whose was it if not mine?" he asked with the finality of unshakable belief. "I knew, on that long miserable trip, that it was hopeless. She tried to be brave, to hide the pain, but I knew."

"You couldn't have—"

But maybe he did, she decided, looking into his eyes. They seemed filled with ages-old knowledge. At any rate, he'd taken the blame upon himself and there it resided, buried in pain too deep for her to reach.

"So you're never entitled to happiness again," she concluded as darkness gathered inside her.

"Happiness?" The planes of his handsome face hardened until the bones jutted against the skin. "I don't want it. I don't want the responsibility."

"Yes," she murmured. "It's hard to let go."

His gaze was sharp. "Of what?"

"Grief. Guilt."

Standing, he faced her. "What do you know of it?" he asked so softly it was scary. "What can you, viewing life from your gilded cage, possibly know?"

He strode across the waving sea of grass and disappeared into the forest, blending into his surroundings like a creature of the mountains, untamed and angry and so very dangerous because he was so very wounded.

Time. Only time would heal him. Maybe.

But she wouldn't wait. Tomorrow, if all went well with her sister and nephew, she would leave.

Time. It was all she had to fill the emptiness.

"Loneliness," she said at last. "I know loneliness."

Chapter 13

Travis whacked the nail holding the hinge on the new barn door with the hammer, then cursed when it bent.

"You have to hit the nail straight on, bro," Trevor advised, coming up behind him.

Travis yanked the nail out, threw it on the floor and drove in another with three strikes. He ignored his brother, hoping he'd go away.

No such luck.

"Tomorrow's Saturday. You're free, aren't you?" Trevor continued.

"So?"

"You could go down to Boise. There's a fancy political fund-raiser going on, I understand."

"Huh." Travis pounded another nail.

Haunted by memories, he'd worked every spare minute of every day. Oddly, the memories were recent ones, not the old ones that had taunted him with failure.

"I happen to have a ticket," Trevor continued.

He whirled on his brother. "Butt out," he ordered.

Trevor shrugged. "You're a fool if you don't go."

"For what? What would be the point?"

"Your future." Trevor sat on a sawhorse and gave him a hard stare. "Ask her to marry you. She might say yes."

The abyss rolled uncomfortably. Travis saw no need to see Alison and ask her anything.

"Funny," his twin continued, "I thought your marriage was a good one, that you were happy. I guess not."

"It was. I wouldn't trade the three years I had with Julie for a million dollars in the bank," he said stiffly.

"Even if you'd known at the time what was to come?"

"Sweet Jesus," he muttered, a prayer for strength not to hit his intrusive twin with the hammer. He flung it on the ground. "I don't need this."

"If marriage was so great, why are you such a coward about trying it again?"

"Get out of here before I…" He couldn't think of a worthy retaliation. Fighting was stupid.

"Before you let the chance of a lifetime slip right

through your fingers? Think about that. Think about what Julie would want for you.'' He laid a ticket on the sawhorse. ''Zack asked me to take over the poacher watch, so I'm heading for the hills.'' He left in his truck.

Travis picked up the ticket, intending to tear it into pieces. After a long minute, he stuffed it in his shirt pocket and got back to work.

As he picked up the hammer, the sun reflected off it and into his eyes, dazzling him for a second.

In the shiny metal, he saw his face, thinner than it had been two weeks ago when Alison packed and Beau drove her back to the city. Staring into his eyes, he saw only darkness, a calm darkness. That was the way he wanted it.

The sun caught the edge of the hammer and blinded him once more. Through the reflected radiance he saw something...a golden aura that started his heart to pounding...the enchanting outline of a woman... He knew she was smiling...and that she held her arms out to him...to welcome him to the light...

Did he dare step into the circle of brilliance?

''Yes, right there,'' Alison said.

The men put the enormous ice sculpture in the center of the table. The frozen mermaid erupting from the waves was beautiful. She'd watched the chef carve the mythical figure, fascinated by his skill.

After directing the men in arranging the flowers

around the base of the mermaid, she glanced around one more time, satisfied that all was being done as planned.

"The red carpet is out," Greg, one of the young movers and shakers who worked for her father, announced.

"Good. Thanks for helping with the details."

Glancing at her watch, she saw it was time to go to her room. She found it easier to stay at the hotel rather than run back and forth to her family home, which was a distance from town, during events such as this.

"Can you keep an eye on things here for a few minutes?" she asked. "I need to get dressed."

"Sure."

She wasn't unaware of the admiration in his eyes. As she rode the elevator to her floor, she wondered why she'd never fallen for someone like him. He was handsome, well-spoken, intelligent and ambitious.

Because she'd known her married life would be like the one she'd been born into? Fund-raising. Campaigning. Months in the nation's capital. It wasn't a terrible life, but it wasn't the one she wanted for her children.

What children?

Rolling her eyes at her ridiculous musing, she quickly showered and dressed in a pale blue–green evening outfit of silk chiffon with a satin slip and cummerbund waist. The sheer sleeves were pleated and gathered into satin bands that fastened with pearl buttons at her wrists.

Her hair had already been set into an artful Grecian cascade of curls at the back of her head, with flirty tendrils floating at her temples and nape. With a simple pearl necklace and earrings and an iridescent sheen in her eye shadow and powder, she was ready.

This was an important function, the kickoff dinner for her father's drive to be governor. And the last event she would plan for him. She'd been accepted to teach at Lost Valley High starting in September.

Her insides clenched into a ball of uncertainty. Not for the first time, she wondered if she was doing the right thing. Maybe her heart would be broken, but that foolish organ was set on one of the seven devils who lived in the mountains, Travis Dalton by name.

Amelia had already promised her a room at the B&B for a very reasonable price. Heading for the elevator, Alison admitted finding an apartment in a small town had proven more difficult than in the city, which was going through a boom in construction at present.

Entering the ballroom, she made a last sweep of the room and saw that all was in order. The dais for the six-piece combo was in place. Spotlights highlighted the dessert tables, while the rest of the ornate room was cast in a soft glow. All of the one hundred tables was decorated with a lovely floral arrangement

that some lucky person at each one would take home
as a gift.

"All is in order," Greg assured her, coming to her
side as soon as he spotted her. "You look beautiful."

She hardly noticed the compliment. "Thanks. Do
you think it's too warm in here? The ice sculpture
seems to be melting fast."

"No, it's just right." He chucked her under the
chin when they reached their table. "Quit worrying."

His seat was next to hers, she saw. Probably her
mother's doing. Her parents were at the main VIP
table. The state political manager and her husband
were to preside at a second. She and Greg were part-
nered at the third.

She made herself look at him, really look. He was
successful and well on his way in his career as an
economic adviser in government affairs. He would
probably run for office someday. Some woman would
be lucky to get him.

She wasn't that woman.

Along with a new knowledge of herself had come
an insight into her family. Her father was ambitious,
but it was her mother who directed the family in serving that ambition. With her father's unspoken con-
sent.

A husband and wife should be supportive of each
other, but that didn't mean manipulating your children
into living their lives focused on the same goals.

People were individuals and had to find their own

reasons for being, thus her move to Lost Valley. If it didn't work out, maybe she would move on. All that could be decided later.

That was another thing she'd learned. She didn't have to have a plan for every moment, with a contingency plan to back up the first.

That elusive plan B.

If people could look inside her, they would see an odd mixture of sadness and joy. She smiled as she recalled her sojourn in the mountains. She'd found more than her errant sibling.

Peace. Happiness. Love. They had seemed within her grasp for a time…a very short time.

Laying her evening bag on the table, she went over her list one more time, then spoke to the catering manager. Everything was proceeding as it should.

Travis stood near the entrance to the ballroom and watched the activity. The attendees reminded him of ants rushing about in an anthill, busy as could be. The room wasn't crowded by any means, nor hot, but he felt stifled and uncomfortable.

Taking a quick check on what the other men were wearing, he saw dark suits were the order of the evening. Good thing. He didn't own a tux. Neither did anyone in his family that he knew of. Again he wondered if he was in his right mind for coming.

This was Alison's world, and it didn't take a genius to know it wasn't his. Not that he had anything against the people here. Politicians were as necessary as cops.

He dodged the reception line where Senator Harvey, his wife, Alison and another man welcomed people with a gracious manner, completely at ease with the task. By holding a side door for a waiter, then entering behind the man, he ducked into the huge room where a couple hundred glamorous and influential people were gathered.

Glancing at his ticket, he found a matching table number in the middle of the room, two rows behind the VIP tables. He chose a chair where he could keep an eye on the front and accepted a glass of wine from a waiter.

Dinner was served on time. He had to admit the meal was good. The beef fillet was tender, the chicken in a wine sauce delicate, the vegetables crisp.

After the tables were cleared, Alison's father gave a brief talk and thanked them for coming. He announced his candidacy for governor. The audience stood and cheered. Then Alison invited the guests to visit the dessert "stations" located around the room.

Travis's breath froze in his lungs at his first direct view at her. She looked like a princess, one made of ice like the sculpture in the middle of the room. Her dress was as filmy as sea foam and the pale color of a tropical ocean.

She was everything he'd dreamed of the past two weeks and looked as remote as a mermaid on an ice floe. He swallowed hard as an ache formed in his chest.

The low background music stopped and a group of musicians took their places onstage.

He'd noted the guy hovering close to Alison all evening, apparently with the approval of her family. The senator had clapped the younger man on the shoulder in a friendly gesture and Alison's mother had embraced him like a long-lost son earlier.

Glancing around the ballroom, Travis knew Alison had done the planning and supervising of the event. One of the hotel managers approached as he watched and consulted with her. She discussed the problem, then smiled and nodded.

Travis's heart went into overdrive. What the hell was he doing here at a five-hundred-dollar-a-plate function? He counted the tables and did the math. Her father stood to raise a cool quarter-million dollars tonight for his campaign, minus the cost of the food and trappings.

Deciding to skip dessert and the rest of the event, he headed for the door. Unfortunately, everyone else also stood and started milling about. He was stalled halfway to his goal by several men who greeted each other heartily.

To either side of that group, people blocked his progress. He did an about-face, intending to try one of the side doors. His eyes met startled green ones.

Everything in him shifted and brightened, as if the sun came up at that moment.

Standing in a circle of light, she was as radiant as a crystal, reminding him of the first time he saw her, that day in the forest. He'd known then she was going to be trouble. He should have heeded the warning.

She blinked, then nodded without smiling. He returned her acknowledgment with a dip of his head.

His insides burned. An ache sprang into being as he surveyed her against this rich, luxuriant background. He wished he'd never come here. Listening to his twin had always gotten him into trouble.

Three chatting women came between him and her. When they had passed, Alison was engaged in conversation with her escort and an older, prosperous-looking couple. He realized it was a senator from an adjoining state.

Desperate for a way out, he wound a path through the crowd and came upon the ice sculpture.

The mermaid resembled Alison in her cool, remote beauty. However, Alison wasn't cold or remote. She was warm and passionate and responsive.

The ache bloomed into a piercing pain that reached all the way to some lost part of him. A woman wearing diamonds at her ears and throat swept by him. Turning, he nearly ran another woman over. His hands went to her shoulders.

"Sorry," he said and stepped back. His heart stopped, just stopped.

"That's okay," Alison said, her heart skipping several beats as he released his hold on her. "Have you tried any of the desserts yet?"

"Uh, no. I was just leaving."

She struggled with a smile, forcing it to stay in place. Why had he come? Why was he leaving?

"I'm going to try the cream tarts. Sure you can't be tempted?" She gave him a flirty glance because that was easier than letting herself cry.

His chest moved as he drew a deep breath. "Yes," he said in an oddly resigned voice. "I can be tempted."

When his eyes met hers, she looked for answers to his presence there, but it was like looking at a wall. She handed him a clear crystal plate and took one for herself. They selected a variety of artfully decorated concoctions.

"This way," she said, leading him to her table. "How is Uncle Nick?"

"Fine." Travis took the seat next to her. "What happened to your date?"

She looked puzzled. "Oh, Greg. He isn't a date. He works for my father. Right now, he'll be pressing the flesh, as they say in political circles."

Travis nodded. He watched her take a bite of tart. He went into meltdown when she licked a smear of cream off her lower lip. He couldn't look away.

"Don't," she protested, her lashes fluttering down over her eyes.

He wanted to take a bite out of her. He wanted to kiss her breathless. He wanted to grab her up and run off to someplace quiet and soft.

Near them the woman draped in diamonds laughed. The stones sent off flashes like Fourth of July sparklers.

Travis took a breath. "I came here with a crazy idea," he began, then stopped. He'd never known he was a coward.

"Yes?" Alison couldn't help the hope that surged in her. She wished everyone would be quiet…or better, just disappear.

"I thought I'd ask you to marry me," he said doggedly, "but I didn't realize what I'd be asking you to leave behind." He gestured at the opulent ballroom and the distinguished guests.

Alison couldn't breathe. She couldn't have heard him right. "Marry?" she repeated.

He shrugged. "Forget it. It was just a thought."

Her heart dropped to her toes. Then anger rushed over her. "No, I won't forget it." She glared at him. "Did you mean it or not?"

He glared right back, then his gaze softened. "I meant it. Crazy, huh?"

"I really wish you'd take me away from all this," she said. Happiness made her giddy. She laughed. "I'm a mountain woman, and I'm much happier there."

Memories flashed between them. Travis felt a glow

start deep inside, like a candle in the wind, holding out against the storm. "Can we go somewhere private?"

"I have a room here."

He took her hand and helped her out of the chair. "So do I, but I don't trust myself with you."

"*I* trust you."

"You shouldn't," he muttered, leading the way toward a side door.

"Alison, where are you going?"

Alison blinked at her mother. "Home," she said and knew she didn't mean here.

"You can't leave—"

"Greg has everything under control," Senator Harvey interrupted smoothly, appearing at their side. He winked at Travis and Alison, then told his wife, "I'll circulate and find out which way the political winds are blowing."

"Thank you," Alison murmured.

"Go on, you two. My blessings," he whispered.

"What is going on?" Virginia Harvey demanded.

"A wedding, I'd say." The senator grinned. "This will be good for my political future. After all, the public loves a romance."

"Well, yes," her mother said, her face lighting up.

Alison couldn't keep the smile off her face. It radiated from her heart. She kissed her mother and father on the cheek, then spoke to her beloved. "Come on."

Travis nodded at the older couple, then followed his love out the door. His love. The words made him nervous. If he said them aloud, The Fates might get jealous.

He realized that was a coward's thought and pushed it away. The glow increased to a shimmering radiance. He'd realized during the long night that he couldn't continue without her warmth.

She led him to a service elevator. In less than five minutes they were in her room. He eyed the bed, then turned to her. There were things to be talked out between them.

"I stopped by the police department this morning and picked up an application. They need men since the town started booming as a new Silicon Valley."

She shook her head. "I start as a teacher at Lost Valley High in September. I'll be taking over for another teacher who's going out on maternity leave."

"What?"

"I'm going to—"

"I heard you. When was I going to know about this?"

"Well, I assumed I'd run into you in town."

He laid his hands on her shoulders and gave her a little shake. "I've been going crazy since you left. I devised a million plans on how we could be together and a million reasons for why we couldn't." He paused then added softly, "I'm not very good at cherishing and protecting."

She stroked the thick dark hair from his forehead. "Yes, you are. Look how you helped me. Look how you helped Janis and the baby. Life happens to everyone. We can't change that."

He touched her dress and ran a finger along the neckline. "You're silk and satin. I'm denim."

She heard the questions. She'd felt the same doubts while she waited to hear about the teaching position, afraid he wouldn't want her, that the attraction was only sexual on his part or a misunderstanding on hers.

"Money and lifestyle are not issues between us," she said. "Love is. And the future. I want children."

Travis saw the undaunted certainty in her eyes and was humbled by her courage. He knew he had to be as brave. "I do love you. I think I have from that first meeting in the mountains when you were so determined to carry out your search, no matter what it took."

She nodded, not at all surprised. "I fell in love with you when you shared your tent and food with me, a little more each time it happened."

"Don't lie."

"There was an attraction from the first," she reminded him. "We just had to work through all the other stuff."

Her smile was gentle, her gaze direct and clear. He knew her to be a loyal and honorable woman. "The average net earnings of a rancher is forty thousand.

In a good year.'' He had to be fair and make sure she knew what she was getting.

''The average starting salary of a teacher is less than thirty thousand.'' She grinned.

So did he. He couldn't help it, not when she looked at him like that. The doubts faded. He drew her into his arms. Maybe he didn't deserve it, but he was getting another chance. No way he'd let it go, not now.

''How soon can we be married? Where do you want to go for a honeymoon?'' he demanded.

''The cabin? It's already stocked.''

He groaned, then chuckled. ''My brother will think he brought all this about.''

''Uncle Nick told me the abduction was his idea.''

Travis, about to kiss her delectable mouth, stopped. ''What?''

''He confessed all my last day there and apologized to me. He felt really bad about everything.''

''That old codger,'' Travis growled. ''I ought to...'' He couldn't think of any retaliation worthy of the old man's conniving ways, well, maybe a million dollars, but he didn't have that.

Alison laid her fingertips over his lips. ''We'll thank him and tell him he was absolutely right.''

She snuggled close and the warmth in him became a threatening volcano.

''Would you kiss me now?'' she asked.

It was a request he couldn't refuse. Later there would be other things to talk about. He ran a finger along the edge of the silk dress. "You look like a princess."

Alison knew what he was thinking. She unzipped the dress, stepped out of it and flung it on a chair. The slip followed. Her heart danced at the fire in his eyes. She pulled the pins out of her hair, one by one, until the strands slipped down around her face.

"I'm simply a woman, my love, one who was lonely until she met someone wonderful."

Then she melted in his arms, demanding his kiss. He gave her his all—body, heart and soul.

Much later, she laughed softly.

"What?" he murmured.

"I was thinking about our children. Will they be little devils or angels?"

"Some of both. They'll give us grief and they'll give us joy. We'll weather it." He touched her face and saw the glow in her, felt it inside him. "Together."

Together, they'd teach their children to be decent, caring people, to fulfill their own destinies and to find a home wherever their hearts led them.

Alison knew she'd been lucky. She'd gone into the mountains to find her sister. She'd found adventure and romance. She'd also found her true love, just as Janis had.

"It was worth it," she said aloud.

Travis raised himself to his elbow and peered into

her eyes, marveling at the love he saw there, all for him. "What was?"

"The journey into the Seven Devils Mountains."

He had to agree. He'd faced his own demons there, and he'd found his treasure. Not gold. His true treasure.

That of the heart.

* * * * *

The SEVEN DEVILS *are getting matched
up if Uncle Nick has his way!
So what happens when
Zack meets his match?
Find out in*
SHOWDOWN!,

*coming this April from
Silhouette Special Edition.*

In April 2003
Silhouette Books and bestselling author

MAGGIE SHAYNE

invite you to return to the world of
Wings in the Night
with

TWO BY TWILIGHT

Enjoy this brand-new story!
Run from Twilight

Savor this classic tale!
Twilight Vows

Find these seductive stories, as well as all the other tales of dark
desire in this haunting series, at your favorite retail outlet.

Silhouette®
Where love comes alive™

Coming in April 2003

baby and all

**Three brand-new stories about
the trials and triumphs of motherhood.**

"Somebody Else's Baby"
by *USA TODAY* bestselling author Candace Camp

Widow Cassie Weeks had turned away from the world—until her
stepdaughter's baby turned up on her doorstep. This tiny new life—
and her gorgeous new neighbor—would teach Cassie she had
a lot more living…and loving to do….

"The Baby Bombshell" by Victoria Pade

Robin Maguire knew nothing about babies or romance.
But lucky for her, when she suddenly inherited an infant, the sexy single
father across the hall was more than happy to teach her about both.

"Lights, Camera…Baby!" by Myrna Mackenzie

When Eve Carpenter and her sexy boss were entrusted with caring for
their CEO's toddler, the formerly baby-wary executive found herself
wanting to be a real-life mother—and her boss's real-life wife.

Silhouette®

Where love comes alive™

Visit Silhouette at www.eHarlequin.com   PSBAA

If you enjoyed what you just read,
then we've got an offer you can't resist!

Take 2
bestselling novels FREE!
Plus get a FREE surprise gift!

Clip this page and mail it to The Best of the Best™

IN U.S.A.	**IN CANADA**
3010 Walden Ave.	P.O. Box 609
P.O. Box 1867	Fort Erie, Ontario
Buffalo, N.Y. 14240-1867	L2A 5X3

YES! Please send me 2 free Best of the Best™ novels and my free surprise gift. After receiving them, if I don't wish to receive anymore, I can return the shipping statement marked cancel. If I don't cancel, I will receive 4 brand-new novels every month, before they're available in stores! In the U.S.A., bill me at the bargain price of $4.74 plus 25¢ shipping and handling per book and applicable sales tax, if any*. In Canada, bill me at the bargain price of $5.24 plus 25¢ shipping and handling per book and applicable taxes**. That's the complete price and a savings of over 20% off the cover prices—what a great deal! I understand that accepting the 2 free books and gift places me under no obligation ever to buy any books. I can always return a shipment and cancel at any time. Even if I never buy another The Best of the Best™ book, the 2 free books and gift are mine to keep forever.

185 MDN DNWF
385 MDN DNWG

Name	(PLEASE PRINT)	
Address	Apt.#	
City	State/Prov.	Zip/Postal Code

* Terms and prices subject to change without notice. Sales tax applicable in N.Y.
** Canadian residents will be charged applicable provincial taxes and GST.
  All orders subject to approval. Offer limited to one per household and not valid to
  current The Best of the Best™ subscribers.
® are registered trademarks of Harlequin Enterprises Limited.

BOB02-R   ©1998 Harlequin Enterprises Limited

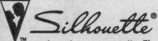

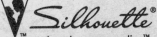